Mastered

With This Collar
On His Terms
Over the Line
In His Cuffs
For the Sub
In the Den

Bonds

Crave
Claim
Command

The Donovan Dynasty

Bind
Brand
Boss

Master Class

Initiation

Impulse

Shockwave

Homecoming

Unbound Surrender

Halloween Heart-throbs

Walk on the Wild Side

Clandestine Classics

Jane Eyre

Sexy Snax

Her Two Doms

Anthologies

Naughty Nibbles
Night of the Senses
Subspace
Bound to the Billionaire

Single Titles

Signed, Sealed & Delivered
This Time
Fed Up
S&M 101
Voyeur
Bound and Determined
Three-way Tie
Bared to Him

The Donovan Dynasty

BRAND

SIERRA CARTWRIGHT

Brand

ISBN # 978-1-78686-074-3

©Copyright Sierra Cartwright 2016

Cover Art by Posh Gosh ©Copyright 2016

Interior text design by Claire Siemaszkiewicz

Totally Bound Publishing

Published in 2016 by Totally Bound Publishing, Newland House, The Point, Weaver Road, Lincoln, LN6 3QN, United Kingdom.

Printed and bound in Great Britain by Clays Ltd, St Ives plc
1

BRAND

Dedication

For amazing friends who challenge my thinking—Michelle Wilson, aka Ms. Romantic Reads, Kimberly Penn, Professor of Sociology. I appreciate the intellectual discussion with you and value your contribution in my life.

For BAB—as always! Tanja—there's a scene here that you asked for.

Whitney—the best PA in the world. And Emmy Ellis—your genius amazes and delights me.

1

"He's a fucking badass. A *hot* fucking badass. But still, a fucking badass."

"Who?" With a scowl, Sofia McBride looked up from her clipboard and glanced at her assistant.

"Cade Donovan."

She followed the direction of her assistant's gaze.

Sofia wasn't the type to swoon, but...

He was standing next to the registry station near the front door of the country club and was dressed in an athletic-cut black tuxedo that emphasized his broad shoulders and trim waist.

Rather than a typical bow tie, a sexy Western bulldogger tie was fastened around his throat. Intricately crafted leather cowboy boots were polished to a shiny gleam, and he wore a black felt cowboy hat.

Even from down the hallway, she noted his rakishly appealing goatee.

Though she'd never met him, she'd grown up in Corpus Christi, less than fifty miles from the Running Wind Ranch. Because his last name was Donovan, he was local royalty, and she'd heard of his exploits—fast cars, bull-riding championships, women—all the privileges money could buy.

He was mouthwatering. Given how tempting he was, no doubt he'd earned every bit of his reputation.

The woman at the front pointed toward the Bayou Room where Sofia and Avery were putting the finishing touches on the preparations for Lara and Connor Donovan's wedding celebration. Cade touched the brim of his hat with old-world charm.

"He's heading this way," Avery said unnecessarily. "You need to get going."

"How about we switch jobs for the evening?" Avery suggested. "You can go to the Oilman's Ball, and I'll stay here."

"No chance." Sofia's answer had nothing to do with Cade and everything to do with her friend Lara, who'd just married into the family.

Even though there would only be a couple of hundred people at this evening's reception and the country club was one of the best venues to work with, Sofia planned to be there for her friend.

"But, but… That's Cade Donovan." Avery exaggeratedly stuck out her lower lip.

And Sofia wanted to meet him. At dinner last week, Lara had mentioned that Connor was a Dominant. And Sofia was curious to know if the other brothers were as well. "I'll take care of him."

"You never were good at sharing, boss."

"Go."

"If you need anything, anything—"

"Good luck with Mrs. Davis." Honestly, Sofia needed Avery's skills at the Oilman's Ball. Five hundred people were on the guest list, and press would be in attendance.

Zoe, Sofia's sister, had been at a downtown Houston hotel all afternoon, overseeing the setup of the challenging event. Mrs. Davis, the ball's chairwoman, was notoriously demanding, and she'd been making changes to the plans for the last month. Avery's ability to say no while keeping the client happy was a skill Sofia had yet to master. "You're a cruel, cruel boss."

"You might meet a rich oil baron."

"There is that," she conceded with a cheeky grin. Avery was twenty-nine, and she'd set a goal of being married by the time she was thirty. She didn't lack interest from men, but she wouldn't settle for just any man, insisting she wanted a man who could keep her in very expensive shoes and give her a monthly purse budget to match.

After gathering her belongings, Avery headed for the back exit through the kitchen.

Sofia straightened her shoulders and walked toward the front of the room to greet Cade, who had paused inside the doorway. His gaze locked on her. He didn't blink, didn't look away. Instead, he perused her as if she were the only person on the planet.

It was discombobulating and heady.

Her sensible black skirt suddenly felt a bit tight, her patent leather heels a little too tall. Still, she strove for professionalism she suddenly didn't feel. "Mr. Donovan." She gave him her best smile. "I'm Sofia McBride. Lara's friend and the event coordinator."

"I'm early." He offered his hand.

Because it was the polite thing to do, she accepted.

His hand was so much larger than hers. All of a sudden, his presence seemed to consume her. His scent was leather laced with strength. He was exceptionally tall with a chiseled jaw, and it appeared that his nose had been broken, maybe more than once.

She had to look up a long way to meet his gaze, and when she did, she saw that his eyes were a chilly gunmetal. His posture spoke of a confidence bordering on arrogance, and he wore power as comfortably as he did his tuxedo jacket.

The air around Cade all but crackled with intensity, and part of her felt as if she'd been swept into some sort of vortex.

Last week, when she'd met up with Lara, her friend had confessed that she and Connor shared a BDSM relationship. The news had momentarily left Sofia speechless. She had read books and seen a couple of movies about the subject, but other than the fact sex was kinky, she hadn't known much about it, and she'd never known anyone who was into it.

Once she'd gotten past the initial shock, Sofia had started

asking questions. Lara had responded quite matter-of-factly, sharing enough information that Sofia was more intrigued than ever. When she'd gone home that night, she'd powered up her computer and done an Internet search. Some of the things she'd seen had made her flinch, but the idea of being tied up had starred in a few of her recent fantasies.

Now, she wildly wondered if Cade was also into BDSM, and she had a disturbing, naughty image of being over his knee while he spanked her.

With a little shiver—part apprehension, part curiosity—she pulled back her hand. "We're just putting the finishing touches on before Connor and Lara arrive," she said, probably unnecessarily.

Because the couple had married a few weeks before, the order of the evening was a bit unusual. The family was planning to meet at five for pictures, and the cocktail hour was scheduled for six, with dinner following at seven.

"Anything I can do to help?"

The offer caught her off guard. "Thanks, but I think we've got it covered."

"If there's anything you need, let me know."

She questioned if she'd imagined a slight emphasis on the word anything.

The photographer shouted out a cheery hello as she arrived, and Sofia was grateful for the interruption. "There's a bar near the restaurant, if you'd be more comfortable waiting there?"

A hint of a smile teased his mouth. Rather than softening his expression, it only made him look all the more dangerous.

"Are you trying to get rid of me, Ms. McBride?"

Yes. The man definitely unnerved her. "I just want you to be comfortable."

"Can I get you anything while I'm there?"

"Thank you." She shook her head. "But I don't drink while I work."

"Do you always follow the rules?"

Though his tone was light, the question sounded serious. "I like rules," she replied.

"Do you?"

"It helps keep my life in order."

"That's a good thing?"

"Isn't it?" she countered. Even as she answered, she wasn't sure why she was having this conversation, why she was revealing parts of herself to a stranger.

"Have you ever been tempted to say the hell with everything and explore all that life had to offer?"

"When it comes to business, yes."

"And everything else?"

"No." But honestly, she was now.

The photographer placed her backpack on a chair then moved toward them, sparing Sofia from further discussion.

Sofia introduced the pair, then excused herself to greet the DJ and show him where to set up.

Over the next ten minutes, three generations of Donovans began to arrive, and Connor and Lara took her aside.

"We need your help with something," Lara said.

"Anything."

"Julien Bonds RSVP'd about ten minutes ago. He's an old friend of Connor's."

Only professionalism kept her from dropping her jaw. There were a number of high-profile Texans on tonight's guest list, including one senator, but Julien Bonds? The man's genius was legend. She'd waited in line several hours to buy his latest wearable device at the opening of his newest flagship store, and he'd been at the event for a short time. He'd left only minutes before she would have gotten to meet him.

About two years ago, she'd written to the company, wanting an app that allowed her to do more impressive business presentations. Surprising her, one of Bonds' engineers had responded. Within two weeks, two of her favorite programs had been fully integrated. The difference it had made in her success had been phenomenal, and she'd always wanted to tell him.

"He's requested no pictures," Lara continued.

"I see." And since almost every person in attendance would have a cell phone, that presented a challenge. "We can ensure Heather won't take any professional shots," she said. "How would you like me to handle the other guests?"

"I was hoping you'd have ideas."

"That's what I was afraid of." Especially when she, herself, wanted a photo with him. She nodded, hoping to convey confidence she wasn't feeling.

"He won't be arriving until nine."

She checked her schedule. By then, the alcohol would have been flowing for a couple of hours. "Will he have anyone with him?"

Lara and Connor exchanged glances.

"Like security?" Sofia clarified. "An entourage?" He'd had about half a dozen people surrounding him at the store opening.

"Not to my knowledge," Connor said.

"Can you find out?" People blocking views would probably be the best hope.

Connor stepped to the side to make a call.

"How are you doing?" Sofia asked Lara.

"Fine. Happy. Nervous." She said it all in the same breath.

"I'll be your designated worrier." Sofia squeezed Lara's hand reassuringly. "Your job is to enjoy the evening. I'll be nearby if you need anything."

Lara smiled.

"You look beautiful," Sofia said. "The perfect Mrs. Donovan." Lara radiated elegance and sophistication in her short, form-fitting, cream-colored lace dress. "Marriage is obviously still agreeing with you."

"More than I would have imagined." Her friend flushed and fingered the stunning gold choker around her neck.

A series of diamonds descended from the metal to snuggle against the hollow of her neck. Because of their discussion, Sofia knew it was more than a piece of jewelry.

The necklace was an outward symbol of Lara's submission to her husband.

Sofia didn't quite understand it, but she couldn't argue that Lara seemed happy, satisfied in a way she had never been before. Even when Sofia had asked, Lara had said she wasn't sure whether the feeling came from being married, from the strength of her new husband's business acumen, or from submission. After a glass of wine, she'd mused that it was probably the combination of everything.

"It's been a whirlwind, and I couldn't have managed this without you," Lara said.

"I wouldn't have let you," Sofia replied. "Please let me know if there's anything you need."

Connor returned and lightly touched his wife's shoulder. "Julien will have two men with him. And it's my understanding he'll only be here a short time. Mostly he's coming by to gloat. He thinks he had a hand in making the relationship work, and he does enjoy feeling as if he's a genius."

"And did he? Have a hand in the relationship?"

"He's a good friend with good advice," Connor replied.

"I'll talk to the DJ. I'm thinking he can play a song that will engage a lot of people. The twist, perhaps. Other than that, I'll contact the country club personnel and security to see what we can do. Maybe we can bring him in the back way. Keep him on the patio or something."

"You'll work it out," Connor said, his voice holding no trace of doubt.

She asked for a contact number for one of Julien's people. "I'll do the best I can," she promised.

The photographer signaled she was ready for the bride and groom, and Lara and Connor excused themselves.

While the couple was busy, Sofia went in search of the country club security team. They agreed that bringing in the Bonds entourage through the patio was the most feasible option and suggested she have a look for herself.

She greeted other arriving family members then confirmed

the schedule change with the DJ and asked for his help in keeping the focus away from Julien.

"Not a problem," the man assured her. "We can do some things with lighting and announcements about the photo booth and video greeting cards for the couple."

"There's a reason I like working with you, Marvin."

"It's the voice." He dropped his tone until it sounded like honey drizzled over a jagged knife.

"You should have a radio gig," she told him. "Nights, on an all-romance, all-the-time station."

"I have the face for it."

"You're fishing," she said.

"Yeah." He shrugged.

"I'll bite, though. You're a handsome man."

He straightened his tie, preening. Then, professional that he was, he made notes on his schedule as she walked away.

Before leaving the room, she couldn't help but sneak a peek at Cade. Even though he stood next to his handsome brothers, he didn't completely fit. His smile wasn't as genuine as theirs, and his Western-style tux and hat set him apart. He was taller, broader, more... She considered herself pragmatic, but the only word she could think of was brooding.

After shaking her head, she went to check that everything was perfect for the cocktail hour in the other room.

The quartet was in place on a platform, and they were tuning up. Two servers stood behind an open bar. The banquet manager confirmed that hors d'oeuvres would be served at ten minutes after the hour. All the centerpieces and decorations were perfect.

Finally, she went outside to check the patio.

Right now, it was too hot and humid to be pleasant. The overhead beams had pendant fans hanging from them, their blades seeming to slog through the thick air.

Later, though, the lights off the bayou and the view of downtown Houston, combined with cooler temperatures, would make this an ideal spot.

She ordered a sparkling water from the bartender, enjoying the last few minutes of peace that she was likely to get for the next couple of hours.

"Lemon? Lime?"

"Lime, thanks." After she had the drink in hand, Sofia walked around the patio. She found a gate that led to the side of the building. There was gravel there, with pavers. That could be the best way to get Julien into the party with as little disruption to the festivities as possible.

She paused at the back of the patio near a massive potted palm. If she could get some workers to move the plants around, they could block part of the area from view.

Cade emerged from inside. Without hesitating, he headed directly toward the bar.

Sofia told herself that he hadn't followed her, but she couldn't be sure.

The woman wrapped a napkin around a beer bottle and handed it to him.

Sofia watched as he dropped a bill into the tip jar. Judging by the bartender's wide-eyed expression, it had been a good one. If she hadn't already liked him, she would have changed her mind in that instant.

Then he turned toward her.

If she'd had any doubt that he'd followed her, it was erased.

He remained where he was.

Heat and feminine response chased through her. She shouldn't be attracted to him, but damn it, she was.

Maybe she should have handled the Oilman's Ball and left Cade to Avery. Even as the thought flashed through her mind, she banished it. No matter how badly he unnerved her, he ensnared her. Intuition told her to run before she couldn't. Yet her body refused obey her mind's orders.

She curved both hands around her glass as he approached.

"I would have gotten that for you," he said, indicating her drink.

"I think as the event planner, it's my job to make sure

you're taken care of."

"Always the duty of a man to make sure a woman's needs are met."

He hadn't said anything provocative, so why was she responding as if he had? "Thank you. But I'm pretty accustomed to taking care of myself."

She noticed him glance toward her left hand.

"By choice?" he asked.

"That's nosy, Mr. Donovan."

"It is," he agreed.

But Cade didn't relent. Instead, he seemed genuinely interested in learning more about her. How long had it been since that had happened? Months? Maybe years? Then the truth hit her. She'd never had a man be so inquisitive and not back down when she called him out on it. He was unique among the men she'd known. That, more than anything, was what encouraged her to respond. "My mother was abandoned by my alcoholic father when I was very young."

He winced.

"I had to take care of my little sister. As soon I was able, I was helping my mother bake cakes and pies for local restaurants. Sometimes she'd stay up all night. I really don't know how she did it. She remarried a wonderful man a number of years later, but I learned some important lessons early, and I've never forgotten them. I went to school on a scholarship. And I worked my ass off to buy my mom's business and expand it." Traces of irritation buzzed through her. "So it's hard to say that anything was by choice. I've done what I needed to from necessity."

"It appears you've done a fine job." He never looked away. Instead, he tipped his beer bottle toward her in silent salute.

"I grew up in Corpus Christi," she admitted. "I know of your reputation."

"Yet you're still talking to me."

"Some of it was good," she replied.

"That surprises me."

"We come from very different backgrounds."

"Do we indeed?"

There was something in his voice, an ache maybe. Pain, perhaps.

Because of his approval, the expression of his own angst, something went out of her. The fight? The need to explain, justify, defend the way she'd grown up? It hadn't taken long for Cade Donovan to have an impact on her.

Her text message alert sounded, and she put her drink on the waist-high adobe wall while she took her phone from her jacket pocket. It was the country club manager, as she'd guessed.

"Duty calls?" Cade asked.

"Afraid so."

"I hope to see you again later."

She didn't reply. The words sounded more like a promise than a statement, and a secret part of her hoped he was serious. She wanted more time with the darkly mysterious Donovan brother.

He went inside. After collecting her wits, she asked the manager to meet her on the patio.

She offered her suggestions, and the manager nodded and summoned a few members of the banquet crew. They brought out a hand truck to move around the big pots, creating a secluded area not far from the gate.

Once she was satisfied with the result, she informed Julien's team of the plan then found Connor to update him.

The only part she disliked was the fact that once again she wouldn't get to meet the elusive Julien Bonds and get his autograph on her cell phone case. What could be better than his signature right below the Bonds logo?

❤❤❤

Shortly before nine o'clock, she received news that Julien's car had arrived.

After signaling the DJ and receiving Marvin's nod in

reply, she went outside to the gate to greet the party.

A beefy-looking man—security if the earpiece was anything to judge by—had a quick look around before nodding at her and speaking into a microphone on his lapel.

A moment later, Lara and Connor joined them in the makeshift meeting area.

The security guard positioned himself between the bar and the plants. She couldn't have been more pleased with how the plan worked.

Sofia ordered another soda water. The sound of Lara's laugh drew her attention, and Sofia couldn't resist taking a peek.

Julien wore a loose-fitting jacket, a white shirt and a skinny little tie that was knotted loosely. His trademark athletic shoes were an obnoxious magenta color, and the yellow laces quite literally glowed. He'd taken his tacky footwear to a whole new level yet he still pulled off the casual style that he'd become known for.

A woman, tall and willowy, with blonde hair cascading halfway down her back, stood next to him. She wore an electric-blue dress that flared around her in a style Sofia associated with Marilyn Monroe.

Sofia hadn't heard that he was dating anyone, but the way his arm was draped around the woman's shoulders and the way she leaned into him hinted that this was something more than casual.

The bartender handed Sofia the drink, and she turned to see Erin heading toward the private area.

Since she was the groom's sister, Sofia didn't try to stop her, and she nodded to the security guard to let him know that Erin should be allowed to pass.

"Let me know if you need anything," she said to the security guy.

He nodded curtly but didn't respond.

Sofia went inside and stood near the back wall, surveying the festivities. More people than normal were on the floor, showing off their moves, and some were even snapping selfies. How they managed that, she wasn't sure.

It was less than two minutes later when Erin returned, a pained smile on her face, her shoulders slumped a little.

Sofia thought about seeing if there was anything she could do for Erin, but the woman headed straight out of the front door.

Other than that, Julien and his date's visit went smoother than she'd anticipated, but she still breathed a sigh of relief when the country club manager let her know that a limousine had whisked away the Bonds party.

Several times during the next couple of hours, she caught Cade watching her, and she had to force herself to concentrate on her job and not the wild, crazy things he did to her insides.

❦❦❦

"When is it your turn?"

In the waning hour of the reception, with strains of music spilling from inside the country club, Cade thumbed back his cowboy hat and turned to face his younger sister. Half-sister, really. But the fierce and loyal Erin Donovan would protest that distinction. In her mind, as well as those of his half-brothers Connor and Nathan, they were family, no arguments.

Cade loved all of his siblings, but Erin most of all. Ever since she'd been a toddler, she'd been a pest, smothering him with adoration and love even when he didn't want it or deserve it. "My turn?" he repeated, stalling.

"Don't play dumb. When is it your turn to get married?"

"Not happening," he replied, even though he knew she would push the point. Erin worried about him living all alone on the ranch. As far as she was concerned, there was nothing but cattle, deer, horses and wilderness in South Texas. It didn't matter to her that he employed dozens of people, many of whom he interacted with on a daily basis. He also traveled more often than he would like. He drove to Corpus Christi at least once a week, flew to Houston almost every month for family business meetings, and he spent more time in the nearby town of Waltham than he cared to.

"Are you at least finally seeing someone?" she pressed.

"You know the answer to that," he responded.

"I keep hoping."

His father's death had devastated him, shattering his sense of self in ways he was still trying to comprehend. It was almost as if that event had divided the old Cade from the new Cade. In his late teens and early twenties, he'd been a bit reckless. The whispers about him, the way he didn't deserve the life of privilege he'd ended up with, had gnawed at him. He'd set out to banish the voices as well as to prove himself. He'd lived hard, tried to make his mark on the world, taken unnecessary chances bull riding, racing motorcycles then eventually, cars.

When Jeffrey Donovan had been buried, Cade had resolved to be a better man, to live up to the expectations placed on him. He'd thrown himself into his responsibilities and obligations, letting them consume him as he attempted to redeem himself.

He'd shut himself off from distractions, including dating. At one time he'd been active in the local BDSM community. Until this evening, when he'd walked through the door and met the curvy, sexy Sofia McBride, he hadn't had much interest in women lately. His attraction to her had jolted him and he wasn't sure he liked it. Hell, it had been at least three months since he'd attended a leather party, even longer since he'd hosted a submissive at the ranch.

Penance was a bitch.

Realizing that Erin had rested her fingers consolingly on his wrist, he shook off the melancholy. Tonight was supposed to be a celebration of love, of marriage, of the future. He wouldn't be the one to bring it down. "How about you?" he asked, redirecting the conversation.

"Me? Seeing someone? Are you kidding me?" She

dropped her hand. "I'm too busy helping Julie get the corset shop going in Kemah. And trying to find someone to run the foundation. I'm pinch-hitting for now, but..."

"You're exhausted," he guessed.

She shrugged. "It's a lot of hours."

As head of HR for Donovan Worldwide, Erin didn't have an easy job. Filling high-level vacancies was difficult at best, and their aunt's decision to spend more and more time with her younger beau complicated matters. The Donovan Foundation had always been run by a member of the family, but now they would have to look to an outsider to fill her position.

And, in spite of their youngest brother's objections, Erin had gone ahead with plans to assist a friend in opening a fancy lingerie shop. When the woman had admitted she didn't have the funds to open the store, Erin had supplied that, as well. No matter the challenge, she accepted it.

"How are plans coming for the centennial celebration?" she asked, changing topics to one Cade hated only slightly less than the subject of his non-existent love life.

The Running Wind Ranch, which had been in the family for five generations, was going to be celebrating its centennial in early fall. He would have pretended it wasn't happening, but his grandfather, the Colonel, had recently announced that he wanted the family to host a gala, inviting neighbors, friends, vendors and business associates. Many of them had never been to the ranch. Others remembered a time the Colonel and Miss Libby had hosted grand events, the last one about twenty-five years ago. It was a headache Cade didn't want, but a duty he knew he'd fulfill. "My mother said I personally have to check out the caterers."

Erin grinned. "Excellent idea."

"Not sure why she couldn't do it."

"You really expect Stormy to take the blame if the food is awful?"

"Well said." Around Erin, he freely spoke about his mother. Neither Connor nor Nathan had ever said a negative word about her. On the other hand, none of them had ever discussed her involvement in the business, either. The Colonel had spoken fewer than a hundred words to her in over thirty years, and Stormy said she preferred it that way. When Cade's father had gotten her pregnant, she'd been offered a significant amount of money to go away quietly. If she'd been the type to do that, no doubt his father wouldn't have fallen in love in the first place.

"Do you have anyone lined up yet?"

"A new bakery opened in town, a couple of doors down from the pharmacy. So I stopped in."

"And?"

He'd never felt more helpless. Give him a complex piece of machinery to repair or a steer to brand and he had complete confidence. But when two women had started smiling and shoving food at him, flipping through pictures of weddings and birthdays, offering him tiny plates filled with bizarre concoctions, he'd been overwhelmed and speechless. "Buffalo chicken wing cupcakes?"

"Were they good?"

"I don't know. I couldn't bring myself to pull it out of the frosting. How the hell do you eat something like that?"

"I see your point. I guess she was going for something sweet and savory in the same bite."

"Cupcakes should be sweet," he said.

"The whole world isn't black and white, big brother."

"I have rules, Erin."

She grinned. "Got it. Cupcakes are sweet. Women are spicy?"

"Don't you have someone else you can bother?" he asked pointedly.

"Seriously, Cade, you don't have time to put an event together. You need a company to manage it, invitations, decorations—"

"Decorations?"

"Absolutely. Flags. Bunting. Maybe a take-home memento, like a Christmas ornament or something."

He blinked.

"Flowers," she continued. "And entertainment. Perhaps a band. Live music is always good. People will come just for that. Oh, and a bounce house for kids. Margarita machines, for sure. You've only got a few months."

Until now, he'd figured he'd need about ten minutes to put it together. Throw some burgers on the barbecue, smoke some brisket, maybe get some of the ranch hands to roast a pig... But with the scowl on Erin's face, he saw he'd made a huge miscalculation.

"Have you sent out a save-the-date announcement?"

"To whom?"

"Seriously?" She rolled her eyes. "Ask Granddaddy and Grandmother for their guest lists, and Connor. Better yet, ask Connor and Thompson. Thompson has Connor pretty well organized. He'll know who's who. Don't forget Nathan. My mother may want to invite a few of her friends."

He hadn't considered that. But it made sense. Though he'd never spent much time with Angela, she had been married to his father.

"Do you want me to ask her?"

"That's thoughtful of you. But no. I'll do it." Or find someone else to do it.

"I have a few people I'll want to invite. And we'll need to contact the cousins. Granddaddy's the best person for that, too."

"Are you sure all of these people have to come?"

"You'll be haunted to the grave if you forget anyone. No matter what you say, who you apologize to, it will be taken as a personal affront. You're welcome to run the whole thing by me. We probably do need to limit it at some point."

"To a hundred?" he asked hopefully.

She scowled. "I was thinking a thousand."

"People?"

"And horses."

A cold frisson of panic clutched him. "What?"

"People, Cade. A thousand people. I was joking about

23

the horses. Tell me you've at least decided on a date?" she persisted.

"I was thinking about October, maybe November. I don't suppose you—"

"Oh, hell and no. No chance. I can help you find someone, but I can't handle everything from a distance."

"What about Miss Libby?" He'd heard rumors that their grandmother used to host some of the best parties in South Texas. And she'd hosted many of them at the ranch.

"It's been too many years. She can give you pointers, but she doesn't know the companies down in that area any longer."

"Your mother?" he asked desperately.

"Again, too far away. You're welcome to meet with both of them, but your event person may want to do that."

"I see."

"I'll try to have some people for you to interview by the first part of the week."

He nodded. A runaway train was easier to stop than Erin. This time, he was grateful.

"You're going to be fine."

He'd rather climb on the back of a roaring, snorting sixteen-hundred-pound bull than deal with a guest list.

Inside, the DJ announced that it was time for a line dance, and Erin gave a quick excuse then hurried off.

He went to the bar and ordered his second beer of the evening. Other guests were reaching for glasses of champagne, but he preferred to drink Santo, a rich, thick brew that suited his personality.

Because of the heat and late spring humidity, there weren't a lot of people outside, but he still wandered to the far side of the courtyard and leaned against the outer adobe wall. In a crowd of any size, he tended to seek out quiet corners.

Now that the toasts and obligatory pictures were out of the way and the party was in full swing, he loosened his bulldogger tie and unfastened the top button of his Western shirt. He took a deep drink and glanced toward the clubhouse.

Inside, his new sister-in-law was also participating in the line dance. He wasn't sure what radiance looked like, but Lara had to come close. She and Connor had gotten married in a private ceremony weeks before. He'd only met her the previous evening, but he'd instantly seen why his brother had been attracted to her. She was witty, beautiful and elegant, a fitting partner for the ruler of the Donovan empire. Connor was clearly besotted, if the fact he couldn't keep his hands off Lara was any indication. When she'd briefly left the room, he'd followed her movements and momentarily lost track of the conversation.

Until he'd seen the two together, Cade had been a bit skeptical of love. To him, it seemed like an emotion that fucked with people's common sense, something with the power to be dark and destructive.

No doubt his father had loved his mother, but he hadn't been strong enough to tell his own father to fuck off so he could be with the woman he loved. Instead, he'd married Angela Meyer. She was obviously a fine woman, if his half-siblings were anything to judge by, but Cade had seen the way Jeffrey looked at Stormy up until the day he died.

Love for a man she could never have had kept Stormy stuck, and it wasn't until a year ago that she'd even gone on a date.

But watching Connor opened Cade's jaded eyes, just a little.

A few minutes later, champagne in hand and a stupid smile on his face, Connor wandered over.

"Congratulations," Cade said.

"Glad you could make it."

"Wouldn't have missed it," he replied. He'd talked to Connor when Lara had approached him with her bold proposal to save her family's business. Cade had offered his support, but he'd urged his older brother to exercise caution. He'd sacrificed a lot to take the helm of Donovan Worldwide. He should have had years to travel, learn the business, date. But he'd never complained. He'd simply done what he'd needed to. All without blaming Cade for anything. "You look...happy."

Connor grinned like a fool. "I am."

"Here's to many joyful years together." He lifted his beer bottle and Connor tapped the rim of his glass against it.

"You're going back in the morning?"

"Figured I'd head out after breakfast. Get in a half-day's work, at least." Cade didn't have to explain. More than any of his half-siblings, Connor understood him, his need for solitude, to roam the land in endless search of healing. His grandfather, behaving more like a general than the colonel he was nicknamed after, often insisted that Cade needed to spend more time with the family, so it fell to Connor to cover and make excuses. Cade appreciated it. "I'm told I need to ask you for a guest list for the centennial."

"That'll take some thought. I'll try to remember to ask Thompson."

"Since you're technically on your honeymoon starting tonight, I'll get with him. He's here tonight, isn't he?"

"Somewhere. But wait until Monday. This is supposed to be his day off."

"I forget."

"It's a Donovan curse."

Cade nodded. Their father had always told them it was their responsibility not to fail. And none of them wanted to be one to let down the previous five generations. "Speaking of work..."

"I should have guessed."

"When you're back from your honeymoon, I could use some time to discuss some ideas for the ranch."

"What are you thinking?"

"Ah. You mentioned something about this being your reception?"

They exchanged shrugs.

Connor glanced back inside, evidently to ensure his wife was occupied. "Make it quick."

"I'm thinking of offering limited tourism. Maybe seasonal."

Connor took a drink and regarded Cade. "On the whole section?"

He shook his head. "Just section one."

"That one's yours. You don't need to run anything past me unless you're looking for a second opinion."

"It's your heritage, too. But there are fiscal aspects to consider. Could make money. Could lose it."

"What are the net benefits?"

"More people get to enjoy it. It provides employment opportunities for people living in town. Considering allowing tubing on the river. Horseback riding. That sort of thing. If it makes money, we could consider expanding the conservation area into section one."

"Negatives?"

"Because I live there, it could mean some loss of privacy. Increased insurance premiums. Environmental impacts, for sure. We'd need parking, restroom facilities, vans or some way to move people around." They already offered hunting, fishing and birding trips. But those were on the southernmost portion of the land. "There have to be another dozen things I haven't considered."

Connor nodded. "Have you consulted with Ricardo?"

Ricardo was the foreman of that section. More than anyone, he would know some of the pitfalls. "I was going to do that next."

"Good plan. Then have him contact Nathan. Nathan can work on a feasibility study, work up a cost analysis."

"You don't mind me asking?"

"Why the hell would I mind?"

"He's got real work to do for Donovan Worldwide. This would be a distraction."

Connor's eyes, so similar to Cade's, narrowed. "Don't make me knock some sense into you in front of the family." Connor's voice held shards of ice.

"I'm still bigger than you," Cade reminded him.

"But I'm more pissed. And you've fucking had it coming for a long time. Five years, at least."

Cade took a swig of his beer, considering. Connor was right. Something raw and nasty gnawed in Cade's gut. Guilt. Anger at the unfairness of it all. Part of him wanted Connor to take a swing. Maybe it'd give him some fucking release.

Nathan strolled over.

The tension between Cade and Connor continued to roil, just beneath a polished veneer.

"Private party?" Nathan asked.

"Brotherly love," Connor returned. "Welcome to the brawl."

"Damn. We haven't had one of those in what, seven, eight years?"

Cade remembered the fucking miserable summer night in Corpus Christi. Middle of August. Eighty-something degrees, ninety percent humidity, making the air as suffocating as a wet blanket. Only two things had been moving, rattlesnakes and tempers.

"What are we fighting about?" Nathan sounded interested.

"Same thing as last time," Connor replied.

"More or less," Cade agreed. Back then, Cade had been in college, and Connor had recently graduated from high school. Though their father had insisted Cade receive a good education, it had been clear that Connor would inherit the majority of the family's money and interests. Cade hadn't objected. After all, he'd had no desire to move to Houston. He'd liked his life the way it was. All he'd needed was the rodeo, his ridiculously fast cars and motorcycles and a place to stow his gear.

None of them had known that it would be the last time they'd all be together with their father still alive. The four had spent the day on the land. Their father, Jeffrey, had told them the history of ranch, shared his memories, the dreams he'd had for it. And they'd all heard the regret in his tone. He'd loved the ranch, and that he wasn't able to devote time to it had bothered him.

Connor had said that Cade would make it all happen. Cade, feeling like the outsider he was, hadn't wanted something that rightfully belonged to his brother. He'd said he'd be moving along after he'd earned his degree.

Later that night, Connor had sought him out, called him a quitter and told him he had the same obligations as any other Donovan.

All his life, Cade had heard the whispers. He was a bastard, an imposter.

His frustration at being told to step up and behave like a member of the family had made him furious, and he'd thrown the first punch.

Connor had gone down, but he'd grabbed Cade's ankle and yanked him off balance, slamming him to the ground. He might have been bigger than Connor, more accustomed to barroom and street brawls, but he had been dazed, and Connor had taken advantage of that. He'd still been pummeling Cade when Nathan had joined them and pulled Connor away and stayed between them until the tensions had eased.

"I'd prefer not to spill any of this mighty fine cabernet. But if necessary…" Nathan put down the glass on a nearby table. "Whose side am I on? Or am I just supposed to separate the two of you?"

"Your choice, big brother," Connor said to Cade. "You can continue to be a jackass or you can lose the chip on your shoulder and realize no one objects to you owning section one." He narrowed his gaze. "Or the house. If you want to burn the thing down or sell it, turn it into a bordello, that's your right. You owe us nothing."

"A bordello?" Nathan asked. "Now there's an idea."

"Whether you like it or not, we're brothers," Connor persisted. He didn't even bother to direct his gaze toward Nathan. "If you have a personal business idea, we sure as hell should be the people you turn to first, for advice, feasibility studies, financing. It's what family does."

He got that Erin, Nathan and Connor did that for one another. But Cade spent the majority of his time alone. Always had.

"What's it going to be, Cade?" He put down his champagne glass. "You going to take the help? Or are you going to continue to be an asshole with some fucked-up version of reality in your head?"

The laughter and revelry from the reception spilled around them, yet the tension continued to draw and stretch. Cade had no doubt Connor was serious. He'd fight for family, even if Cade didn't think he deserved it. And Connor threw a wicked punch. He'd go for a quick one-two to the gut then the jaw. Cade was fast and big. Both had reserves of anger to draw from. But on principle, Cade wouldn't hit as hard. He wasn't sure he wanted to drive back to the ranch with a dislocated jaw.

In the end, it was Nathan, as always, who defused the situation. "My jacket is brand new. I'd hate for my biceps to tear it."

"Your biceps?" Cade repeated, feeling some of the tension begin to ease from his gut, even though Connor still looked pissed.

"Been keeping myself fit so I have the energy to shoot down the ideas that everyone else thinks will make millions of dollars," Nathan said.

He was damn good at it. Not only did he have the patience to drill down on the most mundane details, he had a sixth sense when it came to evaluating a company's place in the market.

"Takes talent to thrash the wheat from the chaff."

"True," Connor conceded.

"Let me at it," Nathan continued. "You can email me or I could come down."

A few seconds stretched, the silence tenuous.

"That'd be good. It's been a while," Cade agreed.

The angry tension drained from Connor's face, and the knot inside Cade began to dissipate. He was smart enough to realize that he didn't deserve the family who so lovingly accepted him.

"I'll email you on Monday and set up a time," Nathan said. "Maybe stay a couple of days."

"You've got a room waiting." More like a wing, and if he wanted even more privacy, there were an additional three guest cottages on the property. Eighty years ago, the size of the house had made sense. Now it stood mostly as a museum.

No matter what the will or Connor said, Cade believed it belonged to his siblings every bit as much as him.

"Lara and I might come down, too," Connor said, as if Cade hadn't just been on the edge of fracturing their relationship. "When he was here, Julien mentioned he may want some time to ride horses."

"Bonds gets his prissy ass on a horse?"

"Inconceivable," Nathan added.

Connor shrugged.

"He's welcome. I'll keep a guest house ready." The ranch had a short landing strip and a helicopter pad, making it easy in and out for a notorious recluse.

Any lingering emotional strain was shattered when Cade saw Lara and Erin heading toward them. Erin's hand was firmly clamped around Sofia's wrist.

Well, well.

The evening was looking better every moment.

Nathan stepped aside to make room for the ladies.

"We're sorry to interrupt," Lara said, her voice holding no trace of apology. "Cade, I'd like you to meet my friend Sofia McBride. She owns Encore, the events company that put together this reception. Two hundred people, three weeks, one brilliant result."

"We've met."

"You have?" Lara frowned.

After sweeping his gaze over Sofia, he said, "She's been taking good care of everyone."

"Thank you, thank you," Sofia replied, taking a little bow, likely to cover the flush of embarrassment that had crept up her face.

He wondered if anyone else noticed the way she was avoiding eye contact with him. No doubt he'd had the same effect on her as she had on him.

From the first moment he'd seen her, the petite, curvy woman had grabbed his attention. And she hadn't let go.

She wore a jacket over a stretchy white shirt, and a matching black skirt clung to her hips and thighs, tight in a way that made him want to touch. Despite the heat, she had on stockings, and he was man enough to wonder if they were attached to a garter belt. Her pumps were several inches high, but she would still fit beneath his chin.

Vaguely, he noticed that Lara hadn't stopped speaking, and he forced himself to focus on what she was saying.

"Encore Events specializes in pulling off the impossible, which she certainly did tonight."

He hadn't glanced away from Sofia, even though she had

yet to meet his eyes.

"Best of all," Lara continued, "they have several locations in Texas, including one in Corpus Christi. All of your centennial celebration problems are solved."

Understanding dawned, hot with possibility. Sofia had said she was from Corpus, but she hadn't mentioned she had offices there.

"We'll leave you to it." Lara nudged Connor.

"Right," Connor responded. "I think I'll dance with my wife."

"Does this mean we're not having a brawl?" Nathan asked.

"It means you need to excuse yourself," Connor told him. "Unless you want to get dragged into discussions about petits fours and color selection."

"I kept you out of those decisions," Lara replied.

"I owe Sofia my eternal and undying gratitude."

Lara flashed Connor a sunny smile. "You can thank me later. In private."

He skimmed his finger down Lara's throat and across the diamonds in her necklace. For a moment, the two appeared lost in each other.

Nathan cleared his throat. Still, it took Connor a few seconds to drop his hand and stop staring at his wife.

As if nothing untoward were happening, Erin filled the silence by saying, "Cade will need your centennial celebration guest lists."

Nathan groaned.

She glared at him. "By the end of the week."

"It's not too late to burn the whole thing down," Nathan said to Cade.

Erin punched him in the biceps.

"Damn."

"Be glad I hit like a girl."

"Christ. What the hell? Have you been taking boxing lessons?"

"Thought you said you'd been working out?" Cade asked

33

easily.

"She only hurt me because my muscles were sore from pumping iron this morning," Nathan replied, but he rubbed at his arm.

"Uh-huh," Erin said.

A few seconds later, Lara and his siblings returned to the clubhouse.

Then he was alone with Sofia. He thumbed back the brim of his hat so he could get an even better look at her. The glow from a nearby lamp reflected off the coppery highlights in her mahogany hair. She wore it pulled back, in some sort of fancy braid that he itched to free.

Out here, under the filtered lights, he noticed that her hazel eyes were flecked with gold. Unusual and arresting.

"Erin and Lara mentioned you're planning a centennial celebration for the ranch sometime this fall," she continued. "I was told, in no uncertain terms, that there will be no buffalo chicken wing cupcakes on the dessert table."

"She's correct. Turns out planning a party is outside of my usual job description, and I was just informed that I should have already sent out a save-the-date announcement."

"We can do that. And we can handle as much or as little as you want. I have a generic checklist of all the things that need to be considered. I can email it to you. You can decide which things you want to handle yourself and which you want to hire out. If you want to be your own coordinator, it will give you a list of the service providers you may want to consider."

"Caterers, for example?"

"Absolutely. Ones who would never consider putting buffalo wing cupcakes on the menu." She grinned.

Sofia had an easy-going but professional air that appealed to him.

"But I'll also provide options for music, entertainment, videographers, that sort of thing."

"So why would I pay you?" he asked.

"Peace of mind. I imagine there are a dozen things you

do better than anyone else on the planet. Which means you have no time to be a party planner. It would be a waste of your time and energy. Why should you wonder if the caterer has enough chairs for all of your guests to sit on, or enough napkins for dinner and dessert? The truth is, you don't have any idea of all the things you need to be concerned about. Because you're related to Lara, I'm happy to give you a crash course, but I know how big your ranch is. It takes a lot of energy. You don't have time to arrange an event. And you don't want to wake up in the middle of the night thinking about the details."

Plenty of things kept him up. And he could add tantalizing thoughts of her to the mix.

"Of course, you could choose a different event planner, but the truth is, almost no one else in South Texas is as big as Encore. They will end up getting most of their hard goods from us. So, you'd be paying more for markups, as well."

He appreciated her businesslike approach. "That's a hell of a sales pitch."

"It's not a sales pitch. Frankly, we don't need the business and my guess is, because of the remoteness and the fact the celebration wasn't your idea, the timeframe and the lack of a guest list, working with you would be a significant pain in the ass, enough so that I'd probably add a Pain in the Ass Fee to the bid."

"Are you always so blunt?"

"You've already been quite nosy. Why shouldn't we be forthright?"

"You've got a point."

"Besides, I prefer the word direct over blunt. But I was right, wasn't I?"

"About me being a pain in the ass?"

"As I said earlier, I've heard of your reputation. You're not an easy man to work for. Exacting. Unforgiving."

His ego suddenly felt a little bruised. "You also said you'd heard some good stuff."

"That was the good stuff."

He winced.

"I think you intimidate some people."

"But not you?"

She hesitated for just a moment. "On a personal level, yes."

Her honesty impressed him.

After a little breath, she went on, "But when it comes to business, I'm not afraid of you."

"Is that confidence or recklessness speaking?"

"Confidence. I don't leave things to chance. We handle multiple events every week. On the Gulf Coast, we arrange corporate dinner cruises, organize a yearly rodeo and we're the company of choice at the biggest events center in Corpus Christi. All of that means we have relationships with the vendors in the area. We work with them, we know their strengths. Better yet, we know who to steer clear of. I know which pieces of the contracts are negotiable. I can get you people who might already be booked."

"The party isn't until fall."

"Weddings are often scheduled a year in advance. You've actually started planning this at least six months too late."

"Seriously?"

"I can make up the lost time, though, and I have some pull with local musicians like the Matthew Martin band."

Even he'd heard of them. The country-and-western group had recently won a prestigious award and were in the middle of a nationwide tour. "You can get them?"

"If you want them, yes. They will reschedule for me. I can give you a not-to-exceed budget and we can pay all the other contractors so that you only write two checks, one for a deposit and another at the completion of the event."

He glanced around and hooked a thumb toward the clubhouse. "Do you always give this kind of service?"

"Encore does, yes. I don't attend all the events. We have a well-trained staff, so I usually attend the more complicated ones."

That appealed to him. "Do you offer net terms?"

"I prefer not to. Our top clients get three days, max," she replied.

"Three days it is. Any discount for payment at time of service?"

"Never."

He raised an eyebrow, but she didn't relent. "Are you expensive?"

"Very."

Her answer was so fast that he knew the answer to his next question before he even asked it. "Are you worth it?"

"Every penny."

"I like your style." He took out his business card and offered it to her.

She slid it in her pocket without glancing at the information. "I'll be in Corpus this Tuesday and Wednesday. Would you like to set up an appointment? I'd like to see the ranch, the facilities and any amenities so that I can get some ideas going for you. I know you're busy, so if you can have someone show me around, that would be fine. But if you're planning to hire us, the sooner we sign the contract, the better."

When he wanted something, he went after it. He saw the same resolve in the set of Sofia's shoulders and he admired it. "Tuesday afternoon is fine."

"Three? At the ranch?"

"Contact me and I'll send you detailed instructions. One point of clarity. You said you typically handle the more complicated events."

She nodded.

"I want you to personally handle this event."

"Of course."

"When I call, I want you to answer." Then he clarified, "Not an assistant. I want you to select all the vendors and make sure the food is perfect."

"That's not the way we do things." She smoothed her hand down her skirt. "I generally allocate my time between the three offices, and my home is here in Houston."

"Your point being?"

"You're already a pain in the ass, Mr. Donovan. I assure you that Encore has a very capable team. The Corpus Christi project manager is wonderful, and our foreman has been with the company since its inception. I'm happy to check in on progress during our weekly staff meetings, and I receive daily status reports, and of course I'll be at the event itself. You'll be well taken care of."

He crossed his arms over his chest. "Is there a part of what I want that's unclear?"

She exhaled and met his gaze. "I understood what you said. But that's a level of service that's unreasonable. It's not something we're set up to offer."

"So add it."

"Mr. Donovan—"

"Cade."

As if he hadn't spoken, she went on, "You may need a smaller company, one that has time to give you what you need."

He continued to meet her stare. "I think I was clear. I want you, Sofia."

Silence hung, stretched, grew taut. Finally, finally, she exhaled. "If I have to oversee everything, it will cost you more. A lot more."

"I'm always willing to pay for excellence." He extended his hand. "Do we have a deal or not?"

"After you sign the contract," she hedged.

"But we have a verbal agreement to meet and proceed."

"We don't need to shake hands on that."

"Perhaps I prefer to do business the old-fashioned way." And perhaps he wanted to know if she felt as soft and feminine as he imagined.

She regarded him for several seconds.

"It's going to be a pleasure to work with you."

"I think I'm going to regret this," she replied.

"Probably," he agreed easily.

She slid her palm against his. He felt her warmth and

38

softness.

Her breath caught as he squeezed just a little, and she looked up at him through her impossibly long, dark eyelashes.

She blinked then extracted herself from his grip.

The sounds of a country-and-western ballad spilled from the clubhouse. He recognized the song from the radio, knew how to pick a few of the chords on his guitar. And because there was something about a wedding, something about being alone when other people had partners, something about the temptation of a beautiful woman on a starlit evening and the fact he wanted an excuse to talk with her a little longer, he asked, "Do you dance?"

"I love to. But I rarely have the opportunity. Occupational hazard."

"You're the one making sure the party is a success, not the one enjoying it."

"Precisely."

"Dance with me."

Her mouth parted. He could tell he'd caught her off guard.

"With..." Sofia glanced over her shoulder then back at him. "I'm working."

"I know the boss."

"That's true," she conceded.

He couldn't look away from her mouth and her inviting red lipstick. "It's just three minutes. Four at the most."

"That's also true."

"And you want to."

"I..." She took a breath.

Cade glanced at her left hand. "We've ascertained that there's no Mr. McBride and that you haven't had a lot of opportunity to color outside the lines."

She hesitated, seeming to choose her words. Obviously she'd noticed the way he'd looked at her and she realized she had a choice in how she wanted to respond. She could shut him down, or she could take the chance he was offering.

She fingered back a stray wisp of hair.

"What harm could there be?"

"Honestly?" she asked. "About five things come immediately to mind."

"Only five?" He kept his tone light.

"At least five."

"There's hardly anyone out here. No one will notice."

"I'm not your type, Mr. Donovan."

"What type is that?"

He didn't step back or give her any space. Instead, with uncharacteristic patience, he waited.

"You know what I mean."

"No, I really don't. Enlighten me."

"Someone who…" She paused. "I'm not trying to insult you."

"As you were saying, why stop being blunt now?" He gave a little wave, indicating she should continue. "By all means."

The color on her cheeks darkened a little. It made her even more appealing.

"This is more about me, not you." She drew a breath. "You've had a lot more experience than I have."

He couldn't help but grin at that. "Are you calling me a manwhore?"

She had the good grace to blush, and he was glad to see it. Her not-so-delicate assumption had pissed him off a little.

"I can assure you, I am not. Nor was I. I dated a lot in college, on the rodeo circuit, but I've never been a fuck 'em-and-leave 'em guy."

"I didn't mean to imply that," she protested.

"I believe you did. Without knowing me."

"You're right." She exhaled. "I apologize."

"Accepted. Next objection?"

"I picture you with a socialite."

Cade couldn't have been any more taken aback. "Are you calling me a snob?"

"You're a Donovan," she said, as if that explained everything. Maybe to her, it did.

"Which means?"

"You're the town's elite. Someone who keeps to his own kind." She lifted a shoulder.

"Such as?"

"Senators. Business leaders. Other landowners. The Running Wind isn't exactly an ordinary ranch."

That much was true. He recalled the first time he'd seen the house, when he was five. He and his mother had been living in a small one-bedroom apartment above a garage near the stables where she'd worked in Kentucky. His father, a man he hadn't known, had shown up one day, and Cade still remembered the shouting and his mother's sobs.

Soon afterward, they'd all been piled into his father's gargantuan pickup truck, with its oversized tires and soft-leather interior. They'd had to stop overnight at a hotel with an air conditioner that worked, making the room so cold he had been able to snuggle under a blanket.

Now he realized it had been a place designed for road-weary families, with a swimming pool and a breakfast buffet. But as a child, it had been unimaginable that he could have enough food to get full and he could make his own waffles.

Afterward, his father had driven them the rest of the way to the Running Wind. Cade had a vague recollection of a Garth Brooks song playing on the truck's stereo when he'd encountered his first-ever bump gate.

It had seemed to him that they'd traveled forever before the big house came into view. To his mind, it had been about the size of the hotel they'd stayed at the previous night. And when his father had said that he was supposed to live there with his mother, Cade had stared in wide-eyed disbelief.

Then he'd noticed the man at the top of the stairs. Imposingly tall, frightening in his far-reaching power.

His mother had looked out of the side window, refusing to speak, and Jeffrey had said the man was William Donovan—the man most people called the Colonel—

Cade's grandfather. Cade remembered standing there mute and paralyzed. He hadn't known he'd had a dad, let alone a big, tall grandfather who wore a suit coat and massive black felt hat and never smiled.

For at least the first week Cade had been so overwhelmed that he'd sneaked into his mother's bedroom and slept on the floor.

As time had progressed, and without his conscious awareness, the palatial space had become his home, part of him. It had been built to endure the harsh Texas weather, unbearable summer heat, relentless tropical storms, never-ending wind.

He appreciated the craftsmanship of the structure and the fact it had been designed with family in mind. "Even Miss Libby wears boots when she's at the house. That's the reality of ranch life. When it was built, my great-great-grandmother said that the big house had to withstand people living in it, employees dropping by, visitors showing up. There's no carpet, and no fussy collectibles. More than one set of spurs have gouged the floors. And that's the way it should be." He hesitated. "So, other than me hanging out with socialites, whoring around and the fact I'm a snob, tell me about my type."

"Mr. Donovan, I come from a hardworking family. Even now we live a moderate lifestyle. I was the first to go to college, and I couldn't have done that if I hadn't gotten a scholarship." She exhaled.

"And I'm illegitimate."

She blinked. "Meaning?"

"As in my mother was not married to my father."

A smile teased the corner of her mouth. "Well, I can assure you that I've heard you called a bastard, and never once did it refer to your parentage."

He raised an eyebrow in appreciation of her boldness. "Well said, Ms. McBride. So tell me again about how I'm not your type."

After a quick exhalation, she said, "You have me there."

"You said you had at least five reasons we shouldn't dance together. We got rid of number one. What's next?"

He knew he was making her a little uncomfortable, probably because she wanted to be in his arms as much as he wanted to have her there.

Her cheeks now held streaks of embarrassment. "I think what I'm trying to say—badly—is that I don't sleep around."

"And you've heard that I do?"

"Actually…" She scowled. "No."

"I don't date. Haven't in the last few years."

"You know, I think I've made some assumptions."

"And?"

"Maybe I've underestimated you."

Vaguely he was aware of other people around them. There was an air of intimacy, though, about the way he was standing near Sofia. People stayed away from them, and it was as if it were only the two of them outside. "Since you're clearly at a loss for words, shall I tell you about my type? Then we can take it from there?"

"I've done a really bad job of this."

"My type is a woman who is honest, who knows what she wants and isn't afraid to go after it. My type is someone who is comfortable with who she is, not trying to impress anyone. She's tall. Or not. She's curvy. Or not. Perhaps you meant to say I'm not your type."

"That would be rude."

"But true?"

"You know it's not."

"Yeah." He did know. A thread of sexual attraction wove between them. He was a warm-blooded man, and she was a lovely, brave woman. "What are the other three reasons?"

"I'm not really dressed for it."

He felt a smile tugging at his mouth. And she was biting her lower lip. "You've given me a lot of excuses, yet you haven't said you don't want to," he pointed out.

The song ended and another took its place, this one a bit

43

more uptempo.

She continued to look at him. Another few seconds ticked away. How long had it been since he'd asked a woman to dance then waited with this kind of anticipation? College? Maybe he had once or twice in the couple of years after, before everything changed.

"I think I'm more concerned because I do want to," she admitted softly.

Her admission slammed his libido into overdrive. "A two-step," he offered, to put her mind at ease and to put some boundaries up for himself. "I'll be a gentleman."

Her eyes darkened.

From her reaction, he couldn't tell whether she liked that idea or had hoped he'd misbehave a little.

"Yes," she said. "I'd like to dance, Mr. Donovan."

He raised her hand a couple of inches and placed his left palm just above the small of her back. She hesitated only for a moment before lightly touching his biceps.

Cade moved them into the dance, and she effortlessly followed his lead. Once they'd found a natural rhythm, he guided her into an outside turn. Her movements were flawless, but she hesitated as she came back toward him. "Well done," he said.

"It's been a while," she replied. "But I took some lessons a couple of years ago. I was at an event, and the DJ was having a difficult time getting people out onto the dance floor. And I didn't know enough line dances to try to lead one. I figured it was a skill that could come in handy. I'm not an expert, but I know enough to encourage people to get out of their seats."

He took a chance and raised his hand slightly, signaling an upcoming inside turn.

She executed the move perfectly.

He brought her back to him. It jolted him how right it felt to have her in his arms, so close that he could inhale her scent, something light, fresh—a direct contrast to the emotions churning in him. "You are good."

44

"Thank you," she said. "But a two-step isn't that difficult."

Cade looked down at her, scowling.

"And what I mean is, you lead well. Is your ego soothed now?"

"It would have been if you had stopped talking after your first sentence."

Her smile was quick and a bit sassy. "I've heard that my whole life."

"Have you?" It had been years since he'd enjoyed this kind of easy exchange with a woman. He appreciated it more than he expected.

"I would never have suspected you were such a good dancer," she told him, jolting him from his thoughts.

"More preconceived notions?"

"Maybe I should have worn boots. I keep stepping in it, don't I?"

"I spent some time on the rodeo circuit. I learned very young that girls like to dance. So my aunt taught me how. Wait until you see me line dance."

She raised her eyebrows. "Really?"

"I'll show you at the party."

"Is that one of the ways you're hoping to entice me to take the job?"

"I don't know. Would it work?"

He was aware of her gaze on his chest, maybe directed at the ends of his bulldogger tie. If he'd had any idea he would have a beautiful woman in his arms, he'd have stayed dressed up.

"Ms. McBride? I was asking if my line dance would entice you to take the job."

"It certainly doesn't hurt," she admitted in that husky voice of hers.

The song neared the end and he brought her a little closer.

Her breath caught as she swayed, almost missing a step.

She looked up and met his gaze. The gold flecks in her eyes appeared brighter. The longer he held her, the longer their gazes held, the more her hesitation and reserve seemed to melt.

For a moment, he thought of kissing her. He trailed his thumb across her upper lip, and her breath caught.

The darkness in him was attracted to the lightness in her. It was seductive. Relentless. Consuming.

Fuck it.

He moved them to a quiet corner.

"I want to kiss you, Sofia."

"I…" Her eyes were wide, the gold flecks pronounced.

"Tell me no," he encouraged her.

"Kiss me," she said instead, stunning him.

She raised onto her tiptoes and leaned toward him. More than ever, he wanted to work his fingers into the luxurious length of her hair. It was long, thick and enticing, perfect for a sex scene. When they had more time, he would delight in pulling out the assortment of pins and removing the band at the bottom. For now, he settled for wrapping his fist around it, pretending, for a moment, he wasn't a caveman.

He skimmed a finger across her lower lip before he kissed her. Then he demanded more.

She moaned. Rather than pulling away, she moaned.

God damn fucking wonderful response.

Once he touched his lips to hers and she surrendered, he was filled with a need that he'd never experienced.

She tasted of the freshness of citrus, and more, promise and hope, things that had been absent in his life for so long that he barely remembered them.

He breathed in her innocence, basked in it. It wasn't enough. He wanted more. Wanted her.

As she responded by linking her arms around his neck, he kissed her harder, with more passion, all but devouring her. She met him boldly, accepting everything he offered. It was as if her innocence were wrapped in an inviting package of curiosity.

He wanted to be the one to show her. But that would be a mistake. Even though he'd been the one to encourage this, he needed to keep the enchanting Sofia in the off-limits category.

Slowly, reluctantly, he ended the kiss, but they remained wrapped together. Surprising him, she didn't pull away. Surprising him even more, he didn't encourage it, even after the music trailed off.

In the background, he heard the DJ announce that Lara was going to toss her bouquet and that all the single ladies were requested to gather around.

"I should go." Her voice had a huskiness that spoke of the South and seductive summer nights.

"Are you hoping to catch the flowers?"

"No," she said quickly. "I just want to be sure the photographer gets the right pictures." She lowered her hands and took a step back.

"Thank you for the dance."

"You were a perfect gentleman, as promised," she said.

"I was tonight," he told her. "In the future, I might not be." In fact, he couldn't help but picture her attached to a beam in his barn, mouth gagged, her hair gloriously loose around her shoulders as she waited for his commands.

The image—bright, vivid—startled him. It knocked him off balance, and it wasn't as unwelcome as it should have been. "In fact, you'd be wise to keep your distance from me."

"Would I?" She pressed her fingers to her lips.

Trying to remember the kiss? Or maybe soothe the ache from the intensity?

"Everything you've heard about me…" His voice was gruff, the confession tearing at his vocal cords. He wasn't a good man. "It's true. All of it, and more."

"Is it?"

"I'd be remiss if I didn't encourage you to protect yourself."

"In that case, Mr. Donovan, please be assured that I consider myself warned."

"Sofia—"

"I'm looking forward to Tuesday," she said.

She was either very, very brave or she had a reckless disregard for her safety, and that meant trouble for him.

Sofia turned, picked up her clipboard then walked toward the clubhouse.

Her hips swayed with each step, and he saw her calves flex.

Near the door, she glanced back and met his gaze. Fuck him three ways from Sunday. He wanted her. Hard. Fast. Beneath him. Kneeling for him. And he wanted it now, not several days from now.

Then she turned away and went back inside.

It took every bit of his hard-won control not to go after her.

It'd been a hell of a night—so much more than she'd expected.

Sofia kicked off her shoes in her apartment's entryway and dropped her oversized tote bag on the floor next to them. With a sigh, she shrugged out of her blazer and tossed it onto the coat rack.

Without turning on a single light, she walked through to her bedroom, unfastening the buttons on her blouse as she went.

She'd anticipated it would be an easy event and that she'd be home well before midnight. But she hadn't counted on Julien Bonds showing up, or spending considerable time with the intriguing Cade Donovan.

The dance with him had left her mentally unbalanced and sexually needy.

While she wasn't a virgin, she had never had this kind of reaction to a man. For her, sex had been ho-hum, something she could take or leave. Mostly she did it because a man expected it after they'd dated for a while. She'd never initiated it, and thoughts of it certainly never occupied her mind the way it seemed to for her friends. And she'd never experienced anything like Lara had talked about.

That was, until tonight.

The way Cade had looked at her, as if he wanted to devour her, had made her feel desired. His touch had been masterful, his attitude that of an implacable alpha, and his kiss…

She put her hand on the wall to steady herself.

As if he were there, she recalled the way he'd touched

his lips to hers. At first, he'd been gentle, then insistent and finally, demanding. It had been as complex as the man himself, and it—he—had ignited a dizzying number of emotions in her.

There'd been nothing hesitant about him, and she'd found his confidence appealing. He'd left her wanting more.

In the bathroom, Sofia tugged the band from the bottom of her hair then used her fingers to work the braid's strands free.

Most times, she took a bath to relax after a long night, but tonight she opted for a shower. Without much conscious thought, she removed her blouse and dropped it on the floor. Her bra followed. Then she shimmied out of her snug-fitting skirt and rolled down her stockings. Irrationally, wishing Cade were there to finish undressing her, she wriggled out of her sensible panties.

She stepped beneath the lukewarm spray then took down the handheld showerhead.

With her eyes closed, she allowed her mind the freedom she'd denied it all night.

She recalled the initial nervousness when Cade had taken her in his arms. He was a big man. But his size offered strength, rather than intimidation.

As they'd moved together, she'd had a stray, wild compulsion to stroke her fingers across his face, outline the trimmed, well-kept goatee. Sometime after the wedding pictures had been taken, he'd unknotted his tie but left the ends dangling. He'd also opened the top button of his shirt. His casual elegance had intrigued her.

His skin was tanned, no doubt from time spent outdoors. And for a scandalous moment, she'd wanted to know what his chest looked like.

More than anything, though, the pain in his eyes continued to haunt her.

What they'd shared had ignited a dormant flame in her. None of it had been enough.

And yet…

He was dangerous. He'd advised her to stay away from him, and intuition told her she'd be smart to heed him.

But to her heated body, the warning meant little.

She all but felt the metal of his belt buckle against her bare skin as she moved the nozzle up her body, across her abdomen, over her breasts.

Sofia parted her legs and directed the spray toward her pussy.

The sensation was nice, sweet, but it didn't match the demand that swarmed through her. She opened her eyes to change the setting to pulse.

As the water jetted against her, she took turns squeezing her nipples, imagining it was Cade's grip twisting and pulling on them.

She closed her eyes, allowing the fantasy to morph.

She saw him securing her wrists in one of his big hands before he tied her face down on a bed. Even though she tried to keep still, she moved her ass in anticipation. Before she was ready, he brought down his belt, searing her.

Sofia cried out. An orgasm gathered force, stunning her.

She didn't masturbate often, and she'd never gotten aroused this quickly.

Then she realized she'd been turned on since Cade had introduced himself. Her climax was the culmination of all the sensations he'd evoked in her.

Still picturing Cade touching her, making her respond, she allowed the spray to hit her clit, and she gasped. Again, frustrating her, it wasn't enough.

After tugging each of her nipples a final time, she used her free hand to part her labia and expose her clit.

Worrying her lower lip, she moved the showerhead closer to her pelvis. This time, the combination of the heat and pressure was enough. She jerked as it pounded her, and she was filled with thoughts of Cade doing this to her, this... Individual feelings coalesced, merging, and she couldn't sort one from another. All she could think of was Cade. Her clit ached. This... She wanted him...his mouth, his tongue, his cock...

She screamed.

Then she put a hand out to steady herself as she came.

It wasn't until much, much later—when the water was chilled—that she could rouse herself to turn off the faucet.

With only a towel wrapped around her, she fell on top of her bed.

Sofia always slept well.

Tonight, though, she dreamed of eyes so dark they seemed to devour, of being held down and fucked hard. Before she could climax, everything splintered into a nonsensical kaleidoscope of careening, unfulfilled desire, dropping, plummeting, gnawing on the edges of her consciousness.

〰〰〰

When she woke up, she felt a bit blurry, as if she'd never been to sleep.

Washing her face in cold water, getting dressed, even a cup of hot tea didn't help her throw off the lingering effects of the night before.

Thank goodness she had a full day today, getting ready for her usual Sunday morning brunch with her sister, going into the office, reviewing the week's financials from the three Encore branches.

After dressing in shorts and a tank top, she whipped up a quiche and popped it in the oven. While she waited, she opened a bottle of sparkling wine, grabbed a bottle of orange juice, pulled out a carton of raspberries then made herself a mimosa. Maybe the bubbly would help her banish thoughts of Cade Donovan. Or, if not, at least move them to the side so that he occupied fewer of her brain cells.

Before she was quite ready for company, her sister Zoe knocked on the door, called out a greeting then used her key to let herself in without waiting for a response.

Sofia had rarely been happier to see anyone. Over the years, having Sunday brunch together had become a ritual.

They'd talk about work, catch up on all the personal things they didn't get to discuss during the week.

By nature, Sofia was a family person, so her travel schedule was a challenge. She would love to spend more time in Corpus Christi, especially since one of their younger half-sisters now had six-month-old twins. This connection with Zoe helped sustain Sofia.

"So, what's he like?" Zoe demanded.

"What? Who?"

"You know who." Zoe plopped down her purse then slammed the door behind her. There was nothing subtle about her younger sis. "Avery said Cade Donovan was heading right for you when you shooed her ass out the door."

"I didn't—"

"Diversionary tactics will not work. I'm on to you."

"How do you know Cade?" she countered.

"I don't. Not really. I saw him in town a couple of years ago." Zoe gave her a quick hug before sliding onto one of the stools across the granite bar from Sofia. "He's one of those people you know on sight, even if you've never met them. Well, I suppose all the Donovans are. They're in the society pages often enough. Or at least they used to be, a few years ago."

Again without waiting for an invitation, she splashed a dollop of orange juice into a flute then filled the rest with the sparkling wine. If Sofia had been pouring, she would have used considerably more juice than Zoe.

"Come on. Tell me all." Zoe picked up a plump raspberry and plopped it into her glass. "Avery said he looked edible."

Edible was a fitting word. Cade had been unlike any other man at the reception. It went far beyond his good looks. When he entered a room, he dominated it.

But she wasn't going to tell her sister about her haunted fantasies and dreams.

"When I saw him, he reminded me a bit of Mr. Rochester."

"Mr. Rochester?" Sofia repeated.

"You know, from *Jane Eyre*?"

That Mr. Rochester.

"It wasn't long after his father's death. He didn't say much, and he struck me as being a little lost. In his own world."

While Sofia was pragmatic, Zoe could be a bit of a romantic. Most of the time that worked well for their business partnership.

Sofia checked to be sure the oven timer was set then picked up her drink. "I'm meeting with him Tuesday to talk about the ranch's centennial celebration."

"Get out." Zoe put down her flute with a tiny thud. "Seriously?"

"Erin Donovan, that's his half-sister, was talking to Lara about the event. Lara mentioned that Encore has a Corpus Christi office. So in answer to your question... What's he like? A shrewd businessman." Sofia looked across at her sister. "He may not know anything about parties, but he asked for terms and a discount."

"He's not a corporation. Wait..." Zoe stopped and frowned. "Come to think of it, he probably is. How many people are we talking about?"

"According to Erin, about a thousand."

"At the ranch? Or are they going to rent someplace? Maybe the rodeo grounds?"

"They're planning to hold it at the Running Wind."

"That could be a logistical nightmare," Zoe said. "Figuring out parking will keep you up nights."

"I'm thinking of running shuttle buses from Waltham."

Zoe nodded. "Good thinking."

"There may be other options. I'll know more when I see the ranch."

"Anyway, back to Cade."

Sofia had been hoping Zoe had moved on. She should have known better.

"Where are you meeting him?"

She pretended that her heart wasn't suddenly thudding

out of her chest. "At his place."

"Just the two of you?"

"And the dozens of people who work for him." At least she assumed so. The idea of being alone with him was one notch under terrifying.

"You're being ridiculously silent. I'm thinking you liked him."

Too damn much.

She was aware of Zoe regarding her, waiting. "He is intense," she said. "Knows what he wants and is determined to have it. No seems to mean maybe. We danced."

"Seriously? What, a waltz?"

Sofia scowled.

"Okay, okay. Go on." Zoe had a small sip from the flute but somehow managed not to break eye contact. "He asked you to dance and you said...?"

"I gave him a list of reasons I shouldn't. Including the fact I'm not the type who associates with the Donovans, or, rather, they're not the type who associates with us."

Zoe groaned. "Please tell me you didn't mention that Mom used to be a server for Miss Libby's events."

"Shockingly, I was able to keep the confession from pouring out," Sofia said wryly.

"Whew. So. Keep going."

"He responded that he was a bastard."

"To which you replied..."

"I'd heard that but I'd never had the impression it had anything to do with his parentage."

Zoe lifted her glass to clink against Sofia's.

"Is he a good dancer?"

"He is."

"And?"

Sofia shook her head. "That's it." The rest was personal and private.

Obviously sensing she wasn't going to get any more information, Zoe returned to business. "Okay, we know that working with the Donovan family could be really good for Encore. It could give us an intro into another echelon of contacts, which means long-term growth. So what are the potential pitfalls?"

"Besides capital expenses? If a thousand people RSVP, we may need to buy more sections for our party tent. And we'll need to know soon so that we can get them ordered." They rarely got requests for events of that size. Of course, they could advertise the additional capacity, in all the cities they served. "And he wants me to handle the details personally. All of them."

Zoe fished out her raspberry and popped it into her mouth. "Did you mention you don't have time for that?"

"More than once, actually."

"And? Come on, sis. Do I have to drag every stinking detail out of you?"

"Well, if you'd quit interrupting, we'd get through it faster." Sofia took a drink. "I told him we had a capable team, and that if he wanted that kind of personalized attention, it would be costly."

"If you're not spending as much time at the Houston branch, we may need to hire extra help. I can work a few more hours, but I have to stay focused on sales when possible."

"True." Sofia had moved to Houston for college eight years ago. When Zoe had been accepted into the same school two years later, they'd become roommates. It had been natural for Zoe to join Encore, even more natural to promote her to general manager when Sofia had opened the San Antonio branch.

Somehow Zoe managed to juggle all kinds of responsibilities. But there was a limit to how much more they could handle. "On the other hand, it could be good for me to spend more time in Corpus." The team was doing an exceptional job, but if she were there more often, she could perhaps generate additional sales. "Am I insane for even considering it? Should I cancel Tuesday's appointment?"

"We have other high-maintenance clients."

"Not like this."

"And it's temporary," Zoe said. "Six months, max. And it could be a good opportunity to find out who our best employees are, where we have weaknesses. I can spend a bit more time in San Antonio, as well."

"I don't want you to get burned out." Even with excellent people in each location, driving the vast distances between the three sites each week grew tiresome. She needed Zoe to be her very best.

"Maybe we can see if there's someone who's ready to be promoted over there?"

"It's an idea. You sure you can handle more?"

"As I said, it's temporary."

The more she thought about it, the more Sofia liked the idea. A little extra time in Corpus Christi might be good, and things would be back to normal before the busy holiday season.

"Just make sure you price it well," Zoe added.

"I told him it may include a Pain in the Ass Fee."

Zoe lifted her glass once again.

The timer buzzed and Sofia pulled out the quiche she'd put together that morning.

"What's in it?"

"Red, green and orange bell peppers as well as spinach, onions and mushroom. I'm calling it rainbow quiche."

"Which means I'm the taste tester for a new recipe."

Sofia grinned. "Yep." She put the dish on a rack to cool.

While she placed an assortment of berries and mint on white plates, Zoe refilled the glasses.

For the next few minutes, Zoe chatted about her lively social life. Zoe had a wide circle of friends, and she was dating several different men at the same time. "Anything serious with any of them?" Sofia asked.

Zoe took a fork and started spearing the pieces of fruit that Sofia had arranged on the plates. "No. So many men, so little time."

That had been the main reason she'd moved out a few

years ago. Sofia wasn't enough of a party animal to keep up with Zoe.

When Zoe aimed for a strawberry on Sofia's plate, Sofia smacked away her sister's hand.

Once the quiche was cool enough to cut, Sofia served them each a slice.

After taking a bite, she said, "Maybe I should add a hint of cayenne pepper."

"You could." Zoe nodded. "Nothing wrong with it as it is."

"But it might give it just a little more jazz."

"At some point, sis, it's okay to admit something is fine as it is and quit trying to improve it."

She frowned. "I don't do that."

"Yeah. You do. You edit proposals until the last possible minute before the deadline. You tweak a recipe every single time you make it. You'll mop the floor then rinse it again."

Sofia winced. "I'm that bad?"

"You should ease up on yourself. Sometimes good enough is good enough."

The words stung a bit, but she wasn't sure there wasn't some truth to them.

After they were finished eating, they turned on the webcam and set up a video call.

Their mother, Cynthia, looked tired but happy, holding one of the twins. Their stepfather John held the other baby, and Delores, their half-sister, was pulling two pies from the convection oven.

"They've grown since last week," Sofia exclaimed.

"But they haven't slept," Delores protested.

Sofia missed the mayhem, and sometimes the video chats made it worse. The family still lived in the humble house where Sofia and Zoe had grown up. She remembered the zany years of too many people in too few rooms.

At first, after her alcoholic father had abandoned the family, things had been horrible. Instead of just working as a server for a local caterer on the weekends, Cynthia had taken a full-time job and had started baking pies and cakes for local restaurants.

After juggling it all as a single mother, she'd met John McBride at a local hall where he'd been repairing the building's air conditioning. She'd offered him a bottle of water, and he'd been smitten. Cynthia had insisted she had no time for men, but John had been persistent. Her divorce had been long and messy, but John had stayed by her side.

And when it was over, he'd married her then adopted both Sofia and Zoe, moving them from a one-bedroom apartment into the small house and providing his new family with stability while Cynthia had built her own catering business. They'd had three kids together, all girls.

Even though Sofia felt sorry for John, being surrounded by all those children and estrogen, she'd never heard him complain. He'd worked hard all his life, and he'd spent a lot of his evenings driving the catering van for his wife.

"Are you coming to town this week?" her mom asked.

"Yes. Tuesday. I have a meeting with Cade Donovan."

Delores swung to face the camera, a pie still between her hands.

"They're hosting a centennial celebration at the ranch this fall."

"No shit?" Delores asked.

"Language," John scolded.

Though Sofia had never heard him utter a swear word, somehow all the girls had developed colorful vocabularies.

"I was planning to stop by afterward to see the twins." Up until Delores had given birth, Sofia had often stayed overnight when she was in Corpus Christi. But now, with the twins, the only place left to sleep was the pull-out couch, and since the twins rarely slept for long periods of time, it was occupied almost all night.

"We'd love to see you," Cynthia said as she moved her tiny bundle to her shoulder.

"I'll let you know."

Cynthia frowned. "Zoe Michelle, what is that on your

neck?"

"Nothing, Mom," Zoe said quickly as she moved her hair forward.

John squinted at the camera.

Sofia took a closer look. "Busted," she whispered.

"She has eyes like a hawk," Zoe replied. "I thought the fucking thing was gone!"

"What did you say?" Cynthia demanded.

"It's getting late. I need to be going...to church. Yeah. Church."

Cynthia started to protest but John waved her off and spoke over her, "You need to come see us, Zoe. Sofia makes the effort."

Sofia promised to call on Tuesday when she was at the office then disconnected the call. "Church?"

Zoe shrugged lamely.

"And a love bite?"

"I'm going to hell for all my lies."

"I think you'll have plenty of company while you're there," Sofia replied while sliding off her chair. She moved to the other side of the counter to cut off a large slice of the quiche. "Who's the vampire?"

"Might have been Todd."

"Might have been?" Sofia asked, pausing with her knife halfway through the egg dish.

"Probably."

"Probably?" she repeated.

Obviously Zoe couldn't keep a secret and gnawed on her thumbnail for a second before adding, "Maybe Marcel."

"I haven't heard about him." Sofia finished the downward motion with the knife then drew it toward her.

"Is that for me? It is, isn't it? You're taking pity on me so I don't have to cook this afternoon."

"You're not getting out of telling me this story," Sofia countered.

"Nothing much. A bunch of us went to dinner on Thursday night then headed for dancing at the Top of the

City."

The nightclub had opened a little less than a year ago. It occupied the top floor of a downtown high-rise, and there were reportedly bouncers at the door on the street level to check the invitation list before allowing guests the privilege of waiting in line to get on the elevator.

"Marcel is the manager, and I might have thanked him for letting us cut the line. You could join us some night."

"I'm in bed by then."

Zoe rolled her eyes. "We arrived just after ten."

"Like I said…"

"Sis, I may drag you there myself. You've got to get out. Live a little."

She wished she had an argument for that. Zoe worked as hard as she played.

She put the slice of quiche into a plastic storage box then pressed the lid into place.

"Any more of those berries left?"

"You could go to a farmer's market sometime. Or even a grocery store."

"A…what?"

Sofia filled a second container with fruit, stacked it on top of the first then slid them both into a paper bag.

"I don't suppose you have—"

"Out. Go home. Or better yet, go to church."

With a grin, Zoe stood. "Seriously, I've got your back if you decide to go ahead with the Donovan deal."

"I know you do. That means a lot."

"But I'll want to know what kind of kisser he is."

"Go to church. Twice."

After Zoe left, the apartment seemed laden with emptiness. Zoe's life always seemed so exciting in contrast to hers, and generally Sofia enjoyed listening to the stories. Today, though, the silence and emptiness felt like a shroud.

That damn Cade Donovan had gotten to her. And she couldn't wait to be with him again.

"Are you freaking kidding me? The Donovans? *The* Donovans?"

Did everyone have the same reaction when they heard that name? Sofia was sitting at the wooden table that served as the warehouse's lunch area, conference room, prep space, even an extra office in a pinch. Encore's Corpus Christi project manager, Vivian, sat across from her. Tyrone, the branch's foreman, was seated at the far end.

Sofia plucked the last cookie from a white platter. Since they managed the majority of the area's events, it wasn't unusual for restaurants, bakers or caterers to stop in with samples, much to the delight of her mouth and horror of her hips. She'd learned one thing—people only provided their very best treats.

She hesitated before putting it in her mouth. Common sense urged her to skip it and go somewhere for a salad. But the fact she'd eaten a stale protein bar for breakfast was tipping the odds in the cookie's favor.

Her alarm had chimed at five a.m., and she'd prepared two cups of coffee for the road before making the four-and-a-half-hour drive to Corpus Christi.

After arriving, she'd said a quick hello to her staff and promised to be ready to meet just after they returned from lunch. Then she'd shut herself in her office to reply to emails, check each scheduled event's progress, look at budgets as well as sign a couple of purchase orders and checks.

While she was there, she'd put together a presentation for Cade. She'd added pictures of other events they'd done, including some from last year's rodeo and others showing photographs of tents and table displays, even cakes.

She'd finished with her checklists and her company's Gold Star Satisfaction Guarantee. After emailing the whole thing to herself just in case of technical glitches, she'd sought out her managers.

"Eat it already," Vivian insisted, jolting Sofia from her

musings.

Finally, Sofia closed her eyes and took a bite of the chocolate chip deliciousness. "Bliss. I have no idea what's in this, but damn, it's good."

"It was everything I could do to save that one for you," Vivian said.

"I'm not sure whether or not to be grateful."

"Next time, Tyrone, I won't throw myself between you and the plate."

"You did that for me?" Sofia asked Vivian.

"Tyrone said you'd never know what you were missing."

Sofia scowled at her foreman. In his late thirties, Tyrone stood well over six feet tall. He was as broad as a tree, had a tribal tattoo on the upper part of his left arm, wore a bandana around his head and had a ferocious look, but a quick smile. She'd seen him devour a dozen brownies without blinking. "Did you say that?"

"Trying to protect you from yourself, boss." He lifted one shoulder. "Part of my job description."

"Uh-huh."

"I sacrificed my body for you, boss," Vivian continued.

"Your heroics have made it taste even better." She savored every bite. "Keep this company in mind as a backup for boxed lunches," she said. Most of that business went to her mother, but occasionally extra help was needed.

Vivian jotted a note.

"So where were we?" Sofia brushed her hands together to dust off the crumbs.

"The Running Wind," Tyrone prompted.

She filled them in on the centennial celebration and told them about Donovan's specific demands.

"How much personal attention does he want?" Vivian asked.

"My involvement in every detail. Which will necessitate longer visits to Corpus Christi."

"Meaning you'll be spending less time at the Houston office," Vivian said. "Which might not be a good thing."

"For a number of reasons." Because Houston was the fourth largest city in the United States, Encore's operations there were bigger. That meant margins were thinner. "Zoe has offered to put in some extra hours."

"Awesome," Vivian said. "She's good, but her putting in extra time won't be the same as having the two of you work on things together. And she's damn good at sales. You don't want her taking too much time away from that."

"We're at a juncture here," Tyrone said. "We've been talking about this for what, eighteen months? We need to expand."

But they needed more money to expand.

For certain events, they had to subcontract suppliers for tables and chairs, even flatware. Those services left them at the mercy of other companies, and Encore paid a premium, especially during the summer months.

On the other hand, owning all that meant capital expenditures and a larger warehouse.

The eternal business conundrum.

"This could be the opportunity we've been looking for," Tyrone continued. "We outgrew this warehouse well over a year ago."

Tyrone had been pushing for growth for several years, and she valued his input. He'd started out loading vans for her mother years ago. He was the only person who'd been with the company longer than Sofia had. And everything he said was correct. They'd erected several metal buildings for extra storage, but she knew managing inventory and getting trucks ready for deliveries was more complicated because of it.

"On the other hand, it could overextend us and put us at financial risk," Vivian countered.

"We don't have enough information to work with," Sofia said.

"I'll run some numbers when we know more," Vivian suggested. "Put together some scenarios."

"Agreed." Sofia nodded. Vivian wasn't just an excellent

project manager, she had killer spreadsheet skills. Since they'd been working together for a couple of years, she knew the business well and had developed an uncanny ability to anticipate Sofia's questions and concerns.

"I'll put together some projections about the event, but also about Tyrone's expansion." Vivian paused. "And having an actual showroom where we could bring potential customers would be excellent."

They had that in Houston, and Vivian was right, it made a big difference. Having more room meant they could host tastings, leave tables set up as examples, drape the ceiling, display arches and columns. "We could host an open house," Sofia mused.

"That's what I'm talking about," Tyrone agreed.

"Let's not be too hasty." Sofia said the words as a reminder to herself as much as her staff.

"Mind if I solicit some bids?" Tyrone asked.

"You'll need to for Vivian's projections." Sofia experienced the same burst of adrenaline and dread she'd felt when she'd signed the contract to buy this property nearly three years ago. "Anything else for me to think about before I head out?"

Vivian ran through the upcoming weekend's events and provided updates on future bookings. Outside, thunder rumbled.

Tyrone said he'd hired on extra help for the summer.

She nodded, glad for her team's competence.

"You're not coming back today, are you?" Vivian asked.

Sofia shook her head. "I'm not sure how long I'll be at the Donovan place, and I want to spend some time with my mom and the twins. And I'm a road warrior tomorrow."

"Off to San Antonio?"

"Yeah." Since she'd be at a hotel at least one night, she had a bag in the vehicle.

"Tell your mom I said hello."

"I will."

"How is it working out with everyone under one roof?"

"I think my mother's in her own little part of heaven. She loves having the babies around."

"So you'll be in tomorrow before you head out?"

"Yeah. I'll want to give you an update." In the far distance, thunder rumbled again.

"Be careful out there."

Tyrone checked his phone. "Radar is showing light rain moving our way."

She nodded. There was nothing unusual about unsettled spring weather in South Texas.

After saying goodbye, she headed outside to her SUV. Printed instructions to the ranch were on the passenger seat. In an email exchange, Cade had warned her that her GPS wouldn't do a lot of good once she left the local highway. The ranch had miles of roads, and most of them weren't paved.

He'd informed her that house itself was more than a mile from the first gate. Taking wrong turns could lead her deeper onto the property, so he'd suggested she memorize the directions.

Once she was free of downtown Corpus Christi, Sofia pushed a button on the dash to dial Cade's phone number.

As she listened to it ring, a frisson of nerves skated through her stomach.

No matter how much she'd tried to shove thoughts of him away, they'd returned relentlessly, teasing her senses, making her want more, making her wish he hadn't been a perfect gentleman Saturday night.

Just when she thought the call might go to voicemail, he answered. "Donovan."

Since the phone was connected to the car's sound system, his deep voice surrounded her in a rumbling, masculine tone that took her immediately back to their conversation on the terrace at the country club. Now, as then, every feminine reaction flared. Instinctively she reached to turn down the volume. "It's Sofia McBride," she said, a bit amazed by how steady her voice was. "I'm confirming our three o'clock appointment."

"That's brave."

His tone contained an edge that should have scared her, but instead intrigued her. "I told you I'd be there," she said.

"Where are you now?" he asked.

"On Highway 44, a few miles west of Corpus."

"Right on time. I'll see you in less than an hour. Unless you'd like me to meet you in Waltham?"

"I should be fine." A fat raindrop splatted on the windshield.

"And have you worked a bump gate before?"

"Well…" She hesitated. "No." In his email, he'd explained that in many cases on the ranch roads, they'd opted to use gates that swung open when you hit them with a bumper. According to Cade, it saved a tremendous amount of time. "But it seems pretty straightforward."

"You'll have seven seconds to get clear before it swings shut. It's plenty of time, but if you dawdle, we're not responsible for the damage to your car."

"Did your lawyer tell you to say that?"

He laughed, the sound low and deep, filling the inside of the vehicle with intimacy.

"I've seen plenty of vehicles damaged over the years. When I tell people to hurry, they don't. Warning them that a thousand pound hunk of metal will smack 'em in the ass gets them moving."

"Is that your version of a motivational speech?"

"The threat of an ass smacking gets most people moving."

She shivered at the image of his big hand landing on her butt. Her breath caught, and she couldn't tell whether or not he was teasing. And what if he wasn't?

"Tell me the directions once you leave the main road," Cade instructed, breaking into her thoughts.

"First right," she said after shaking her head to clear it. "Third left. Then it's about a quarter of a mile farther in. Follow the dirt road until it becomes paved. Park in front of the house."

"You memorized it like I told you to."

Warmth and approval deepened his voice, and something inside her unfurled. "I figured it was easier than trying to drive and look at a piece of paper at the same time."

"Buzz me from the intercom when you reach the main gate," he reminded her.

"Will do." She disconnected the call.

Sofia checked her speed and focused on the road to regain her equilibrium. She forced herself to focus on the fact he was a potential client. This was nothing different than a dozen other sales calls she'd been on over the years. She'd inspect the site, listen to the client's ideas, ask as many questions as needed, do some brainstorming, discuss budgets and options then formulate her plan.

But a niggling voice told her this was different because she was attracted to Cade.

A sudden downpour with brisk bursts of wind forced her to concentrate, and before long, she exited the highway toward Waltham.

Originally, Waltham had been built as a stop on the railroad. Now it was home to a college and a sleepy tourist town. An old-fashioned drugstore with a soda fountain had been her favorite stop as a child.

The storm eased and she turned off the windshield wipers. Quick moving clouds darted past to reveal blue skies.

She stopped for one of the town's three traffic lights then continued north several miles, slowing as she searched for the road that would lead onto the Donovan property.

After finding the small green sign, she flipped on her blinker. Unless she had known where to turn, she would have missed it entirely. Considering that the ranch holdings were vast enough to be spread out over several counties, the Donovans didn't appear to broadcast its location.

As she worked her way deeper onto the property, she noticed miles and miles of barbed wire fencing, as far as she could see. She continued to follow the paved road and took the first right. Cade had been correct to suggest she memorize the directions. The juncture was four-way, with no indication where any of the roads led. Trees, some palm, others she recognized as mesquite, obscured the view, giving the area the feel of a maze.

After only a hundred yards or so, she saw an industrial-looking gate. Obviously the bump gate he'd referred to.

It hadn't seemed difficult, but as she approached, knowing she had to hit it with the front of her vehicle unnerved her.

Gently she nosed in and touched her bumper to the metal. It didn't move.

She backed up. This time, when she moved forward, she nudged it a bit harder.

The spring released and she sat there, a bit stunned. Then, remembering he'd said she'd only have seven seconds to clear the entry, she hit the accelerator.

In her rear-view mirror, she saw the gate swing closed behind her, right on cue.

She continued on and, a few seconds later, the paved road ended. Though the dirt was well-groomed, she had to slow down so chunks of gravel didn't gouge her vehicle.

The sun vanished completely behind a cloud, casting shadows across the ground.

She took the third left. This road was paved, and imposing wrought-iron gates loomed in the distance.

Since the day continued to darken, she pulled off her sunglasses.

She braked to a stop near the wrought-iron gates. An ornate R was crafted on one, and a W adorned the other. Massive pillars flanked each side, and there was an impressive concrete statue of a horse with a cowboy on top. The animal's hind legs were slightly tucked under, and the cowboy was throwing a lariat. She couldn't think of a more perfect way to welcome visitors to the property.

Sofia pushed the call button. She expected the gates part, but instead, Cade's voice greeted her.

"Welcome to the Running Wind," he said.

The gates swung inward, revealing beautifully trimmed

trees and sculpted flowering bushes.

With each moment, her heart added an extra beat.

She followed the road as it snaked along, passing three cottages before she rounded a final curve and the ranch house came into view.

Unable to help herself, she paused to take it all in.

It was as if she'd stepped back into another time.

The home's lawn spanned at least an eighth of an acre and featured a small pond. The area was shaded by several gorgeous live oak trees.

The house itself was stunning. And she realized it really couldn't be called a house. It was more of a mansion and shaped like a horseshoe, and it had a turret. The structure was whitewashed stucco that had faded to a soft, inviting cream tone. Bright-red Spanish tiles covered the roof, and two sets of stairs were also red, adding vibrant splashes of color. The building was all the more imposing because it was set quite a bit back from the circular driveway.

A sudden movement caught her eye. She glanced over to see Cade standing on the walkway.

Today he wore tight, tight jeans, a brown Western shirt with the sleeves rolled up, a belt with an oversized buckle and a summer-weight straw cowboy hat. The sight of Cade Donovan made it impossible to string two thoughts together.

She'd expected to see other people, but since she'd left the main road, she hadn't glimpsed another car. Despite what she'd told Zoe, it seemed they were alone.

Swallowing deeply, she drove on. After she'd parked, he came around to the driver's side and opened the vehicle door.

"Ms. McBride," he greeted. He tipped his hat and she had to remind herself to breathe so that she didn't swoon. "You made it safely."

"You give excellent directions."

"Things go better when people do as I suggest," he agreed.

Again she questioned whether or not he was a Dominant.

His tone, his easy confidence that bordered on arrogance, made her wonder. She looked away to shut off the vehicle. Then, keeping the conversation light, she admitted, "I was gawking." She quickly clarified, "At the house."

"At the house," he repeated. A long, slow smile sauntered across his lips. "I do the same thing every time I come home."

Being casual was incredibly difficult when he stood this close, branded with the clean scent of the outdoors and the spice of a hot Southern night. "You never get used to it?"

"No. And honestly, I hope I don't," he said.

Finally, he took a step back to give her some much-appreciated room.

She reached into the passenger seat for her phone, tablet and clipboard before exiting the vehicle to stand next to him.

"It's an honor, and a big responsibility to live here. All the expectations and ambitions of my forefathers are here for the world to see." He looked off into the distance. "I can't be the Donovan to fail, to lose Maisie's Manor."

"Maisie's Manor?" she repeated.

"My great-great-grandmother was named Margaret, but my great-great-grandfather called her Maisie. According to what I read in a newspaper article, their original house burned down, somewhere around 1909. So when he rebuilt, he wanted to be sure it would survive anything. They moved in on their fifth wedding anniversary."

She looked up at the house, ideas forming, helping her to focus on business and keep naughty thoughts of him in the background where they belonged, until she could banish them entirely. Excitement gathered inside her. "Is there a written history of the land and the ranch somewhere?"

He shook his head. "The only thing I found was that newspaper clipping. I think it was from the 1950s, just a local feature on homes in the area."

"We could have something put together for the event," she said. "Maybe as part of the program."

"Program?"

"Since it's a centennial celebration, I figured you'd want to at least say a few words. You know, you'll want to welcome people, let them know how glad you are that they came, maybe acknowledge relationships that have helped ensure the success of the ranch. Perhaps your grandfather could talk? Or your grandmother? Long-time employees? Vendors? Community leaders, like the mayor, talking about the importance of the Running Wind. Maybe a video presentation, if you have pictures of the ranch as it was a hundred years ago? And we can find a photographer to recreate them from the same angle today. Of course, we'll want press coverage. You know, we may want to consult with a PR firm about the whole thing. And of course, we'll need an audio-visual budget."

"Whoa. This started as some hot dogs and burgers on the grill."

"The ranch and its history are, in a way, the history of this part of Texas. As you said, it's a huge honor and responsibility. It could be good for your image to show it off, let it be featured in the press."

"Why do I feel as if I'm losing control?"

"Don't worry. It won't hurt a bit." She smiled sunnily. She hadn't had the chance to handle many events with this much significance, not just because of who the Donovans were, but because of the history. If she recalled, his great-great-grandparents had donated the land where Waltham had been built. Zoe had been right. If they pulled this off, it could gain Encore much-valued publicity. All of a sudden she wanted to get a contract signed so they could get busy. She worked to tamp down her excitement so that she didn't appear overeager. "As I said on Saturday, you're getting started at least six months late. For a project of this scope, a couple of years would have been ideal."

"Maybe we can forget this one and plan to celebrate the one-hundred-and-twenty-five-year anniversary?" he suggested.

A big fat raindrop splatted on her belongings then another smacked her on the shoulder.

"It's been smelling like rain for a couple of days," he said. "Keep getting teased by glimpses of it, but we haven't had a downpour."

"Fine with me."

"Spoken like someone who doesn't depend on the weather for their livelihood."

"Not true," she countered. "My business can live and die on the weather. Hell hath no fury like a bride whose wedding reception gets rained on."

He winced.

"But that's better than the other option. Her crying," she added.

"You're right. I'll keep my problems."

She slid her phone into the back pocket of her slacks.

"Where would you like to start?" he asked.

"Do you have any special requests that I need to take into consideration? For example, are you going to have the house open for tours? If so, what parts? Are you going to try to keep people outside?"

He shook his head. "Hadn't thought about it. I don't have ideas, but my grandparents might."

"I was assuming we'll need a tent that will be able to seat everyone, maybe big enough for a dance floor, as well."

"I was wondering if the barn would work?"

"I'd have to see it to give you my opinion. We've done plenty of parties in barns. What's it used for now?"

"It's mostly empty, except for some storage. I have a garage for my machinery and vehicles. I found it easier to keep everything all together."

She shrugged. "I'd like to see it. Barns can be a success as long as you have air conditioning."

"Hadn't thought of that."

"We can still have plenty of heat in October or November. Especially when you get that many people together. At the very least, you'll need to have fans to move the air around."

He nodded.

"We have cooling units that can be used, so it's really not a problem. We'd be doing the same thing for a tent. Have you thought about a theme?" she continued. "A dress code?"

He took off his cowboy hat and ran his palm down his face. "Dress code? I have to tell people what to wear?"

"If you don't, some people may assume you want sequins and tuxedoes. Others will show up in jeans or shorts."

"I'm trusting your guidance as a professional."

"I've already warned you, I'm not cheap."

"You'll earn every penny." With that, he replaced the hat. It seemed to change him, as if it were part of his dominant aura.

"Why don't you walk me around the property? Show me what we have to work with? I have a few ideas already loaded on my tablet, and we can sit down and go through them."

"It seems like you should be asking other people. I didn't even show up to my high school graduation party."

"I can. If you hire me, I'll be happy to contact your family members myself, get their ideas then make my recommendations to you."

"Yeah. You're definitely going to earn every penny you're paid."

From nowhere, a gigantic, seemingly unkempt, barking dog raced toward them. She took an instinctive step back.

"That's Loopy. My mother got her when she was about a year old. She got too big for her previous owners and they were going to abandon her. My mother couldn't let that happen, so Mom took her in."

"What is it?"

"A mutt. We know she's part Old English sheepdog."

"And part polar bear?" she asked.

"Could be."

The gargantuan four-footed ball of fluff skidded to a stop in front of them, tail wagging furiously and her tongue hanging out.

"Does her name have any significance?"

"You tell me," he replied.

"I'm guessing she wasn't the pick of the litter?"

He grinned, showing his affection for the pup, and allowing her to see another side of him. How many grown men adored crazy dogs?

"Loopy, say hello to our guest."

Obediently, the dog lifted her giant paw in Sofia's general direction. Overgrown hair covered the animal's eyes.

"How does she see anything?"

The dog whined and batted toward her.

"Her feelings will be hurt if you don't shake," he informed her.

"Are you serious?"

"Oh yes. She'll resort to licking and jumping up on you if you don't say hello."

Grateful she'd worn black pants instead of the white ones she'd considered, she handed her belongings to Cade then bent to accept the proffered, muddy paw.

Apparently still not satisfied, Loopy lunged forward to lick all of Sofia's face, from bottom to top, in a single swipe.

"She likes you."

She wiped off the affection and accepted Cade's help to stand. "Does she greet everyone that way?"

"If she doesn't like you, she nips your heels to herd you back into your vehicle."

"You're making that up."

"No, ma'am."

Cade still held her hand. His gaze was riveted on her, and she realized he was judging her based on her reaction to his dog. He adored the animal, clearly. That he had such affection for an overgrown mutt endeared him to her. "I'm guessing the dog might be your mother's but you offered to keep her."

"Might be some truth to that."

Loopy leaned her head toward him and he dutifully scratched behind one of her ears.

"She likes attention," she observed.

"Loopy thinks everyone was put on the earth to love her, dog fan or not."

The land, the connection, the dog, it all mattered to him. Even though she'd been behind the ornate gates only a short amount of time, she felt as if she knew him just a little bit better.

On Saturday night he'd warned her away, but the truth was, she wanted to know him on a deeper level, no matter how ridiculous that urge might prove to be. "Tell the truth," she said. "Your mom wanted to take the dog, but you wanted to keep her."

"We have an understanding, Loopy and I."

"I can tell." Slowly, she extricated herself from his grip.

"Shall we?" he said, indicating a four-wheeled ATV parked a little farther down the driveway. It resembled a golf cart with a canopy, but with bigger tires that had plenty of traction. A metal brush guard was attached to the front. The tough-looking vehicle was painted white and each side was emblazoned with the Running Wind's horse logo.

"We're not walking?"

"You'll be grateful," he promised her.

Thunder grumbled and big clouds, mostly white with patches of gray, moved across the sky.

Before getting behind the wheel, Cade handed her into the passenger seat then gave her back her belongings. Loopy bounded up and lay in the small space behind the backseat.

"Hang on," he said, looking over his shoulder, more at the dog than at her.

He took off so fast that Sofia slid backward. The dog barked excitedly.

"You do that often?"

"Yeah. Loopy loves it. It's part of our routine."

"I think there's a hidden side to you, Mr. Donovan."

"There is."

He said the words flatly, acknowledging that there was more to him than he let the rest of the world see.

To distract herself, she readjusted her grip on her belongings.

He braked to a stop and Loopy hopped up onto the backseat and sat with her head hanging out the side to catch the wind.

"You two really could have a comedy act."

"She's talking about you, girl."

Loopy gave a single woof.

Weather stirred up the wind again, made worse by the speed they traveled. She brushed hair back from her face.

"These are guest cottages." He indicated the buildings she'd passed on the way in. "The first was originally a bunkhouse." He pointed. "That one is where Maisie and Humphrey lived before the Manor was built. The other was always meant for visitors. According to what my father used to say, Maisie always had room for travelers, workers, anyone stranded by a storm. She had a heart as big as the land, and she even built a one-room schoolhouse on the property to educate the children of her workers. At that time, the Sykes Ranch was like a town within a town."

"Those are exactly the kind of stories that would make an excellent handout or commemorative book."

He slid her a glance. "You think?"

"Yes. We could find someone to do the research. Newspaper articles, interviews with…" She paused. "I don't know the whole history, but you have cousins and there was originally more land?"

"You've made me curious about my own heritage," he admitted. "When Phillip Sykes died —"

"Your?"

"Great-grandfather," he supplied. "The land was divided between his children. I don't know if it was equally or not. But my grandfather and Miss Libby inherited the portion with the house."

"Which you now own?"

It took him a while to answer. "Yes."

Cade was quiet for so long that she wasn't sure if he was

77

going to say anything further. Eventually he continued, "After my father died, the Colonel moved forward with sorting out the land situation. Connor and Nathan control most of it, and it's tied up in the corporation."

He stopped less than a minute later in front of a red-painted barn. It was an enormous wooden structure. Cade exited the ATV, and she gathered her phone, clipboard and tablet. She and Loopy waited near him while he slid one of the massive doors open.

The interior immediately captured her imagination.

The floor was concrete and a huge loft was perched at the far end of the open space. The metal roof was corrugated and she heard occasional raindrops spattering against it, adding to the ambience. Possibilities for its use crowded through her mind, each idea quickly chasing away the previous one. "This really has some potential, Cade," she admitted.

"I understand the Colonel and Miss Libby hosted some events here."

"You mean your grandparents?"

"Yes. Years ago, before my father and I used to work on cars out here."

"What kind?"

"Race cars, mostly. A couple of collectibles." He adjusted his hat. "It was a long time ago."

"Where are they now?"

"Gone." His tone was gruff, letting her know he wasn't inviting any further conversation.

She nodded.

"We've done yearly maintenance on the barn, to keep nature at bay. But it would need some improvement."

"Do you have the dimensions?"

"I can get them for you."

She wandered around. "Mind if I take some pictures?" she asked, glancing back at him.

He was resting a shoulder against a post, watching her, his eyes partially hidden by his straw hat. "Feel free," he replied.

After wandering around for bit, Loopy went back outside, so Sofia felt comfortable putting her clipboard on the floor while she used her tablet to shoot a few pictures. "You know, a few windows in here would be incredible."

"Are you remodeling the place already?"

Sofia glanced over at him. "It's not a bad idea. You could turn this into a rental, if you wanted, make it a place for church gatherings, weddings, meetings. It could produce income, rather than sitting here empty."

"I actually have a meeting set up with Nathan to discuss utilizing the ranch more."

"You ought to consider it. There are plenty of civic groups in Waltham, and there aren't a lot of places like this in the county. I can tell you that not all brides want to go to Corpus Christi or San Antonio to host a big event. You know…" Her thoughts tumbled. "I'm sorry. I'm getting ahead of myself. I'm here to discuss your event."

"I'm interested. Go on."

"You could do a bed-and-breakfast option. Brides could stay overnight. Or the honeymoon couple. Corporate retreats."

"Do you see me as a host?"

"I don't know." She pretended to consider him somewhat. "You have a certain charm, I suppose. Maybe we could get you lessons in deportment or something."

"Deportment?"

"Yeah. Even I'm not sure what it is."

"Manners."

"You could be taught."

"Know any teachers?" He grinned.

Cade himself would be part of the attraction. She could only imagine the success of the endeavor if his picture was on the website or trifold brochure.

She used her tablet to fan herself.

Not for the first time, she realized that being here, alone with him, was dangerous to her libido.

She forced herself to refocus and she considered the loft. A band could be featured up there, or a DJ. Or perhaps it could be used for additional seating or dancing. It could also be a great spot for people-watching or, even better, pictures. It would be a fun spot to set up a photo booth or as a place to video guests who were commemorating the event.

Sofia headed toward the stairs but when he spoke, she stopped.

"It's mostly used for storage," he told her.

"That's okay. I'm more interested in how it might be utilized during the centennial celebration." Undaunted, she continued on.

"I'm not sure how safe it is," he warned her. "Let me get someone out here to check."

"How soon can that happen?"

"Tomorrow, maybe."

"Not today?"

"Are you always this—"

"The word you're looking for is direct," she reminded him with a cheeky grin.

"Direct," he repeated.

"Direct," she affirmed. "Not blunt. Not bossy. Not demanding."

"Got it," he said with a slow, stimulating smile.

"Since I'm here today and I'm not sure when I can come back, I'd love the opportunity to have a look."

"Are you asking me to get my ass over there and check it out for you?"

"Why, Mr. Donovan, thank you kindly for making the offer," she said with an exaggerated Southern drawl. "I declare, I don't know why I didn't think of it."

"Why do I feel as if I've been nicely manipulated?"

"I can't begin to imagine."

"Has that worked for you your whole life? The Southern belle act?" He pushed away from the beam and walked toward her, his boots sounding a bit formidable on the floor.

"You'll have to tell me. I've never tried it before."

"I'm a bit embarrassed by how well it worked on me," he admitted.

He stopped next to her. Though he said nothing, she felt that indefinable *something* flare between them the same way it had Saturday night. She'd never experienced it with another man. It wasn't just a pounding heart or a shortness of breath. It felt as if every one of her nerve endings were tingling with awareness.

Sofia had never been madly in love, and sex had never been a pulse-pounding experience for her. It'd been okay, something she could definitely live without. So the arousal he evoked had caught her unprepared.

He stood only inches away from her, looking at her with his gray eyes, which didn't appear as chilly as they had at Lara and Connor's reception. And he made no attempt to move past her.

Slowly, he lifted his hand and brushed back a lock of hair from her eyes.

"The wind," he explained.

"Thank you."

More raindrops pelted the roof, sounding like marbles against the metal, and it seemed to jar both of them.

Without a word, he tested the stability of the handrail before heading up the stairs. "Come on up," he said when he reached the top.

Tablet in hand, she followed him. "They seem to be sturdy enough."

At the back of the loft, huge tarps were draped from the ceiling beams, blocking off the space. He stood near the front railing and she joined him.

"What do you think?"

"It's not as serviceable as I'd hoped, so I'm glad I looked." She wrinkled her nose. "The stage would be below us, so there's no view of the speakers or entertainment for anyone sitting up here."

He nodded.

"But that doesn't mean it couldn't be used for something. I'm just not sure what." She drummed her fingers on the railing. "It does offer some great opportunities for lights and streamers, bunting, that kind of thing." Tablet still in hand, she moved toward the back of the area to see if there was a window.

"Just storage back there," he told her. "Nothing to see. Ms. McBride—"

She brushed back a tarp and what she saw stole her breath. She'd expected garage-type items, maybe boxes, tools, that sort of thing.

Instead, she saw an immense wooden chair. The back had to be over five feet tall. Its padding was all leather. And the huge arms had wild-looking horses carved into the wood beneath them, ferocious and frightening.

Paddles, whips as well as all sorts of things that she'd never seen before hung from the wall. But what made her freeze was a raised table, like a massage table, with sturdy restraints in strategic locations.

Ice froze her blood. He *was* into BDSM.

She'd thought she'd known what that meant, but she hadn't. Seeing everything shocked her. Having her own images come to life in front of her rendered her immobile.

His footsteps echoed, threatened, as he moved across the wooden planks to join her.

"Don't worry, Ms. McBride. This area is by invitation only."

The air around them was charged with the impending storm and it seemed to ricochet through her.

By slow measures, she dropped the tarp and stared at him.

His arms were folded across his chest and his feet were a little more than shoulder-width apart. He appeared resolute, bigger, broader than he had even a few minutes ago. He made her nervous, but no matter how ridiculous it seemed, she didn't feel threatened. "You're a..."

He waited, making her say it.

She turned to face him. "A Dominant?"

"I am." He continued to regard her. "Do you know what that means?"

"I'd say the table gives me a hint," she said wryly. When he didn't smile, she went on. "Honestly? No. I don't have a clue. I've read books, watched a couple of movies, talked to a few friends about their experiences." Since Lara had asked her to keep their conversation private, she didn't mention it to Cade. "But I've never been..." How the hell did she say it out loud? She settled for, "Involved in anything remotely resembling..." Again she floundered. "This."

"Despite what you may be thinking, it's about more than sex and pain."

Given the surroundings, she found that a bit difficult to believe.

"Doms are naturally protective and they take charge of situations. Being a Dom is an obligation and a responsibility that is taken seriously."

Those were the same words he'd used when referring to the ranch and the house. Absently she wondered if Cade saw everything in his life in that way.

"Some people only practice their BDSM in the bedroom. One person is a top, the other is the bottom. Others live it as a lifestyle, twenty-four hours a day. Often it's part of a committed relationship and the Dom or Master is in charge of all big decisions. He protects and provides for his sub or slave."

She shuddered. "That sounds a bit extreme to me."

"There's a saying, show me a hundred BDSM couples and I'll show you a hundred different ways to practice BDSM. Some people don't have kinky sex, they simply live in a D/s way. What works for some people won't work for others."

"So what kind of Dom are you?" She was as fascinated as she'd been when Lara had talked about it the other night.

"Since I don't own a collared slave, I'm not a Master."

The term made her squirm, but she wasn't sure it was entirely from discomfort.

"I enjoy sexually dominating female submissives so I occasionally go to clubs or kink events. I engage in what's known as SSC—safe, sane and consensual scenes. You're safe with me." He was silent for a few moments before he added, "As safe as you want to be."

She exhaled to chase away the sudden picture of him choosing an implement from the wall and walking toward her.

"Since you've already found my dungeon, you're welcome to have a look around."

"That'll teach me to be nosy."

"Or you can go back downstairs. If you want to pretend you didn't see anything, that's fine. If you want to ask questions or talk about anything, that's okay." His lips twitched with a trace of a smile. "And if you want me to take you back to your car so you can get the hell off the property and pretend you never heard the name Donovan, I understand."

Though he'd given a little smile, there was no doubt how serious he was. "There was nothing wrong with the stairs, was there?"

"No."

"This is the most unusual sales call I've ever been on."

"Is it?" he asked. He thumbed his hat back just a little so that she could look him in the eye.

"Of course, I typically don't dance with clients, either."

"Or kiss them?"

"Or kiss them," she conceded. "I've never met anyone like you. You intrigue me. This intrigues me. You're a client. A *potential* client. And I don't want to screw this up."

"Let's agree that what happens up here has nothing to do with us potentially working together. We'll keep business separate from this discussion."

"I'd appreciate that."

"I'm a man, a Dom, and you're an attractive woman. It can't surprise you to know I want you."

"Want me?" she asked. Her heart thumped so hard in her

throat that she could barely force out her next question. "In what way?"

"Don't be coy, Sofia. You know exactly what I mean."

She did. "You're saying you..." She took a breath. "You want to fuck me."

4

"That, certainly. Yes," he confirmed, making her knees knock together. "And more."

The thought consumed her. Attraction raced through her. She shouldn't have any interest in what he was offering. Someone like Cade Donovan was outside her realm of experience. He was worldly, sophisticated, with a sexual nature that unnerved her.

She was aware of the wind howling, the rain lashing, yet it was only the two of them here, shut off from the rest of the world. "So you'd want…"

"I would."

Absently she rubbed her upper arms. As she was coming to expect, he waited for her to continue. She glanced back toward the tarp. "Like I said, I've never done any of that stuff."

"You've never been spanked? Maybe been blindfolded or tied up?"

Her stomach dropped to her toes. "We are so not having this conversation."

"And again, like Saturday night, you haven't run away, even though I've warned you that you probably should. You haven't reached for your phone to call nine-one-one. You haven't asked me to take you to your car."

He made no move toward her. Instead, he stood still, as if he had all the time and the patience in the world.

"No. I've never been…spanked. Or blindfolded." What else had he asked? She met his gaze. Though his eyes were still gray, they seemed somewhat lighter, the color more molten. "Or tied up."

Suddenly rain beat harder on the roof.

"Until now," he said.

Loopy dashed into the barn and she looked over to see the sheepdog shake herself off, spewing water everywhere. Then she raced toward them, tongue still happily hanging out of the side of her mouth.

"Wait," Cade said to the animal.

At the bottom of the stairs, she whimpered.

"Stay." His voice was quiet, but forceful.

The dog tipped her head to the right.

Cade raised his right index finger. Then he pointed toward the floor and Loopy lowered herself to the floor. Sofia might have imagined the dog sighing.

"Good girl," he said approvingly.

Loopy thumped her tail and kept her gaze focused on him.

Returning all his attention to Sofia, he said, "It's your choice entirely."

A battle waged within her. She was curious, as he'd suggested. A little nervous, as well. If they proceeded with using the barn for the event, no doubt he would have to move everything. In the end, fascination trumped fear. "Yes," she said. "I would like to see your…"

"Dungeon."

"That sounds fierce."

"It's supposed to."

Despite the heat, she felt as if the temperature had cooled a few degrees.

She put on a brave face. "Lead on, Mr. Donovan."

He nodded then took a step forward to pull back the tarp. It required a tremendous amount of courage to walk past him.

Because of the storm and lack of windows, the area appeared small and somewhat foreboding.

He followed her and switched on an overhead light. It demystified the equipment, made it less intimidating.

"Unfortunately, it's rarely used. It doesn't have a lot of

equipment, but it's serviceable."

"Maybe we can take a few pictures for the commemorative book," she teased.

"You might want to ask the PR firm that you referred to."

He was smiling, and that helped her pulse return to a more normal rate.

"I acquired this chair from a defunct club in Dallas. The Dungeon Master was the only one allowed to sit in it."

"Dungeon Master? Seriously? He was actually called that?"

"Most of us in the lifestyle are very serious about our BDSM," he assured her. "That doesn't mean there aren't lighthearted, enjoyable exchanges, but safety is the number one concern."

Sofia took a step toward the chair, then stopped. "It's imposing."

"It's meant to be."

"Do you sit in it? Or is it just for show?"

"Nothing here is just for show," he replied.

For a moment, she imagined him in it, hands curved around the ornate arms. She realized the chair wasn't just tall at the back, the seat was a bit higher than normal, and it was significantly wider than a normal chair. Even if other people were nearby, its occupant would be slightly above everyone else. "So…"

"Go on. I promise I won't be offended."

"What do you do in the chair, if it's not for show?"

"Often I contemplate a submissive. Maybe as she strips, or kneels and waits for a command, perhaps dances."

"A woman really does that for you?"

"Yes."

"Kneels naked and waits?"

"With grace and patience." He nodded toward a circle on the floor. "There."

She sucked in a breath. Though she tried to banish the image, she pictured herself doing exactly that.

"Or I can enjoy the sight of her on the table."

"You just sit there and watch?" she asked, incredulous, wondering what it would be like.

"I find there's something exquisitely sexy about the sight of a woman's nude body — my submissive's nude body — as she's strapped down waiting for my attention, my touch."

His voice had strokes of sensuality that painted a vivid, breathtaking picture.

"Across the room, I can watch her every movement, see her ribcage rise and fall as she breathes. I can tell whether or not her nipples are hard. If her feet are in stirrups, I know if she's wet with anticipation."

My God.

"As I mentioned, it's not just kinky sex. It's more complex than that. For me, transcendence matters. Can a sub quiet her mind enough to remain still? To be fully present in the moment? I want my sub to focus on pleasing me."

She couldn't believe she was here, listening, and yet she couldn't make herself move.

"If I've blindfolded her, can she keep her head from moving even if she hears a movement off to her left side as I approach the wall?"

Unable to stop herself, she looked. At the paddles. Some had round heads, a few were oblong. Most were crafted from wood, others from leather.

The rich timbre of his voice drew her back.

"Sometimes I may instruct her to keep her eyes open, but to focus on an overhead beam. Maybe on that crystal."

Until now, she hadn't noticed it. The exquisite piece of glass was shaped like a teardrop, and it hung from an overhead beam, unmoving.

"Other times, I may request she keep her eyes closed. That can be a real challenge. A sudden sound, like a smack" — he clapped and she yelped — "might tempt her to disobey."

Desperately she wanted to know what happened if the sub didn't do as she was told.

As if he hadn't just startled the hell out of her, he continued, "I can see whether or not she tests the bonds. Does she need to see if they're tight? Is she hoping she can escape them? Or praying she can't?"

Sofia's wrists seemed to chafe.

"Or perhaps I have positioned her in a way that's pleasing to me and I've instructed her not to move. Depending on the sub, that can be all the more challenging."

She could imagine it. Vividly. The waiting. The anticipation. Wondering if he'd touch her, when he'd touch her, and would it be a caress, or something harsher? This, her reaction, couldn't be happening to her.

"Alternatively, my sub can be draped over my knee while I please her." He paused. "Maybe I'd tease her clit. Maybe I'd put a finger up her ass."

Her mouth dried. She'd never been with a man who was this frank, and she'd never had a guy even suggest trying anal sex. And he spoke of it so casually.

"Depending on my mood, I might spank her. It could be a pleasure paddling, but perhaps it's something more serious, a transgression that needs to be rectified. My imagination is my only limitation."

His words seemed to swim in her mind. No matter what she did, she couldn't banish the images that had formed. Instead, a wicked part of her yearned to be the nameless submissive, doing as he commanded.

"Would you like to have a closer look at the wall?" he asked.

"It makes me think of a medieval torture chamber." Still, she was intrigued enough to walk toward it. She'd never stepped foot in an adult-themed store, but she'd looked at so many sites online that she could guess what the things were and how they were used. "It's a little scary," she admitted.

"It doesn't have to be. Domination is more about control than anything else. Would you like me to show you?"

She told herself she wasn't going to do this. She wasn't. *No way.*

"Any Dom who's worthy will insist you use a safe word,

something that immediately stops play."

"You have an interesting definition of the word *play*, Mr. Donovan."

"Do I? It's a lot of fun."

"For whom?"

"Both parties," he said. "Why else would a sub do it?"

"Because it pleased her Dom?" she asked, glancing over her shoulder.

"That's a hell of an answer and not altogether incorrect." His voice was hoarse in a way that made a thrill slip down her spine. "But I'd say a lot of subs wouldn't do it more than once, let alone often, if they didn't get something out of it."

"I'll be honest, I'm a bit skeptical." Even though Lara had told her the same thing.

"I can't blame you." He took a few steps and stopped near her. "Communication is the key to success. Each person needs to have clear expectations."

"It's the same way in business."

"It is."

Even though he wasn't uncomfortably close, her senses blazed.

"Before a scene, individuals talk about what works for them. The submissive will let the Dom know if she has hard limits—things she refuses to do. There can be soft limits, as well, things she likely doesn't want to do but is open to talking about or considering, depending on the situation. She also lets him know if she has physical issues that prevent her from doing certain things. It's the Dom's responsibility to ensure she's kept safe at all times."

"It sounds very serious."

"You're right. But it doesn't have to be a long talk. It can be informal. And the more you're with a particular person, the less you need to go over."

A part of Sofia couldn't believe she was standing in Cade Donovan's barn – *in his dungeon* – having this discussion.

"As I said a minute ago, a sub will have a safe word.

Because it's easy to remember, many choose the word red. But if you want to go any further with me, you can use anything you wish. I prefer that my partners let me know if they need to talk about something, even during a scene. You can say yellow to get me to pause or to let me know something is too much or to take a short break. Green lets me know everything is okay."

Cade looked at her, captured her gaze, mesmerized her. She wasn't sure she could have looked away, even if she'd wanted to.

"Are you ready to continue?"

Her gaze was continually drawn toward a pretty pink paddle. It appeared to be sturdy and made of wood. It reminded her of something she'd used when she'd played ping pong. "I don't see how anyone gets pleasure out of that. It looks as if it's meant to hurt someone."

"It certainly can. It doesn't have to be used that way, though. If you'd like to experiment, take it down and give it to me."

His vocal chords were taut, and his tone held no trace of humor.

She hesitated, and she was reminded that, once again, she hadn't said no. Thunder ripped apart the atmosphere but even it didn't drown out the sound of her heartbeat.

Realizing she may not get this chance to be with a Dominant ever again, Sofia put down her things then removed the pink paddle from its hook and offered it to him.

"Very good," he said, thrilling her.

Rather than instructing her to bend over, or at least turn around, as she expected, he mesmerized her by tracing a callused finger down the side of her cheek, then he gently outlined her lips. "Tell me what you want to use as a safe word."

Right now, she had a hard time remembering her own name. "The colors are fine."

"Close your eyes," he said.

For the first few seconds, all she could think about was the fact he towered over her and held an implement of pain.

Then he fisted his hand in her hair. "I've been thinking about this since Saturday night."

He had? The knowledge that she'd affected him melted the last of her resistance. She exhaled a breath she hadn't known she'd been holding.

Cade eased her head back. She could open her eyes, but keeping them closed enhanced her other senses.

He touched her lips with his and she moaned.

"You're beautiful," he said.

Sofia knew she wasn't, but his tone was so serious that for a moment she believed him.

He deepened the kiss and she responded, tasting the freshness of spearmint. He smelled of the elements—rain and wind—and she felt consumed.

He ran two fingers down the column of her throat then paused at the hollow. She'd never felt this gloriously alive.

By slow measures, he pulled back from her then eased his grip on her hair.

"Continue to keep your eyes closed. I'm going to turn you around."

It took some trust, but she gave it.

His grip was light on her shoulders as he turned her. Then he slid his forearm across her chest.

"Stick out your rear a little more for me."

Nerves almost failed her.

"You can say no," he said. From his tone, she knew he wouldn't judge her if she did. "Or yellow. Or red."

"Scared."

He laughed in a gentle way that she found oddly reassuring. She appreciated that he wasn't trying to frighten her.

"That's not one of the acceptable answers, Sofia."

She reached up to curl her hands around his arm before doing as he'd instructed. "Fine. Do it. Get it over with."

"Tell me green," he said.

After a moment, she said, "Green." Then she waited.

He spanked her across both buttocks with the sturdy paddle.

She barely felt it. "That's it?" she asked, strangely disappointed. She opened her eyes, and everything in the room looked as it had before. Part of her had expected that the world would appear differently.

"Control," he reminded her. "I wanted you to know that nothing has to be horrifically painful."

"But it was...nothing." She turned her head back to look at him.

"Did I give you permission to open your eyes?"

She gasped. "No."

"Close them."

Immediately, she did.

"Another one?" he asked. "A bit harder?"

She nodded.

"Tell me."

"Yes."

He brought the paddle across the middle of her ass, harder this time. As soon as he pulled back his hand, the pain abated and he kissed the side of her neck.

"One more? Harder?"

"Yes," she whispered.

He delivered the third with more force, making her rise on to her tiptoes. She yelped, but he distracted her by brushing a hand across her breast.

Shocking her, Sofia's body felt more relaxed than it had, as if tension had seeped from her.

"A good Dom asks, reads, senses what his sub wants," he said.

He'd snared her interest, making her wonder what else there was to it.

"Now open your eyes."

He turned her to face him.

The steel in his eyes had been tempered. "And?" he prompted.

"That last one...and the way you..." She looked away, but he took hold of her chin.

"One very important thing about anything BDSM is the honesty. If you're going to play with anyone, you have to be transparent. There can be no hiding, especially from yourself."

She wasn't accustomed to this. In fact, the opposite was true for her. More than once, she'd lied and said she'd had an orgasm so she could spare a man's feelings.

"Tell me what you're thinking and feeling."

"The last one stung a little," she admitted. "The pain went away quickly, especially once you brushed your hand across my chest."

"Are you sexually aroused?"

Lord save me. "I'm getting there," she admitted.

"How sensitive are your nipples?"

She wondered if she'd ever had a conversation this personal. "I'm not even sure how to answer that."

"Can you come from having them touched?"

"I honestly have no idea," she confessed. "I'm totally embarrassed."

"Don't be. That's not my intent. I just want to know about you."

"I'm sure you're accustomed to..." She took a breath then began again. "I'm sure you're accustomed to playing with women who are far more experienced than I am."

He raised his eyebrows. "Are you a virgin?"

"No. But there's no way anyone would consider me worldly."

"If you want to proceed, we can go as slow as you want."

The world felt a little bit as if it had tipped.

"I'd start by getting you naked," he said, as if sensing her unasked question. "Ask you to stand still while I looked at you. I'd touch you, learn what you like."

"What about sex?"

"It can be part of a scene for some people. For us, now? No. I wouldn't want you concerned about that. I've already told you I want to fuck you. I would prefer it be part of a BDSM scene but that's not a requirement. I'd happily give you vanilla sex if you wanted it."

She wasn't certain what to say.

"There's no pressure, certainly no hurry. If you don't want to sleep with me, I won't hold that against you."

The problem was, she did want to. It would be smart to go back to the house, go through her presentation then get back on the road. But she knew she'd always wonder. She hadn't gotten to be a success in business by being afraid of risk. "I didn't think I liked pain at all until that third swat." The paddle still hung from one of his fingers. He was standing in that commanding stance of his. No matter how reassuring his tone, there was an underlying steel that she now knew was part of his dominant nature. "I'm curious," she finally admitted. "Curious but cautious."

"You have a right to be. Trust is built over time."

She scowled. "So you're saying I shouldn't trust you?"

"I'm saying you should ask for whatever you need to feel safe. Avoiding restraints? Keeping your underwear on initially?"

After leaving work yesterday evening, she'd stopped by the Galleria and bought some new bras and panties from a fancy boutique. She'd rationalized that she needed some since she hadn't purchased any in at least a year. But the truth was there. She'd been thinking of Cade when she'd slid her credit card across the counter.

"Having me undress you? Would you like that? Or would you prefer to strip for me?"

"I…"

"You can say yellow or red at any point," he reminded her. "Or walk out the door."

While she decided, he put the paddle back on the wall.

"I want the help, this time," she said when he returned. "And I want to stay in my underwear."

"Let's begin with your boots." He offered his forearm for balance.

She wrapped one hand around his wrist and removed her cowboy boots and socks. The couple inches of height that she lost felt suddenly significant. He seemed so much bigger and more powerful.

He moved in front of her and unfastened the top button on her pants before lowering the zipper.

"Ready?"

She wiggled as he lowered the pants. She stepped out them, feeling exposed.

"Gorgeous," he said.

"You keep saying things like that."

"To me, you are."

"I need to work out more." *Or avoid chocolate chip cookies. Maybe both.*

"There's nothing more exquisite than a woman revealing herself," he told her. "I appreciate everything. And I like women who have some curves. Turn around for me."

Surprising herself, she didn't hesitate.

"Spread your legs as wide as you can and grab your ankles."

Sofia thought she would feel ridiculous, bent over like that, but she didn't.

He walked around her, his footsteps loud, a bit ominous. Her pulse fluttered but she remained in place.

"Good, now stand."

After she did, he unbuttoned the top buttons on her blouse. Then, his gaze fixed on her, he trailed his finger from the hollow of her throat, down her sternum then stopped where the fabric was still held together.

Without saying a word, he continued until the blouse hung open.

She shrugged and he pulled the material away from her, letting it float down to rest on top of her pants.

"How does it feel?"

Knowing he wouldn't settle for a half-answer, she said, "Not as scary as I thought it might." But she didn't tell him that she'd been hoping, dreaming of him sexually dominating her.

He traced the lacy outline of one bra cup then the other. Her nipples hardened and she wanted him to touch her. "Yes," she whispered.

"Yes, what?"

She looked up at him. "Are you going to make me say it?"

He gave her an annoying, frustrating grin. "I am."

Sofia would have preferred he make this easier for her, but she was glad he wasn't. "Touch my breasts."

His gaze still on her, he lightly brushed the fingers of one hand inside her bra. With exquisite gentleness, he moved across her nipple.

She gasped.

"Tell me how you like the pressure."

"I do… I mean, it's fine."

He brushed again. "More?"

"Harder," she said, realizing it was the first time she'd ever asked a man for what she wanted.

Cade circled the tip with his finger before pressing hard.

"That's even better," she admitted. The moment she started to close her eyes, he moved to the other side, repeating the motion. Her pussy tingled. Without conscious thought, she jutted her hips forward.

"This is what I was referring to," he told her as he placed a palm flat on her belly. "You're communicating with me silently. If we had been in a sexual relationship for a long time and you trusted me, I'd give you what you're asking for. As it is, I won't violate our agreement."

She scowled. "You're starting to annoy me."

"Good."

"Good?" She couldn't tell if he was teasing her or being callous.

When he spoke, she realized that neither guess had been correct. "It means you want more. So ask."

"All I know is I'm turned on."

"Remove the rest of your clothes."

Wordlessly, fingers trembling, she did, tossing her bra on

top of her shirt, then pulling down her panties and using her toes to drop them on top of the pile.

Sofia lowered her head but managed to resist the impulse to cover herself.

"You're exquisite. I want you to present yourself to me."

She cocked her head to the side in question.

"Go stand in the circle with your legs apart."

Even minutes ago she might have balked at the command, but there was something reassuring and compelling in his tone that made her yearn to obey.

"Hands behind your neck."

Aware of him watching her with great intensity, she moved into the circle and did what he'd instructed. With her hands behind her, her breasts were thrust forward. But because of what he said earlier about focus, she forced herself to look straight ahead, even as he walked around her. She was uncomfortable knowing that he could see all of her flaws, but when he stopped in front of her, his eyes were smoky with approval.

All of a sudden she understood why a woman—a sub— might want to make this man happy.

"How are you doing?"

"Mostly green."

He grinned.

Nervousness was banished. He'd seen her flaws and still desired her. That knowledge was intoxicating.

He cupped each of her breasts and she sighed.

"Sounds are okay, but I want you to remain in this position. Muscle fatigue is a reason to say yellow or red."

"Yes."

Still cupping her breasts, he flicked his thumbs across her nipples.

Staying in place was more difficult than she could have imagined. Then he rolled each between a thumb and a forefinger and slowly increased the pressure.

"Keep breathing," he said. "And tell me when it's too much."

She closed her eyes and enjoyed the sensation of him twisting, tugging then squeezing. As he did it harder, her breath came in little spurts and she felt herself starting to get damp.

Right when she was tempted to say the word yellow, he backed off.

"Ask me to touch your pussy, to give you an orgasm."

He'd shocked her so much that she almost broke position. "I might die if you don't."

"Sofia, Sofia…" He held a finger in front of her mouth. "Suck it. Get it wet." He didn't argue or ask again. Instead, he waited for her compliance.

A full thirty seconds ticked by, filled with shuddering thunder, relentless rain, sizzling lightning strikes, but he didn't relent. Finally she opened her mouth.

"Very, very good."

How could she deny him anything?

He placed his finger in her mouth and she sucked on it, swirled her tongue around, got him wet.

He made her do it longer than she'd expected, turning it into a completely erotic experience of its own.

"Almost," he said, even when her jaws were beginning to ache. He moved his finger around, plundering her mouth, making her think of a good, hard fucking.

Without conscious thought, she moved her body, undulating slightly.

"Oh yes," he murmured, words approving.

Until this moment, she'd never thought of herself as a sexy woman. It was an exhilarating feeling.

"Stay in position," he reminded her.

She stayed where she was as he pulled out his finger. He slowly trailed it down, past her bellybutton, over her pubic mound. It became more and more difficult to follow his order. With each second, she understood more about what he had meant about transcendence. It took a lot of effort to follow such a simple command. She wanted to writhe, demand, grab his hand and thrust it between her legs.

"Such excellent control."

"It's because I'm gritting my teeth."

"Are you?" he asked, sounding completely unconcerned.

Finally, finally, he stroked between her labia. Her knees buckled and she reached for him.

"Position," he reminded her.

Madness.

Then, with a bit more sharpness, he repeated, "Position, Sofia."

"But..."

"Yellow, red, or get your ass back in position."

After gasping, both from the overwhelming need and the harsh demand in his tone, she did what he said.

"Keep your hands in place while I play with your pretty little pussy."

Mortification raked at her.

He teased her clit, smoothing his fingertip across it then flicking it from side to side. She had to lock her knees in order not to touch him. He circled, rubbed, abraded with his fingernail. With each stroke, no matter how hard or how soft, she got wetter.

"I'm going to fuck you with my finger."

"Today?"

"Brat." He pinched one of her nipples and she yelped. "We move at my speed."

Frustrating her, he pulled away.

"That's cruel," she protested.

"Let me know when you're ready to proceed."

She looked at him and saw his face was set in implacable lines. "I'm not sure I like this part of it."

"Which part?"

Sofia was still aroused. "I just want you to touch me."

"Being a sub isn't always easy. As I said, it takes a lot of focus."

"I'm learning." Then, realizing he was waiting on her still, she added, "I won't say anything else."

"Let's start over."

The man frustrated her.

"Take a breath. Shake out your arms."

She inhaled then she lowered her arms. He rubbed her skin, maintaining the connection between them.

Sofia realized she'd never had a man spend this much time with her while she was naked. Most of the time, they hopped into bed with the lights off. At first Cade's demands had seemed a bit unnatural, but she was starting to enjoy them.

When she was ready, he cupped her breasts as he had earlier and teased her nipples until they were taut.

Then he held his finger in front of her mouth.

This time, she tasted her own essence. It was startling in its eroticism.

As he had earlier, he drew his finger down her body. It was all she could do to keep her mouth shut and wait on him.

It seemed to take him forever to touch her clit again. She sighed.

"Ask me."

"Fuck me with your finger." She looked at him. "Please?"

"My pleasure." He placed his finger in her, just a fraction of an inch. Then he pulled it out to torment her clit.

Though she'd never admit it to him, it had been worth the wait.

"I could play with you all afternoon."

"I would let you," she said. She squeezed her internal muscles, searching for an orgasm that was so, so far out of reach.

"My pace," he reminded her.

She had a feeling that she wouldn't need to tell him whether she'd had an orgasm or not.

He took his time, leisurely stroking then entering her again. She closed her eyes and gave herself over. Until now, she hadn't been aware that she'd been fighting—herself as well as him.

"That's it."

His words became part of the hypnotic spell that he was weaving.

She couldn't believe she was standing naked in Cade Donovan's barn while he pleasured her. Yet there was no denying the exquisite torture.

"Play with your nipples."

She blinked away her confusion and did what he said. As she did, he increased the tempo, fingering her faster, deeper, going as far as his knuckle before pulling out.

Sofia curled her toes into the wood beneath her, seeking stability that she couldn't find. Even though he'd cautioned her to remain still, she jerked her hips.

"Pinch yourself," he ordered, voice guttural.

"Cade!"

"Do it." He pressed his thumb on her clit.

"Ow," she protested.

"Yellow?"

"No, no." It hurt, but in a way that brought her more pleasure.

He inserted a second finger, forcing her apart, making her take more.

"Twist your nipples," he said.

She was hyperaware of him standing so close, fully dressed, commanding her, tormenting her as the storm raged. Perspiration dotted her skin, and she'd never been more overwhelmed.

"I want to hear you whimper."

She was lost somewhere inside her own mind. Overwhelmed yet seeking more.

He crooked one of his fingers, finding that sensitive place in her, and he pushed against it.

That, along with the ache in her clit and the pain in her nipples, made her fall forward as an orgasm washed over her.

He was there, catching her, holding her up, pressing a kiss against her ear.

Before she was aware of what he was doing, he'd scooped

her from the ground and carried her to his chair. He sat and continued to hold her against his chest.

Sofia stayed snuggled there for long seconds, until she heard the thud of his heartbeat, and felt soft cotton and hard muscles beneath her face.

"Welcome to your first taste of a BDSM scene."

She leaned away from him and turned to look at him.

"How was it?"

"I'm still processing."

"Take as much time as you need."

"I'd like to put my clothes back on." Now that the scene was over, it felt strange to be cradled, nude.

He helped her up and kept a hand on her until he was sure she was steady.

Cade didn't look away while she dressed.

She expected him to get ready to go, but if she'd learned anything in the last few minutes, it was that he rarely behaved as she anticipated.

"Come back here."

Slowly following his order, she went to stand in front of him and the Dungeon Master chair.

Even though she was fully dressed, wearing heeled boots and standing, she was still aware of the dynamic between them. He was every bit a Dom, and something deep down inside her responded to that.

"Part of a scene is aftercare," he explained. "Making sure you're okay."

She nodded.

"A lot of couples debrief, talk about the experience. What went right or wrong. What worked for them. How they're feeling. Oftentimes something comes up mentally or emotionally that should be discussed."

"I'm fine," she said, hoping the words would reassure him as well as herself. The truth was, she'd never been at a more fevered pitch. It had made her feel as if she'd been on a knife edge.

She'd liked being naked, the way he'd looked at her

and touched her, the paddling. The combination of his gentleness and gruffness had turned her on. After-effects from the orgasm still ricocheted through her. His seduction had been complete when she'd curled into him for comfort afterward.

The whole thing had been more fulfilling than she could have imagined. It scared her to realize there would be no going back. She craved more. She wasn't sure what the hell to do with that knowledge. All she knew was that being with him had changed her.

"What did you enjoy?"

She exhaled. "Do you ever stop?" Sofia might not say it aloud, but his determination to talk to her, draw her out, was part of his charm.

Without responding, he tapped a finger on the arm of the chair.

"It's a lot to take in. I feel somewhat overwhelmed."

"In what way?"

She blew a wisp of hair back from her face. "Do you have to stay in your role as a Dom? It has me a little discombobulated."

"That's always my role. It was Saturday night when we talked, danced, kissed. I can't separate it out from my personality. But we can talk inside the house if it's more comfortable," he agreed as he stood.

Right now she wasn't quite sure how to tell him that she was hoping he'd command her to crawl up onto his medical table and stay still while he secured her in place and did unimaginable things to her very willing body. Actually, she realized, he might not be surprised at all, but she was stunned.

He gathered her electronics then moved past her to pull back the tarp and she couldn't resist one last look at the medical table with its threatening-looking restraints.

5

Pretending she didn't feel feverish, Sofia went down the stairs.

She had to step over the dog, and Loopy barely lifted her head. Sofia picked up her clipboard then kept walking until she reached the door. Since the rain was coming in, she stopped there.

When Cade stepped off the staircase, Loopy roused herself and trotted after him.

"Did you get everything you need here?" he asked when he joined her, as if she hadn't just been naked while he'd fingered her to an orgasm. "Do you need any more pictures?"

She'd taken hardly any, but she was pretty sure every detail was indelibly etched in her memory. "If you can just get me the dimensions, that will be fine. I know approximately how many square feet we need for a thousand people. Of course it depends on the setup we use, for example, round or banquet-style tables." The return to reality felt abrupt. She'd been the one to ask him to step out of his Dom role, but she was still wrapped in her sensual delirium. "Once we have a sense of the actual number of attendees and the type of event you're having, we'll be able to make a judgment call. Alternatively, if you're set on using the barn, we can make it work by limiting the people and having a less formal meal. Either way is fine."

Wind gusted and she took a step back.

He reached out a hand to steady her and she realized that he was always polite, solicitous, even during the scene when he was unrelenting in his demands.

"Wait here."

There was no way she was going to make it the few steps to the golf cart without getting drenched.

He dashed out to the cart, Loopy chasing after him.

The two hopped into the vehicle, with Loopy in the back.

Cade drove into the barn and stopped next to her. He grabbed a towel from the floorboard and wiped off her seat. "Your chariot, ma'am."

"That really wasn't necessary."

He waited.

"But it was gallant. Thank you." She climbed in and took a seat.

He exited the ATV for a moment to roll down some sheets of plastic, then fastened them to the side of the vehicle.

"Brilliant," she said.

"Not our first rainstorm," he replied.

The makeshift doors in place, he unzipped his side to slide behind the wheel. "Good?"

This time, she knew to hang on to the small bar in front of her.

After checking on Loopy, he hit the accelerator. This time he didn't pause. Instead, he continued down the path at full speed.

He took a turnoff and headed to the rear of the big house. The back door was protected by a portico, and he stopped beneath it.

They each unzipped the doors then he had to unhook his side to let Loopy out.

"I need to close the barn door and secure a few things from the wind. Go ahead into the house," he said. "The door leads into a mudroom then into the kitchen. Make yourself comfortable."

For a second, she debated what to do.

Part of her wanted to put some real distance between them so that she could do some more research on BDSM. Now that she'd had a taste, she had another dozen questions. Unfortunately, since Lara and Connor had left for a honeymoon, she couldn't ask her friend for advice.

But she had to remember she was here on business and still had to go over her presentation with him. Seeing that he was looking at her, waiting, she nodded.

"Stay with Sofia," he said to Loopy.

The dog wagged her tail and barked.

He drove off at his usual quick pace.

Loopy dashed up the stairs and looked back, tail wagging furiously, as if she were encouraging Sofia to move faster.

Even though the area was covered, wind blasted through, bringing rain with it.

She held on to the door so it didn't slam open and Loopy bolted inside, through the mudroom and into the kitchen, sliding across the floor like an oversized, fluffy mop.

Laughing, she forced the door closed.

The mudroom was a well-organized space, with an oversized sink, stacked washer and dryer, laundry hamper, a bench, cubbies for storage of shoes, towels and flashlights, thirsty mats and pegs for jackets and, obviously, cowboy hats.

She toweled dry, kicked off her shoes. Then, pushing away the feeling of being an intruder, she went into the kitchen. Here, at least, she felt more at home.

Over the years, especially while she'd helped her mother with the catering company, she'd been in a lot of big kitchens, but she wasn't sure she'd seen anything quite like this. The appliances were industrial-sized, and a butler's pantry stood off to one side. No doubt the house had been used for entertaining on a grand scale at one time.

Most likely, when the house was built, the kitchen would have been in a separate building. So that meant extensive remodeling had been done. And that could be another interesting addition to any book about the ranch.

She put water in the kettle using the pot filler above the stove. When she eventually bought a house of her own, that would be a necessity.

Going through the motions soothed her. Not only was it

homey, she was accustomed to being the hired help and finding her way around. At least for a time, she was able to forget about what had happened in the barn, as if she'd temporarily been someone else.

Sofia turned the stove's flame on high then wandered into the pantry to look for teabags. She found a glass jar with a few miserly bags in it, but thankfully, it was a brand she knew and liked. She located the brown sugar and honey, and she chose a ripe lemon from the fruit bowl. But she couldn't find a bottle of whiskey.

Whoever had set up the kitchen had done a good job. Several mugs hung from a wooden tree next to the stove. After putting down the items from the pantry, she found spoons and a teapot.

Cade returned to the house, and Loopy blasted by to greet him as if he'd been gone for a month. She shook her head, rubbed against him, barked. It was amazing he could keep his balance.

"What a good girl," he told her.

Sofia watched him remove his hat and shake it off before slamming the door closed.

With Cade in the house, the respite from her thoughts vanished. She was once again the woman who'd felt his paddle and been held against his chest.

"Hellish storm," he said.

"The weatherman's version of twenty-percent chance of rain." Because of the unanswered questions between them, normal conversation seemed inane.

He tossed his hat onto the bench then plowed a hand through his damp hair, dislodging a single, mesmerizing lock. She continued to watch as he shucked water from his shirt.

For a short time she'd lived with a man, but she'd never stood, riveted, and watched him undress. To be fair, he'd been nothing like Cade. This cowboy exuded confidence and masculinity. Especially after what they'd shared, he was a force as menacing as nature herself.

Cade wiped the bottom of his boots on a mat then started to unsnap the pearl buttons on his shirt.

He wore a white T-shirt beneath, and she wasn't sure whether or not she was disappointed.

The kettle gave a soft whistle and she moved toward the stove before she got caught, again, staring at him. He really did muddle her thought processes. It wasn't just him, though. It was her and the aftershocks still zipping through her.

She moved the kettle to the back burner and turned off the flame.

Concentrating on what she was doing, Sofia plonked teabags into the pot and filled it with the hot water. She was just putting on the lid when he joined her in the kitchen.

It shouldn't have been possible, but he was even broader, more devastating in the white T-shirt and well-worn jeans.

Her voice was a tad higher than usual when she asked, "Do you have whiskey?"

"A case of it, at least."

"I didn't see any in the pantry."

He blanched. "Whiskey doesn't belong in the pantry."

"Are you serious?"

"There's some in my study. I'll get it."

He returned in less than three minutes and handed the whiskey to her.

"That's a gorgeously shaped bottle."

"Connor left it here. It was a gift from Julien."

"Now I'm really impressed. Not only does he show up to the reception, but he sends this kind of gift?"

"And damn good stuff," he replied.

Focusing on anything but his hands as he removed the cap, she grabbed a cutting board from behind the sink and pulled a knife from the nearby block.

He put the bottle down near her. Rather than moving away, he propped his hips against one of the marble countertops and swept his gaze over her in a way that reminded her of the loft and heated her from the outside in.

She forced herself to concentrate on slicing the lemon, aware of the way he watched her every movement. Trying to make small talk to dispel the unaccountable tension crawling through her, she pretended nothing was unusual by saying, "When someone tells me to make myself at home in a kitchen, I'm afraid I can't help it."

"I like to see someone get some use out of it. All I need is the grill and a beer."

Why did that not surprise her?

She coated the bottom of two cups with the honey then spooned in a hint of brown sugar before drenching the mixture with fresh-squeezed lemon.

"Is this your version of a hot toddy?"

"I experiment with recipes. The brown sugar highlights some of the whiskey's finer notes. Speaking of which"— Sofia indicated the fancy-looking bottle—"are you sure you want to use this? I typically choose something less expensive."

"Swill?"

"You're a whiskey snob?"

"Indubitably," he replied.

She grinned, liking this side of him, less nerve-wracking than the Dom who'd commanded the loft a few minutes ago. Still, she knew a thing or two about alcohol. As she eyed the amount she was adding to his cup, she realized he was going to be drinking a ten-dollar cup of tea.

After pouring tea into the mug, she gave it a gentle stir. "Cinnamon is a nice touch, if you like it."

"No. Thanks." He accepted her proffered cup.

She waited while he tried it.

"Damn."

"Well?" she asked while pouring tea into her cup.

"Better than I expected. Thank you." He gestured toward her mug. "Not putting whiskey in yours?"

"No. I still have a long drive back to Corpus."

"You'll be here a bit. Should at least give it a try." He extended his hot toddy to her.

Accepting it, drinking from it, implied intimacy. And yet, as she'd been telling him, nothing about their time together had been normal.

Their fingers brushed as he handed off the mug.

She blew on the surface of the hot toddy then took a small sip. The alcohol seeped through her and she felt its soothing effects creep up the back of her neck. The flavors leaped to life, and she tasted a layer of peat then the sweetness of maple. "Really palatable."

He accepted the mug back.

She picked up her own and took a drink.

"Not as good?" he guessed.

"A let-down," she agreed. The disappointment had her reaching for the bottle. She splashed about a quarter of an ounce into the wannabe toddy, enough to add flavor, but not enough to affect her judgment or reactions.

"Let me show you around," he said. "But don't think I've forgotten that you owe me some answers."

Her hand shook.

"Bring your drink," he encouraged. "This will take a while."

Around them, wind continued to pound the house.

"That would be an *occasional gust*," he informed her.

"Yeah." She looked out of the back window and saw the wind stripping some pink blossoms from oleander bushes. The rain was even fiercer than it had been earlier, and lightning ripped through the air.

A shocking clash of thunder sent Loopy scurrying under the kitchen table. She knocked a chair back and curled up, her head buried under one paw.

"I'll check the weather radar when we we're in my study," he said.

She followed him into the dining room and her mouth fell open in shock. Ornate windows overlooked a courtyard and a picture of the Alamo dominated the far wall. A massive wooden table filled a good portion of the space. "How many people does it seat?"

"With all the leaves in the table? Fifty."

What surprised her the most was that furnishings were sturdy, rather than ornate.

"Great-great-grandfather was very much a product of his time, I'm told. He believed in using what was available and making certain things were built to last, especially after the fire. Most of the original furniture is mesquite, and the finishings on them are brass and copper. All the leather used is from the hides of ranch cattle."

"So this is original?"

"As old as the ranch," he confirmed. "Of course, through the years, we've re-covered some of the pieces."

"It's impressive."

"At Grandma Maisie's insistence, he built the house in the hope that all of his kids would stay here and raise their families."

"How many kids did they have?"

"Five. Only my great-grandfather Phillip continued to live here, along with his bride, Anabelle. But everyone returned on the holidays. I'm told that Maisie was never happier than when everyone was home."

He kept on talking as he led her toward the front of the house.

"The architect designed it as a horseshoe, essentially, so that all interior rooms face the courtyard."

She moved in for a closer look, but the view was obscured by the driving rain. A concrete fountain and wishing pool were in the middle, and the wind whipped the falling water horizontally. Two small palm trees leaned sideways, and bougainvillea petals blew everywhere. "That has to be a thirty or forty mile an hour gust," she said. "Good thing they're only occasional."

"Let's head to my study."

As he'd said, the floors appeared battle-scarred, worn from years of boots and spurs.

History and masculinity defined the room that was on the other side of the hallway. An ornately framed portrait hung on the wall between two windows. Humphrey Sykes, she assumed. On another wall was a rendition of a woman from the same period. Perhaps the man's wife, Maisie.

"Have a seat," he invited as he sat behind a substantial desk, something she guessed the original Sykes owner had built. From everything she observed, it appeared that being a Dom was in his DNA, not that something like that was possible.

This office, in color, size and scope, suited him. She couldn't imagine anything more fitting.

She slid onto a leather chair that faced him and glanced around while he powered up his computer. The wall space was covered with pictures of the ranch—drawings, photos, aerial shots. There were paintings of horses, of cattle. A branding iron was displayed on a shelf.

There didn't seem to be many mementos belonging to Cade, though she could be wrong about that.

Every time he walked in, he had to be reminded of who he was and the weight of his responsibility. No wonder he took things so seriously.

Her hot toddy had cooled enough so that she could take a long drink. Thunder rumbled, accompanied by a bright flash of lightning. A few seconds later, the overhead lights flickered. "Ominous," she said.

He looked over the computer screen at her. For a few heartbeats, their gazes were locked. His eyes appeared dark and his expression was unreadable.

The computer made a sound like a bell and he glanced away, severing their connection.

A few seconds later, he crooked his finger, indicating she should come around the desk. Even though she realized that being so close to him was a spectacularly bad idea, she went to stand behind him.

A picture of the local radar filled the screen. The storm cell was enormous, covering most of the county. Most of it was in green, signifying rainstorms, but several patches were yellow and several were red.

"We have a flash flood and tornado watch until eight p.m." He pushed a button to set the radar into motion. "And it's moving east."

Which meant that if she left now, she would be driving through the potentially treacherous weather the entire way back to Corpus Christi.

"I have about fourteen bedrooms you can choose from," he offered, turning his chair slightly to look at her.

Her heart dropped.

"Or the guest house if you're more comfortable."

She wanted to protest, say that she'd just head out when this band of rain eased. But she knew the power of Texas storms, particularly near the coast. And if the computer predictions were accurate, there were more powerful winds to come. "I'll have a look at the radar again later."

"The ranch roads can wash out in places if we get a lot of rain in a short period."

She hadn't considered that possibility. "I know you were only planning to have me here for an hour or so."

Looking over his shoulder, he said, "Ms. McBride, I can assure you, I have no objection. You're anything but an inconvenience."

Uncertainty rippled through her as she moved away from him. "Do you mind showing me the rest of the mansion?"

None of the house was ostentatious. As he'd said before, it was intended to be lived in. Furnishings were sturdy. And for a house that had been occupied for most of a hundred years, there were surprisingly few personal items. The parlor had a library of hardback books, all lined up alphabetically behind glass-fronted doors. Family portraits hung on many walls. Most of the other paintings depicted either landscapes or Texas historical sites.

"Is it what you expected?" he asked when he led her upstairs.

"No. I thought it would be much more..." She sought for the right word. The place seemed a little austere, unlived in. The courtyard with its bright, tropical plants, flowers, roses, provided a stark contrast. Finally, she settled for, "Grandiose."

"Humphrey Sykes' father was a lawyer who left Virginia to find a better life for his family. He moved them all to Texas, took advantage of some land grants, but he died shortly after. Yellow fever, I believe. The family wasn't rich, and Humphrey grew up knowing that everything he had could disappear in a moment."

"The fire reaffirmed that?" she guessed.

"It did." He nodded. "So he never overspent. When my great-grandfather Phillip died, all of his personal possessions filled a shoebox. Money went into the land, into the kids' educations, purchasing cattle and horses. An obligation to the future."

"Is that ideal something that you share?"

At the top of the stairs, he paused and turned toward her.

She stopped a step below him. "In your office, I didn't see anything that might belong to you."

"I grew up really poor the first few years, and not because my dad wanted it that way."

"So you don't feel as if any of this is really yours?"

His eyes darkened again. When he spoke, his voice was ragged, a bit raw with emotion. "You might say that."

Without another word, he headed down the hallway.

More interested than ever about him, she followed.

"This is for storage," he said, indicating a door. "When the house was built, trunks were kept here, for traveling, for extra clothing. That type of thing. Generations since have kept holiday decorations, unneeded furniture. If indeed we do a pamphlet, there may be some things of interest in there."

He pointed out bathrooms and bedrooms, and the transom windows so that air could move between interior spaces. "Many of the windows facing the courtyard open all the way so you can walk out them and onto a sleeping porch. Of course, now that we have air conditioning, the only people who do that are kids."

"Did you?"

She had a difficult time picturing him as a little boy.

"Yeah. More often than my mom might have liked. She used to say she was afraid the mosquitoes would carry me away."

"I think my mother used to say something similar." She grinned. "Where does she live?"

"Waltham. She opened a leather shop. Saddles, furniture, that sort of thing. Mostly with leather from our ranches."

He paused. "This one is my room." The door was closed and he didn't offer to open it.

"When I pulled up, I noticed a turret. Is it just for decoration?"

"No. It's functional. It's actually part of the master bedroom."

"Yours?"

"As I'm the only master here, yes."

"I thought you didn't consider yourself a Master?"

"I said I hadn't collared anyone," he corrected. "There's a difference."

"So if you did, you'd want her to consider you her Master?"

"Yes."

The word seemed to hang between them. Her mouth dried.

He rested his shoulder against the doorjamb and gave her a smile that tantalized, captivated and frightened her a little. "Why else would I offer my collar? Protection? A commitment? To me, it would be every bit as meaningful as a wedding ring."

Nervous, she smoothed imaginary wrinkles from her pants. "I didn't realize it was that significant."

"To me, it is." He curled his hand around the doorknob. "Would you like to see the turret?"

Part of her knew she should refuse, but she seemed to have become a different person since she'd arrived at the Running Wind and fallen under its master's spell. "Yes. I would."

Sofia expected his bedroom to be austere, so the sight of the bright-blue quilt was a pleasant surprise. Two chairs were grouped in front of a fireplace. And this room had the personal effects she hadn't seen downstairs. Big belt buckles sat on top of the dresser. At least some, she imagined, were rodeo-riding awards.

Small, framed pictures adorned a shelf. In one, he was on a horse, smiling widely, revealing a missing tooth. "May I?"

He shrugged, and she took his non-answer as a yes. There were photos of Cade with a woman who appeared to be his mother. Horses featured in almost all of them. "Is this your father?" she asked, picking up a picture of Cade standing near a motorcycle.

"It is."

He had photos of his half-siblings, but nothing that appeared more recent, as if he'd stopped living his life at some point.

"Bathroom is over there."

She glanced over to see him pointing. Obviously he'd been watching her, and she had the sense he wanted to distract her from prying.

"My grandparents had a wall removed. So the suite is actually the size of two original bedrooms."

And with it being at the far end of the house, his private area was like an oasis.

She looked in the large bathroom. While it was modern, it had been remodeled in keeping with the historic feel of the rest of the house. A chandelier hung from the ceiling.

"It was repurposed from one of the guest houses."

"Smart and frugal."

"The turret is this way." He opened a door, and she breathed him in as she walked past.

Every moment, she was more and more attracted to him, more tempted to ask him questions about his loft.

Sofia led the way up the circular iron staircase to the

turret.

When she reached the top, she was astounded. The area felt like a home within a home. There was a small sitting area, with a leather couch and a couple of chairs. A steamer trunk served as a coffee table, and a well-used guitar leaned against a wall.

"Do you play?"

"I pluck a few chords," he said. "But I'm no musician."

He had a small area for a coffee service.

"So I don't have to go downstairs to have my first cup," he explained.

She walked over to one of the oblong windows. Wind continued to pummel the shrubs and trees, and through the rain she could see that verdant land swept in every direction. She thought she could see the cuts made by the river and the roads, but the rivulets of water running down the panes of glass made it difficult to tell.

"Before cell phones, this was a great way to see if someone was drawing near."

She continued to walk around the small space. From another window, the ornate front gate was visible, and she realized he'd probably watched her arrival.

"Because it has a three-hundred-sixty-degree view, I can watch both the sunrise and sunset from here."

It lacked a desk, which meant he couldn't work in here. "It's peaceful. And…"

"And?" He had a shoulder braced against a windowsill.

"A little wild." She waved her hand toward the window. Clouds seemed to tumble over each other. Others collided. In the distance, lighting snapped across the sky.

"Best vantage for a storm, for sure," he agreed.

And to survey everything he owned. He really was lord over his domain.

"I've had a fantasy," he said.

She turned.

"Of having my submissive in the window, naked when I came back in from the range. Or maybe displayed for a bit

119

for anyone who happened by."

It wasn't likely that anyone would happen by, she realized, but it was the image that tantalized.

"I think about flogging my sub while she's spread wide. Maybe secured to the wall on either side."

"When you say that, I feel a little fear."

"Fear can be an aphrodisiac."

"Can it?"

"Can't it?" he countered in return.

Perhaps it could be, she mused. If the sensation of fireworks rocking through her was anything to go by, he was right. It sure as hell had been in the loft.

"Ready to talk to me?" He folded his arms across his chest.

She didn't know whether it was intentional or not, but he was blocking the doorway. Since she realized he would persist until he got what he wanted, she decided to tell him everything.

"Was fear part of your arousal?"

"It was," she admitted. "What happened back there confused me. I liked it. More than I anticipated. It turned me on." She blushed. "Obviously."

He nodded and remained quiet.

She pulled her hair into a mock ponytail before letting it go again. "I told you I don't have a lot of experience."

"Go on."

"Coming like that isn't something I've done often. But you made it happen quickly."

"Because most of a woman's sexual arousal comes from her brain. Thinking about what we were doing excited you. Making you touch the paddle created a tactile reinforcement. Even when your eyes were closed, you knew I was looking at you, only you."

Even his voice, smoke and sex, aroused her again.

"I engaged all of your senses. And I did it deliberately," he said.

She dug deep to find the courage to answer him. Still the confounded man waited patiently, and she knew he wouldn't push her. "I've read books," she continued. "Erotic ones. And I've seen some movies. I'm intrigued by some of it. And parts of it scare the shit out of me."

"Yet you never needed a safe word, never said yellow and you didn't say no."

All of that was true.

"Forget for a moment that we played. Imagine instead that you arrived and I took you to bed. Would you have been nervous?"

"Probably," she admitted.

"Would it have stopped you?"

"No." She exhaled. "But being in your dungeon isn't exactly the same thing as having sex. I was a little freaked out."

"Okay."

"Okay?" She scowled.

"Acknowledging your feelings is a good thing. There's no shame in being nervous. And you can choose to scene any way. You can try different things and see what works for you."

Like being naked in his window.

With patience she'd never seen from anyone else, he waited. Working through this seemed important to him. Finally, she asked, "How did you know that you were into it?"

"For me there was never a question. I sought out BDSM clubs as soon as I was old enough to drive. When I walked through the door and witnessed my first scene, I knew I belonged."

She rubbed her upper arms.

"There was a woman, sub, tied to a St. Andrew's cross. She was being flogged, and she seemed lost. It wasn't until later that I learned about subspace."

"I've never heard of it."

"The submissive mentally, emotionally flies, soars, goes someplace inside her head, mostly because of a release of endorphins."

"Back to what you said about transcendence?"

"Exactly. I wanted to bring a woman that much pleasure. And I was impressed by the way the Dom was so in tune with his sub, checking on her, making certain she was all right. I realized then that D/s was about more than controlling someone else, it was about controlling myself, my impulses, behavior, actions. It took some time for me to totally understand it."

"If I hadn't met you, I'm not sure I would have known what to look for." But she did know that she'd felt restless.

"Ready to go back downstairs?"

She nodded.

Rather than going first, he stepped aside and waited for her to pass.

The lights flickered a number of times as they picked up their empty mugs from the study and made their way back to the kitchen.

They found Loopy where they'd left her, under the table.

In the mudroom, he showed Sofia where batteries, flashlights, matches and candles were stored.

"I have a generator, but I use it mostly for the freezer, my laptop computer and as a way to keep my cell phone charged."

"I hope it doesn't come to that."

"We're prepared if it does."

Thunder crashed. Loopy whimpered. Lightning ripped apart the sky. Being stranded with Cade Donovan was beginning to look like a possibility.

They moved into the kitchen and he asked, "Did you want to show me your concepts?"

"Yes. Is there a place you want to sit?"

"This is fine."

She sat at the kitchen bar and he pulled another chair close to hers. Pretending this was an ordinary sales call, she turned on her tablet then touched the icon for her presentations.

"That's the ranch logo," he said, and there was a warmth

in his voice she hadn't heard before.

"I save each client's presentation with their logo. It makes it easier to find. And this one, I particularly like looking at," she said.

"Do you?"

"Your graphic designer is talented."

"I drew the rough draft."

"Did you really?" She looked over at him. "That's impressive. I love the definition of the horse's mane, and its face looks fierce, as if nothing will stand in its way." All of the same characteristics Cade had.

Loopy scooted out from beneath the table and padded toward them. With a shudder, the dog plopped down behind both of the chairs.

Even as Sofia went through the slides she'd prepared, she noticed him watching her more than the screen.

Their scene in the barn, combined with the picture he painted of what he wanted to do in the turret, replayed in her mind, making it difficult to focus.

"The presentation?" he reminded her.

She shook her head before touching the screen. Automatically she moved from picture to picture of the various tent options. Some were self-supporting, others were framed and a few had poles. "As for specific ideas… If you wanted to do an informal afternoon event, you can have a presentation on a stage, either in the barn or in one of these tents. Then turn that area over for entertaining. Or, if you want something more upscale, there's this option." She advanced to pictures of a formal party inside a climate-control century tent.

"Good God. I had no idea they came in so many different sizes."

"This one includes windows, and you can add real French doors."

"Are you joking?"

"No. We can add sections based on the number of people in attendance." She showed him various layouts, for plated meals, old-fashioned Texas barbecues, buffets.

"Bottom line, what do you recommend?"

"This idea was your grandfather's, wasn't it?"

He nodded.

"I think we need to ask him before we go much further. Of course, things will change if you can utilize the barn." She shot him a sideways glance. "And you'll need to wall off the dungeon or move the equipment."

"But not immediately."

Something hot unfurled in her veins.

"Plenty of time for it to get some use."

Striving for professionalism, she cleared her throat then said, "Regardless, this will not be an inexpensive event."

"With the Pain in the Ass Fee," he added.

She pointed to the screen. "That number is likely to be the biggest line item and the one most subject to change." Finally, she quoted some ballpark figures for the celebration.

"Fuck me to Sunday. Repeat that."

Without flinching, she did. If he wanted to hire her, he'd have to pay for it.

"You realize how many bulls I could purchase for that price? Hell, I could buy another fucking ranch."

"Do you know much advertising you'll be buying?"

He frowned.

Undeterred by his reaction, she opened her checklist as a spreadsheet to show him each item and a price estimate, high to low, of each. Then she saved it as a PDF and emailed it to him. "You're welcome to find your own people for each of those things. But be sure your quotes also include tax and gratuities."

"There's at least a hundred things on there."

"More, if you count the signage, parking and shuttle buses," she said with a cheery smile.

"Has anyone ever had a heart attack at this point in your presentation?"

"Calls to nine-one-one are extra. And I don't give mouth-to-mouth."

He raked a hand through his hair, dislodging a piece, making him look younger, more rakish, momentarily less frightening.

"Over the years, I've dealt with the shrewdest business people. I've never met anyone like you."

"What's worse is I don't negotiate."

"Take it or leave it?"

"Green or red, Mr. Donovan."

"Your pretty little butt cheeks will pay for that comment," he promised.

Suddenly the air between them pulsed. It had gone from all business to part sensual. The man was a master at changing her focus. And she was taken aback at how much she wanted just that.

"Let's talk to the Colonel. When will you be in Houston again?"

"Thursday night."

"I'll set up an appointment for you on Friday if that will work.

"Morning to midafternoon is fine." Her phone rang and she plucked it from her back pocket. From the ringtone, she knew it was her mother. "If you'll excuse me? Mom doesn't usually call if she knows I'm in a business meeting."

"Go ahead," he said.

She slid off the chair and crossed into the dining room, aware that Cade could hear every bit of the conversation.

"Where are you?" her mother demanded without saying hello.

"The Donovan ranch."

Cynthia let out a heavy exhalation. *"Gracias a Dios."*

"What's up?"

"Flooding. And a ten-car accident on the highway."

She paced the length of the room, captivated by the sight of the rain and the way the trees leaned and the bushes thrashed. "It's no better here," she said. "It would be insane for me to try to leave anytime soon. Everyone safe there?"

"Waiting for your sister to get back."

One of the twins was fussing, making it difficult for Sofia to hear everything her mother was saying. "Someone sounds unhappy."

"It's Bella. She's tired and won't go to sleep."

"Tell baby Bella that her Auntie Sofia loves her."

The crying stopped.

"She heard you. Her eyes are wide."

Another streak of lightning burst down. It was followed by an ear-splitting sound, like an explosion. Loopy whimpered. Sofia jumped, and the phone momentarily buzzed with static. "I'm going to have to go, Mom."

"Promise me you'll stay put."

She remained patient. It didn't seem to matter to her mother that Sofia was an adult. She worried ceaselessly. "I will. I'll let you know if anything changes."

After ending the call with her mother, she returned to the kitchen and he was nowhere in sight. She heard noises in the mudroom, so she walked over there. "What happened?

"Sounded like the lighting hit something," he replied as he fastened up his slicker. "Stay here. I'll be back as soon as I can."

The sight of a man in a bright-yellow slicker and plastic-wrapped hat should not have been sexy, but it was.

The lights flickered three times, then went off and stayed off.

"I think that settles the matter of whether or not you're staying."

"Could be worse," Cade said nearly half an hour later, as he forced the door shut behind him.

Sofia and Loopy met him in the mudroom, and the kitchen was filled with the rich scent of something cooking.

He'd told himself he liked living alone on the ranch, just him, the dog and the wide-open spaces, but now he wasn't so sure. A long-denied part of him appreciated the difference between a house and a home.

She grabbed a couple of towels from the top of the dryer and put them on the floor.

"Thanks." He stomped water off his boots then tossed his hat on one towel and dropped his slicker on the other.

At her request, he'd removed her small duffel bag from the SUV, and he put it on the bench. "Kept it as dry as I could."

"Thank you."

"We have most of a live oak tree down, and it looks as if it may have done some damage to the roof of one of the guest houses. From the inside, I didn't see anything leaking. Power poles look okay. My foreman is checking on the cattle and horses. As soon as the weather clears, we'll be able to better assess the situation." After wiping off his boots and hanging his wet coat and hat from pegs, he said, "Something smells good."

"Stir fry. I wasn't sure how long the power will last, so I figured I'd make us something to eat."

"Thank you." He tucked back a wayward strand of her hair. As he did, he imagined it bound with rope and secured in a hog-tie. The thought of her bent in that exquisite arch

127

was enough to make his cock hard.

After toweling dry his hair, he followed her into the kitchen. "Wine with that?"

"A red would be wonderful," she said.

While she tested a vegetable for crispness, he pulled out a bottle of merlot from the under-counter cooler then uncorked it.

It hadn't taken her long to find her way around the kitchen. And she'd put two place settings on the counter, complete with napkins. Just in case, there was a candle and a lighter nearby.

She transferred the food to a platter and moved it to the island. He watched her all the while.

He put food in Loopy's dog dish, but when the thunder rumbled again, she dashed off to hide under the table.

"Poor thing," she said.

"As soon as the storm passes, she'll be hungry." He washed his hands then carried the wine glasses to the island.

She slid onto one of the bar stools and he took the other.

Her tablet was in front of her and he saw that she'd been looking at a BDSM site.

"Learn anything interesting?"

She blushed and quickly turned off the screen.

"Don't." He put his hand over her wrist. "I want to know what you're looking at."

"An article on being a submissive." She pulled back, shoved the tablet a few inches away then busied herself with filling their plates. "As well as some pictures of bondage."

"And?"

"I'll admit I'm intrigued by it."

"You've never tried it, correct?"

She paused, holding the spoon above the serving dish. Her eyes were wide and her mouth open a fraction of an inch. Suddenly he couldn't banish the idea of seeing her beautiful body secured with gorgeous hemp.

"No, I haven't. Some of the stuff is a little extreme for my tastes. The inverted positions, for example."

"After dinner, show me what you were drawn to?"

She sucked in a breath. "You definitely unnerve me. I can't say that I've ever looked at porn with a man before."

"I'll happily be your first. Tell me about the article."

"Well, honestly, I saw bits and pieces from a few different sites. It seems odd that I got so much pleasure from the pain. And I wanted to learn more about the power exchange."

He said nothing.

"You were right about endorphins. One person said it was like a runner's high." She grimaced. "Which is something I'd never know anything about."

"You can get it from a lot of things. Anything risky, edgy."

"Thank God." She sighed. "Otherwise I'd never experience it."

He laughed.

"It helped to realize that I'm not all that strange in liking it."

"I'd say you're quite normal."

"You would. It's in your best interest."

He shrugged in concession.

She filled a plate and offered it to him. "But what I'm still struggling with is understanding other aspects, like service, genuinely wanting to please your Dom."

"Again, not all that different from a vanilla relationship."

"Meaning one that doesn't have BDSM?"

He nodded. "All good relationships have the element of genuinely wanting to please the other, wouldn't you say?"

"If not, they should," she replied.

"Take this for example."

She looked at him.

"The meal."

"We both need to eat," she said, as if dismissing her efforts.

"But coming in from the weather, hungry, and not having to cook, is spectacular."

"Really, Cade. I love to do it. It's something creative,

but also mindless, if you know what I mean. It helps me unwind after work."

"And that does nothing to diminish my appreciation."

She looked away. "In that case, you're welcome." After spooning food onto her plate, she stuck her fork into a piece of meat then took a bite.

She sighed in a way that reminded him of her orgasm.

"Is this beef from the ranch?"

"It is."

"I haven't had anything this good in months. Succulent. Melts in your mouth."

"Glad you approve. You're welcome to take some back with you."

"Seriously?"

He nodded then took a bite of his own. "It's not just the beef," he said. "It's your cooking."

They finished dinner and he insisted on cleaning the kitchen, not that there was a lot to do. "You're not a messy cook."

"I learned early. I hate to clean up afterward." She topped off their wine glasses.

"Would you like to join me in the turret? It's the best place to watch the storm." And it was cozier, more intimate than the parlor or living room.

"Is that where you spend most of your evenings?"

"My study, generally. No matter how much I get done, there's more needed."

"I'm happy to do some work of my own, or read a book."

He shook his head. "I'd enjoy the company."

The specks in her eyes brightened and he wondered if she were imagining herself naked in the window, as he'd suggested earlier. Sofia's eyes were more revealing than she probably realized. "In that case, yes. Thanks."

"Grab your wine and bring your tablet as well. I'll grab your duffel bag."

She glanced at the tablet then back at him before she picked it up. Once he had her bag in hand, she followed him out of the kitchen. Loopy jumped up and padded behind them, all but knocking them aside in her haste to pass them on the stairs.

"Excuse her manners," he said.

At the end of the hallway, he opened the bedroom door. He'd rarely had a woman sleep in here with him, but he pictured her in his bed, hands secured over her head and attached to the iron headboard as she squirmed, silently wondering what he was going to do next.

With abundant energy, Loopy raced ahead of them up to the turret, which was fine with him. After placing Sofia's bag on the floor near the bed, Cade took his time following so that he could watch her hips sway. If she were his submissive, he would have instructed her to drop her clothes in his bedroom. Of course, if she did that, he may never give them back.

This woman, with her curves, appealed to him on all levels. He appreciated her business savvy, her occasional sass, her ability to make herself comfortable in his family home. Especially, though, he liked that he was the first to touch her with a paddle.

She curled up on the couch, tucking her legs beneath her while cradling the wine glass between her palms.

He took a seat across from her, legs stretched in front of him. Thunder rumbled again, and Loopy wedged herself between the steamer trunk and the couch. *Traitor.* Generally, she stayed near him, but since Sofia's arrival, the dog had been attached to Sofia. "Show me some of the pictures that you liked."

She put down her wine glass on the end table next to her.

He noticed she was a little flushed, but she did what he told her.

After touching a series of icons on the screen, she turned the tablet to face him.

"It'd be easier if you came over here."

With obvious reluctance, she stood. He offered a hand for balance so she could safely step over the dog. Loopy cracked open an eye—or at least he thought she did—but she made no attempt to move out of the way.

Sofia perched on the arm of his chair before enlarging a picture of a woman bound with rope and attached to a bed, spreadeagle.

"Easy enough to do," he told her.

"It's pretty elaborate, don't you think?"

He looked up at her.

"I mean, you could have the same effect with cuffs, couldn't you?"

"And a lot faster," he agreed. "But bondage is as much art as it is restraint. Exposure. For some people, it can be cathartic."

"For the sub, you mean?"

"For the Dom as well. It takes concentration. If I were doing it to you, I'd take my time to ensure it didn't cut off your circulation. I'd want it to be strong, sturdy and beautiful. It requires patience from both partners."

"Honestly, I'm not sure if I'd have the patience. I think I mostly like it because it's beautiful, as you say."

"I've been picturing you in a hog-tie."

"Really?" She met his gaze.

"Red rope, with your coloring," he replied. "Maybe purple, if you prefer it."

Her eyes were wide, fringed by impossibly lush lashes. The color he liked so well was darker than it had been earlier. "When you're ready," he said, "let me know. Show me more."

It took her a moment to refocus, as he'd hoped.

She scrolled through a few pictures and he told her to stop on one. "That's a hog-tie. See the arch of her back?"

"It's intimidating. I know it matters to you, but I'm not sure my body can do that. The models look as if they do yoga. Or something. Maybe they're double-jointed."

"And they have plenty of experience," he confirmed. "I have no expectation that I'll be able to fold you like a pretzel on your first attempt. You'd look every bit as beautiful, I can promise you that."

She frowned. "It looks complicated."

"More so once I tie your hair into it."

Even more color seeped into her face. "Are you serious?"

"Absolutely."

"I'm not saying yes."

"But?" he prompted.

"Maybe."

"Totally fair. There are other things we can do in the meantime."

She was so close he heard her breath catch. "Such as?"

"I have a few toys in the steamer trunk."

Her eyes widened.

He waited, watching her as she considered his unspoken invitation.

It took her at least ten seconds to put down her tablet. Then she worked around the dog before leaning over to open the wooden lid.

"In the plastic box."

She took it out, closed the trunk then put the box on top before taking off the lid.

He watched her consider the contents. Finally she pressed her tongue to her upper lip.

"Well, the handcuffs and blindfold are obvious. This..." She pointed to a slender silicone plug and broke eye contact.

"Butt plug," he said.

"That's what I was afraid you'd say."

"Anal virgin?"

She shifted in a way that told him she'd squeezed her buttocks. "Is nothing sacred?"

"Do you really want it to be?"

She glanced over at him. "No," she whispered.

"Then answer the question."

"Yes. I'm an anal virgin."

"Not even a finger?"

"Cade..."

"Sofia."

She inhaled. "Not even a finger," she confirmed.

"We'll take care of that soon enough. If you were my sub, you'd have a plug up your ass most days. I'd want you thinking of me all the time, when you sat, when you walked. And I'd want you wondering when I was going to take it out, and if I were going to fuck you there because your ass would already be stretched open."

She didn't blink. And he knew she was thinking of it, just as he was.

"Being my submissive would mean you were always available to me, and I would make damn sure you wanted it as much as I did."

"I've never had a man seduce me in quite this way before," she said wryly.

"You have no idea how much that appeals to me." Until her, he'd never played with a novice. His women had already been in the scene when he'd met them. He'd had no clue how enticing it could be to introduce someone to all the aspects he enjoyed, or how fucking turned on he would be to watch it unfurl for her. He didn't expect that she'd like everything he suggested, but her willingness to offer her trust gave him a rush he'd never experienced. "The other thing is a Wartenberg wheel."

"It looks devilish."

He nodded. "As well as delicious. And potentially devastating. It's all about the pressure, from a light tease to actually piercing the skin. Sensation play at its finest."

"You're scaring me again."

"Give me your hand."

The storm still raging outside, rattling the windows in their casings, she reached across and offered her hand. He cradled it to hold her steady. Before he could touch the metal to her skin, she flinched.

He tipped his head to one side. "Really?"

"In my defense, I never said I wasn't a coward."

"Hold still." He gently traced it across her palm.

"That was like a feather."

"Now a little more." He did it again. Then again, then again, criss-crossing, using more force to leave behind a little trail of dots.

"I could imagine that I might like that."

"On your nipples, I'll bet. Show me."

"What do you mean?"

"Take off your shirt and bra and tease yourself with it."

She opened her mouth but closed it without a sound emerging.

"I'll help." He unbuttoned her blouse and took the pinwheel from her.

She pulled off the blouse. "I can't believe I'm doing this."

Her bra was white, more lace than substance. "Pretty and feminine," he said. And a nice contrast with her suitable black work pants and cowboy boots — something he would remember as he masturbated.

He exercised control while she took it off. "Trade you," he said, offering the wheel in exchange for her lingerie.

The more he thought of it, the more he was tempted to keep her naked all the time. He'd never tire of looking at her body.

Her nipples were already starting to harden as she brushed the metal spikes across the first.

She sucked in a breath.

"Nice." The metal-on-skin image made him hard. Her nipple became taut as she moved over it. "Go harder."

"That's mean."

"Harder."

She blinked at him but complied without further argument.

Her body twitched beneath the pressure.

"Now, my turn."

"I'm not sure I'm that brave."

"Yellow or hand it over. I don't like arguments."

"Sometimes you're a real hard-ass."

"Sometimes?"

"All the time?" she guessed.

135

"Anything else is a waste of energy." He stood and held out his hand. After only the slightest of hesitations, she put the implement in it.

Cade angled his body so that it was easier for him to cup one of her breasts.

She murmured and closed her eyes.

"Watch," he told her. He made an X on the tip. The nipple got harder. "Now this." He circled the nipple then the areola with the biting spikes.

She put a hand around his wrist.

He moved on to her other breast and her knees weakened.

"I love it," she confessed.

"Is your pussy getting wet?"

"Yes." Her eyes closed.

He made Xs over each nipple with more and more pressure until she began to whimper.

"Cade...Cade!"

He eased off and she exhaled a shuddering breath. "Very nice," he praised.

"That was incredible," she said a few moments later, opening her eyes. "Better than I might have imagined."

"There's a smorgasbord of things for you to try," he said. "Some you'll love, some you'll like, others you'll endure just for me."

She cast a glance at the butt plug. "That, for example."

"You don't know that you won't like it."

"I can guess."

"We'll see." He put the pinwheel down and picked up her blouse.

With a small nod of thanks, she accepted. She shrugged into it, forgoing the bra. Then she returned to the couch. Loopy had never budged.

"I'm curious about something," she said.

After he sat, he took a drink of his wine. "Go on."

"When I was looking at those websites and earlier when we scened... I don't understand what you get out of it." She fell silent, as if she was trying to put her thoughts in order.

He waited.

"What we did in the barn," she went on. "I mean, I came, but you didn't. And you said that some people never have sex."

"What do I get out of playing with you, specifically? Your pleasure is my pleasure. Watching your eyes widen or close, smelling your arousal, hearing your gasp, is heady stuff. The act of dominating a submissive—you—is its own reward."

She picked up her wine glass.

"In BDSM, we talk about a power exchange. You give me control, but as the sub—my sub—you have the ultimate decision about what happens. The scene only lasts as long as you say. Your words, yellow and red, trump everything."

He crossed his ankles and waited.

"I honestly had no idea it was this complex."

"It is. Conversely, it's elegant in its simplicity."

"I hadn't realized it had such emotional implications. That makes it sexier, I think."

Watching her, feeling her internal muscles convulse around his fingers, had given him an erection. His cock had been hard for two hours, throbbing and insistent.

"So what we've done so far, is that enough for you?"

He smiled. "Obviously I'd like to have sex with you. Fuck you hard. Watch you ride me, suck my cock."

Eyes wide, she regarded him over the rim of the glass.

"But, yes. I will play with you, whether you want to have sex or not."

"And if we do?"

"We'll use condoms."

"That wasn't my question."

He waited.

"It will be kinky?"

He couldn't help but smile. "Do you want it to be?"

"Yeah."

When she looked at him like that—wide-eyed and guileless—and when she spoke to him with a husky

137

vibration in her throat, he had to fight for control. "My bedroom," he told her. "Now."

In spite of the storm, Loopy remained where she was even when Sofia stood and headed toward the stairs.

"Wait."

She stopped and looked back at him, her eyebrows drawn together in question.

"Indulge me if you will. Take off your clothes."

She turned back toward him. "All of them?"

"All of them." If he had his way, there would be a time in the near future when she wouldn't question him. Instead, she'd be so comfortable with him, with herself, that she'd simply do as he bid. Drop her garments, and maybe add a respectful, "Yes, Sir."

Her hands shook as she undressed and he found that sexy. This time he didn't help her, instead, he watched.

She sat on the wooden trunk to take off her boots. Then she removed everything else and put it all on the couch.

"Better," he said. "Much, much better." Slowly he stood. Then, unable to resist, he traced his forefinger down the column of her throat. For a few moments, he was mesmerized, and obviously, so was she. After shaking his head to clear it, he waved toward the stairs. "After you."

He heard her shaky breaths, but she didn't argue.

He followed, appreciating the sight of her naked body as her hips moved, her breasts swayed and her hair brushed her shoulders. The reality was even more erotic than his imagination had been.

In his bedroom, he said, "There are condoms in the cabinet beneath the right-hand sink."

She paused long enough to take a breath, but she didn't question him.

He fetched a couple of lengths of silk rope from a dresser drawer and placed them on the nightstand before removing the quilt and draping it over a chair. She returned a moment later, the small packet in hand. "Put it there," he instructed.

The moment she saw the rope, she swung her gaze to him.

He didn't speak, and neither did she. Instead, she put the condom where he'd suggested. "Now undress me," he said.

She glanced at the floor then back at him. Her footsteps were silent as she closed the distance between them.

Her hands were steadier than he expected as she unsnapped the pearl buttons. He rolled his shoulders to dislodge his shirt and she hung it from the bedpost. Then she watched as he tugged off the white T-shirt and dropped it on the floor.

She trailed her fingers across his bare chest.

"Am I allowed to tell you how sexy I think you are?"

"As much as you want." He brushed hair back from her face and tucked it behind her ears.

"Now my boots." He sat on the side of the bed, leaving her no choice but to crouch to remove the first one. "I might hire you to do this full-time," he said.

"I think you're depraved."

"Merely allowing you to experience the full joy of submission."

"Mmm-hmm."

He fisted his hand in her hair and pulled back her head. Her lips parted slightly as she looked at him. The flecks in her eyes were more pronounced than they had been earlier. Her sensual movements soothed the beast in him. "Continue," he told her.

She took off each boot. Then instead of rising, she scooted back, still on her knees. He wasn't sure whether she'd done it on purpose, but it was so perfectly submissive that he felt a flare of masculine possession.

He stood.

With deft motions, she unfastened his sterling-silver belt buckle. "I hadn't noticed earlier." She traced the horses on the metal. "It's the ranch logo."

"Observant."

"This close, it's hard to miss." Her voice held a hint of sass.

"I don't mind having your mouth that near to my cock,

ever," he said.

She pulled the belt from its loops then placed it on the nightstand.

Then, taking her time, she unfastened the metal button at the top of his jeans before lowering the zipper.

She eased the denim from him, then the boxer briefs.

"Damn," she said.

His cock was erect, throbbing.

"It's... You're well-endowed."

He gripped her shoulders. "Your nakedness has an effect on me, my sweet Sofia."

"I think I'm scared again," she said.

"I'm sure you'll manage." He grinned.

She wrinkled her nose, as if she wasn't sure she believed him.

"Up," he said, putting his hands on her shoulders.

Instead of responding, she resisted a little.

He scowled.

"May I?" Without waiting for an answer, she swirled her tongue around his cockhead.

He dug his fingers into her skin. "Sofia, I don't think you have a fucking clue what you're doing to me."

Never acknowledging that he'd spoken, she took more of him into her mouth, sliding up and down, back and forth. "Woman..."

She wrapped a hand around his shaft. She squeezed as she stroked. Outside, lightning slashed the sky.

His balls drew up and tightened. Cum, hot and heavy, threatened. "Enough." The word was more growl than actual speech. "I mean it." He captured her wrist. "Immediately."

The confounded vixen continued for another few seconds before pulling back, yet her heat remained. "You're flirting with danger," he warned her. "Be sure it's worth it."

"It is."

"Is it?" He raised an eyebrow at her as he helped her to stand.

"I've never done that for a man before. Haven't wanted to."

If she had been touching him, he would have ejaculated. *Damn.* "I set the pace," he told her, his words tight with tension.

"Do you?"

"That's it." He sat and pulled her over his lap. She clenched her muscles. Instead of spanking her, he stroked between her thighs, urging her legs apart. He touched her clit and her pussy, teased her.

"Oh, oh…" She squirmed, trying to get him to give her more.

He didn't respond and kept his ministration light, intentionally maddening.

"Cade!"

"Do you want to come?"

She arrowed her feet toward the floor then pushed off, offering her pussy to him.

"I can't hear you, Sofia."

"Yes. Yes, yes, yes."

"No."

She cried out an unfulfilled sob.

He refused to allow the plaintive wail to dissuade him. "My pace," he repeated. "Acknowledge what I said."

"Your pace," she repeated, but not happily, if her clenched jaw was anything to judge by.

"Good." The musk of her arousal intoxicated him. He fought against his own base instincts. Right now, he wanted nothing more than to throw her on the bed and fuck her senseless in a ritualistic mating. This woman…

He helped her to stand, and he looked at her.

Her cheeks were red, her hair a riotous mess and her eyes flashed with gold. The storm raging outside couldn't compare with the one inside him. "I want you on the bed."

She nodded.

"In the middle, on your back."

Even though she did as he asked, she did it slowly,

exaggerating her motions. "Arms above your head, spread out. And splay your legs, too."

He secured her wrists and checked to be sure they weren't too tight. "Comfortable?"

She tested the bonds. Her eyes widened a bit when she realized she couldn't extract herself. "Yes."

Before tying her ankles to the footboard, he asked, "You know you can stop this at any time?"

"I don't want to." She shook her head.

"If you change your mind…"

"Thank you. But please…" She flicked a glance at his rigid cock. "Put it in me."

"Fuck you?" he clarified.

Boldly she met his gaze. "Fuck me."

Motions deft and sure, he attached her ankles to the bed. "Are your muscles okay?"

"It's a little uncomfortable. Not bad, though."

"You wanted to suck my cock, sweet Sofia?"

"Yes."

"Then do." He moved over her then reversed positions so that his cock was near her mouth and his face was all but buried in her pussy. He parted her labia and licked.

She jerked, thrusting her hips up as far as the bonds would allow, and he moved so that his cock entered her mouth. "That's my girl," he approved.

He was careful to keep most of his weight off her while he exerted enough pressure to fuck her mouth.

She whimpered and moaned, and she was even louder when he flicked his tongue rapidly over her clit. He pulled back for a moment then plunged his tongue into her tight cunt.

Since it wouldn't take long for him to explode, Cade forced himself to focus on Sofia, pleasing her even as he demanded the honesty of her physical responses.

He felt her body strain as she pulled on the ropes, but he refused to give any quarter. After a full minute of tonguing her, he changed his position a little so he could thrust his fingers into her.

As she sucked him, keeping pressure on his cockhead, he found her G-spot and pressed against it.

She bucked and moaned, thrashing her head as much as she was able. He ate her pussy until her mouth stilled on his dick and she gave a muffled scream.

He continued to torment her, giving her aftershocks that made her twitch.

Finally, eventually, he withdrew his cock from her mouth and removed his fingers from inside her.

He climbed off the bed to stand next to it and look down at her.

She shuddered, helpless in her bondage.

His cock was erect, throbbing.

"Cade, I want you," she said.

He pressed a finger to her mouth. "On my terms," he reminded her.

Other than a soft exhalation, she didn't protest.

He went to his closet and returned with a number of plastic clothespins. Her eyes widened and she pulled at the bonds.

He bent to suck one of her nipples into his mouth. Once it was hard, he put a clip on it. She hissed a breath between clenched teeth.

"Looks beautiful."

"It hurts like a bugger," she protested, looking at him again.

Thunder rumbled outside, matching his mood.

He walked around to the other side of the bed and repeated the process, clamping her other nipple. She wiggled her feet. And she stared in wide-eyed fascination as he moved to the foot of the bed.

"Ah..."

"It'll be more uncomfortable than painful," he promised as he affixed clothespins to her smallest toes.

She flexed, as if trying to dislodge them. "They're annoying," she said.

"I meant for them to be. They'll distract from the ache in your nipples, and they will intensify your orgasm."

"Any more intense and I'll come out of my skin," she insisted.

"I can only hope."

"You do have a sadistic streak."

He twisted the pins. She cried out and he grinned. "It's more than a streak, I promise you. How do your nipples feel?"

"I'm noticing the clothespins more and more."

"I might just stand here and look at you, wait until the color darkens. Watch you squirm. Wonder when you'll cry out and beg me to take them off."

As he'd intended, she shifted. "Do you have any idea what you look like there, secured in my bonds, to my bed, with a wet pussy, wondering when I'll fuck you?" He showed her that he still held two clothespins. "Suggestions as to where I should put these?" He swept his gaze over her body.

"Cade…"

"How about on your pussy lips?"

She attempted to roll to one side, but the silk rope made it impossible for her to move much more than an inch either direction.

In turn, he plumped each of her labia before affixing a clamp.

She whimpered.

"How's that?" he asked.

"Wicked," she insisted.

He climbed onto the mattress and gripped each pussy clamp then pulled them wide to expose her cunt. "Beautiful," he told her.

Her breaths came in ragged, desperate little bursts, the heady stuff of his fantasies. He knew it had to be uncomfortable, not entirely painful, but annoying. "Should I lick you again?"

"You should fuck me," she replied.

For a woman who wasn't very experienced, she was

figuring this out fast. "Tell me you want to move at my pace."

She lifted her head for a second before dropping it back down on the pillow with a tiny moan. "I want to move at your pace," she repeated.

"Now relax."

"When my whole body feels as if it's on fire?"

"Especially then." He released his grip on the plastic pins. Since they still kept her lips parted, he stroked her, dipping inside her vagina to moisten his finger then drawing it up over her clit.

Her scent filled the air, making it more difficult for him to contain his own energy.

He brought her to orgasm then pushed her over the edge with his tongue.

She screamed his name. "Now! *Please?*"

Those words.

He plucked the pins from her labia then dropped them on the mattress before leaving her to roll a condom down his cock. He didn't even have to stroke himself to be sure he was hard enough.

She closed her eyes and worried her lower lip when he moved between her legs.

To get her attention, he twisted the makeshift clamps on her nipples.

She screamed. "That's going to make me come again."

"You're more wonderful than I could have hoped," he told her as he placed his cockhead at the entrance to her pussy.

"I'm still not sure about this," she said, her voice skeptical.

"You're wet, and we'll go slowly."

He kept his weight off her and used the smallest motions, going only a tiny bit deeper with each stroke as he sought to coax a response and make her forget her apprehension.

"This is…"

"You okay?" he asked, staring down at her. Her eyes were wide, and the flecks seemed to flare as lightning continued in the distance.

"It's amazing. Yes."

When he was balls deep, she sighed.

"*Yes*," she whispered. She did her best to raise her hips, but the force of his forward thrust pinned her down again.

"I want to be able to put my arms around you," she protested.

"Another time," he promised. Beneath him, he felt each of her muscles strain. And he loved the fact she couldn't do anything other than submit.

He found a rhythm he could maintain for more than a few strokes. Gingerly, he shifted so that he could reach between them to press against her swollen clit.

She began to convulse.

Then he moved so that he could play with the pins.

"I... This..." Whatever else she was going to say was drowned in her scream, and her internal muscles squeezed him.

Sofia said his name over and over, making it into a chant.

The sound pitched him over the edge. He drove into her and allowed himself to spurt, coming in a hot rush.

Then, drained, he forced himself to get off her. It'd been so fucking long since he'd had sex that hot, it left him momentarily depleted.

He shook his head to get some oxygen back into it so he could check on the beautiful little submissive whose curious innocence had given him so much. "You okay?"

"I'll let you know tomorrow." But she smiled.

He removed the clamps, taking time to suck each nipple until she stopped wincing and the circulation returned. After removing the ones he'd placed on her toes, he told her, "Move your feet around."

"Thank you. You were right. They did add something to it, but now they're irritating as hell."

"I'll get you out of the rope, too." It didn't take long to free her from the restraints, and he made gentle circles on her skin to ease the chafing. "Move slow," he cautioned.

Cade went into the bathroom to dispose of the condom then immediately returned to her. He sat on the mattress then rested his back against the headboard before pulling her against him.

She snuggled right in, as if they'd done it a dozen times. He smoothed her hair from her face and he appreciated the way its length trailed across his chest. "Talk to me," he encouraged when he heard her breathing take on a normal, relaxed rhythm. "Too much? Do you hurt anywhere?"

"I'm okay," she said. "Really." She maneuvered so that she could look at him.

"Nothing's overly sore?"

"My legs are a bit tired, but they'll feel better once I move around."

"Your pussy?" he asked, putting a hand above her pubic bone.

"Never fear. I survived the attack of the gargantuan cock."

He tugged back on her hair, forcing her to look at him. A playful smile danced in her eyes and on her mouth. Definitely not the look of a woman with negative after-effects from a scene.

"I may never walk straight again. Does that feed your ego?"

"Oh, my sweet Sofia, you will regret your comment."

"Will I?"

He shook his head. They needed to have a conversation about bratting, one he reinforced with leather. But for now, he wanted her right here.

"I liked the whole thing," she assured him.

"No questions? No concerns?"

"Like earlier, it may take some time to work through it."

He held her as the storm continued to batter the house. She stayed curled against him, offering her total trust. It wouldn't take much to convince him to stay here the entire evening, learning about her, exploring her, tormenting her, but his phone rang. "Duty calls." He eased himself from the bed and leveled a look at her. "But don't think for a moment that I'm done with you."

Cade's eyes matched the stormy outdoors, and a shudder went through Sofia. Not from fear, but from anticipation.

Even though his phone had gone silent for a few seconds only to begin its insistent demands again a moment later, he took the time to stroke his finger over her cheekbone. His touch was gentle, yet she knew how forceful it could be.

After placing a kiss on the top of her head, he climbed from the bed.

She turned onto her side and propped her head on her hand, watching him dress, her thoughts filled with lust. It seemed impossible that this man had dominated her just mere minutes ago.

"You're not making it easy to leave," he warned.

"Good."

He gave her exposed buttock a hard spank that made her wince.

Cade was still fastening his shirt as he left the bedroom.

Loopy must have heard his footsteps since she scampered down the stairs and skidded into the bedroom. She stopped long enough to ensure Cade wasn't in the room before she raced down the hallway, yipping as she went. Sofia laughed. She hadn't been around a lot of dogs, but she'd never known one with this kind of personality.

Alone, she sat. Since it was uncomfortable without him, she plumped a pillow and placed it behind her. She collapsed against it before drawing the sheet to her chest. Every part of her body seemed alive, from the slight pressure in her toes where the clothespins had been affixed, to the throb in her breasts, to the tenderness of her pussy.

Even though she'd talked to Lara, read numerous articles, looked at a lot of pictures and videos, none of it had given her a sense of what it would really be like for her.

It was, more than anything, personal.

How could she ever explain her internal reaction when a man instructed her to strip before walking down the stairs? She'd been so very much aware of his gaze on her, heating her body. Because they'd played in the loft, she wasn't as self-conscious as she might have been, but it had still been a bit unnerving.

Then...

The sight of his naked chest had thrilled her. She hadn't been with a man who was so finely muscled. She doubted he went to a gym, but he was so broad, muscular, with defined abs.

Exhaling, she tipped back her head.

She'd been unprepared when she had removed his jeans. She'd told herself that his tight boxer briefs had made him look bigger than he was, but when he'd taken them off, she'd been shocked to realize just how significant his cock was.

Still, kneeling there, in front of him, something had come over her. Maybe she had been inspired by the pictures they'd looked at together or their conversation about him being a Dom, but taking him into her mouth had seemed to be her next obvious move, even though it was the first time in her life that she'd initiated a blow job.

By the time he'd finally taken her, she'd been out of her mind. Being spread wide and bound had made her feel both sexy and vulnerable, making her very much aware of her role.

Sex with him had been nothing like she had imagined. Because of the way he'd engaged her brain—something she had no doubt he'd done on purpose—everything else had been magnified.

And when they were done, he'd held her, stroked her,

talked to her. It was as if their lovemaking hadn't ended after he'd climaxed.

Sofia expelled a breath. What they'd shared so far hadn't been close to enough.

Not more than a minute later, she heard his footsteps and the scrabble of dog nails on the hardwood.

"Heading out for a bit. Need to give the guys a hand with some fence," he told her. "Make damn sure you're here when I get back."

"Cade—"

"It's dangerous out there, and I don't want to think about you getting stranded."

"I was going to wait for it to ease off."

"Would you like me to tie you to the fucking bed?"

"Ah, isn't there a rule about not leaving a sub unattended when she's in bondage?"

He folded his arms across his chest. He was the picture of implacability, and his words were no softer. "Not if it's for her own good."

Arguing would net her nothing, she realized. And worse, she was delaying him. "I'll be here."

"I meant it when I said I wasn't done with you."

She shuddered.

Quicker than she would have believed possible, he moved. He grabbed her hands and momentarily pinned them to the wall above her head. The sheet tumbled, leaving her naked and exposed. Her breaths came in ragged gulps.

He devoured her with a kiss, pinching one of her nipples and pulling on it. No way could she resist this man.

He left her then, trembling with need.

Loopy raced after him. In the distance, she heard a door slam.

She had no idea how long he'd be gone, and she knew she couldn't spend the evening in his bed waiting for him.

Loopy returned and Sofia considered what to do.

Using his shower seemed really personal, and yet, how much more personal could they get?

She went into his bathroom and took a shower.

When she returned to the bedroom, wrapped in an oversized towel, Loopy was there, head resting on her outstretched paws. "You lost, too?"

Thunder rumbled again and the dog scooted across the floor to wedge her head under the bed.

Sofia petted the dog before getting dressed.

She went downstairs, sent a couple of emails from her phone, called her mother to let her know she was spending the night as a guest of the Running Wind. Her mother was concerned about her being so far away but said she was glad that the house had so many bedrooms. She hadn't burdened her mother with the information that she might be sharing Cade's.

After promising that she'd stop in to see the twins before going to Houston, she ended the call.

Restless, not only because she was alone but also because of the storm, the uncertainty of when she'd leave and the submissive experiences she was still thinking about, she wandered around. The house was enormous and she realized her first impression had been accurate. It wasn't really lived in. Because so little had changed over the years, it was more like a museum than a warm, welcoming home. She wondered how he did it, staying out here, all alone, with all it entailed. It was a lot for anyone.

Even though she'd just slept with him, she really knew nothing about him. Cade Donovan was as much of a mystery to her as he'd always been.

When she walked into the kitchen, Loopy followed her. The dog plonked herself down behind the bar stools, keeping an eye on Sofia.

Sofia looked again and realized she really had no idea whether or not the dog actually had her eyes open.

She resorted to her usual method of coping, this time, by baking cookies. Fortunately, she found chocolate chips. Even though it was oversized, she decided to use the entire bag.

Not wanting to go all the way upstairs to reclaim her unfinished wine, she grabbed another glass and filled it with the merlot. After a long sip, she gathered the ingredients and began to make the dough.

Over time, the storm eased. Thunderclaps were spaced farther apart. Flashes of lightning didn't appear as bright. Rain still fell, but it let up to a drizzle for a while before returning again in force.

Even after she'd baked three batches, he still wasn't back, and night was drawing closer.

Other than the vintage books in the parlor, there was nothing to read, no magazines, no paperbacks.

She ate a couple of cookies, put the rest on a plate and covered them with plastic wrap then decided to go to the turret to read a book on her tablet.

Once up there, she couldn't help but look for Cade. She saw nothing. Again, she wondered how he managed the sense of isolation.

She read for a while, looked at a few BDSM sites and played a game of solitaire before restlessly returning to the window. In the distance she saw the ATV's lights.

Her heart did a slow, thudding beat.

She told herself that there would be no way he could see her from the distance. There was no reason for him to look that direction, and the occasional rain would obscure the view.

There were a dozen reasons she couldn't, shouldn't take off her clothes and expose herself in the window. Among them was the fact that she didn't do things like that. Sofia McBride, staid, boring business owner, didn't set out to seduce men.

As he approached, she amended her thought.

Hadn't.

Until now, she *hadn't* behaved that way.

With Cade, she was letting her emotions and instincts guide her more than she ever had. Not questioning what the hell had come over her since she'd driven onto the

Running Wind, she toed off her boots even as she pulled the overhead chain to turn on the light.

It might have been her imagination, but the ATV seemed to slow.

Succumbing to the feeling of urgency, she finished undressing then she moved to the window.

Gulping back trepidation and nerves, she spread her arms wide, as if she were fastened to restraints as he'd said earlier.

The ATV stopped.

Cade—*please God let it be Cade*—unzipped the side and exited the cart.

He tipped back his hat and looked up.

She told herself she couldn't see his eye color from here, but she fancied that she did—dark, steely, intent.

He gave her a thumbs up then returned to the cart.

Now that she'd done that, she wasn't sure of her next step.

Stay there until he returned? Get dressed? Pretend it hadn't happened?

The back door slammed. With a few yips that seemed too high-pitched for a dog that size, Loopy took off with a shuddering skitter.

She glanced at her pile of clothes and frowned with indecision. Since she rarely went naked, she felt odd. Even at home, after a shower or bath, she pulled on a robe, and she kept it on until she dressed.

From what he'd said, though, he'd probably prefer she always be nude.

She heard sounds from downstairs, the rumble of his baritone as he spoke to the dog. Then there was silence, followed sometime later by the echo of his footsteps on the stairs then in the hallway.

As he drew closer, she settled for merely donning her shirt and leaving it unbuttoned.

His stride on the metal stairs sounded purposeful, and nerves almost compelled her to cover herself or sit. Instead, she chose to remain standing.

When he entered the turret, boots and jeans still damp, she was glad she had. He had eyes only for her and his intent was purposeful

Cade sank his fingers into her shoulders and drew her up onto her toes. "You are so fucking sexy," he told her before capturing her mouth in a kiss that left her ragged.

It was as demanding as it was powerful, his tongue hot and plundering. He tasted of dominance and untamed desperation.

Everything this man did with her—to her—was over the top, from his desire to have her naked to the way he so physically handled her.

He moved one of his hands to her hair and held her fast so he could deepen the kiss. Her back was slightly bent. The combination of being helpless and protected seeped into every part of her body.

She now had a sense of why no other relationship had worked out for her.

Even though she loved family and being around people, no one had insisted on this kind of response from her.

But this man—Cade Donovan—was anything but ordinary.

With a ribbon of panic, she realized she could never go back to a regular relationship after this.

He broke the kiss long enough to ask, "How's your pussy?"

She felt heated again, even though she knew she shouldn't be shocked. "It's a bit tender."

"Too bad."

She smiled.

"I was going to come back and spend some time talking with you, find you something to sleep in, give you some time to recoup, but I'm telling you straight up, that isn't going to happen."

Her tummy did a somersault.

He released her and said, "Grab the plastic box."

While she'd been waiting for him, she'd put it back in the

steamer trunk, mostly because looking at the butt plug had made her nervous. The handcuffs and blindfold interested her. The plug was intimidating.

Knowing he wouldn't tolerate her procrastinating, Sofia lifted the lid and pulled out the box.

"We'll give your pussy a bit of a break."

This time, her stomach felt as if it were in a freefall.

He moved away to hook his foot around the leg of a chair and dragged it toward one of the windows. "Sit here."

With a nervous frown, she did so.

"Put on the blindfold."

Her hands were shaking so badly that she dropped the piece of lightweight black fabric. "This feels a bit like asking a condemned man to put on his own noose."

"Get on with it."

She did as he'd said.

"Take off the shirt."

Suddenly things felt edgier to her. She'd had no idea that a simple blindfold could change her experience so much.

Wondering if he was looking at her, she shrugged out of the shirt.

"Spread your legs wide."

With a little trepidation, she did.

"Now part your labia so that you're showing me everything."

She hesitated.

"No secrets from me, Sofia." His tone allowed no argument and it made her pulse a bit sluggish.

"This feels obscene." But she took hold of the tender flesh as he'd instructed.

"It's sexy," he countered. "I told you in the loft that I'm a voyeur. I like to look at what's mine."

His words ricocheted through her.

She forgot how to breathe.

She knew she wasn't his, not really. But for the moment, this moment, she yearned for the fantasy.

"I'm going down to the bedroom. I'll be back in less than

two minutes. I want you to stay exactly where you are."

When she didn't respond, he asked, "Do you understand my instruction?"

Did he have any idea what he was asking from her? This was one of the most difficult things she'd ever done. The position was uncomfortable mentally as well as physically.

The man knew exactly what he was doing. "Yes," she whispered.

Wearing a blindfold, with him gone, all of her other senses seemed keener. She heard the occasional raindrop on the window, the rustle of a light wind through the bushes, even the hum of the air conditioner.

She was tempted to lift the blindfold and to move her hands. She considered doing both, rationalizing that he'd never know. It was only his command that made her do his bidding. But the truth was, she wanted the experience, all of it, every nuance, no matter how far away it was from her comfort zone.

Sofia tried to picture what he was doing, but the sounds were muted by the distance.

When he returned, though, every step seemed magnified. And her pulse throbbed harder as he drew closer.

"Perfect."

She exhaled.

"Are you wet?"

"No." She shook her head. "I'm too nervous."

"Then maybe you should play with yourself."

It wasn't a suggestion, she knew. She rested her head on the back of the chair as she considered.

"Now." He spanked her pussy and she screamed, clenching her legs together against the sharp and sudden pain.

She realized he hadn't done it all that hard, but the shock of not even being able to see it coming had startled her.

"Do you need another?"

"No!" But before she could react, she felt his damp finger slide between her folds.

Tension drained from her shoulders. When he pulled away, she continued what he'd been doing.

"Much better."

Again stunning her, she felt his mouth on her pussy. Being sightless disoriented her, adding a thrilling, terrifying dimension.

At some point, she stopped thinking, stopped the internal battle and instead surrendered.

"Slide your fingers in and out," he encouraged.

She held her labia apart and fucked herself with her fingers while he used his mouth to suck and to lick her clit.

Never had she experienced something so totally overwhelming.

She became lost inside her own mind, seeing nothing but laser beams of neon-colored lights.

"Tell me when you're close to coming."

Repeatedly he drove her to the edge only to yank her back.

"Oh. This."

"Almost?"

"Yes."

He moved away entirely, leaving her gasping for air. "Cade," she protested, reaching for him.

"A little orgasm denial will keep you on edge."

"I already am. Have been the whole time you were gone."

"That's nice to hear."

Despite his words, she knew he wouldn't change his mind.

She schooled herself, drawing in half a dozen really deep breaths. "Anything you say."

"Oh, sweet Sofia. You have no idea how much I wanted to hear that."

She hoped that meant he'd give her an orgasm, but she heard a rustle indicating he'd moved away. She closed her legs.

"I didn't give you permission to do that."

Behaving submissively was more challenging than she

would have ever believed. It was about much more than following his dictates, it was also about tamping down her own instincts, even those for preserving her modesty and vulnerability.

Without further prompting, she spread her legs again.

"Keep touching yourself. But no orgasm."

Her clit was so sensitive that the lightest of touches made her squirm.

"I could get used to this."

She wondered what he was doing, why he'd gone down to the bedroom, how much more of this she had to endure.

Too quickly, she found out.

He clamped his hand around her wrists. "Now stand." Cade pulled her up. "Shuffle step to the right."

After she'd done so, he guided her to turn.

"I'm going to bend you over the side of the couch."

His touch was firm, helping her maintain some confidence that she wouldn't topple over.

"Put your hands on the arm."

She felt around until she was able to grip the leather.

"The butt plug is going up your ass."

In mute protest, she stood.

"Back into position. Unless you'd like to be punished?" His voice, surprisingly, was more gentle than harsh.

He slid a hand between her thighs to touch her pussy. Since she was already so aroused, the lightest brush reignited her, making her want to please him.

He put a hand on the middle of her back to ease her down. "We'll go slow," he promised soothingly. "And you always have your safe word."

She nodded.

"I'm going to start with a finger."

She scrunched her nose.

But when he started, all thoughts of fighting vanished. She should have known she could trust him.

He inserted a finger in her cunt, teasing her, making her wet, bringing her to that razor point of anticipation.

159

Then she heard the squirt of a liquid. Lube, she guessed when she felt the cool, wet smoothness of gel when he fingered her anus.

"Every time you feel me, bear down."

"I'm not going to like it."

"Uh-huh," he replied unconcernedly. He pressed against her tightest hole again.

All the while, he continued to talk to her and play with her pussy with his free hand. She wasn't sure she'd ever been more turned on.

"Yeah. A little more." He eased a finger into her ass, a fraction of an inch. Then he pulled out.

While she was still relaxed, he penetrated her again, deeper.

"I'm in up to my knuckle."

She felt unbelievably full.

He moved his finger around.

"I'm feeling embarrassed," she said.

"Quit thinking. Focus on pleasing me."

"It might be easier if you didn't have your finger up my ass."

He smacked her left cheek with the hand he'd had on her pussy. "Your choice. A spanking? Or I can play with you so that you enjoy the anal more."

"Sorry," she said, unrepentant.

"Then we're agreed. A spanking it is."

"No!"

He brought down his hand hard on her flank as he drew out his finger and plunged it in again, twisting, prying apart that reluctant muscle.

Being spanked while being anally finger-fucked was the most overwhelming thing she'd ever experienced. She whimpered and cried and begged him not to stop.

Abruptly he did.

She collapsed on the arm of the couch, shuddering.

"You were about to come from anal," he said. "Tell me again how bad you hate it."

Sweat drenched her, along with the shock waves from his repeated denial. "You're a beast, Cade Donovan."

"I'm still getting started. Back into position."

"Can I have a moment?"

She heard a terrible scraping noise, and she realized he'd moved aside the steamer trunk. Since she was blindfolded, she had to guess what he was doing, and he'd either crouched next to her or he was bent over, since he spoke directly into her ear.

"You're so much more than I could have hoped. Tell me yellow and I'll remove the blindfold."

She shook her head. "I don't want you to stop or change it up. I just need to catch my breath."

"There's no shame in saying it."

How could she make him understand? If she looked around, at him, the moment wouldn't be as intense. "I don't want to go backward from here."

He trailed his fingers down her spine and the tension began to ease. Then he surprised her more by wiping her with a cool, damp cloth. He even lifted her hair to soothe her neck before blotting her forehead.

As he continued, she unclenched her feelings and allowed her body to elongate. "I'm not sure how much I like orgasm denial." It felt as if tiny needles were pricking her.

"When I let you come, it will be all the more powerful. And you'll do it with my cock buried in your cunt."

She shivered.

"Let me know when you're ready."

"I am." She spread her legs and adjusted her weight.

"That's my perfect little submissive."

His submissive. The words seemed to bounce around in her head and she gripped the seat cushion.

She could never be Cade's submissive. He'd said he played with women at clubs, that he'd never had a sub of his own, and she knew that was because he hadn't wanted one. Women would line up for the opportunity to be with a man like him.

But for now, he'd chosen her. For now, that was enough.

"You liked the spanking," he said.

"Yes."

"Can't wait to get you in the loft, attached to a beam." He slapped her hard, right on top of where he'd landed the previous blows.

She yelped.

Arousal clawed at her, blistering and insistent.

His strong hands were on her legs, forcing them apart so he could adjust her position, allowing him better access. He licked her pussy and gently bit her clit, making her cry out and forcing her body forward as she tried to escape.

He began to fuck her pussy with a finger, keeping her distracted while he placed the slick plug against her ass.

"You're already stretched."

"Not convinced."

He moved aside the plug and put his finger there. It amazed her how easily it went inside. "You're more ready than you want to admit." There was an annoying note of triumph in his voice. This man, this Dom, seemed to know more about her than she herself knew.

When he started to slide the plug in, she again tried to crawl up the side of the couch.

"It'll be less difficult if you stop struggling."

To her, there was nothing more natural than trying to escape.

"Thrust your hips back."

"I..."

He worked his arm between the leather and her body. With his strength, he essentially held her immobile. "After this, it'll be the medical table for you. It was made for squirming bottoms."

He spanked her hard until she almost felt limbless. All the fight remaining in her vanished.

"Bear down. Now."

Before she was totally ready, he pushed it in even as he jerked her pelvis back.

She screamed.

"You're there. Relax and let it settle in."

"Fuck, fuck, fuck, fuck. *Fuck.*"

"I'll get the bigger one next time."

The flexible silicone moved just a little as he tugged on it. But now that the thickest part was in, her sphincter closed around the small shaft and the momentary pain receded.

"I want you totally helpless."

She felt as if she already were.

"Hands behind your back, please."

The handcuffs.

Since she was bent over, it was difficult to comply, but he reached over to help her, holding her right hand at the small of her back while bringing her left to meet it.

He ratcheted the metal into place, and she felt him put a finger beneath each to make sure they weren't too tight.

As if she weighed nothing, he moved her, inching her forward so that her toes no longer touched the ground.

He left her long enough to undress, and she'd never felt more exposed than with her legs spread, a plug stuffed up her ass, unable to move or see.

She fully understood what was demanded of her. It wasn't just her physical compliance, it was mental as well. The struggle to stay still was real. She wanted to test the cuffs, adjust some of the weight from her shoulders, push herself back so that her feet were firmly on the floor. Transcendence, he'd called it. She wondered if it was something she'd ever fully achieve.

Striving toward it, she counted her breaths.

"Any part of your body overly stressed?"

"No."

"Say yellow immediately if it happens."

"Promise," she replied.

He parted her labia, pinching where he'd placed the clamps earlier. No matter how she tried, she couldn't escape.

Then he began the slow, torturous build-up again,

touching, teasing, moving the plug, making her forget everything including her name.

Within a minute, he had her back to pre-orgasm. The feeling was part bliss, part agony, and the tiny pinpricks returned.

Having cuffed hands hampered her movements more than she would have guessed possible. She was helpless but to wait on his pleasure.

"Your ass needs to be a little redder." He rubbed her buttocks and her thighs, then he rained down dozens of spanks, everywhere, on top of each other, six inches apart, left side, right side, making her burn, making her flesh jump.

She was breathless, and her eyes ached from the tears scorching them. "I want. Need."

"Me, too, sweet Sofia."

Finally, finally she felt his hard cock at her entrance.

She gasped at his first shallow thrust.

With the plug and his girth, the wind was knocked from her lungs. She wasn't sure she could do this. She tried to protest, but she couldn't even come up with the words.

"You can," he said, as if reading her mind.

Not without being torn apart.

She heard the squirt of a bottle, and she knew he'd applied the lube to his cock.

He put his hands on her hipbones and repositioned her, forcing her chest across the couch a little, abrading her tender nipples.

Cade—her Dominant—pushed deeper with each slow movement. Even though she'd thought it impossible, she began to accommodate him.

"So damn tight." He stroked the outsides of her thighs with his fingertips. And since parts of them were already sore from the spanks, the touch was enough to make her jerk.

When he sank his dick all the way inside, she lost the remaining air in her lungs. She imagined what she looked like with her buttocks pried apart, and that cock inside her while she was helplessly cuffed over the arm of the couch.

"I've got you."

As he fucked her, she gave herself over, trusting that he would make sure she was safe.

She allowed herself to drown in the sensation of being full, being taken by a Dominant, thoroughly gorgeous cowboy.

Cade Donovan was everything she would have imagined him to be, but so, so much more.

His sounds drove her crazy. The knowledge that she held any power over him made her delirious.

This time, the orgasm that built seemed to come from a different place inside her, as if her whole body were involved, not just her sex organs. "Ahh..."

"Try to wait."

She wasn't sure she could. And she wasn't sure how to communicate that.

"Just a few more seconds."

His fingers dug into her hipbones. She felt the movement of their bodies, her front pressed into the leather couch, the backs of her thighs against his muscular legs.

Surprising her, he dragged her back as he thrust inside her.

"Come for me, sweet Sofia."

She exhaled as the climax claimed her. Maybe because of the series of denials, it rocked her, making her dizzy. She sobbed out his name.

Moments later she felt him pulse inside her. He shifted one hand and plowed it into her hair as he continued to jerk his pelvis.

She had no sense of how long she stayed there or how long he held her. Time lost meaning as the earth seemed to hurtle through space.

It could have been minutes later when she realized he was speaking to her in soft tones.

"Sensational, Sofia."

She turned her head to the side.

He eased his cock from her then she felt him tugging on the plug.

"I can do that."

"I'm sure you can," he replied. "You're not done with the scene until I say you are."

Since she was still helpless, she had no choice but to let him, even though part of her wished the couch would open up and swallow her.

He used a damp towel to wipe her.

Eventually he removed the cuffs, taking time to massage her skin and urge her to move slowly.

She shrugged several times before stretching out her arms.

Then he took off the blindfold.

She opened her eyes to see him crouched next to her, wearing nothing other than a pleased smile.

He smoothed a finger over one of her eyebrows. "You were submissive perfection," he said.

The approval magnified the experience for her.

"The window thing? Do that anytime you want."

She grinned.

"Let me help you up." He lifted her, and she put her arms around him. "Hold on."

"What?"

He walked toward the stairs.

"You can't carry me the whole way," she protested.

"According to whom?"

She held on tighter as he negotiated the metal staircase. "You are at least half crazy."

"At least," he agreed easily.

He deposited her on the floor near the bed. "Join me in the shower?"

Even though she'd already taken one, it sounded refreshing.

He led the way and turned on the faucet to adjust the water. "Tell me if the temperature is okay."

She stuck her hand in. "It's fine." Then she entered the

stall.

When he joined her, the space suddenly seemed too small. Though it had appeared big enough for both of them, Cade wasn't an average-sized man. She couldn't move without bumping into him.

He took down the showerhead and wet her before putting it back and reaching for the bar of soap. "Shouldn't I be doing that for you?" she asked.

"You can. When I'm done."

"I think I'm confused about submission then. What about the acts of service?"

"I consider this aftercare. And there's no rule that says a Dom can't care for his sub."

That word again.

He put down the bar before he covered her in white lather. She closed her eyes.

When he circled her nipples, she winced.

"Tender?"

"Very."

"That's the way a sub always should be. Aware that her Dom has used her."

How did he do that? Unravel her with a single comment?

"Turn around."

He traced over the marks on her buttocks. She squirmed, trying to get away, but the shower unit wasn't big enough for that.

"Now spread your legs."

She sighed. "Will it do any good to argue?"

"Want to sleep with a butt plug in your ass?

She spread her legs.

"We need to talk about bratting," he said. "Later."

"I'm not sure I like the sound of that."

"Quite sure you won't," he agreed.

But she did like the way he cared for her, washing and rinsing her thoroughly.

"You've got a very sexy body, Sofia."

"I might start believing you."

When he was finished, she asked, "May I?"

This wasn't an act of service, she realized when he turned his back to her. It was pure, unadulterated pleasure. She loved touching his skin, feeling the hard planes of his body, his taut muscles.

She took her time, and when he faced her again, his cock was at least semi-hard. Sofia was satiated and sore, but she still ached for his possession.

"You can use a bit more pressure on my testicles," he said.

She frowned up at him. "I thought they were fragile."

"Even after what I did to you in the turret?"

She took his balls in hand and used a firmer grip.

"That's enough," he warned.

She stroked his shaft with the lather, pressing her thumb pad to the underneath as she moved up.

By the time she was finished, he was fully erect.

"You could be in danger during the night," he warned.

Which meant he expected her to sleep in his bed. She'd hated to assume, since he had said he had a number of bedrooms. "I'll take a chance."

He caught her hand. "One of many," he informed her.

She met his eyes, and in them she read something dark and determined.

Cade steepled his index fingers and stared out of the window of his study. Tonight, condensation from the rain and humidity ran down the panes of glass, distorting his view.

Three a.m. was a familiar time of day, one he both loved and despised.

The silence soothed. And because it was so dark, all the millions of things he needed to do could wait. Had to wait.

It was too late for alcohol. Too early for coffee.

Insomnia was a demon, one he danced with all too God damn often. Tonight he hadn't expected to. Sceneing with Sofia, being with her, should have soothed him and allowed him to sleep the peace of the worthy. She couldn't have been more willing or enthusiastic.

He'd anticipated she'd say yellow at some point. Hell, he'd even encouraged her to do so. But she'd gamely done everything he'd asked of her, and the stunt in the window? Beyond anything he might have imagined. At first he had thought he was looking at a shadow. It had taken several seconds to realize a beautiful woman was standing there, someone all but a virgin, unfamiliar with his lifestyle, filled with only the potent desire to please.

And please him she had.

Again and again.

Which left a jagged tear in his conscience.

He knew better than to play with a neophyte. He liked subs already in the lifestyle who had no expectations. Since he'd introduced her to his version of kink, he had a responsibility to ensure she was okay.

After their shower, he'd offered her a shirt from his closet. It had drowned her, reminding him of how small and vulnerable she was.

In a way that was out of character for him, he'd climbed into bed and pulled her against him, cradling her, stroking her hair until she yawned sleepily. She'd turned onto her side, and she'd fallen asleep with her hand on his bare thigh.

He'd liked it. Too damn much. It had felt as natural to him to protect her.

She was lightness to his dark. He didn't deserve someone like her. Hell, he'd heard her cooing and seen her smiling when she'd been on the phone. She needed laughter, family, her friends.

He dropped his legs from the windowsill and stood, pushing the guest chair back into position.

Despite the hour, he crossed to the sideboard and poured himself a jigger of Julien Bonds' whiskey. As he did, he admitted the truth. Sofia McBride wasn't the problem. He was.

Ever since he'd moved onto the Running Wind as a child, there'd been something fucked up inside him.

His dad hadn't visited often, but every time he had, he'd brought Cade into this office, sat him down and very seriously recited his obligations to the land, to the family line.

It hadn't been until he was older that he'd understood everything. Why his mother cried herself to sleep, why she stayed even though she hated living on the ranch in isolation, why she vanished when the Colonel visited.

The night he'd turned ten, after an awkward dinner in town with his parents, he'd come into the office on a night much like this, after a storm. His father had been sitting in near darkness, with only the desk lamp on.

Jeffrey Donovan had had a drink in front of him, had said he'd fucked up a lot of things in his life, taken his eye off what was important. He'd warned his son not to do the same.

Cade had been expecting the lecture about sex, not that he would have listened to his old man about it. Everyone knew Cade was a bastard, that his father had knocked up his mother and never married her.

But Jeffrey had never preached, at least not to him. Instead, he'd told him to grab life by the balls and squeeze every drop of excitement he could out of it.

Jeffrey's visits had gotten further apart after that. And Cade had never known why. Maybe because he was busy with three legitimate kids and a high-society wife?

The less time he'd had available, the more determined Cade had become to impress his father. He'd started competing on the rodeo circuit, and his poor mother had hooked up the horse trailer and driven hundreds of miles and stayed overnight more times than he could count in rundown motels.

He'd figured if his dad was proud of him, he'd come around more. To his credit, Jeffrey had done his best to attend Cade's events.

From broncs, he'd moved onto bulls and motorcycles then cars, spending the money his father threw at him for anything with a motor. That was something else he and Stormy fought over. Money, and the amount Cade received. She told Jeffrey that he couldn't make up for his absence with dollars and gifts. There were always fights, Cade remembered. Screaming. Passion. Slammed doors. Tires spinning on the truck as Jeffrey roared toward the exit and Stormy sobbed.

Over the years, Cade had taken bigger and bigger risks. He'd bought his first car before he'd even had a driver's license.

The first time he'd raced, he'd done it illegally—a drag race down a backcountry road not far from Waltham.

Later that winter, someone had ratted them out to the local police. Cade had been caught and hauled to jail. Since his father had been out of the state on business, the Colonel had collected him. He'd said nothing other than Cade needed to bring honor, not disgrace to the family name. As far as he knew, it had never shown up on his record.

His grandfather had left him in front of the gate, and his mother had been waiting on the porch after he'd done his version of the walk of shame.

The event hadn't stopped his racing, but it had encouraged him to channel it in a legal direction. To his mother's horror, he'd started hauling his own stock car to the local dirt track and fearlessly pitting himself against drivers twice his age.

He'd ended up with a broken leg when he was seventeen.

That had slowed him down long enough to pick up a new hobby, restoring old cars. It was something his father had enjoyed doing as well. To Cade, it seemed his old man had spent more time at the ranch once they'd started tinkering on them together.

"Is this a private party?"

Without taking a drink, he put down his glass and turned toward Sofia.

The shirt he'd given her was so long on her that it hung past mid-thigh. She'd rolled up the sleeves and had only fastened a couple of the buttons.

He'd rarely had women out here. None had spent the night, so having her walk in startled him, but not in an unpleasant way. "Sorry I disturbed you," Cade said.

"Mind if I join you?"

He did. He liked his solitude, hated to be bothered when he was ruminating. *Ruminating?* Even in his own head the word seemed ludicrous. He was being morose, nothing any nobler than that. But he didn't want to be an ass and say it out loud, especially since she'd been so accommodating.

Without an invitation, she came in and perched on the windowsill where he'd had his feet propped. "Did something wake you?"

"Nothing out of the ordinary."

"Do you do this frequently?"

Now he knew why he didn't invite women to stay. And maybe he shouldn't have let this one sleep in his room. As

172

soon as that thought formed, he dismissed it. Sofia wasn't a typical woman. She was a determined, resourceful one. There had been no question in his mind that he'd wanted her in his bed. "More than I'd like, yes."

"Ranch business?"

He picked up his glass and went to his chair. He put his bare feet on the desk and regarded her. "Sometimes."

"Tonight?"

"You're being—"

"Direct." She grinned. "The word is direct."

With the force of a combine, she cut through his defenses. Over the next few seconds, her smile faded. "I know it's not about me."

"What in the hell? No." He leaned forward to slam the glass on the wood.

"I watched you for a while before interrupting. And I went over everything. I know you want to talk about me being a brat—"

"Sofia, that's not—"

"I know that," she reaffirmed. "Everything between us was fine...the sex. The shower. But there was something in your eyes..." She met his gaze again. "I thought I was being fanciful, making it up. I'm not, though, am I? It's still there."

"I warned you to stay away."

"Yeah. You did. Brats aren't always well behaved, I'm guessing."

Despite himself, he gave her a half-smile.

"I'm still here."

"You should go back to bed." He picked up the whiskey then took a sip and waited for the liquid amber to warm its way down.

"Still here."

"Doesn't surprise me." He rolled the glass between his palms.

She eased herself from the windowsill and moved toward him.

"Sofia." The word was a growl, a warning, a plea. "Don't."

She sat on his desk, crowding his space, only inches away. "Whatever it is, the night makes it worse."

"Does it?"

"That's when my birth father would come home, sometimes in drunken rages."

Now he wanted to soothe. Men were made to protect those they loved, not make them live in fear.

"During the day I could go to school, pretend everything was wonderful. At night, there really was a monster, and he would come out."

He heard no self-pity in her tone, only the harsh reality no child should endure. Not just in the BDSM they'd shared, he admired her strength.

"It took us all years to learn how to sleep peacefully, without an eye on the door, jumping at every little sound."

"I'm sorry you went through that."

"We got closer because of it, the three of us. The day he abandoned... Well, Mom didn't really know at the time that he was gone, that he'd stay gone. It's her I admire. She moved us to Corpus Christi, and she eventually met John McBride." She had a small smile. "I learned some men were hard workers, that they gave a damn, that they could be trusted. He took in another man's children and helped provide for them. When I look back, that's what I remember. The good."

"It's not always that simple."

"No? Tell me about your dad."

This was a thin, dangerous place for her to tread. "You should go back to bed."

For a moment, he thought she was going to obey. She slipped off the desk and went toward the door. But instead of continuing through it, she stopped. She took a framed picture from the wall then turned to face him. "Is this your dad?"

He should spank her, distract her, make her put it back, anything, including making her go away. Should. But he didn't.

"Your eyes are like his. Yours and Connor's both."

The photograph was one of Jeffrey sitting behind this same desk. His grandfather, the Colonel, was in the guest chair. Cade guessed his father to be about nineteen, maybe twenty. The oldest son about to come into his inheritance and obligations, a symbolic transfer of power from one generation to the next. William was smiling for a change, his chest big and proud. The future looked bright for the Donovan dynasty. And it might have even been the same summer he'd met Cade's mother.

"Do you ever let anyone in?" she asked.

"No."

"Whatever it is, it's not made better by harboring it."

"There are things you can't understand."

"Are there?" She tipped her head to the side. "You may be a Donovan and all that entails. You may be larger than life to some. You may be a badass Dom. You may have cut yourself off from the world. But there's still a world out there. All of us have pain. All of us suffer in some way. And a whole hell of a lot of times, there are people we can gain strength from. A burden shared is a burden halved."

As if anything could undo the past, bring his father back. "Do you really believe those platitudes?"

"Yeah. A long talk and a piece of my mother's chocolate cake helps a lot of things."

Chocolate cake and conversation? "Are you trying to be insulting?"

"No." She winced. "That was never my intention. I only wanted to help."

Now he felt like an ass.

"I apologize for intruding." She put the picture back then took a moment to make sure it was perfectly straight. "No, actually, that's a lie. I don't apologize at all. Come back to bed."

"I'll be there soon."

She moved toward him in her bare feet and barely covered

body.

Since he knew she was going to be persistent and because he was experiencing an unwelcome twinge of remorse, he dropped his legs to the floor.

She pushed his chair back from the desk then straddled him. This woman might have been sexually inexperienced, but she was braver, bolder than any other woman he'd been with. His remoteness kept others at bay. But it seemed to beckon her.

With infinite gentleness that was stronger than anything he'd known, she placed one palm in the middle of his chest, over his heart.

It was just the two of them, in the nighttime silence, no words needed. This was a form of intimacy foreign to him. It made him nervous. It gave him peace.

In all of his relationships, he'd been in total control. Even as a kid, he'd rejected his mother's comfort. None of that seemed to matter to the persistent Sofia.

"Come to bed," she repeated.

Denim separated them, but his cock responded when she rocked forward to hug him.

And now he didn't know what in the hell to do.

In a sexy move consistent with a more experienced woman, she gyrated her hips, stroking herself over him. That got through to him. "Your pussy is going to be so sore you won't want sex for weeks."

She pulled back and looked at him. "Big words, Cade."

"That bratting conversation is coming," he vowed.

"Can it wait until after you put your dick in me?"

"I'm not made of granite, woman."

"No?" She moved herself over his dick. "Feels like it to me."

He shifted abruptly, keeping his hands on her waist so that she didn't fall, but he put her on her feet. "Go."

She waited for him.

On the way out of the door, he glanced at the picture of his father. All the guilt was still there, gnawing at his stomach, at his mind. But for now, its intensity had been turned down a notch.

She bent at the waist and flipped up the hem of the shirt, showing him that she wasn't wearing panties.

"Fuck me," he swore softly.

"That's the idea."

Before he could grab her, she scampered away toward the stairs.

He wasn't sure where Loopy had come from, but she was there, barking happily in a way he'd never heard before.

With a laugh, Sofia took the first few stairs two at a time. He shut off the desk lamp then followed her.

Halfway up, he found the shirt she'd been wearing. He scooped it up. Despite himself, he held it to his nose, inhaling the sweetness that was Sofia, strength wrapped in femininity. *Frustrating, beautiful woman.*

She was already in bed when he entered the room. She'd left a nightstand light burning, and it created just a small amount of ambiance.

Her hands were curled around the iron headboard and her legs were parted in silent invitation.

He dropped the shirt that she'd discarded then shucked his jeans. Loopy snatched them up and took them into the closet where she most often slept.

Cade grabbed a condom from the diminishing stack and tossed it toward her. It landed on her belly. "Put it on me."

After releasing the headboard, she picked up the square packet and crawled across the mattress.

"Did you spend all your time this evening reading about submission?"

She shook her head and her hair fell in an enticing disarray. "Pictures."

Her back dipped slightly, making her rear stick out.

He helped her off the bed. Without being told, she knelt in front of him. She ripped apart the packet and pulled out the condom. Her innocence was evident in the way she studied it, as if trying to ascertain how to put it on him.

177

The contradiction between this side of her and the woman who'd climbed into his lap was startling. He couldn't allow himself to forget just how little experience she had, especially with men like him.

She finally placed the latex on his cockhead and rolled it down.

He picked her up and tossed her on the bed. She squealed and Loopy came to see what was going on.

"It's okay," he told the animal. "Back to bed."

She cocked her head to the side.

"Bed," he repeated.

After standing there for a moment, she finally lost interest and wandered back to the closet.

"Where were we?" He climbed onto the mattress and forced Sofia's thighs apart. "Put your legs on my shoulders."

She did, and that tilted her pelvis.

"Now lift your ass a little."

Once she'd pressed down on his shoulders, the position left her hips suspended and opened her for him. He licked her pussy, more gently this time since he could see her flesh was swollen and red.

She moaned, turning her head to the side.

"Hold on to the headboard. Consider my order to be your bonds."

"Yes..."

Even though she had sassy, bratty moments, when things were important, she was amazingly obedient.

He dampened a finger then slid it inside, moving it, getting her wetter. Then he pulled it out and eased it inside her ass.

She tightened her muscles.

"Give yourself to me."

So, so sweetly, she did.

With his finger knuckle-deep in her rectum, he licked her to climax.

She tightened her thigh muscles on his shoulders, leveraging herself a little as her ass squeezed his finger.

Then he moved her so that he was between her legs, cockhead at her pussy entrance.

"You're such a great lover," she told him.

He grinned, not having expected a compliment from the pretty little sub. He plunged into her heat.

"Please let me wrap my arms around you."

One reason he liked dominant sex was that he could keep the woman somewhat distant from him. Sofia, though, he suddenly wanted close. "Yes."

She held on to him, hard, tight, and he pulled out to sink in again.

Without his bidding, she linked her feet behind his back, inviting him deeper. "Yeah."

Everything he offered, she accepted. And she demanded more.

"Cade!"

"Come," he whispered in her ear.

With a whimper, she did.

Her pleasure fed his. Even though he hadn't been sure that he could actually ejaculate again, he did, as if it were their first time.

When he was done, he had to fight not to collapse on her. He was finally, totally exhausted.

He left the bed long enough to clean up then returned to her.

Instead of putting the shirt back on, she'd remained nude. The idea of being skin-to-skin appealed. He climbed in and pulled her against him, wrapping his body completely around hers.

She reached for his hand and didn't stop her movements until their fingers were intertwined.

Not for the first time, he recognized how utterly determined she was, not just to be with him, but to ensure a connection.

She wriggled backward and tugged harder on his hand, as if making sure he wouldn't leave her again.

And he wasn't even tempted.

"Bacon?"

Sofia looked over from where she stood in front of the stove. "I figured you had a lot of work to do today and would appreciate a cooked meal. I hope that's okay?"

Jesus.

He'd awakened suddenly a few minutes ago, slightly disoriented. Part of him had known he wasn't supposed to be alone in the bed, but since he'd never had a woman sleep with him, it had taken a while for reality and dreams to merge.

Memories had bowled into him. Sofia's arrival yesterday, her foray into submission in the barn, the storm, the image of her in the turret window, the way he'd thoroughly dominated her, the late night discussion in his study, the tender sex in his bed and the trusting way she'd pressed herself to him in the early morning hours.

He'd wondered if she'd left, and he'd gone to the window to look. A stupid grin had plastered itself to his face when he'd seen that her SUV was still there, covered in leaves, oleander blossoms, twigs, water.

The scent of food had permeated the air in a way it hadn't since his mother had moved out. He'd been taken aback to realize how much he appreciated it.

He'd gone into his closet. His most loyal companion had abandoned him. *Traitor.*

Cade had dressed in his oldest jeans and a pair of old boots. With the amount of work he had ahead of him, it promised to be a hell of a long day. He'd barely taken time to drag on a long-sleeved shirt before heading down the stairs.

What a sight.

Her hair was pulled back into a ponytail and she was wearing tight blue jeans and a black T-shirt. Better still, she wore his Texas apron. She'd had to wrap the cloth strings around her twice. And he couldn't think of anything more appealing. Loopy sat near her feet, gazing up hopefully. She never even looked at him.

"I brewed coffee. I figured that's what you drink since the pot's the size of my apartment."

"I enjoy a cup in the morning."

"A cup?"

"Or a gallon."

He filled a mug while she transferred the bacon to a platter. She scooped scrambled eggs into a bowl. A few seconds later, the toaster sent bread flying into the air.

"Need to get that fixed."

"I'd say." She'd grabbed one but missed the other.

"Loopy's," he said, shaking his head. "Coffee for you?"

"I've had tea. Thanks."

He realized she'd set two places at the bar.

His phone signaled a message and he checked it. "The guys are working on the tree removal."

"Good. I already let my mother know I'll be there later today. I checked the highway conditions and all the roads that were closed have been reopened."

She placed the food on the bar then hopped up on a stool.

He joined her. "Thanks for this. It wasn't necessary."

"Honestly? I needed something to do."

"Everything okay?"

"The return to reality," she said.

He thought he knew what she meant. For her, it probably seemed they'd done extraordinary things.

For her?

Fuck.

For him.

He'd played with women for a lot of years, and none of them had evoked an emotional reaction from him. And he had been stunned by the surge of possessiveness that had hit him this morning.

♡♡♡

181

Even when he was working with the crew to cut the storm-ravaged live oak into manageable pieces, Cade's mind kept drifting back to the house, to her.

They hadn't signed a contract yet for the centennial celebration, but he was going to get it done. He wanted an excuse for her to return to the ranch.

"Boss?"

He shook his head, realizing his foreman was speaking to him.

"Want me to drive her SUV out?"

Cade nodded. That would give him a few more minutes with her.

Once the road was clear, he returned to the big house.

She was at the island, her tablet and phone stacked next to her purse and duffel bag. The kitchen was clean and Loopy lazed on her back with her belly exposed.

"I think she's in a bacon coma."

"You gave her—"

"I did."

Neither the woman nor the dog looked apologetic.

"You're a spoiled girl, Loopy."

The dog yawned.

"Tough life," he said. "I remember when she was a hard-working ranch animal."

"When was that?"

"Yesterday. Are you ready to go?" he asked. "Before you ruin my dog forever?"

Sofia slid from the stool. "Too late."

For him, as well, he was afraid. "Can I have your keys?"

She fished them from the cavernous depths of her purse.

"What the hell do you keep in there?"

"All the known secrets of the universe."

He raised his eyebrows.

"And lipstick."

Some of which she'd obviously used, considering her lush red mouth was an invitation that he wasn't sure he could refuse. On the other hand, if he started, he might not stop.

He grabbed her duffel bag and held open the back door for her. "If you can rouse yourself, you can come, too," he said to Loopy.

The dog stayed where she was. Until Sofia walked out of the door. Then Loopy flipped over, scratching her nails on the hardwood as she scrambled to catch up.

He shook his head.

Outside, he opened the vehicle door for her to stow her belongings on the passenger seat while he placed her bag in the back where he'd found it.

She extended her hand for the keys.

"I'm going to have Ed drive it out for you because of the washed-out roads. You're with me."

She opened her mouth.

"Don't argue." He put a finger beneath her chin.

Smartly, she remained quiet.

Earlier, he'd wound up the weather doors, and now Loopy bounded up into the back of the ATV. When Sofia was also sitting, he took off. Loopy yipped and Sofia shook her head.

The main gate opened automatically, but the bump gates were tricky because of the amount of mud he had to deal with. The vehicle bogged down, making it difficult to gather enough speed.

"It really is worse than I thought," she said.

"Was a gully washer," he agreed. "No one predicted this. I still have to check on the guest house and ride the fences."

When they met up with the foreman near the main road, Ed turned to her and said, "Your car's going to need a wash."

"Or two," she replied. "Thank you for driving it out."

Cade walked with her to the SUV and opened the driver's side door. But before she could slide inside, he grabbed her hands, pinned then behind her and used that point of contact to nudge her closer to him.

He spread his legs wide, bringing them pelvis to pelvis. "Open your mouth for me." He didn't care who was watching.

He kissed her, devoured her, made damn sure she wouldn't forget him anytime soon.

9

"I'm not sure how you do it," Sofia said to her mother. "They're perfect."

She'd arrived at her mom's house an hour ago and the twins hadn't given them a moment's peace. Unless they were being held, they fussed.

Her sister was taking a nap, so Sofia and her mother hadn't put them down. And since they were so active, trying to crawl up her, Sofia began to feel as if her thighs were a trampoline. Considering that she was still sore from the night before, that didn't feel good.

"How did the meeting with Cade Donovan go?"

"Lots of possibilities. There's a barn..." She pretended that one of the girls had captured her interest. "Depending on the setup, it could be used. And honestly, I can't see why he doesn't have an events center out there." Well, except for his privacy.

And that mattered to him, even though she hadn't respected that when she'd crashed his party of one at three o'clock this morning. Part of her had been surprised that he hadn't lost his temper and thrown her out. But she was more saddened that he hadn't opted to share his pain, even after she'd told him of her childhood.

After last night, she knew that whatever bothered Cade was deep. Serious stuff.

While he'd been out earlier, she'd started an Internet search to learn about his past, but she hadn't looked at the results. She wished he'd open up to her, and she vowed to wait until he did.

The babies finally fell asleep. Before they could wake,

Sofia and her mother put them in their cribs. Sofia lingered in the doorway, watching them with a slight feeling of awe for a few minutes before rejoining her mother in the kitchen.

"Did he sign a contract?" Cynthia asked, handing her a glass of sweet tea.

Sofia sat at the table and pushed aside the newspaper and pen. For as long as she remembered, John had worked the crossword puzzle every day. If he was too busy, the pages would pile up and wait for the weekend. It was a lovely, predictable rhythm that had helped define her life, comforting after the chaos of her birth father.

"The contract," Cynthia repeated, bringing Sofia back to the present.

"I'm meeting with his grandfather and Erin next week."

"The Colonel," her mother said. "You know he wasn't a real colonel?"

"No."

"I think he was a captain. But he was so assertive that he was nicknamed the Colonel, and it stuck. He sure carried himself like a commander. He and Miss Libby were a fine-looking couple. I remember... When was it? Thirty-two, thirty-three years ago? Before I had the catering company, I was hired on as a server for one of Miss Libby's fundraisers."

Even though Sofia had heard the stories her whole life, she listened with renewed interest.

"She'd decided to host a British-themed event. Victorian... No. Edwardian. Well, one of them. It doesn't matter, I suppose. She had it on the lawn. It could have been something out of a movie. All the ladies wore long dresses and carried umbrellas."

"Parasols?"

Cynthia nodded. "The gentlemen wore top hats. They played croquet."

"That sounds like a nice idea."

"Except there were arguments about the rules. And it had rained. So the women had mud on their gowns. And the mosquitoes..." She shook her head.

The challenges of an outdoor event.

"The food was a disaster. No one really knew what to do with the clotted cream. One woman put it in her tea. The finger sandwiches went limp, and the chocolate melted off the strawberries. Which didn't go well for the women who'd worn gloves. Everyone was trying to crowd under the few tents that had been set up. I'm afraid Miss Libby ended up letting people go into the big house to cool down in front of the air conditioner. Heard she never tried anything like that again. Went back to barn dances and barbecue."

She answered a few of her mother's questions then brainstormed ideas for the centennial celebration before giving her a goodbye hug.

♥♥♥

After stopping in at the Corpus Christi office to give the no-update update, she hit the highway toward San Antonio. She spent a couple of hours with Manny, the branch's general manager, updating him, contemplating what would happen if Zoe spent more time there.

Manny had some excellent suggestions about moving staff into different positions, including promoting their current bookkeeper to a project manager. Evidently, she'd taken a course and had received her certification. Since Sofia was already there, she called the woman in for an impromptu discussion. She expressed an interest in the opportunity and agreed to shadow Manny for a few weeks to see if she had an aptitude for the job. Manny said he would put an ad online to begin collecting resumes for a new bookkeeper, in case the change became permanent.

Sofia checked into her hotel then wandered down to the River Walk to have dinner at her favorite Mexican restaurant. She managed to grab a patio table. They gave her a basket of tortilla chips and salsa, and she ordered a margarita.

As she licked salt from the rim, the previous twenty-four

hours caught up to her. All day, she'd had some success keeping thoughts of Cade at bay, but now she was no longer successful.

With the distance of both time and space, mortification seeped in. What had she been thinking? Sleeping with him, sceneing with him, wasn't something someone like her should do.

The first night they'd met, at Lara and Connor's reception, her self-preservation instinct had been strong. She'd given him a host of reasons why she shouldn't be involved with him. Of course, he'd dismantled her arguments.

Being with him had been an amazing experience, but probably one she should have resisted.

She knew nothing about submission, didn't have any experience in separating her emotions from her actions. As a result, everything felt like a jumbled mess. The nurturer in her wanted to help take away his pain. But the realist in her, who'd taken several psychology classes in college, realized that wasn't possible. No one could be all things to anyone else. Unfortunately, her heart seemed to be cut off from her brain.

Truth was, she liked Cade. With his breathtaking good looks and mad sex skills, he appealed to every part of her, especially the newly discovered naughty bits.

She gave in to the impulse to grab a tortilla chip and dipped it in the salsa.

This was one of her favorite places in San Antonio. She loved watching the pleasure boat pass by with its entertaining captain and waving tourists. Tonight, though, she felt restless. She was accustomed to being alone in the city, but the feeling of being lonely was new.

Her phone beeped. She dug it from her purse and checked the message.

She sucked in a breath when she saw Cade's name on the screen.

Meeting with the Colonel and Erin this Friday, ten a.m.

Donovan Worldwide headquarters downtown. Confirm?

Sofia swallowed her disappointment. What had she expected? That their time together had meant the same to him as it had her? With the day he had planned, she should be grateful he'd even thought about the centennial celebration.

Opting for the professionalism he obviously wanted, she typed her response.

I've marked my calendar.

The waiter brought her meal. Since no response appeared to be forthcoming from Cade, she put down her phone and picked up her fork.

The enchilada flavors burst in her mouth, and she wasn't sure that melted cheese and sour cream had ever tasted more appealing.

A large party was seated on the patio near her and the mariachi band wandered over to serenade a birthday girl.

She even put aside her disappointment to clap along with a lot of other people.

After dinner, she skipped dessert, but she enjoyed every sip of the margarita. She avoided temptation and didn't order a second. Instead, she opted to take a stroll around downtown. Maybe that would help her relegate thoughts of Cade to the back of her mind.

On the way to the hotel, she passed the Alamo. But even the site of the iconic mission made her remember him.

With a sigh of frustration, she headed back to her hotel.

Zoe's ringtone shattered the room's quiet.

"What the hell? No call from you?" her sister demanded, jumping in without any pleasantries. "And you spent the night with Cade Donovan?"

"You must have talked to Mom."

"You *spent* the night."

"At the ranch," Sofia agreed. She couldn't help but smile.

"So give."

"There are fourteen bedrooms."

"And which one did you sleep in?"

When Sofia didn't immediately respond, Zoe let out a triumphant, "Ha!"

"It's not like that."

"You had breakfast together."

"And?"

"You spent the night with one of the Donovan brothers and you had cozy time in the morning."

"I'm telling you, it's not like that."

"But you wouldn't admit it even if it was," she guessed.

"True."

"You are one cruel, evil, terrible sister."

"So who did you go out with last night?"

That question was enough to derail Zoe. "Marcel. And about eight hundred other people. Okay, five other people. Might as well have been eight hundred. We went to a comedy club, some great improv."

"But?"

"Well, there was no vampire attack."

"Wasn't that Todd?"

"I was pretty sure it was Marcel. I'll find out. Tonight, it's just the two of us. I'm cooking."

"That's a way to a man's heart."

"A way to get him alone is more like it," Zoe said.

Even across the miles, she heard the smile in her sister's voice.

They spent a few more minutes discussing business, and Sofia let Zoe know that Cade had confirmed her meeting with William and Erin Donovan.

"Do you want me to join you?"

"I think I've got it," Sofia replied. "But I'll want to go through the new presentation with you. Seeing the ranch and talking to Mom gave me some things to think about."

"Will you be in the office tomorrow?"

"I'll be there after lunch, yes."

A few minutes later, they ended the call.

Sofia watched a little television but couldn't concentrate on the plot line. She responded to emails and reviewed a couple of contracts each branch was getting ready to send out before admitting she was still restless.

She changed into a swimsuit and headed to the pool for a few lengths, and even that didn't help.

Finally, later, in the shower, as she lathered the soap, she allowed herself to remember her time with Cade, the spanks, the three times he'd used the paddle, the cuffs, blindfold, a plug up her ass while he fucked her with his big cock.

In surrender, she tipped back her head, moved her palms over her breasts and tweaked her nipples. Unbelievably, she was still tender from the pinwheel and from the way he'd squeezed and tugged on her. She moaned from the pressure.

Eyes closed, she slid a hand between her thighs and touched her clit. She gasped and jerked. Their lovemaking in the middle of the night had been exquisite, but it had left her sore. Even the gentlest touch was enough to make her gasp.

But she didn't stop. She wanted to come again, and the rawness allowed her to almost, *almost* believe he was there...

Sofia slipped a finger inside her pussy and rested her forehead on the ceramic tile.

The beginnings of a climax made her stomach clench and she plunged a second finger inside and fucked herself hard.

Crying out his name, she rose onto her toes, pressed against the wall for more support and shuddered as she came.

Even as the aftershocks assailed her, she knew it wasn't enough.

Cade had changed her, rocked her. She was starting to fall for him.

The recognition that she meant little to him was devastating. It would take all her resolve to forget about him and keep her own thoughts in perspective.

She turned off the faucet and wished she could turn off her emotions as easily.

∿∿∿

Sofia lost her breath.

She stepped off the elevator at the eighteenth floor of Donovan Worldwide to see Cade standing in the lobby area, legs spread shoulder-width apart. He had on a blue Western shirt covered by a black blazer. His jeans hugged his thighs, and his expression was partially hidden by his cowboy hat. The sight of him devastated her.

In the forty-eight hours they'd been separated, she'd told herself their time together hadn't been as incredible as she'd remembered. To him, she was certain, she was a woman interchangeable with any other sub.

But when he moved toward her, she realized she'd been lying to herself.

The experiences at the Running Wind had indelibly affected her, changed her, and she was grateful to have had the opportunity. It had exposed her to a whole new dimension of sexuality, and she felt more confident as a result. Or had, until he put a finger beneath her chin.

"I didn't expect to see you," she said.

"I figured it would cut down on a lot of back and forth. I'm told we've lost too much time as it is."

"That's true." She wondered, though. He didn't need to be here. He could have attended via conference or video call. As she wasn't sure what his presence really meant, if anything, she tightened her grip on her shoulder bag.

After a few seconds of silence, he moved his finger. "This way."

He led her down a hallway to a room with a small, round table.

A peach hibiscus bush appeared to be in danger of taking over an entire wall. Three peace lilies sat on the windowsill and a fourth was perched in the middle of the table. There was a counter with bottles of water and a single-cup beverage maker with about a dozen different choices of tea, hot chocolate, coffee. With the greenery and amenities, the space felt homey, not like a place to make decisions in the country's fourth largest city.

"Can I get you something to drink?" Cade asked as the door closed behind him.

"No, thanks."

"I want something."

Frowning, she turned to face him.

Before she could react, his hands were on her shoulders and he had her against the wall.

Her insides melted.

He nudged one of his legs between hers and she complied with his unspoken demand, bringing her pelvis against his thigh.

Mindless of her bag, he pinned her arms at her sides.

Her mouth parted, more in welcome than protest.

To him, *for* him, she was helpless.

His eyes were that determined gray, and he held her gaze ensnared.

"I haven't been able to stop thinking about you."

She shifted, and that brought them closer. "Cade—"

With his ruthless mouth, he cut her off, silencing her words and simultaneously devouring her.

In instant capitulation, she closed her eyes. She'd needed this, dreamed of it.

Helpless, she responded, giving herself over his to aggressiveness.

She jerked, already aroused.

The damnable, frustrating, astounding man brought her to orgasm with only his leg and his kiss.

She went limp, collapsing into his strength.

He released her left wrist so that he could thumb his hat back. And he grinned down at her.

"The meeting," she said, glancing at the door.

"I locked the door. I didn't drive five hours this morning to not get a kiss."

"You...?"

"Got up at three o'clock."

He had wanted to see her. Her heart raced, even as she urged herself toward caution. "I'm not sure what to say."

"How about thank you for the orgasm? Unless you'd prefer that I don't get you off in the future?"

She swallowed, realizing how tight his grip was on her right wrist. How was it possible that a single sentence re-established his dominance?

"I'm waiting."

"Thank you."

"Still waiting."

"Thank you for letting me come," she said quietly.

He finally released her wrist and took a step back. She rubbed the place where his thumb had bitten into her skin while he went to unlock the door.

Struggling to get her breathing under control and make sense of what had just happened, she placed her bag on the conference table.

A moment later, Erin breezed in.

Her confidence was stunning, so very different from what Sofia had witnessed when Erin had fled out the front door of the country club.

Sofia guessed that the Donovan sister was about five foot four, but that was before she slipped into unimaginably tall heels. Sofia knew she'd topple over if she tried to wear something like that. But Erin rocked three-inch heels with sequined butterflies just above the peep-toe front.

Her form-fitting skirt couldn't draw attention away from the bustier beneath a black blazer.

Her smile welcomed, but Sofia was focused on Erin's hair. She had the light-blonde length piled on top of her head, secured with a couple of pens. For the reception, she'd had dark-blonde highlights. Today, she had fire-engine red ones.

The ensemble wasn't entirely corporate, but she managed to look stylish and edgy.

"Nice to see you again," Erin said, extending a hand.

Sofia accepted, but the greeting was short-lived once Erin noticed her brother. "Cade! What are you doing here? You didn't say you were coming. Did you?" She hurried toward him and launched herself into his arms for a massive hug. "How long are you staying?"

"I'm not."

"Well, shit."

Sofia had the same reaction. Not that his plans should concern her.

"I was here last week," he said.

"For the reception?" She waved a hand, and half a dozen thin bracelets jangled. "That doesn't count. You were here five minutes."

"Twenty-four hours."

"We didn't even get to go out."

"You know where the ranch is," he said.

"It's like that thing has tentacles that keep you tethered to it."

"Roots," he said.

Erin looked at the hibiscus and shuddered. "What is it with you people? There's nothing wrong with the concrete jungle."

"Unless you want to breathe," Cade countered.

"Fine," she protested. She turned back to face Sofia with a smile. "Sorry. I didn't mean to ignore you, but I never know when I'm going to get a minute with my big brother."

"I totally understand." More than she could know. Sofia distributed folders in front of each chair. "Is it okay to move this plant?" she asked, knowing she'd never be able to see everyone comfortably with it sitting in the middle of the table.

"Is Aunt Kathryn coming?" Erin asked Cade.

"Not to my knowledge."

"In that case, yes, we can move this monster," she said.

195

"Be grateful she hasn't gotten around to bringing in a goldfish bowl."

"Really?" Cade asked.

"They promote a tranquil environment." Erin shrugged. "Supposedly."

"Can't blame her for trying," Cade said.

Erin scooped up the peace lily that was on the table and moved it to the windowsill and jammed it in with the others. "Can I get you something to drink?"

"Coffee," Cade replied.

"I didn't ask you."

"Want a noogie, pest?"

Sofia lowered her head to hide her grin at their easy banter. She appreciated seeing the softer side of him. From what she knew of Cade, he was overly serious, weighed down by life and a past he refused to talk about. Almost all of their interactions had been intense, and she'd only seen a few genuine smiles and even fewer laughs—and those had been because of Loopy.

"Sofia?" Erin asked.

She shook her head. "I'm good."

Cade brewed his own coffee. "Don't suppose Thompson's around?"

"He should be. He's hardly left the office since Connor has been on his honeymoon." Erin shrugged. "Text him."

"Thompson?" Sofia asked.

"He's Connor's admin. The place couldn't run without him. He's Donovan Worldwide's secret weapon, but his coffee is the worst on the planet. *The* worst. I heard it was once confused with ninety-weight gear oil. I think the stuff's in his veins. It's why he's able to stay at his desk something like twenty hours a day."

"He was in the military," Cade offered, as if that explained everything.

"Special super-secret something," Erin added.

Despite Erin's dire words, Cade sent a text message.

"He'd bring you a coffee, really?" Sofia asked.

"Oh, yes," Erin replied. "It's one of his greatest delights. He admires anyone who can put it in their gullet. Mark of masculinity or something."

"It's really pretty good."

"You and Lara are the only two who can actually drink it."

The three were seated at the table when William Donovan entered the room, leaning lightly on a cane.

Cade stood, and so did Sofia.

"Cade," the man said with a sharp nod.

"Colonel."

"Didn't know you'd show up. About damn time you took an interest in something to do with the family."

"Granddaddy," Erin said, obviously trying to distract him. "Can I get you something to drink?"

"What in the Sam Hill are you wearing?"

"This?" She stood and removed her jacket before doing a little pirouette. "It's a bustier."

"Since when do you work as a stripper?"

"It's casual Friday." Erin laughed easily. "I'm modeling one of the lines we'll be carrying at the corset shop."

"Put the jacket back on. Cade, give her yours, as well. Christ, does anyone have a fucking blanket?"

The man lowered himself gingerly into a chair.

"I've already had one stroke," he explained to Sofia. "And my granddaughter's trying to give me another."

"A lot of women wear them," she said. "Aunt Kathryn ordered one."

"Jesus, Mary and Joseph. Was your trust fund not enough? Now you're trying to kill me off?"

"You'll live longer if you loosen up," Erin said, sounding unconcerned. "Coffee? Tea?"

"Valium," he replied.

"Tea it is."

"You're as intolerable as your aunt."

"Green tea," she said, unperturbed. "Not black."

Sofia's finger had been hovering over the Running Wind

icon on her tablet, and she'd been looking at each Donovan in turn. All so amazingly alike. Stubborn. Committed. Resolved. Proud. And family. Loving in their own ways. Despite the words, there was an underlying affection she recognized.

While Erin brewed a green tea for her grandfather, Sofia touched the Running Wind icon to open her presentation. "I had the opportunity to visit the ranch this week. It gave me some ideas. Before I get started, can I hear what everyone has been thinking?"

Cade remained quiet.

Erin said, "I don't have a lot of suggestions, as long as the right people get invited."

William nodded.

"Let me show you a couple of slides." She advanced to a picture of a tent. Then she showed some mockups of the barn, decorated for an event. "We have some realities. Weather in South Texas in fall is likely going to be beautiful. But it might not be."

The Colonel nodded.

"I'd considered a formal. The more I thought about it, something more casual seemed to fit."

Though Erin had said she had no real opinion, she wrinkled her nose at that idea.

"The event is significant, and so it should be special," Sofia continued. "I think we need to start with a formal presentation." She went on, showing the barn set up with rows of chairs and a stage up front. She had an American flag on one side, the Texas flag on the other. A banner with the Running Wind logo hung from a back beam.

"The whole ranch is turning a hundred," the Colonel corrected. "The Running Wind is only part of that."

"Of course. Those details are crucial. That's why having you involved is important to the success of the event."

She caught Cade's quick smile and drank encouragement from it. "You should consider being first on the evening's program. You'll need an emcee. Erin, that may be a good role for you. Of course, the program is something that you all should figure out."

Everyone nodded.

"A plated meal is cumbersome, formal and expensive. And buffet lines can be unwieldy. So I'm recommending you have food stations in a party tent. Of course, with ranch beef." She showed pictures of what she meant, and she'd included pictures of Santa Gertrudis and Brahman cattle. "And maybe flavors of South Texas, including Mexican favorites. And of course, desserts. I'm thinking an ice cream sundae bar for the kids."

"I'm not seeing chicken wing cupcakes on here," Erin teased.

Cade shuddered.

"It would be tricky, time-wise, but while your guests are dining, we can reset the barn for dancing. The band can use the stage. We can set up photo booths in the loft."

Erin nodded.

"You can decide if you want outdoor activities for the kids. Maybe a bounce house. You can have a mechanical bull, as well." She flipped to her final slide, of a couple. The man was in a stylish suit jacket and bolo tie. The woman had on a short black dress and turquoise leather boots. Behind them hung a sign that read *Denim and Dazzle*.

"I like it," Erin said. "So ladies don't have to wear heels if we get rain."

"How much does something like this cost?" the Colonel asked.

She took price sheets from her folder and distributed the first two pages together. "A plated sit-down meal is on the first page. The second is for a food station." She handed out more pages. "Here you'll find costs for the presentation, including audio-visual and a program. Then the entertainment options are on the second page. Logistics are on the fifth page. This includes things like signage, security, buses to shuttle people to and from Waltham since we don't have parking available for over two hundred vehicles."

"Another option is to park over by the corral and bring people in via golf carts," Cade said.

She nodded. "That could knock down the price."

"And take a lot of carts and drivers," Erin said. "People will be pissed if they have to wait in long lines. Could we set up the event over there?" Erin asked.

"Also a possibility. If that's something you'd like to consider, we can. And I don't know how long it would take you to put together a rodeo?"

Cade shook his head. "Too much work on the bleachers, the pens."

William nodded.

"Again, if you're looking for moneymaking options, it may be something to have a look at for future use." Continuing, she brought out her last page. "Here are the beverage options. I suggest iced tea, soft drinks, kegs of beer and wine. Hard liquor isn't really necessary at the event, and it adds another expense, including the need to have additional bartenders. Of course, we're happy to arrange it if that's what you would like to do."

She took a breath, trying not to be deterred by the sudden silence. Over the last few days, getting the bid had started to matter to her. And it bothered her to realize it was only because of Cade. Her company was really the only choice when it came to an event the size of the Donovans'. But she wanted to keep working with him. Continuing on as if this were any other event, she said, "Here's pricing for alcohol." With that, she distributed the final piece of paper.

"Someone hand me a pill," William said.

"I'll get you a paper bag to breathe into," Erin replied. "Now stop scaring Sofia."

"Maybe we just turn all our third quarter earnings over to…" He flicked a glance at the top of the page. "Encore."

"Oh. Plus tax," Sofia added.

Cade lowered the brim of his hat. Erin grinned.

There was a knock at the door and a big man entered.

Thompson, she assumed. He had massive shoulders, a bald head and an impressive scar. His broad smile served as a contrast to his intimidating posture. He carried a tray, a silver coffeepot, several mugs, a pitcher for creamer and a sugar bowl.

"Thompson," Cade said. "Our savior. Not sure how this company ever ran without you."

"Brought a couple of extra mugs."

"I'm drinking tea," Erin said, clutching her cup suddenly. The Colonel moved his cup closer to him.

Cade poured a mug and offered it to Sofia. Everyone turned to face her.

"Uh…"

"No shame in refusing, miss," Thompson said. "Not everyone has the same kind of moral fortitude that our Mr. Donovan does."

"Moral fortitude?" Erin asked. "Now it's not just about physical prowess?"

"Always is," he affirmed. Thompson grinned at her. "Being a winner is both physical and mental, and the whole thing is strengthened by having a decent character."

Cade offered her the mug.

"You better give her some cream. Maybe some sugar," Thompson cautioned.

The two men exchanged glances.

"What am I missing?" Sofia asked.

Erin took pity on her. "Thompson always says sugar is for pussies."

With a desperate gasp, the Colonel clutched the head of his cane.

"Present company excepted, of course, Colonel," Thompson assured. "I would have never said such a thing in front of the ladies."

"Is this like some sort of secret handshake?"

"It is." Erin nodded. "I'm afraid I'm not a member. But there's a list on Thompson's computer with those he's deemed worthy."

"And a very short list it is, Ms. McBride," he confirmed.

She couldn't tell whether or not they were serious.

"Dead serious," Erin confirmed.

"Hand it over," she said.

"Cream or sugar?" Cade asked.

"Black." Her fingers brushed Cade's and something potent went through her.

Everyone watched as she took a drink.

It started slowly, a burning sensation down her esophagus. Then it spread, up and down, singeing her sinuses, making her stomach plunge. She coughed. Then gasped.

Just in time, she managed to get the mug back onto the table without sloshing the coffee over the rim.

Thompson and Cade shook their heads in mock misery.

"Another one down," Cade said.

"I'm afraid so, Mr. Donovan."

"Is that steam coming out of your ears?" Erin asked Sofia.

"I think it could be my brains."

Cade poured himself a cup and took a long drink before letting out a satisfied sigh. "You sure you don't want to move out to the Running Wind?"

Cade and Thompson high-fived.

William rapped his cane.

"Anything else?" Thompson asked.

"What more can one man do than be a superhero?" Cade asked.

Rubbing his hands together, Thompson left the room.

"Where were we?" William asked. "Are we getting other bids?"

"I sent Cade all of my information ahead of time, in case he wanted to."

"One was a no-response," Cade said. "Another's quote was incomprehensible. If someone else wants to be in charge, they're welcome to. But I'm not working with multiple vendors."

"We saw the job she did for Connor and Lara," Erin replied. "And we're already six months behind on this.

And since it was your idea, Granddaddy, you're welcome to be in charge. Maybe Grandma Libby might help."

"Barn needs some updating before the event," Cade added. "Rotted timbers, paint. That kind of thing."

"Do we have any full-time positions at Donovan Worldwide?" the Colonel demanded. "I'm going to have go to back to work to pay these bills."

"And what he means is, thank you for such a comprehensive proposal," Erin said.

"That's exactly what he meant," Cade added.

Sofia worked to hide her grin.

She brainstormed a few more ideas with them, then asked, "Do you have guest lists?"

"I'm still going over that," Erin said. "In fact, I'm meeting with Thompson later for his suggestions."

"I can get a save-the-date card going."

"Is that in the budget?" the Colonel demanded.

"Yes, sir. Under logistics. Up to you if you want to do both an email blast and a printed card. Or we can save money and only use email. At any rate, we'll need a graphic designer."

"Please," Erin said. "Let's get it going. Email as well as print. Maybe two hundred and fifty of those?"

They discussed the time of the event then William Donovan stood. "How long are you staying, Cade?"

"Heading back."

"Did you fly?"

"Too short of notice."

"You coming for next week's family meeting?"

"That's a possibility."

The Colonel nodded and drew his bushy eyebrows together.

But Cade was looking directly at Sofia.

She swallowed. Was he honestly considering coming to Houston because of her?

Erin confirmed that she'd be available if Sofia needed anything, and she promised that the family would discuss all events and have the contract signed by next week.

"Thank you."

Erin followed her grandfather from the room, leaving her alone with Cade.

"When are you back in Corpus Christi?"

"Midweek."

"Come to the ranch."

"Why?" She frowned. "Is there something I missed?"

"Come because I want you to."

Breath heated her lungs, making her lightheaded.

"We can have dinner in Waltham. Or I can throw something on the grill."

"I'd prefer that," she replied. And with the answer, she realized she'd agreed to see him.

"I haven't been able to stop thinking about you."

She didn't dare confess she felt the same way. "You could have called," she said instead, letting him know it had mattered to her.

"Then I would have had to decide what to say."

She was tempted to lick her lip, but she didn't want to betray herself.

"And I might have used an excuse instead of telling you that I want you on my medical table."

Sofia pressed her hands together.

"I want to lick your cunt and make you come while you're helplessly bound. I want to rip orgasm after orgasm from you."

Unbelievably, she was getting turned on.

"Tell me you'll come."

"I have a busy week." Even though she knew what her schedule looked like, she decided to stall by pulling out her phone and opening the calendar app. In order to free up time, she could start the week in San Antonio then go onto Corpus Christi. It meant leaving home on Sunday afternoon rather than Monday morning, but the change was possible. "I could be there Tuesday afternoon."

"That will work."

His slow smile did quirky things to her insides.

"Pack a bag."

Which was his way of inviting her to spend the night. And her response was her way of agreeing. "Since I spend several days a week on the road, I always have a bag with me."

"Do you get tired of it?"

"Not usually. Windshield time is synonymous with creativity for me. Because my brain is free, I put things together in ways I can't when I'm near a computer. It helps me to see the business and strategy as a whole, rather than focusing on problems at a particular branch."

"I get impatient when I'm in a vehicle."

"Doesn't surprise me. Bet you're not impatient on the back of a horse."

"Perceptive," he said.

He moved closer and put one hand in her hair. With his free hand, he stroked the column of her throat.

"Hey, I forgot..."

The sound of a female voice startled them both. Sofia took a quick step away from Cade's grip.

"Oh," said Erin. "It's like that, is it?" Her eyes were wide.

"Get lost, pest," Cade said.

"Yeah. I can see you're occupied."

"Five seconds to get out."

"Come see me?"

"Three seconds."

"Fine. Fine." She held up her hands. "My office."

"Out."

Sofia scooped up her folder and stuffed papers back inside.

"I apologize for embarrassing you," he said.

"I'm..."

"What?"

"I don't want her to think this is why I'm getting the bid."

A grin made the corners of his mouth twitch. "She saw you in action last weekend."

"Cade…"

"What?" He took her shoulders and stared at her intently.

"I don't want…" She took a breath. "I've told you before, I'm not in your league. I wasn't going to mention this, but my mother was a server for your grandparents' events."

"And? Almost everyone works somewhere. If you think anyone is judging you, I'm offended on their behalf."

"Do you mean that?"

"Erin wants me to be happy. My grandfather wants me to be more involved with Donovan Worldwide. If you're responsible for either of those things happening, my family is going to build a shrine to you. Mention this again and I will paddle you." He punctuated his statement with a sharp nod.

She exhaled and he slowly released his grip on her shoulders.

"I brought you something."

She wanted to vanish when he pulled a sleek metal butt plug from his pocket. The base had dozens of glittery amber jewels that she might have found pretty under other circumstances.

Instead of reaching for it, she stared at it in horror.

"I want you to have it in when you arrive at the Running Wind."

She looked at him, eyes wide, scandalized. "You want me to drive with it in? You want me sitting on it for hours?"

"Yeah. And call me so I can fantasize about it." He paused. "Will you do that?"

"I am making no promises."

He curled her hand around it.

Her heart was in her throat and she could think of nothing but the weight of the thing in her palm. "Cade."

"Think about it. You'll need lube. Plenty of it. And some patience."

She couldn't believe they were even talking about this. "It about twenty times bigger than the one you made me wear the other day."

"Twenty-five." Then he grinned. "Really, it's not." He held up a finger. "About twice the size that you had up there. And it's still smaller than my dick."

"Oh no. No, no, no, no, no, no. No. And if you missed the memo, hell no."

∾∾∾

Sofia was still thinking about it hours later, even after they'd said goodbye, even when she was in a meeting with Zoe.

Zoe snapped her fingers in front of Sofia's face.

It took that to jolt away the image of Cade's smile that had been haunting her.

"So the deal's signed?"

"Next week. But we have a tentative agreement."

Zoe nodded.

"We need to get going on a save-the-date announcement. And they seemed to like the Denim and Dazzle theme."

Zoe gave her a high-five. "Are you going to get the graphics done, or do you want me to chat with the designer?"

"Go ahead, if you don't mind. You can send her the presentation and my pictures to get an idea for a font and design. If we can have something by Monday, Tuesday at the latest, that would be great."

"Another day, another miracle demanded of our people." She nodded.

At the end of the day, she drove home, still thinking about Cade, still thinking about the plug that was sitting in the bottom of her purse, as if it were part test, part question. Was she willing to give Cade what he wanted? And what would it cost her to do so?

If she gave into this demand, it would be tantamount to admitting she was willing to be submissive to him.

But for how long? How often? And would she get anything other than heartache in return? Cade had never made any promises, and his words indicated he likely never would.

Not for the first time, common sense urged her to flee, stay way the hell away from him. She wondered if she were smart enough to heed the warning.

Loopy blasted past Cade, dashing down the back stairs and leaping over the last one in an effort to get to Sofia first.

She exited the vehicle and he caught a glimpse of her.

Her beautiful, dark hair hung around her shoulders, a tempting invitation. Today she had on a red, come-get-me-and-fuck-me form-fitting T-shirt and a black skirt that hugged her body and left her legs bare, except for short cowboy boots.

Cade got an instant hard-on.

Then, when she crouched to accept Loopy's enthusiastic greeting, his heart softened a bit.

"Take it easy, mutt," he commanded when he reached the pair.

Sofia was laughing, rubbing Loopy behind the ears, encouraging the bad behavior. He finally put a hand on the dog's collar and more forcefully said, "Down."

With obvious reluctance and heartbreaking whimpers of protest, she plopped her bottom on his foot.

"That's quite a welcome," she said.

"You haven't seen the one I have in store for you yet."

"Really?" she asked. "Show me?"

Damn. What the hell had he gotten himself into with her?

Until she'd contacted him from the call box at the gate, he hadn't known how important her visit really was, how bad he had it for this woman.

"You, stay," he instructed Loopy.

She cocked her head to one side, as if trying to decide whether or not she was going to obey.

He released his grip and the animal raced off, chasing a

rabbit.

"She's very well behaved," Sofia said.

"I'm lord and master of everything at the Running Wind."

Sofia raised skeptical eyebrows. Their gazes met and they both smiled.

"When others let me be," he added.

Then something imperceptible shifted. The air sizzled with supercharged sensuality.

He extended his hand. "Come here."

She took it, sliding down almost directly into his arms.

Cade kissed her like he meant it. He plunged his tongue into the heat of her mouth, plundering, demanding, tasting, dominating.

He pressed a palm against the middle of her back to hold her close and curved his fingers into her right ass cheek. He was tempted to put his hand between her buttocks and feel for the plug's hilt. But he resisted. He wanted privacy, wanted to see for himself.

Last Friday in the conference room, when he'd put the stainless-steel plug in her hand, the look on her face had been priceless — part horror, part scandalized.

He'd known that if she complied, it would be a powerful sign of her submission.

Even though they'd talked a couple of times on the phone, she'd never mentioned his request, and he'd tried to guess the thought process she'd been through.

He knew she wasn't comfortable with anal play, and she'd been correct when she'd pointed out that the metal plug was considerably bigger than the silicone one he'd used on her. The metal was not at all pliable, which meant getting it in would take time and patience. No doubt it would also cause some frustration.

For the last ten hours, since he'd gotten up this morning, he'd wondered whether her desire to please him was stronger than her reluctance.

He'd been with plenty of subs over the years, but he'd never had this kind of emotional reaction to a woman.

After she'd left last week, he'd told himself he was interested in her because she was new to the practice. Everything was novel to her, and he was pleased to be the Dom who introduced it to her.

By Thursday evening, he'd realized it was more than that. He hadn't stopped thinking about her, and he'd spent an inordinate amount of time considering the numerous ways he wanted to play with her.

His family had been shocked to see him at Donovan Worldwide on Friday. If he were honest, he'd admit that he, too, had been shocked. He hadn't made the decision until he had been sitting in the turret, with dawn still at least an hour away. He'd remembered being with her in the early morning hours only a couple of days before, the way she'd been nosy about his life, yet at the same time caring, gentle in her questions.

Though he hadn't told her much about his background, it was more than he'd shared with anyone else.

He'd liked taking Sofia back to bed, fucking her with a tenderness he hadn't known himself capable of.

There was something about the gorgeous, sassy, determined woman that had stayed with him. And after she'd gone, he'd noticed, really noticed how lonely the house was.

He ended the kiss. Her chest rose and fell quickly as her breaths came in ragged bursts. He fucking loved how she responded to him. "Let's get you inside," he said.

Today was one of those rare South Texas days with bright-blue skies and no hint of the prevailing southeast wind to give relief from the relentless June sun and humidity.

He grabbed her bag from the back of the vehicle and she reached into the passenger compartment for her purse.

Once she heard the back door open, Loopy raced across the distance, beat them inside then threw herself down in front of an air-conditioning vent.

"Watching her exhausts me," Sofia said.

"Something to drink?" he offered.

"What time is dinner?"

"You hungry?"

"Not really, just trying to decide whether to have wine or iced tea."

"You'd have to brew the tea."

"That's fine." She opened a cupboard and filled a large glass jar with water.

"What are you doing?"

"Making sun tea."

He watched her move confidently around his kitchen and he savored having her there. She grabbed tea bags from the cupboard then plopped a handful of them into the jar and screwed on the lid before carrying it outside.

"Won't that take a while?" he asked when she came back in.

"Yes. So I'll have wine for now. We're having steaks, right?"

"Yeah."

She selected a bottle of cabernet and extended it to him.

"That was decisive."

"Why fool around when you know what you want?"

"Why, indeed?" He uncorked the bottle then took down two glasses.

"I sent you, Erin and your grandfather a sample of the save-the-date email and a couple of drafts of a logo."

He nodded. "I saw."

"And?"

"Impressive. I liked the combination of the Running Wind logo, the ranch house and the picture of the entire four sections. And the verbiage worked for me, too." *A century of success.* He was beginning to see how she was going to draw the various elements together, the history, the present, the future, for the presentations and the program. Erin had been correct. The centennial celebration was much more complicated than he'd expected. At every turn, he was glad Sofia was handling the event. He had confidence in her abilities, and he'd appreciated the way she'd handled the

Colonel at the meeting. Not only was she competent, but her outward gentleness was wrapped around a steel core.

"I hope the others like it, too. I put a call in to your grandfather, but I haven't heard anything back yet."

"He goes to his trainer on Tuesdays. He's planning a five-k race this fall."

"Good for him. He's really a remarkable man."

He felt something in him go cold again. His whole life, he'd had an uneasy relationship with the Donovans. All except Erin. For the most part, he was willing to accept the blame. He refused many of the invitations to the family meetings. But the truth was, he'd never forgiven the Colonel for the way he'd treated his mother.

Jeffrey had been expected to marry well, to a woman who was a strategic match. And to her credit, Angela had loved Jeffrey, remained faithful while he'd gone to college and learned everything he could about the family's varied interests.

But he'd met Stormy.

Stormy was every bit a ranch woman. She loved the land as much as Jeffrey did, maybe more. It was easy for Cade to see why his father had fallen for her. But it wasn't as easy for him to understand why she'd refused to marry him when Jeffrey had proposed.

Cade didn't doubt that his birth had contributed to his father's recklessness. In all, it was a fucked-up mess.

"I'd love to hear more about it," Sofia said. "You know, the family dynamics."

"Leave it."

She didn't seem overly concerned by his reaction. Instead, she reached for the wine bottle and poured them each a glass.

He took a sip, waited for his irritation to pass. It wasn't her fault, he knew. It was his. Like it had been his whole life.

"This is good," she said after taking her first drink. She turned the bottle to face her so she could read the label.

213

"This is a Texas wine?"

"Yeah."

"Something you own?"

"A very small interest in it," he said.

"We need to serve this at the event."

He nodded. "Excellent idea."

"Do you have contact information? I may need to find a distributor, depending on how many bottles we need."

"Remind me if I forget."

"Oh, I will."

"Speaking of forgetting?"

She regarded him over the rim of the glass, her hazel eyes wide.

"Show me," he said.

"Show you?" Her voice was strained, with embarrassment, maybe fear?

Impatient, tired of waiting, wanting her, he put his glass on the counter. "Bend over, lift your skirt."

"Uhm…"

He plucked the glass from her hand then twirled one of his fingers. "Turn around."

Without a word, she turned. Then she caught the hem of her skirt with both hands and drew it up her thighs.

Black lace panties covered her derriere.

After putting her glass next to his, he pulled down her underwear.

The plug was there, its tiny amber jewels reflecting the overhead light. "Beautiful." Only at that moment did he admit to himself how much it had mattered. "Thank you." He stripped off her briefs and stuffed the tantalizing undies in his pocket.

Then he helped her to stand and turned her to face him.

He kissed her in appreciation for the gift she'd given him.

She wrapped her arms around his neck and leaned into him.

"I want to take you to the loft. Manny and his crew installed a couple of window air conditioner units, so the barn should be comfortable enough."

"Yes," she agreed with a slightly breathless note in her voice.

"Do you need anything?"

"I'd like to freshen up."

He'd caught a faint whiff of her arousal and his baser instincts were already urging him to claim her. He preferred dirty, raunchy sex. Instead of telling her that, he carried her bag upstairs to his bedroom and she used the master bath.

"You sure you don't need food, something else to drink?" he asked when she rejoined him.

"Just you."

His nostrils flared. It was all he could do not to pick her up, toss her on the bed and sink his dick into her.

She left the room ahead of him, showing more restraint than he was capable of at this moment.

Loopy scampered after them when they went out back and she jumped up into the ATV.

"She's so smart," Sofia said.

"I think it's more that she's eternally hopeful."

After they were all seated, he took off.

Though she was holding on to the bar in front, Sofia looked back so that she could watch Loopy. "I may never get tired of this," she said.

After the quick start, he backed off the accelerator.

At the barn, Loopy jumped out then vigorously wiggled her whole body as she waited for him to open the door.

Once they were all inside the barn, he closed the doors behind them and told Loopy to wait at the bottom of the stairs. As she had the previous time, she reluctantly lowered herself and put her head on her outstretched paws.

"How's the temperature?" he asked Sofia once they were in the loft.

"Cooler than I expected."

He didn't anticipate that any of his men would come looking for him, but he'd left the tarp in place regardless. "Please stand in the circle."

She exhaled, and he realized it was to steady her nerves rather than a silent protest.

He'd been up here earlier to prepare for her arrival with condoms, sanitary wipes, sections of hemp, bottles of water.

He took a seat in the Dungeon Master's chair and looked at her.

The longer he went without saying anything, the more uncomfortable she seemed. She shifted, curling and uncurling her hands at her sides.

"Think about how much I'm enjoying this. My pleasure."

She met his eyes and nodded.

"Take off your boots."

He was gratified she'd worn a tight-fitting skirt. Otherwise it might have ridden up as she bent over.

She kicked the boots to the side.

There was something unbelievably sexy about a barefooted sub. He liked looking at a woman in heels, but barefoot was even better. "Now the shirt."

She pulled it up and off then let it drift down on top of the discarded boots.

Her bra matched her panties, he realized. Black, ultra lacy, a little low-cut. He ached to touch her, but delay was its own reward. "Now the bra."

She reached back and slowly unhooked it. She held a strap from her finger for just a moment before moving her hand and allowing the fabric to flutter to the floor.

Her dusky brown nipples were already hardened, arousing him even more. "Skirt," he said.

He loved watching her movements as she worked the clingy fabric down her body. "Beautiful."

When she was fully naked, he pressed his palms together and regarded her. "Now turn, bend and part your buttocks so I can see my plug in you."

He noticed that her hands shook a little. But she did exactly as he'd asked.

"That thing is going to feel intense for both of us once I put my dick in you."

She sucked in a breath and remained in place even when he knew her muscles had to be feeling the strain.

"Now my table," he said. "Climb up. I want you on your back."

He'd remained in place while she walked over to it and sat on the edge.

"I'm not exactly sure…"

"Lie back. I'll direct you."

She looked at him, as if seeking reassurance.

"You're perfect."

"I want to touch you."

He'd never had a sub ask that of him before and the statement startled him a bit.

"The connection," she said.

Immediately he stood and went to her, plunging his hands into her hair, bringing her head against him.

She sighed deeply as she wrapped her arms around him.

"Better?"

"Yes," she whispered.

He held her until her breathing evened out. Then, simply because he wanted to, he kept her in his arms a bit longer. "Remember to say yellow," he told her as he eased away.

She put her hand on his forearm. "I didn't know I was at yellow until I was at yellow. I know that sounds weird."

"Not at all." He stepped away. "Are you good to continue?"

"Yes."

Once she was on her back, he shackled her wrists to the sides. Then he attached the stirrups to the table.

"Now you're scaring me."

"Yellow?" He touched her thigh in a reassuring grip.

"No. It's just… I have no idea what to expect."

"That I'm going to leave you so satiated that you won't remember your name."

"That's a pretty bold statement," she said.

He parted her legs and tucked the heel of each of her feet into the stirrups. Then he used cuffs to hold her in place.

"Brace your weight on your heels." Once she had, he slid a portion of the table back.

She gasped.

Her bottom was unsupported and her pussy was exposed, meaning she was at his mercy. "You okay?"

"It's... Yes."

"Tell me," he encouraged.

"Strange. But..."

He waited.

"I like it."

"Tell me how this was," he said, tapping the plug. "And yes, you have to answer."

She struggled to lift her head so she could look at him. "At first, awful. I started practicing Friday night when I got home. I actually had to stop at the drug store for lube. I didn't get it in, and I got frustrated. I almost called you to tell you what I thought of you."

He struggled to suppress his amusement. He kind of wished she had.

"I decided to try again as I was masturbating on Sunday."

"You played with yourself?"

She squeezed her eyes shut. "I didn't mean to tell you that."

"I'll have to watch sometime."

"How did I know you were going to say that?"

"Go on," he prompted, gently trailing his finger down her belly, then lower, between her legs.

"Cade!"

"Keep talking."

She squirmed, but her bonds prevented her escape.

"Anyway," she went on, "I was able to get it in. I wore it for a while, but yesterday, I skipped it because my ass burned."

He grinned. "And today?"

"I put it in at lunchtime at the San Antonio office. I'm about ready for it to come out."

Which meant he needed to change up the scene he'd

planned and fuck her first so that he could remove it from her. That suited him fine. He'd last longer, have more patience later.

He trailed his fingertip over her clit, teasing her, reveling in the way she struggled and strained, trying to force her pretty pussy against him more. "How are your nipples?"

She shook her head.

"I think they'd look more beautiful with clamps on them."

He left her for a moment and she gave a very impatient, unladylike grunt.

"I don't think I like parts of this," she protested.

"No. I don't expect that you do." He grinned. "Breathe."

She closed her eyes.

"Concentrate on pleasing me."

He returned with a pair of lightweight clamps. He took his time playing with her nipples, sucking on them, plumping her breasts then pinching them.

He placed the teeth of each metal alligator near the more sensitive tips.

She sucked in a sharp breath. "They're evil," she protested.

"And they look sexy." He stroked her clit. "Can you endure them for a few minutes?"

She tossed her head to one side, as distracted as he'd hoped.

"Sofia?"

"Yes," she replied.

He licked her pussy.

"Oh my *God.*"

"How do the clamps feel now?"

"Amazing."

He licked, sucked, used his fingers in her, on her, to bring her to orgasm.

She screamed and he captured the sound with his mouth, but not before Loopy dashed up the stairs.

"Tell her you're okay," he suggested.

Her breaths were ragged and she had to clear her throat before reassuring the dog.

He raised a finger and Loopy lowered herself to the floor. "I'll have to leave her in the house next time," he said.

"I don't think she'll like that, either."

"Then it's a ball gag for you."

"I was afraid of that."

"You are so beautiful...submissive," he approved. Her responses were much more than he'd imagined.

He plucked off Sofia's clamps in turn and sucked her until the blood returned and she stopped arching her back off the table.

She looked so exquisite with her tortured nipples and wet pussy that he had to have her.

He toed off his boots then stripped from the waist down before releasing her right wrist. "Get me hard," he instructed.

She turned her head to the side and her eyes widened. "Yum."

That was a reaction he hadn't expected, and one he liked very, very much.

With obedience, she curled her hand around his semi-hard cock and stroked him. "Harder," he instructed.

She continued to move with agonizing slowness.

"How's that?" she asked.

He tipped back his head.

"I'll take that as approval," she said.

As he got harder, she stroked a little faster.

"I like doing this."

After another couple dozen strokes, he knew he had to stop her before he spilled all over the floor. "That's enough."

"Put it in me?"

"Demanding sub."

"I can see why you like to look, to watch. Will you take off your shirt?"

It was an interesting switch to be the subject of adoration. He'd never had a woman drink him in with such appreciation. "Are you objectifying me, Ms. McBride?"

"It would seem so," she replied unapologetically.

He pulled up on his shirt, opening each button in turn.

"All men's shirts should be made that way," she said.

He shucked it then pulled off his T-shirt.

"Can we have a rule that you have to be naked if I am?"

"Nice try." He captured her wrist and re-secured it in place.

"Now are you going to fuck me?"

He raised an eyebrow. "Is that a request, a question, or a demand?"

"I…"

"Rephrase it," he suggested. "As a request."

"Will you please fuck me, Cade?" Her voice was slower, more seductive — impossible to deny.

He fished a condom from his jeans' pocket, tore open the packet then moved between her legs. Cade took the time to tease her back to arousal before tucking his hands beneath her to give her some support while he slid into her.

She moaned when he entered her. "Too much" — she shook her head — "you… The plug."

"You can."

"Cade!" She clenched her hands.

He pulled out before easing back in.

She dug her heels against the stirrups. "Never, never," she protested.

"We can do this."

"There's no *we*."

"You," he agreed. "You can do this." He parted her buttocks to give him a little more room. "Better?"

"You're too fucking big."

He continued on, going deeper with each stroke. "Relax." He adjusted his position so he could torment her clit with gentle touches. "Give me a second."

"Cade!"

He slid the table's section back into place then crossed to the bench he'd brought up today. He picked up a small suction-type vibrator shaped like a petal.

"What…?" She frowned.

He squeezed the thing open and placed it on her clit. Once he was satisfied that it wouldn't slip off, he turned it on, watching her eyes widen as its two tiny jellied tongues licked her.

"Damn, Cade! There's no way I can take this," she insisted. "*I can't.*"

"No?" He stroked himself to hardness then finger-fucked her until she arched and cried out.

Cade entered her a bit at a time. "How are you doing?"

She made a sound that was incomprehensible.

"Sofia?"

"Good." Her body jerked.

The position was sensational. She was spread open for him. The plug up her ass made her cunt impossibly tight, and the shivers from the vibrator rippled through both of them.

She began to move with him, whimpering, chanting his name. Cade had never been this connected to a woman. It wasn't just physically, it was more, something he couldn't identify. He wanted to protect her, brand her as his.

"I'm going to…"

He squeezed her ass cheeks hard. "Come."

She yanked against her bonds, strained to drag her thighs together. Then as the orgasm claimed her, her muscles clenched around him. He gritted his teeth, making sure she reached release before he sought his.

The motions, her convulsions, the vibrator and the plug shoved him into erotic overload. Momentarily, he felt as if he were in freefall with no parachute.

Then, suddenly, the orgasm urged him on. He grunted. Holding her tighter, needing the connection as much as she did, he spilled deep inside her.

For long moments, he stood there, his body rigid with tension.

Then his limbs went numb.

He drew a breath to regain control. "Hey," he said to her. Realizing the vibrator was still in place, he quickly turned it off then used a finger to ease its grip on her.

"Until right now, I wasn't sure what the definition of shattered was."

That went for him, as well.

He slid the table section back into place. "You may have bruises from the way I gripped your ass," he apologized.

"I'll wear them proudly."

Another impressive response, one he hadn't been expecting.

After discarding the condom and placing the vibrator on the bench, he returned to her. "Would you like me to remove the plug?"

"No." A look of horror settled between her eyebrows. "Do you mind if I take it out in the shower?"

"That's fine." He unfastened her ankles before moving on to her wrists.

He scooped her from the table and carried her to his chair. He sat and cocked a knee so that she rolled slightly toward him.

She shifted a bit. To avoid sitting on the plug, he realized.

"You make me do things I don't think I can," she said. "Your cock is somewhat intimidating all by itself, but when you make the fit even tighter…"

He trailed his fingers up and down her spine.

"I don't understand why you want to hold me after every time we have sex."

"Doesn't every man?"

"Excuse me? No. No one, actually."

"What a missed opportunity. It's important to me to connect with you, talk about what we did, see if there's anything you'd want to change the next time. Sometimes emotions can be triggered while having a scene, and I want you to feel safe." If he were honest, he'd also admit that he did it as much for him. He always had. His mentor had stressed the need to provide adequate sub aftercare. It was part of a Dom's responsibility. Cade had learned that a slow return to normal life also benefitted him. He learned a sub's most intimate secrets that way, and offering comfort filled a need in him.

The connection with Sofia, however, was something he'd never experienced with anyone else. She seemed as reluctant to receive his care as he was determined to provide it.

She put her hand on his chest and eased away from him. "You know, I may not be capable of giving you any more sex for a month."

"Forget the shower. I forbid it. I'll run you a bath. Epsom salts."

"That sounds a little self-serving."

"It is." He grinned.

He helped her to stand then scooped up her clothes. Starting with her bra, he handed her each item individually.

Despite what they'd shared, she still blushed a little.

"Underwear?" she asked.

He was tempted not to give the panties back, but he relented and tugged them out of his jeans' pocket.

"Thank you."

He dressed while she finished putting on her boots.

"Would you like me to do that?" she asked when he started to clean the table with a sanitizing wipe.

"Not necessary."

"I'm confused by the acts of service," she said. "That seems like something you should ask me to do."

"My scene. My equipment. My responsibility. There are other Doms who feel differently, but I see it the same as I do any of the things that matter to me. From the house to my horse to my riding equipment. And there's a satisfaction in caring for things." Including her.

Satisfied, he returned to the bench and cleansed the vibrator.

"That thing is diabolical."

He looked over his shoulder. "Did you like it?"

She'd mentioned that it took her some time to process the things they shared. Giving her the space she needed, and him the reassurance he needed, was a balancing act.

"It was almost overload," she said. "I was sort of afraid I wouldn't be able to come at all." She paused. "But when I did... It was one of the most powerful orgasms I can remember. You're spoiling me, Mr. Donovan."

"The pleasure is mutual. I'd never used anything like it before."

"On a woman...sub, ever?"

"I should tell you, those kinds of intimate toys are yours. I bought it for you, specifically."

"I'm... Thank you." She ran her fingers through her hair. "So..."

He waited. Even though he'd rather encourage her along, he continued what he was doing, guessing it would be easier if he wasn't looking directly at her.

"What was it like for you?"

"I think I wore down my back teeth."

"No. Really?"

He lined up everything meticulously then faced her. "The tightness was incredible. I don't generally have to work to hold back an orgasm. This time I did. With the vibrator on your clit—"

"You could feel that?"

"Yes. Believe me, sweet Sofia, that was every bit as powerful for me as it was you."

She pulled her hand out of her hair.

"I would keep silent rather than lie," he assured her. After this afternoon, masturbating might never be enough again.

Once the area was in order, he indicated she should precede him down the stairs and out to the ATV. He whistled and Loopy appeared from nowhere to jump into the back.

"Where was she?"

"It's always a mystery. I think she's at least one-eighth ghost."

In the house, she went upstairs. He lit the grill then refreshed their wine glasses and carried one up to her.

Since the bathroom door was closed, he knocked but then

walked in without waiting for a response.

She was sitting in the tub with the faucet running at full blast. Her hair was piled on top of her head and secured with a barrette bearing the Texas flag. "Are bathrooms not sacred?"

"In the vanilla world, maybe." He crouched next to the tub and noticed that she'd put a bottle of body wash and a pretty pink razor on a ledge. The sight of her personal effects startled him, and not in a bad way. Other than a few stays in a hotel room, he'd never shared space with a woman. He should have thought to ask if there was anything she'd like to keep at the ranch. But that would have required him thinking of something other than her submissive surrender.

"As long as you're bearing gifts, you're welcome to barge into the bathroom." She sat up to accept the glass then took a big sip. "Okay, this is officially more pampered than I've ever been."

"Ever?"

"Ever. Wine. Bathtub. Hot man bringing it to me. Oh, yeah, amazing sex. And he said he'd cook."

"It does sound like a pretty good deal," he agreed. Having her here wasn't so bad for him, either. He'd found himself looking forward to her visit. Making sure that he had his work done so that he could enjoy the evening had kept him sharper and busier than usual.

She reclined. "I might stay in here forever."

"Do you have a hot tub?"

"There's one at the apartment building, but I rarely use it. Too many kids. And it's a hassle to switch into a swimming suit, go down, get wet, shiver all the way back..."

"Tomorrow I'll introduce you to true decadence."

"You're doing pretty well so far." She wiggled her toes beneath the spray.

"Dinner will be about twenty-five minutes. Maybe half an hour."

"Do you need help?"

"Next time."

"Good. I wasn't planning to get out of the tub, but manners said I should at least offer." She reached forward long enough to turn off the faucet.

"I'll let you know when dinner is served, Your Highness."

The smile she gave him? He'd crawl through cut glass to see that again.

He had dinner nearly ready when she joined him in the kitchen. The scent of her reached him first—like a spring morning after a rain. It was intoxicating. Almost as potent as the smell of her arousal.

He turned and glanced at her. Her hair was still piled up, leaving her neck bare. A few damp tendrils escaped to curl alluringly along the side of her throat.

She had on a black tank top. Her shorts were skimpy enough that they should be outlawed. He appreciated them in the house, but he wouldn't allow her into town wearing them. The feeling of possession that swamped him caught him off guard, but he didn't question it. This view was his. Only his.

Her feet were bare and she'd only applied a hint of mascara to her honest, hazel eyes. Everything about her was guileless. Sofia McBride was the fresh air he'd needed in his life. He was captivated.

She moved across the room to stand next to him. "What can I help with?" she asked while brushing a finger down his forearm.

"Do you want to eat on the patio or at the island?"

"Outside is nice, as long as it's cool enough."

"We have an overhead fan and it's shaded."

"Then outside." She gathered plates, silverware and napkins and carried them out to the courtyard.

They met back in the kitchen. "I'm not sure that I'd ever be inside if I had that courtyard at my disposal," she said.

Except for in the mornings, he rarely took time to enjoy it.

"Miss Libby had the fountain put in, but it was my mother who did most of the landscaping. She has a thing for color, design, the height, ground cover, things I'll never understand. She'd look out the window and say, you know, that banana tree should be moved. So Manny would send over a worker, and it would be moved. She was always right."

"Maybe because she didn't feel comfortable making changes to the house? And there's not a lot of color in here."

He'd never thought of it that way, but she might have a point.

"Do we need any other condiments?" She glanced over and saw he'd put together a salad. "Oil and vinegar okay for that?"

"That'll work."

"Do you have steak sauce?"

He swung his gaze toward her before realizing she was grinning.

"One simply does not adulterate Running Wind beef," she said, stealing the words before he could utter them.

Cade shook his head.

"Teasing, Cade. I made stir fry last week," she reminded him. "There was no need for anything other than a light hand with the seasoning."

"You horrified me."

"The expression on your face was priceless."

They worked together effortlessly. She brought in the pitcher of sun tea and did a taste test. "Another hour would be better, but it's not bad. Want some?"

He viewed the weak-looking stuff with skepticism. "Does it come with whiskey?"

She frowned at him. "It could. I hear it's good with wine."

He shuddered. "Definitely not."

"You sure?"

"I'm not ruining a good cabernet with that stuff."

"Suit yourself."

He fed Loopy, and by the time he joined her in the courtyard, the table was set. She'd shaken the leaves off the seat cushions, transferred the salad to a blown-glass bowl and she'd clipped a couple of hibiscus blooms and put them in a jar as a centerpiece.

It was an unnecessary though homey touch that he appreciated. Ordinary was anything but with her around.

After she took her first bite, she closed her eyes. "It melts in your mouth," she said.

He felt an odd sense of pride. Throughout the years, his family had worked to cultivate this kind of beef and it was some of the best available. When he thought about it, which he'd rarely done, it was astounding that he was part of this legacy.

"Tell me more about your mother?" she invited after taking a bit of salad.

"Hell of a woman. Not many people stand up to William Donovan."

Sofia put down her fork.

"He offered her a significant amount of money to go away quietly when she got pregnant. I think her *no* had a *hell* in front of it."

"I'm confused." She frowned. "I thought the Colonel wanted you to be more involved with the family."

"He does. But it wasn't always that way."

Wordlessly, she waited.

Cade had never told anyone this story, and he wasn't quite sure why he was now. "For the first few years that I was alive, Mom continued to work at a ranch, as a riding instructor and wrangler. She left me with an elderly neighbor most of the time. Because she didn't want the Donovans telling her what to do, she vanished. It wasn't until I was five that my dad found us. I remember the yelling. Days of it. Finally, he must have worn her down. He moved us out of the horrible place we'd been living. Single-room garage apartment. Plenty of bugs, in spite of my mother's best efforts. No air conditioning. A piece of crap heater in the winter."

Color drained from her face. "I had no idea."

"The life of privilege you accused me of? In the early years, nothing could have been further from the truth. I still appreciate everything."

She took a long drink of her tea.

An opportunity to look away, he guessed.

"I owe you an apology," she said, meeting his gaze.

"You couldn't have known." He waved her off. She wasn't the first to have preconceived notions of him. "My mother told my father that we were fine, told him to go away, promised she'd never ask the Donovans for anything. To Dad, that wasn't the point. He wanted to know his son, be involved in his life. Mom told me a few years ago that she eventually believed him." He placed his knife on the serving platter. "When she refused to join him, he threatened to sue her for custody. She had no doubt that he would take her to court, but he told her he didn't want it to come to that. He wanted to take care of her, as well. The Colonel was waiting for us at the house. On the front porch. Mom stayed in the truck. Dad had his hand on my shoulder and he made me go meet him."

"You were five," she whispered.

"He told me he was my grandfather, that I was part of the family, that I had obligations. My dad, who I didn't even know at that point, kept his hand on me so I couldn't run away." He put down his steak knife. "I saw the Colonel irregularly after that, but my dad quite frequently. My grandfather and I had a discussion, once, after my father…" *Was killed needlessly, recklessly?* "Passed. He apologized for the way he'd behaved. He'd overreacted, believed my mother was a gold-digger, that she'd tried to trap my father when he was supposed to marry someone else. When she'd vanished, he realized the truth. He said it had haunted him, kept him awake nights, that his grandchild was out there somewhere. He hired a private investigator to find us. My mom didn't make it easy for him. And when Jeffrey contacted her, she changed her phone number. But she wasn't entirely surprised when he showed up. Bottom line to her was that I was entitled to my inheritance, and she realized she could stay with me at the Running Wind, or that William would use his resources to take me away. To her credit, she never said anything bad about either of them. And she's never taken a dime of their money for herself. That's my mother."

Sofia moved her plate aside.

"I'd like you to meet her." The words were out of his mouth before he'd fully thought them through. Much to his mother's annoyance, he'd never introduced her to anyone he'd been involved with. Then again, no other woman was Sofia.

"I would enjoy that, too."

Together, they cleared the plates. While he loaded the dishwasher, she put away the leftovers and the jar of sun tea that he intended to dump as soon as she left.

Then they went back outside to finish their wine.

She stretched out on a chaise and he pulled over a chair to sit near her.

"It's like another world out here. Peaceful."

How long had he looked without seeing the bushes, the mockingbirds, the butterflies? Maybe he never really had, he mused. He'd been so concerned about being an imposter, proving himself worthy, carving his own damn place that no one could take from him.

"You really should consider opening up the barn for events," she said. "This place is a little slice of heaven. You can bottle it and sell it. Even have a gift shop with mementos." She rolled her wine glass between her palms. "No reason the ranch logo can't be on these, and on a host of things. Coasters. Koozies."

"What the hell is that?"

"Those neoprene or foam protectors for aluminum cans. To insulate them? Keep your beer cold?"

"Beer comes in bottles or on draught."

"Snobbery, Mr. Donovan."

"Snobbery and good taste are not synonymous."

She grinned. "Anyway, I'll get some samples of things for you. Water bottles, pens, that sort of thing, key rings."

"People would buy that kind of stuff?"

"Mementos. You create an experience here for them and they will want to remember it."

"Want to see some more?"

"What do you mean?"

"Let's go to the river."

"Seriously?"

"Do you have jeans?"

"What's wrong with what I'm wearing?"

"Any man on the ranch will turn into a caveman if they see that much skin."

She self-consciously tugged on the hem of her shorts. "They're not that risqué."

"They are."

"Are you trying to dictate what I wear?" She scowled ferociously.

"As well as protecting you from bug bites."

"Oh. That."

"That. If you're getting sucked on, I'll be the one doing it."

The golden flecks in her eyes seemed to blaze. Maybe it was the early evening sun, or maybe it was a reflection of the impact his words had on her.

Cade had told her to grab a long-sleeved shirt. Since she didn't have one, she'd selected one of his before going out back to meet him near the ATV.

As always, he looked ruggedly handsome.

He hadn't let her into the private sanctuary of his innermost thoughts the way that she'd hoped, but each time they were together, he offered her a different glimpse. She saw him as more complex, even vulnerable. She knew he would object to that word, but that didn't change the fact he'd told her about the five year old who'd stepped into a massive responsibility.

"Ready?"

Loopy was already onboard and ready for his takeoff.

Sofia enjoyed the dog's howl of delight as much as Cade's carefree grin.

He drove her past the barn and she felt a blast of heat that she told herself was from the sun. What he'd done to her in that building had left her limp.

Having her ass and pussy so full had made it impossible to breathe. Then he'd added the sucky, licky, confounding vibrator. Even without any other stimulation it would have driven her insane, but with his dick and the thick plug, it had been close to overwhelming.

They exited Cade's private part of the ranch and passed through a couple of bump gates then traveled at least another five or ten minutes before arriving at the river.

She pulled out her phone to snap pictures once he'd stopped beneath a tree. "Can you imagine a gazebo here?"

"Always remodeling," he said.

"Trying to make you money," she countered while climbing out of the ATV. "Brides would love the pictures. Especially at sunset."

He came to stand next to her while Loopy dashed to the water's edge. Cade whistled, but the dog ignored him and happily scampered in.

"I'll have to get her groomed after this," he said.

"Let me guess, she only does that every time you're at the river."

"Something like that. I have a few towels in case something like this happens."

She adored the patience he had with the mutt. It, too, revealed more about his character than she suspected he realized.

"You could build a bridge here," she said.

"Do you ever stop?" he asked.

"When I'm sleeping."

"A bridge would be great until after a rain and it washes out. Or when we're in a drought and there's no water flowing at all."

"Stop being a pessimist. It's just a few pieces of wood, a hammer, some nails. How difficult can it be?"

"Could you be tied to it so I could fuck you?"

She sucked in a breath and turned to him, unsure whether or not he was serious. "Let me see your eyes."

Dutifully he pushed back the brim. There were no smile crinkles next to his brooding gray eyes, which meant he was serious. She lifted her phone and took a couple more pictures of the river, just to distract herself from the image suddenly occupying every single one of her brain cells.

"So, still up for the bridge?" This time, he grinned.

Her tummy slowly completed a turnover.

"You can follow the river back farther," he said. "More private." This time when he whistled, Loopy ran from the river.

He grabbed a towel, but before he could use it, the dog gave several massive shakes, sending water spewing all

over her and Cade. Sofia could have sworn the animal
smiled as she got back into the ATV.

"Sorry," he said.

"Are you?"

"It made her happy," he said by way of explanation.

He drove them back into the more heavily wooded area,
through dense mesquite trees. "If I had it cleared, it would
be easier. But it would be less private."

She saw why he liked it. There was a small clearing,
along with a few rocks. There was a dam of sorts, causing
the river to pool, creating an inviting watering hole. A few
wildflowers covered the ground, and she heard a twig snap
as a critter, maybe an armadillo, scurried away.

Loopy was the first out of the ATV and she took the
plunge, sticking her head under the clear water in search of
a darting fish. Sofia gave in to the temptation to slip out of
her boots and socks. Then she sat on the bank long enough
to roll up the hem of her jeans until her calves were exposed
before she finally waded in.

The water had been heated by the sun, so it wasn't quite as
refreshing as she'd expected. But it was still several degrees
below the outdoor air temperature, and that made it feel
wonderful. She curled her toes, enjoying being barefoot.

Cade sat on a rock, stuck a blade of grass in his mouth and
watched them.

"This really is perfect," she said. "There are so many
possibilities for you to keep your privacy, but also let others
enjoy it."

"I'm enjoying plenty right now," he said.

She waded for a while and Loopy splashed over to say
hello. Sofia's pants, as well as her shirt, got wet.

"You might as well take your clothes off."

"What?"

Not for the first time, he'd totally scandalized her. With a
frown, she looked at him.

He was stretched out, legs crossed at the ankle, relaxed
and grinning devilishly.

235

"Out here?" She glanced around. "Skinny dip?"

"Why not? As you pointed out, it's quiet. None of the ranch hands are on this section of land this evening. It's just us."

"But…"

"I have towels."

"You were hoping this would happen," she accused.

"I considered the possibility."

"You really are a shameless voyeur."

"Guilty. Feed my addiction?"

That husk, that timbre in his voice toppled her resistance. Whether he was being demanding or entreating, she was unable to deny him anything. But still, the idea appealed to her. Not necessarily because it meant she was naked, but because getting wet in this heat had definite appeal.

She went back on shore near Cade and pulled off her tank top. He reached up a hand for it and she gave the material to him. Her nipples beaded and she felt sexy, a feeling that was new for her.

Since they were already damp, the jeans were a bit more of a challenge to get out of. He offered no assistance as she wiggled and slithered the denim over her hips and past her thighs.

He captured the jeans that she tossed and folded them nicely. Sofia was reminded that he believed in taking care of things. She appreciated that it extended to her belongings as well.

She peeled off her panties, and said, "My undies don't go in your pocket."

"I'd hate for them to get lost," he replied, ignoring her words and her scowl.

Once she was naked, she stretched. It was more liberating than she ever would have guessed.

Loopy was in a shallow part of the watering hole and Sofia joined her, aware of Cade's heated gaze.

She picked up a twig and threw it in the water and Loopy plunged after it. She snatched it up and returned it, dropping it in front of Sofia. Sofia tossed it at least half a dozen times, even as the dog's tongue hung out of her mouth.

Finally tired, Loopy tromped to the sloping bank then shook before finding a patch of shade where she could cool off.

Sofia wandered in deeper, up to her thighs, before succumbing to temptation and holding her nose before plunging beneath the surface. She came up quickly and pushed hair back from her face.

"Didn't know if you were brave enough."

"I could become a convert," she said. "This skinny dipping is pretty invigorating." She rolled to her back and floated, feeling the sun's rays and gentle breeze. Since she kept so busy in her professional life, this total relaxation was a treat she treasured.

When a massive cloud gobbled the sun, she went under for one last soak before emerging.

At some point, Cade must have gone to the ATV. Her clothes had vanished, but a stack of towels sat next to him, and the long-sleeved shirt that she'd borrowed was draped across his lap.

She grabbed a towel and rubbed her hair while water dripped down her body and dried naturally. "I don't blame you for never wanting to leave this place. It's as if life moves at a different pace here."

"If you let it," he agreed. "Still a hell of a business operation. I was up at four to get it all done to enjoy the afternoon with you."

"I know you work hard, really hard, and the insomnia doesn't help. But there's such beauty here. It restores you."

He nodded. "You have to let it, though."

She'd been rubbing her face with a towel, and she lowered her hand to look at him. Was that pain in his tone, or maybe recrimination? "And have you?"

A shadow, maybe from the movement of clouds, maybe from his internal thoughts, ghosted his eyes. "Maybe not enough. Ready? I want to get to the clearing so you can see the sunset."

He'd been close to letting her in, she knew. Closer than ever before. She tried not to wallow in the disappointment of him shutting her out.

He offered another towel and she dried off her body.

Interested in the goings-on, Loopy pushed herself up and made a huge show of stretching her back legs one at a time before trotting over. How she managed to be a tripod without tipping over, Sofia had no idea.

Cade stood and offered his long-sleeved shirt to her.

"I take it that you're not giving me my jeans back," she said as she stuffed her arms into the overly big shirt.

"You'll be more comfortable like that."

"*I* will?"

He adjusted his hat, smiled and didn't respond.

Sofia rolled up the sleeves and fastened the middle few buttons.

"I may replace your entire wardrobe with men's shirts," he said.

It barely covered her buttocks, but then she realized it was probably as long as her shorts. Except the shorts and panties had kept her crotch covered.

He relented and gave her the jeans back, and she gratefully pulled them on.

She took a step then winced when she stepped on a tiny rock.

Cade scooped her from the ground and tossed her over his shoulder.

He'd caught her off guard and knocked the wind from her.

When he started forward, she suddenly felt dizzy. "Damn it!" She grabbed his waistband for stability. "Put me down."

In response, he smacked her ass.

"Cade Donovan!"

He took another stride and she yelped, reaching to hang on with her other hand. Joining the fun, Loopy ran around them, barking.

At the ATV, Cade jostled her, holding her in his arms for a moment before putting her on the seat. "Thank you. I think."

"You can show me your gratitude later."

"But—"

"Better than hurting yourself."

That was hard to argue with.

He returned to the clearing for the damp towels and ensured everything was secure before taking off.

A few minutes later, he stopped the ATV again, almost in the exact spot he had earlier. This time, maybe because she was exhausted, Loopy merely lifted her head then dropped it back on her paws, content to have a snooze.

Cade went to the rear of the vehicle, opened a box then returned with the unfinished bottle of wine and a couple of plastic cups.

"Very thoughtful," she said as he poured.

They touched the rims together.

The sun set in slow measures and the moment seemed frozen. A fraction of a second at a time the massive orb descended, as if being swallowed by a giant chasm in the earth.

"I'm not sure the last time I did something like this," she admitted. "Do you do it a lot?"

"Not nearly often enough. A lot of times, I'm still working. I'll notice it, but mostly because I'm trying to figure out how much work I can get done before I've burned through all the daylight. I've often wondered, if the sun set only once a year, would we gather around and watch it? Because it's every day, do we take it for granted?"

"I'm guilty," she admitted.

She gathered their trash into a plastic bag and shoved it beneath a seat before climbing in beside him.

He turned on the headlights and headed back. The sky darkened to an inky-velvet color, and the first star appeared. She'd never been one to make fanciful wishes, but tonight, she did. Instead of asking for something specific, she decided she wanted to hold on to the feeling she had right now.

"You're quiet," he observed.

She glanced over at him. Because of the hat and the dim light, he appeared slightly dangerous. In the distance a coyote howled and another answered, making her wrap her arms around herself. "Sometimes you scare me a little."

"Yeah?" He stopped the vehicle in front of a bump gate and faced her. "You scare me a little, too."

The admission stunned her and she wasn't quite sure what to say.

He accelerated forward to hit the metal with the ATV's brush guard.

When they reached the main gate, he keyed in a code. "It's nine-zero-nine-nine," he informed her. "In case you arrive and I'm not around to let you in."

Which meant that he hoped she would come back again, something she wasn't sure was a good idea. She was already starting to care for Cade Donovan. Perhaps a little too much. That self-preservation urge gnawed at her again. If she spent a lot of time here, she'd get even more attached to him, the land and the oversized happy mutt.

The thought of being back in her apartment, all alone, instead of snuggled in bed with him disheartened her. He'd been quite clear that he had a barrier between himself and any relationship. After what she'd learned about him, she couldn't blame him. But where did that leave her?

"Go ahead and take a shower," he told her when he parked the ATV behind the house. "I'll be in after I give Loopy a bath."

"That could take a while," she sympathized.

"Help yourself to another shirt."

"Am I supposed to be grateful you let me wear anything at all?"

"Rope would be fine."

"You're—"

240

"Serious."

Time stopped. How did he manage to keep doing that to her? She should have been accustomed to his outrageous comments, but each one had the ability to unnerve her.

"You might want to show your gratitude for the fact I allow you to wear anything when we're in the house."

The reminder that he was all Dom made blood race through her. Though she never entirely forgot it, there were times he seemed almost tender, then he would say something that would tip her world again.

"Say it," he said, raising his eyebrows.

"Thank you," she whispered.

He took off his hat. "I didn't hear you clearly."

This man never allowed her to hide. She cleared her throat. "Thank you, Cade."

"Thank you, Sir, for letting me wear clothes."

Her heart thudded as she repeated his words. "Thank you, Sir, for letting me wear clothes."

Though he hadn't moved, she felt as if he had. His power was a lethal thing and it claimed her as surely as if he'd dug his fingers into her shoulders.

"Yeah," he said, the word laden with appreciation.

The more he had her under his spell, the more she wanted to be there.

He opened the back compartment and she removed her clothes and the damp towels.

"I'll throw these in the washer," she said.

"Thanks."

She was aware that he continued to watch her as she entered the house. It wasn't until she was in the mudroom that she was able to get her heartbeat back to normal. She sorted through the laundry basket for things she could include in the load. Doing the washing in someone else's house was more intimate than cooking, she realized, as she pulled out a pair of his tight boxer briefs.

After the machine started its cycle, she headed upstairs.

She dropped his shirt and selected another from his closet,

this time a short-sleeved navy-blue one.

Since she'd been in the river, she washed her hair, and was rinsing out the suds when he entered the bathroom. It amazed her how easy it was to be together, how natural. Maybe it was the dominance, the way his confidence affected her. He knew what he wanted, and he was clear in verbalizing it. "Are all BDSM relationships like this?" She slid the frosted-glass door open a bit and steam billowed into the room.

He was in front of the sink with a single-blade razor, keeping the outline of his goatee crisp. In the mirror, he met her gaze. "Like what?"

He looked so fucking handsome with the white towel wrapped around his waist and the blade a mere inch from his skin that she almost forgot her question.

He continued to wait and she mentally shook her head.

"I was thinking about expectations." She closed the door.

"Go on," he said, loud enough for her to hear.

"It's easy to be around you." She lathered the soap, considering what she wanted to say. "I wondered if it was because of the BDSM."

"As I've said, a hundred different couples will have a hundred different relationships. That said, there's a level of trust required in this type of arrangement. Things are purposefully discussed that may never come up for other people."

"Anal sex, for example," she said wryly. She could attest to the fact no boyfriend had ever mentioned it to her. Or spanking. Or hog-tying her, for that matter.

"That," he agreed. "But also negotiations. Safe words. Even the aftercare. There's a lot demanded from the sub, but at times greater demands from the Dom."

"How so?"

"He has to be in control of himself and able to help the sub traverse whatever terrain she's on."

"It wasn't your ass being stuffed full," she protested.

"Nor will it be."

She turned off the faucet. When she exited the stall, he was standing there holding a towel for her.

No man had ever done that, either. She accepted it with a soft, "Thank you."

She dried off then moved to the vanity and took her hairbrush from the drawer she'd put it in when she'd arrived.

"May I?" He held out a hand.

"Seriously?"

He nodded.

"It's not an easy task."

"I'll endure to the bitter end," he promised.

"Start at the bottom," she said. In the mirror, their gazes locked. She saw a smile teasing his face, making him look years younger, more accessible.

"Always good advice when it comes to you," he said.

She gave him a ferocious frown. "I was talking about my hair."

"I wasn't."

He used patience that surprised her, working his way up, easing each tangle, never pulling.

A full five minutes later, when he was done, he put down the brush and turned her to face him.

Her *yes* was silent and covered by the sweetness of his kiss.

She felt his erection against her, insistent, as if they hadn't fucked hard in the barn earlier this afternoon. But the need in her was real, too. No matter how much she got, she craved more.

He deepened the kiss, and she tasted mint, freshness. She lifted her heels off the ground and leaned into him, wrapping her arms around him.

When she was breathless, he ended the kiss, and she succumbed to impish temptation to pull the towel from around his waist then reached for his dick.

He captured her hand.

"But—"

"Remind me to have that bratting conversation with you," he said, his jaw set with purposeful intent.

Cade put his palms on her shoulders and forced her to her knees. She knew what he wanted. All of a sudden, she did too, yearned to draw on the heat he'd stoked.

Hungrily, she reached for him.

He curled a hand around his cock. "Ask."

"I'm sorry?" Leaning back on her calves, confused, she looked up at him.

"Ask permission before you suck me, unless I instruct you to do so." He was looking down at her, his expression focused on her.

It was as if no one else existed for him.

"It's better if you beg."

Even though it seemed somewhat bizarre to her, she asked, "Please?"

He moved his cockhead over her cheek. When she turned to take him, he caught her chin and held her still.

Her breaths were ragged, her thoughts confused. "Please may I suck your cock?" she asked. The longer he denied her, the more consuming her need.

He touched her cheek with the silky-steel shaft. She opened her mouth, hoping for a drop of pre-cum, and she reached for him.

"Hands behind your back."

She moaned in irritation.

"Now."

After she sighed, she did as he'd said.

He continued to torment her with his cock.

She stuck out her tongue and he rewarded her by putting the underside of his shaft there for a second. Sofia pressed against it, but before she could do anything else, he moved away. Frustration warred with desire. She closed her eyes and told herself to enjoy what he was doing.

He curled his hand into her still-damp hair and she opened her mouth even wider. It was unimaginable torture. She lowered her body a little so she could get a better angle only to have him confound her again. Then she knew what it would take. "I… *Please* let me suck your cock, Sir."

"Fucking perfect." He dug his hand into her hair. "Open your mouth."

With her head tipped back, she did so, and he put his cockhead in. She sucked, licked, never ceasing.

Her eyes began to water as he grew harder and took longer strokes.

Measure by measure, she knew he was molding her into the submissive he wanted her to be. The one she suddenly wanted to be.

He spoke to her in reassuring, wonderful tones. There was no place she would rather be in this moment.

"Want," she said, knowing he probably couldn't make out the word.

He stroked his dick and forced more of himself down her throat, making her gag, but she didn't try to pull away.

She felt him go still then his cock thickened even more before he came in her mouth, overwhelming her.

Feeling greedy, she drank as much as she could, and when he pulled out, he left a trail on her cheek and chin.

Savoring the sensuality of the entire experience, she stayed where she was until he offered her a hand up.

He held her against him and she felt the thunder of his heart beneath her ear.

Cade stroked her back, still muttering words she couldn't make out, except she knew they were soothing and conveyed his pleasure.

Eventually she moved away a bit so she could look at him. "That was another soul-shattering experience."

"Soul-shattering?" he repeated, with that trademark quirk of his lips.

"Okay, maybe not. Maybe that's a bit melodramatic. Soul-searing."

Stunning her, he kissed her. "You're God damn hot, Sofia."

He left her to grab a towel from the linen closet. He

dampened the material and blotted her face. "Tell me how in the hell I'm going to let you go home in the morning?"

⌘⌘⌘

How in the hell am I going to let her go home in the morning? Damnation. Better question was, how was he ever going to let her leave?

Cade shut off the water and stepped out of the shower.

Even though he had known her only a short time, Sofia McBride was beginning to matter to him. He enjoyed her easy companionship, the constant influx of ideas about things he could do for the ranch, her confidence and her sexy slide into submission.

For his entire adult life, he'd kept himself closed off from relationships. Then his father had died and Cade had isolated himself even more. Maybe Erin's worry was justified.

He rubbed the towel vigorously over his head, as if that could give him some clarity. *Yeah.* If only it were that easy.

He pulled on a pair of lightweight sleep pants and a soft T-shirt then went into the bedroom. Though the quilt had been turned back, she wasn't in the room.

He noticed that the light was on in the turret, so he climbed the steps.

Sofia was on the couch, her tablet in hand. Loopy, still a little damp, and considerably fluffier than normal, was wedged between Sofia and the trunk. The dog thumped her tail but didn't get up to greet him.

Cade was somewhat surprised by how much he enjoyed having the two of them wait for him. It was beyond normal. It soothed some of the missing pieces of his heart.

As he'd suggested, Sofia had dressed in one of his shirts. "I like it when you do as I request."

"This?" She put down the tablet and touched the fabric near her shoulder.

"Yes."

"It's comfortable."

He took his seat across from her. "You reading anything specific?" he asked, indicating the tablet.

"I was looking at a couple of websites."

"On?"

"Bratting," she said, glancing away.

An appealing shade of red crept up her neck. Damn, he hoped she never lost that compelling air of innocence.

"You told me to remind you."

"Well done." At every turn, she amazed him. He'd also talked to her about a sub pleasing her Dom, and damn, she had that figured out. Of all the dozens of things she could be doing right now, from working, to chatting with a friend, to reading a book or playing solitaire, she'd concentrated on looking up something that mattered to him. "What did you learn?"

She took a breath. "That it's a type of behavior by a sub to get a Dom's attention. Probably intentional, but it's often playful, and not a serious type of disobedience."

"Go on." He curled his fingers around the arms of the chair.

"Some Doms seem to like that." She met his gaze. "Others, not so much."

"Where do you think I fall on that spectrum?"

"I've been wondering that," she admitted. "You've brought it up several times, so obviously it matters to you. But, that kind of connection is part of my nature. After John married my mom, the house was filled with laughter for the first time. He's a bit of a practical joker, and he's always making puns. We groan and moan. But it created a lightness our lives had been missing and, well, with a wife and five girls, it probably saved his sanity."

"Five girls?"

"Afraid so, me and my sister, Zoe. Then he and Mom had three more girls. When Zoe and I moved out, he might have thought he was getting a break, but one of my sisters just had twin girls, and they live at home, as well. There's no testosterone in sight."

"I'm glad you told me," he said. "It helps me to understand you more." Unlike him, she didn't seem concerned about sharing stories of her past. She saw them as part of the fabric of her life, embracing, rather than hiding them. He could learn from that...maybe.

He hadn't realized he'd lapsed into his head until she prompted him. "Cade?"

"What you read is correct. Bratting is often a bit mouthy or flirtatious, but I will warn you that, at times, it will get you spanked or punished in other ways."

"Will I like it?" she asked.

"You're walking a tightrope, sweet Sofia."

"Am I?"

His cock hardened and the need to dominate surged even though she'd given him a hell of a blow job a little while ago.

She failed to heed his warning.

Instead, she stood and stepped over the snoozing Loopy then sauntered across the room to him.

"There are consequences," he reiterated.

"Yes, Sir."

"Bratting?" he asked.

"That was sincere," she assured him. "This is bratting."

She climbed into his lap, straddling him, facing him.

"I've wanted to do this." She pulled off the shirt and dropped it on the floor.

The tempting subbie wore no underwear or bra. His cock hardened.

Sofia put her hands in his hair, leaned forward then kissed him.

Since almost all of his relationships had strict D/s tones that he enforced, he wasn't sure he'd ever had a woman do that. This woman, though, seemed determined to craft her own rules.

He told himself to put a stop to it, or to at least take back control by issuing a few orders, but he was lost in her fresh scent and the feel of her moving her pussy over his crotch. "This is definitely bratting," he assured her.

"Yes, Sir," she whispered in his ear.

"You hoping for a spanking?"

Sofia pressed her breasts against him.

"Or a fucking?"

She moaned and started to grind her cunt on him, reminding him that he'd gotten off but she hadn't. He could take care of that and punish her at the same time. "Offer me one of your breasts."

For a moment she ignored him, but when he pinched her thigh, she yelped and pulled back from him.

The flecks in her hazel eyes were even more pronounced, and he wondered if that happened the more submissive she felt.

She cupped her breast and lifted it.

"Kneel up," he said.

She exhaled and he all but felt the heat of her frustration. *Good. No reason for me to be miserable alone.*

He touched her nipple, toying with it until it hardened. Then he sucked on it. When she was moving her hips in a sex-simulating rhythm, he bit down slightly, making her cry out.

But he smelled her instant arousal. God, she was something.

After releasing her, he moved her and draped her over his lap. "Is this what you want, brat?"

"Mmm."

He brought his hand down hard and she screamed. When he did it again, she tried to squirm away. "Stay still." He massaged her skin to get the blood flowing, though he wouldn't mind if she ended up with a couple of minor bruises, and he suspected she wouldn't, either. He gave no quarter before spanking her again.

"Damn!" She flailed.

He trapped her legs between his then moved his knee to unbalance her again.

She put her hands on the floor to steady herself. "Cade!"

He was ruthless, raining blows all over her delicate skin. She cried out.

"I asked if this is what you wanted."

"Yes," she replied. "Yes."

What in the name of hell had he gotten himself into? This woman wasn't just after his heart, she was entering his soul. He'd never known anyone this determined, this soft, this gentle. No one but her had been strong enough to persist with him, taking everything.

He put his hand between her legs and fingered her cunt. "You're soaked, naughty girl."

"Because of you," she said, words tight and gritty, as if forced through her teeth.

He lubed his finger with moisture from her pussy before forcing his pointer finger inside her ass. She tried to kick, but he held her fast. When she tried to push herself forward he snapped, "Move your ass back onto my finger unless you want my dick up there."

Her frantic cries didn't dissuade him and he spanked her alluring buttocks hard to distract her. Then he raised a knee to force her backward, giving her no choice but to comply with his command. "Beg me to fuck your cunt and ass with my fingers."

As best she could, she turned to face him.

Tears streaked her cheeks. Her hair was in tangles.

"Beg or I let you up and send you to bed without an orgasm. I'll tie you to the bed spreadeagle so you can't draw your legs together and you can't touch your desperate little pussy. Or maybe I'll put the vibrator on you again."

"Cade!" she pleaded. "Sir! Please."

"Three seconds."

"Fuck my ass and my cunt with your fingers please, please. *Now*, do me now!"

How could he resist?

Her pussy got wetter and wetter as he plunged into her, impaling both holes with his fingers.

"My God."

"Ask me to let you come."

Sofia's body shook and perspiration drenched her. He'd never seen a woman get this aroused from a simple spanking and finger-fuck.

She moved her head from side to side, dragging her hair on the floor. "I…"

With his free hand, he gave her six stinging slaps.

She responded by thrusting her hips back and crying out his name. "I'm going to—"

"Oh, hell no, you're not. Not without permission."

Her tremors became more pronounced, her words less intelligible.

"Ask," he snapped.

"Please let me orgasm, Cade. I'll die without one."

"Try again." He pulled out his fingers slightly.

She squeezed him with her pussy. "I beg you. Please." Her body rose as she took a breath. "I've learned my lesson, please let me come."

"That's a good girl." He fisted her hair and pulled back her head a little, holding her in place as he inserted a third finger into her pussy and drove in and out. "Now come for me." On his next ferocious thrust, he spread his fingers.

She screamed and collapsed, her entire body shuddering.

He released his grip on her hair and kept her pinned in place until the final tremor shook her.

Once her body had relaxed, he moved his leg then gently helped her up into his arms, cradling her.

"That'll teach me."

He was afraid it wasn't the lesson he wanted her to have. Though she generally disliked aftercare, this time, she stayed where she was, safe. Secure. "Stay," he said to her. He hadn't planned to extend that invitation, but in that moment, nothing seemed more natural. He wanted to spend tomorrow night with her. And the night after.

With a hand on his chest, she moved back a little so she could look at him. "I'm not sure what you're asking."

"Were you planning to go home tomorrow night?"

"To Houston? No. But I was planning to spend the day working at the Corpus Christi branch then spending the night with my family before heading back to the main branch."

"Would they be disappointed if you didn't sleep over?"

"It might be a bit of a relief for them, actually. Right now, the house is a little cramped."

"So where do you sleep?"

"On the couch. Which typically works fine until the twins wake up in the middle of the night."

"I know the ranch is a hell of a drive from Corpus Christi and the opposite direction from Houston, but I'd enjoy it if you'd spend the night here again."

Her eyes were wide, her mouth slightly parted. She knew what he was asking—for something more than they had. And he'd guessed she was smart enough to hesitate. What he hadn't known was how much her answer mattered to him.

"Join me?" Cade offered, pulling the pillow off her head.

"Could you be any more obnoxious?" she asked.

Dawn had to be at least an hour away but that hadn't stopped him from climbing out of bed and turning on a light. No matter how gorgeous he was, she wasn't amused.

"I'll go without you," he threatened.

She snatched the pillow back. "Where are you going?"

"Outdoor bathtub."

She heard the linen closet open. Curious, she removed the pillow. He walked back into the room carrying two towels, and she noticed he was wearing nothing but a pair of jeans.

"Don't you mean hot tub?"

"No. Bathtub. You fill it up for every use. No chemicals. Cooler water, tepid if you want it. Feels nice this time of the year."

She propped herself on to her elbows. "Where is it?"

"In the courtyard. Behind the grape arbor. Move your tush or miss out. I'd think you'd appreciate a soak before sitting in the car all day."

The reminder of his fingering, the plug being up her ass for half the day yesterday and the spanking made her drop back down onto the bed.

Relentlessly, he yanked the sheet off her.

"I'm never spending another night," she threatened.

"The night's one thing," he said, a smile twitching at his lips. "But you're threatening to spend the morning, too."

"Christ, Cade, it's not even dawn." But damn it, she couldn't resist him. Not his smile, not his demands, not his invitations. Even before the sun came up.

253

He extended a hand. "Last chance."

His voice had dropped an octave and she understood that he was threatening action if she didn't comply. Her butt was still sore from yesterday. "Fine." She accepted his hand.

He helped her from the bed and drew her to him.

For a moment, she basked in his strength, warmth, masculinity. He was starting to matter to her. Too damn much.

"Are you always so pleasant in the mornings?" he asked.

"I don't know. I'll let you know when it's actually morning." Ignoring his laughter, she slipped away from him and went into the bathroom to brush her teeth.

The sight of her reflection in the mirror made her open her eyes wide. Her hair was a fright, as if she'd had a raunchy night. Her skin had a few red spots. Light abrasions from his goatee? Slight shadows from lack of sleep bruised her eyes. Overall, she looked like a well-fucked woman—she made a face—or submissive?

Which was she? A woman or a submissive? *Both?*

"I said move it!" he called from the other side of the door.

"Yes, Sir," she returned, surprised by how easily that rolled off her lips and how much she enjoyed saying it.

When she emerged from the bathroom, he was nowhere in sight. Barefoot, she headed down the stairs.

He was brewing coffee and he'd put on the kettle for tea. "That was thoughtful," she said.

A few minutes later, a fluffy-looking Loopy padded in. Cade poured kibble into her bowl, but Sofia couldn't take her gaze off the dog's flyaway fur.

"She looks as if she's been shocked by electricity or something."

"Humidity. Maybe I should have used some conditioner on her."

"Seriously, she looks as if she's twice the size she normally is. Which is saying something."

"Don't listen to her, Loopy," he said. "You're perfect the way you are."

Sofia grinned. She made her tea while he poured a cup of coffee. After grabbing the towels and putting on a black felt hat, he walked through the side door leading to the courtyard. He hit a switch and flooded the area with muted light.

Mug in hand, she followed, trying not to think how scandalous it was to be walking outdoors in nothing more than his shirt.

With a bark, Loopy made it clear she wouldn't be left behind.

She dashed past them, then ran wide circles while they walked.

He led the way through an opening in the grape arbor.

"This..." She glanced around the lovely area. Grapes grew from the overhead latticework and several plants spilled colorful blooms over the sides of their pots. Pea gravel surrounded the area, for drainage, she guessed. Off to one side, a partition offered privacy for a small shower. But it was the round tub that claimed her attention.

It sat in the middle of the area on a raised deck, a slotted-top table next to it. "I thought you were joking," she said as he turned on the faucet full blast. The tub wasn't overly big, and since he meant for both of them to get in there, it was going to be a cozy fit. "Is it made of wood?"

"Cedar," he confirmed. "Stands up to the elements. I cover it each winter and treat it each spring. Sometimes, after a long, hot, dusty day on the range when even your ass hurts, there's nothing better."

"You do have this decadence thing figured out." She took a drink of her tea and quietly enjoyed the surroundings while the tub filled.

"Ready?" he asked a couple of minutes later.

He held her tea while she pulled off her shirt.

"Better make that water a little colder," he said, "so I'm not sporting a hard-on and only thinking about bending you over the side of that thing."

She'd never had a man be so appreciative of her naked

body before, and she savored it.

"Take your time getting in."

"I do declare, you're being somewhat lascivious, Mr. Donovan."

"I'm a man, sweet Sofia. And you're slaying me with your soft curves and Southern belle charm."

She grinned impishly, knowing she was skirting the edge of brattish behavior. Not that she minded. Their discussion last night had been interesting. He understood her. She understood him. Her behavior would have consequences, but she would know that before she started toying with him. And if they were anything like last night's spanking, she would enjoy it. It had hurt — bad — but the connection they'd shared had aroused her more than she had ever been. At the deepest level, she trusted him.

Sofia dipped her foot in the water. It was warmer than she'd expected, and she climbed into the surprisingly deep tub.

He offered her both mugs, and she held them while he placed her shirt on a hook screwed into the shower partition. Then he stripped. Even though they'd had hot sex yesterday and she'd sucked him off after that, his cock was already half-hard.

She wondered if she'd ever get tired of looking at him.

He hung his pants and shirt next to hers then placed his hat on a third hook.

"Leave it on?" she asked.

"The hat?" He turned to her.

"I think it will look sexy."

"You're objectifying me again," he said, his voice without complaint.

"It would appear that way."

"Never let it be said that I didn't please my woman."

His woman.

The words ricocheted around her brain, making her thoughts go haywire. What the hell did that mean? Was it anything more than a teasing comment?

Obviously it had no meaning to him because he turned away.

She shrugged. Cade had never asked for anything from her, except occasional companionship and submissive surrender.

An image of her on her knees with his cum on her face made her squirm.

When he faced her again, he was grinning. His hand on the crown of the hat, he put it back on. After turning off the faucet, he joined her in the tub.

"I wish I had my phone," she said when he was settled. He was relaxed against the back of the tub. He had one knee propped up with his cup resting on top of it and his hat was cocked at a jaunty angle. With his broad chest, strong jaw and quick smile, he devastated her.

A few minutes later, dawn began to spread across the sky.

"Was it worth getting up early?"

"Most definitely."

He saluted her with his coffee mug. "So will you," he asked, "come back after work?"

She should refuse. Last night, she'd skirted the question, hoping she'd wake up with a definitive answer. But she was no closer to a decision.

The more time they spent together, the greater the risk of her losing her heart.

"Purple," he said.

She took a sip of her tea. "Purple?"

"The rope I want to see you in."

"You're persistent," she said, shaking her head.

"Yeah."

"Can I let you know later this morning?" she asked, hedged, dodged. Maybe some distance would give her some clarity or, even better, resolve.

He nodded.

They sat together in companionable silence for a long time and she was aware of a *hew* sound, most likely belonging to a mockingbird. When it flew, she saw a flash of white on its wings. "We had one in our neighborhood that could perfectly imitate a car alarm. Through a series of whoops and beeps."

He lifted his hat so she could see the skepticism in the set of his dark eyebrows.

"I kid you not," she promised. "They're amazing mimics."

"You're not joking?"

"Look it up," she encouraged. "No, wait. Put fifty dollars on it."

"A wager?"

She smiled.

"You're on."

They each juggled their mugs to their non-dominant hands so they could shake on it.

"They can make dozens of sounds, maybe hundreds. It's one of the ways males attract females."

"Keep talking."

"I'm serious."

"And you're an expert on birds?"

"We did a lot of inexpensive things when we were little, including looking at birds. And we had some in our yard. I used to like watching them. Did you know that they're the Texas state bird?"

"Keep talking," he repeated.

She splashed him. When he looked across at her with dark eyes, she hurried to add, "That was teasing, not bratting."

"I get to decide that." His voice had gotten lower, deeper, sending a corresponding shiver through her.

"I swear," she promised.

"Uh-huh."

"And you can admit it when you hand over the fifty bucks."

He shook his head, but she moved back to the far side of the tub.

She was a little sorry that he didn't hold her accountable, and she kind of expected him to when they went inside. But even while she cooked breakfast then repacked her belongings and dressed for work, he made no mention of it.

"I hope you decide to come back tonight," he said when they stood outside, a foot or so away from her vehicle. He hefted her overnight bag.

"I'll let you know."

"Better bring my fifty dollars."

And she wanted her spanking.

He kissed her deeply, with urgency that left her breath frozen. His pull on her was strong, and her need for him was an addiction.

She climbed into the driver's seat while she was still able.

After he stowed the bag behind the driver's seat, he closed the door then gave the roof a solid rap, punctuating his goodbye.

Sofia couldn't resist the temptation to glance in the rearview mirror as she drove away. Cade moved out from beneath the portico to watch her, Loopy by his side.

A twinge of regret went through her as she left them behind, and in that moment, there was nothing she would rather do than turn around and spend the day with them.

Near the guest houses, the road curved, and she could no longer see them, allowing her to refocus.

She had a life, a job, family outside of the Running Wind. But when she was here, it was difficult to imagine that anything existed beyond Cade and her desire to please him.

Once she exited the main gate, she turned up a country music station so loud that the vibration made the vehicle's interior shake, but it still didn't drown her thoughts of him.

When she drove through Waltham, she turned the radio volume down and mentally ran through her day ahead, including a quick check with Erin to see where they were. It wasn't that Sofia was desperate for the contract—there were still numerous valid reasons to avoid working on the centennial event—but the save-the-date reminder needed to go out. No matter who did the event, having a guest list put together was crucial, as well.

Despite the drive, she was the first one at the Corpus

Christi office. She brewed coffee and found—damn it—a box of cupcakes on the meeting room table.

She'd opened the lid and was still debating the merits of snagging one of the gorgeous lemony-looking confections when Tyrone walked through the door.

"I did my level best to get rid of those for you yesterday, boss," he told her.

"What a hero." Still, she couldn't resist staring at the frosting. It looked to be a mile-high and light as a cloud. And it made her think. Maybe for the Donovan event, they could use a multi-tiered cupcake approach, perhaps a 3D replica of Maisie's Manor.

It would be a showpiece, personal to the family and, if she were honest, to herself, as well. That the dessert would be much easier and quicker to serve than traditional cake was an added bonus.

"What're you thinking?" he asked.

"About the Donovan event."

He folded his arms across his massive chest. Because he wore short sleeves, his tribal tattoos were clearly visible. And his black bandana made him look badass.

"Am I going to get my bigger warehouse?"

"And Vivian wants her showroom."

He grinned. "I'll wrestle her for it."

Vivian walked in, joining them. She shook her head when he repeated his statement. "You don't stand a chance, big guy."

Sofia raised her eyebrows.

"He's a lot of talk," Vivian said behind her hand, her gaze still focused on Tyrone. "But I've kept him out of your cookies and cupcakes. I think he's scared shitless of pissing me off."

Tyrone shrugged. "I'm learning not to get between a woman and her sugar."

"You can say that again." Vivian evidently had none of the same qualms that Sofia did. She flipped open the lid and pulled out a light-green colored cupcake with an emerald-tinged frosting.

Sofia and Tyrone both watched her lick the frosting.

"Lime," she said. "Lordy. Lordy. Even better than the pina colada flavored one I had yesterday."

So if the baker wasn't trying for trendy, odd flavors, that meant that there was a good possibility the yellow one really was lemon. Which made it quadruply hard to resist. "Fine." She snatched one up and tasted it. The sweet and tart tastes exploded on her tongue and the sugar rush was pure bliss. "I have died and gone to heaven," she said.

"I'll order some more for the next all-employee meeting," Vivian promised.

That alone was incentive for Sofia to show up.

The three sat at the table and conversation turned to business. Vivian outlined upcoming events. Tyrone said he'd have a purchase order on her desk later in the morning for a wedding next month.

"I'm following up with the Donovans this morning. I hope to have the entire deal signed by Friday, but we need to get out the save-the-date."

By the time their impromptu meeting was over, others had started to file in, some hitting the coffee pot, others popping open an energy drink.

Within ten minutes, the warehouse and offices hummed with activity.

The sugar she'd consumed buzzed through her, fueling a focus on work that was only interrupted by thoughts of Cade every thirty seconds.

At nine o'clock, her cell phone rang, and Erin Donovan's name showed up on the screen.

Sofia closed the office door before answering.

Instead of a regular greeting, Erin said, "I heard there's a Pain in the Ass Fee buried somewhere in your contract."

Sofia wasn't sure what to say, but it didn't matter since Erin rushed on, "There should be. We haven't gotten started yet and I've already had enough of my family members. Granddaddy has something like eight-hundred people on his list, none of whom can be cut. Grandma Libby wants to invite the garden club. Granddaddy doesn't want Aunt Kathryn's boyfriend in attendance, and she's threatening to boycott unless he can be there. Thompson is still going through Connor's files, and Connor's still trying to catch up from his honeymoon and can't take time to look at it. Cade has sent nothing. Nathan is double and triple checking all his names like he has OCD or something, and I can't pry the list out of his hands." She exhaled.

"And how's your list coming?"

"Don't get me started," she warned, sounding very much like her older brother for a moment. "I told you to put in a Pain in the Ass Fee."

She grinned, already liking Erin.

"Everyone has a different opinion on the logo, but fuck 'em. We're not going to make everyone happy. So I'm making an executive decision, and I'll take the heat for it. Go with the logo you have. Order twelve hundred."

"I'll have to bill you for the printing costs, even if you don't sign the contract."

"I'll sign it today on behalf of Donovan Worldwide. We can work out billing between the Running Wind and the various Donovan branches. Not your concern."

Sofia curled her hand into a fist on top of the desk.

Since she rarely closed her door, she knew it would cause interest. Sure enough, Vivian peered through the window. Sofia waved her manager in and she silently took a chair. "I wasn't expecting this call until Friday after your family meeting."

"Honestly? I've got other stuff I need to be working on. The corset shop, the foundation. I don't have time for another project, especially one that's going to need miracle after miracle if it's going to happen the way we want it to. I drank most of a bottle of chardonnay last night while talking to Aunt Kathryn and Granddaddy on the phone, and I don't have that kind of energy. They'll bitch and moan, but it won't be the first time. Pretty sure it won't be the last."

Sofia gave Vivian a thumbs up, and Vivian gripped the bottom of her chair. The woman all but buzzed with energy. Sofia had to look away so that she could maintain her professionalism instead of jumping up and down.

"Let's go with the Denim and Dazzle theme. If you need me for anything, let me know, but most of the logistics should be worked out with Cade since he's on the property. Promise me you won't ask me about tents and air conditioning and parking. Promise?"

She laughed. "I'll handle the hard goods, if you'll help with the people side."

"I'd rather do neither," she admitted.

"If you're ready to move forward," she told Erin, "we'll need both the signed contract and a deposit check."

"You can have someone pick it up this afternoon, if you want. It will take me that long to go through accounting."

"Perfect. I'll get it countersigned and returned to you tomorrow."

"Fax or email is fine," Erin said.

"As for the save-the-date, I'd like to get it out by Monday, Tuesday at the latest." She got email contact information for each person, including Thompson, so that she could loop everyone in. "I'll have my staff upload each person's guest list into our mailing program, that way we'll catch duplicates and get address verification. Spreadsheets are best, but we'll use whatever you have."

"Even a handwritten list?"

A headache formed at the base of her skull. "Even that."

It wasn't until she hung up that she collapsed against the back of her seat and allowed the importance of the deal to sink in. It represented a hell of a challenge, an opportunity as well as some risk. If they were successful and smart with the way they managed the business, especially in not letting any other event slip, Encore was on the verge of taking their business to the next level.

"I'm getting my showroom," Vivian crowed.

"I think you'd better talk to Tyrone."

"Yeah, yeah. I'll figure out a way to make the budget work so that we can both have what we want. Maybe the showroom *in* the warehouse."

Sofia nodded, possibility after possibility crowding through her mind. And because she couldn't contain herself, she pushed back her chair, moved out from behind the desk and danced around her office.

"That's it. Shake your bootie!"

Sofia fist-bumped Vivian before plonking back into her chair. "Fuck," she whispered.

"Yeah." But they were both grinning.

"Okay, okay. Back to reality." Good thing Zoe was in Houston. Especially with the expansion, Sofia would be spending a whole lot more time in Corpus Christi, which also meant she needed to consider an extended stay hotel for temporary living arrangements. Her mom's house, with its lack of space and a quiet place to work, was not a long-term option. Again, thoughts of Cade flitted through, but since they had no real relationship, she forced them away. He could not be part of her considerations. Couldn't be, even though she was going to be working with him quite a bit in the future.

"Earth to Sofia," Vivian said.

"Sorry." She shook her head. "First things first. Get the files to the printer, get a proof, so I can get it over to Erin. And I'll have Zoe arrange for one of our employees to stop in at Donovan Worldwide for the packet Erin was putting together."

Vivian nodded.

"I'll copy you in on all emails."

"We have some price quotes for the warehouse expansion. I'll get them over to you."

In less than five minutes, Encore had gone from busy to swamped, and adrenaline pumped through her. Risk thrilled her.

After Vivian left her office, Sofia called Zoe with the

update.

Zoe's exuberance matched her own and Sofia promised they'd discuss the upcoming changes as well as toast with mimosas on Sunday morning.

Her brain was still fully engaged two hours later when her phone signaled an incoming text message.

I have your fifty bucks. Cash.

She grinned, her mind instantly jerked away from business.

Oh?

Turns out mockingbirds will even dive-bomb people they don't like. They can remember people. Who the hell knows this kind of shit?

I don't know. Who?

My foreman.

She laughed. Seconds later, another message showed up.

Come and get it?

She exhaled.

Is it tucked into the waistband of your pants?

You being a brat, sweet Sofia?

Even from miles away, he still sent butterflies through her veins.

Could be.

She waited, hardly breathing.

There are consequences to that behavior.

Are there?

See you tonight?

Still deciding.

Still hoping.

From his conversation, it didn't sound as if he knew that Erin had plunged ahead with the contract. And she wasn't sure she wanted to mention it before Erin did.

As she tipped back her head, Sofia decided to be honest with herself. Spending time with Cade was emotionally risky but she was willing to take the chance. She might regret it later, but if she missed out on an opportunity, she would miss that more.

She called her mother, let her know she'd be stopping in on her lunch break. Then she texted Cade.

I'll be there after five.

His response was instant.

Good.

It took all her concentration to review all the pending proposals before heading to her mom's.

The house was filled with the scent of garlic and jalapeños. Cynthia had just finished cooking a fresh pot of beans, and she made up a plate of huevos rancheros for Sofia. While she dipped a tortilla in an egg yolk, her mother put the twins in the high chairs and fed them each a bowl of rice cereal. Sofia was sure the girls were eyeing her food with interest.

She updated her mom on the Donovan deal and shared her idea about the cake.

Cynthia nodded.

"You interested in making it?"

"Maybe in helping," she said. "That many cupcakes plus the design? You need a carpenter, an artist." She shook her head. "Transportation. Set up? Six-hundred pounds of frosting?"

"That's probably an exaggeration."

Cynthia smiled. "And all those flavors? No, thanks. But I'll supply some pecan pies, made with Donovan pecans."

"Awesome idea." After Sofia was done with her meal, she helped her mom with the girls before giving them all hugs and heading back to work.

Mid-afternoon, Zoe called.

"We got the check and the contract."

Sofia twirled around in her desk chair.

"And when are you going to fess up about your relationship with Cade Donovan?"

Her face drained. "What?"

"I have ways of making you talk. Mom said you're not staying with her tonight. You've already been to San Antonio. And your calendar shows you arrive here tomorrow afternoon."

"You've been watching too many detective shows."

"So I'm right!"

"I didn't say that," Sofia protested.

"You didn't have to. You'd have denied it outright if I was wrong. This is your sis, remember? So, when do I get to meet him?"

"It's not like that."

"Fine. Keep him all to yourself."

"I don't have him all to myself," she protested. And that fit her worry-profile. What the hell *did* she have? "We'll talk about it later."

After a few more pointed questions, Zoe gave an exaggerated sigh and hung up.

The closer it got to four o'clock, the slower time seemed to move. When she left, she had even more energy than when

267

she'd arrived.

She reached the ranch and Cade texted to let her know it'd be an hour before he got back to the house, and asked if she'd like him to take her to dinner in Waltham. She replied that she'd rather stay in.

After grabbing her bag from the vehicle, she went inside. The big house was ridiculously large and quiet without Cade and Loopy. Ignoring the silence, she checked the pantry for food options and found alfredo sauce and pasta. Fortunately there was a bag of broccoli and another of peeled shrimp in the freezer. If there was a simpler dinner, she couldn't imagine.

Decision made, she carried her bag upstairs to change.

She traded long pants for shorts, and a long-sleeved shirt for a spaghetti-strap tank top.

On the way out of his bedroom, she paused.

She noticed a snapshot, old and yellowed, lying face down near the back of the shelf. Intrigued, and realizing she might be overstepping a boundary, she picked it up. The picture was well-worn, torn at the upper right corner, as if from repeated handling.

Even though the colors were faded, there was no doubt it was of Cade and his father. They stood side by side with a sleek-looking car behind them. They had helmets tucked beneath their arms and they were grinning widely. Their black race suits had Donovan Worldwide logos on them, as well as a couple belonging to a car manufacturer.

It was almost difficult to believe he'd ever been that carefree.

Her heart heavy once again, she put the picture back.

She returned to the kitchen to open a bottle of white wine and start dinner. A large pan of water was on the back burner, almost ready to boil, when Loopy careened across the floor and jumped up on her.

The oversized mop, tail thwacking the oven, licked Sofia's face.

Looking damp and horny, Cade walked in. "Down, dog."

Loopy ignored him.

It wasn't until Sofia gave the animal a big hug that Loopy settled down.

"I'd be less patient if I didn't understand how she feels," he admitted.

Taking his words as an invitation, she went to him.

He took hold of her hair and pulled back her head. His kiss seared. It was gratitude and promise with an undercurrent of threat that made electricity zing through her body.

"How close is dinner to being ready?"

"Twenty minutes, thirty at the most," she said. "But I'm ready now."

His eyes darkened. He slid his hands down her body to cup her buttocks and press her close against him so she could feel his erection.

The knowledge thrilled her.

Eventually, he released her. "Give me a few minutes to wash the day off me," he said.

He was on his way out of the kitchen when she looked over her shoulder and said, "Aren't you forgetting something?"

He stopped and turned back.

"My fifty dollars," she teased.

"And the spanking you've earned."

Her heart stopped cold.

Before her brain kicked in, he'd scooped her up.

He turned off the burner then strode through to the dining room. Loopy dashed around before running out of the room.

He placed Sofia on her feet and yanked down her shorts.

She opened her mouth to protest, but nothing came out.

Then he stripped off her panties.

She expected him to drag her over his knee, but instead, he bent her over the nearly one-hundred-year-old table.

"How many do you deserve?"

Now that the punishment was actually at hand, courage fled.

"How many for this morning, for this afternoon, for

leaving me wondering if you'd be here when I got home?" He put his hand firmly in the middle of her back and pressed her torso onto the wood. "Don't you dare move."

She heard his booted steps on the hardwood and she had no idea where he was going.

Not only was her courage gone, but trepidation crept into its place. She felt terribly exposed, stretched out, naked from the waist down.

He returned, footfall intimidating, a minute later. "A crop," he told her.

Sofia turned her head so that she could see it and him. "That thing looks fierce."

"It can be. And I want to leave a few marks on you so that you look even hotter when I have you tied up."

"I'm not sure I should have tugged the lion's tail."

"Remorse?"

"Maybe a bit," she admitted.

"It's a little late, subbie."

She squeezed her ass cheeks. "I was afraid of that."

"Spread your legs. I want to be sure I get good solid stripes on the insides of your thighs."

Even though she did what he said, she tightened her hands into fists as the first tendrils of real fear unfurled.

"Did you decide?"

She frowned trying to figure out what he meant.

"How many strokes do you deserve?"

"Don't you get to decide that?"

"That's a decent answer. Five."

Five. She repeated the number in her head. She could manage that.

"On each leg. And three on your ass."

Hell. *That* she wasn't sure of.

He massaged her skin.

Then he moved the leather flapper part of the crop over her pussy. Her physical response was instant. Even though she'd been occupied all day, sexual need had been in the background, distracting her.

He tapped the flapper against her clit. She spread her legs farther in silent entreaty.

Granting her wish, he smacked again, harder, making her cry out.

Cade gave her another, a little lighter, then half a dozen more times, harder before backing off. He had her fevered, moaning.

When she was close to orgasm, he moved away and brought down the crop sharply on the back of her right thigh.

"Fuck!"

Continuing as if she hadn't screamed, he brought it down again and again.

"This isn't what I'd had in mind," she snapped at him.

"Is it not?" He sounded entirely unconcerned.

When he'd finished the first five strokes, he manipulated her pussy with his fingers, bringing her to an explosive orgasm.

"This more what you had in mind?"

Her chest heaved against the table. She couldn't form a cohesive response.

Before she was ready, he gave the second set of strokes. She squeezed her eyes shut against the blinding pain.

If this was the punishment for bratting, she might rethink her behavior.

But then he gave her two fairly sharp smacks to her cunt. Pain slashed at her and she lifted her chest off the table, arching against the shocking strength of her second orgasm.

She collapsed back down. She was so lost, overwhelmed, that she barely registered the stripes he laid across her ass.

Then it was over, he helped her up, turned her over, spread her legs and licked her pussy with gentle strokes. When her breathing eased, he increased the intensity, flicking his tongue back and forth until she came, wrapping her legs around him.

She wasn't aware of him leaving her, but he came back with a cool, damp cloth that he used to bathe her pussy and dab the stripes on her thighs. "I should be careful what I ask for," she murmured.

"I'll ensure you get what you need," he promised.

That much, she believed.

He helped her to sit, and she scooted to the edge of the table. He held her, and she leaned against him, inhaling the scents of leather and sweat.

Damn. Each moment, she drew closer to falling in love with him.

"How was it?"

"Astounding. Fucking damn hurt." She looked up at him. "Do not smile."

"Wouldn't consider it." He held her head against him and she drank in his tenderness. "That was a hell of a way to end a work day."

"For me, too."

They took their time kissing, like long-time lovers. She stayed in his arms longer than she normally did, hanging on to the moment.

Loopy crept back into the room and both of them petted her.

"We may have to start putting her outside so we don't traumatize her."

"Being away from us upsets her even more," he replied. "Don't let that fool you into thinking it means I'm going to stop punishing you."

"I hope not."

"We'll just let Loopy decide when she needs to leave."

He returned her clothing. "All your clothes need to be that easy to get on and off."

"All elastic waistbands. Check."

She was on her way back to the kitchen when his voice halted her steps. "Sofia?"

"Yeah?" She slowly faced him. Damn, he looked so fine, a lock of hair dislodged, a devilish grin on his face, legs spread, cowboy boots and well-worn jeans.

"I gave you what you were asking for. Before the night is

out, you're going to give me what I want."

After dinner, he went upstairs to change. When he came back down, he plucked the untouched wine glass from her hand and said, "It's my turn now."

"I've been picturing you in bondage since the moment I saw you."

As always, when he looked at her with that kind of intensity, Sofia was helpless, even though she still had her doubts. Since they'd met, he'd talked about a submissive wanting to please her Dom. Every day, she more clearly understood what he meant.

He opened the barn door, and Loopy rushed ahead of them at her typical Mach 1 speed. The interior of the space was blessedly cool, and she realized he'd probably stopped on his way back to the big house to prepare things for her.

She climbed the stairs first. This time, the dog stayed downstairs without him telling her to do so.

"Go to the circle."

Would she ever completely get accustomed to that request and her visceral response?

"Say *yes, Sir*," he told her.

"Cade…"

He waited, taking a seat on his throne.

"Yes, Sir." Repeating his words turned on something inside her, simultaneously making her breathlessly acquiescent and deliriously needy. She suspected he knew that.

Once she was standing where he'd said, she untucked her tank top and slowly drew it up, exposing her skin a little at a time. She'd skipped a bra, so it only took seconds for her breasts to be exposed. The cool air beaded her nipples and she exaggerated her movements as she pulled the material over her head.

For a moment she dangled it by one strap from her index finger then dropped it to the floor.

He pressed his palms together. She had no idea what any other Dom looked like, but Cade sure as hell appeared confident, competent, in control. His back was rigid against the chair leather. He had an ankle perched atop the opposite knee. And that cowboy hat... It shielded his features, cast him in intriguing shadows. Every time she was with him was as intense as the first.

Instead of toeing off her boots, she bent so she moved around, allowing her breasts to sway a little.

"You're a quick study." Approval made his voice husky.

She dropped each boot and sock outside her circle.

He put his index fingers under his chin but didn't say anything. Momentarily, she lost her composure. After taking a deep breath to steady her nerves, she removed her shorts and panties.

"Turn your back to me," he said. "I want to see if you still have marks from my crop."

Slowly she followed his order.

"They're faint. But beautiful. You're beautiful."

When he said it like that, she believed it.

"You can sit on the table for now."

As she neared it, she noticed that there was a wheeled metal cart next to it. An oversized wand-type vibrator lay on top. And the stainless-steel butt plug was there too, along with a bottle of lube and a container of hand wipes.

She perched on the edge, already clenching her ass in mute protest.

He slipped a pair of safety scissors into his back pocket before picking up several lengths of purple rope and walking across the room to join her.

"I still have doubts about this. You know that, right?" she asked.

"We'll go at your pace, and I won't push you beyond your limits."

She scowled, quite accustomed to his brand of Dominance.

"You'll take me right up to the very edge, though."

"My focus is on you, sweet Sofia. Nothing and no one else." He put the rope, of varying thicknesses, on the tray before tracing a finger reassuringly over one of her eyebrows. "You have your safe word and you can say yellow for any reason, even muscle fatigue. I'll be talking with you, telling you exactly what's happening, checking in with you at every step. I'll tie the knots so that I can get you out quickly."

"Uhm...so what are the scissors for?"

"Precaution only. In the unlikely event you need out and I'm not moving fast enough, I'll cut you out. Freedom will never be more than a few seconds away."

His tone was gentle, woven with reassurance but, as always, that underlying steel was there. He hypnotized her.

"We're going to start with hair bondage. Then I'll put you in a chest harness. You can stand for both of those. It's not until the very last parts that I'll put you on your belly and attach your ankles and wrists to the chest harness."

She hadn't considered that it was a long, complicated process and that she wouldn't be folded over the whole time.

"Are you ready to proceed?"

Stalling would only prolong the inevitable.

"The plug first."

She wrinkled her nose.

"The image will be stunning. I want you to squat."

"What?"

He regarded her.

"Is that really necessary?"

"Which part? The position or the plug?"

"Either. Both."

"Of course not."

She exhaled.

"But we'll be doing both, nevertheless."

"That royal we again, Cade."

"So it was. Unless you want to experience my leather belt

276

on your ass as incentive, do as I say."

Feeling utterly ridiculous, she did so.

He lubed the plug. It didn't take her long to ascertain his diabolical plan. He crouched behind her and placed the plug against her rear. When she swayed, he reached his free hand forward to play with her pussy. The position and the angle were both unique and erotic.

Rather than sliding the plug in and out, he exerted a constant pressure until the fattest part forced her sphincter muscle to yield. Then he allowed it to sink in.

Confounding her, he left her short of an orgasm.

He cleaned his hands with a wipe, then said, "You're welcome to stand, but I can manage the ponytail while you're in that position."

She stood.

"Back to me."

Cade pulled her hair back into a ponytail and looped a strand of the purple rope around it twice then secured it with an overhand knot. She felt him bend her hair into a U-shape then go around it. After a few more moves, he pulled it until it was secure.

"How's that?"

She rolled her head. "Fine."

"Next…"

Instead of grabbing the rope, he went to the far end of the space and moved aside a tarp. He wheeled a cheval mirror across the floor.

"I want you to watch, to see how gorgeous you are to me."

"I'm a little too self-critical for that."

"In that case, just look at the rope so you know what I'm doing."

She nodded and checked out the hair bondage. It was pretty.

He used a thicker rope for what he called the chest harness.

"How much rope is that?"

"About thirty feet," he said.

He doubled it over. It took him far less time than she'd anticipated, and it was smoother than she'd imagined. He started by wrapping the rope over her breasts, looping it at the back, then going under her breasts.

"What is it that appeals to you about this?" she asked.

"The artistry," he said. "The rope makes a difference, too. Is it hemp? Cotton? Bamboo? Nylon? Silk? What's the intent of the scene? Am I just tying you up so you're helpless when I make you come? Do I just want to look at you? It can be meant as punishment, maybe, so a coarse rope is different. Then you factor in color to the sensual equation. Purple goes with your skin and your dark hair. I'd thought about red, too, and I'm sure that would be just as sensational — deep, dark, blood red."

He was silent for a moment, and she pictured it.

In the mirror, she watched him work, admiring his speed, concentration and competence. He repeated the process before going over her shoulders. The entire time, he checked the tension and ensured the ropes were straight.

When he'd completed that portion, he stood behind her, his hands on her shoulders.

"Look at the way it shows off your breasts. You have to admit that the models you saw were beautiful in their submission, and so are you. You know I'm highly visual, so watching you at every stage is rewarding."

He moved her to the table and told her to lie on her stomach. "Put your arms behind you and cross them." He took each hand and guided them into position.

In less than three minutes, he'd wrapped smaller pieces of rope around her wrists then joined them to the chest harness.

"You'll see some people attach the wrists to the ankles, but I don't do that. I want the pressure to be kept on the chest, not your wrists, so as to avoid injury."

She nodded as best she could.

He wrapped rope around her ankles then began the finishing touches to draw her ankles toward the chest harness.

Her mouth dried.

"We won't go too fast or too far," he promised. "Watch."

Cade pulled to complete the hog-tie, forcing her back into a gorgeous arch.

"How's that?"

"Not as uncomfortable as I feared," she said.

He finished with a simple overhand knot then checked that the hemp wasn't cutting into the side of her neck. "Lightheadedness? Fatigue?"

"No. Neither."

He stepped back, studied her then returned to secure her ponytail to the setup. "Look at yourself."

The image was surprising. She looked...serene. For a moment, she couldn't believe it was her.

With his blunt thumbnail, he scraped the marks his crop had left on her skin, sending goosebumps through her.

"Beyond my imagination," he approved. "Stunning. You asked what appeals to me about this. Do you see now?"

She nodded, pulling on her bonds, reminding herself of her submission.

"It's touch, as well." He trailed his fingers across her skin. "I can't get enough of you."

The sentiment was mutual.

He walked around her, looking at her from every angle. Never had she thought she could enjoy something like that, but she did.

"Do you mind if I take pictures?"

She would have said that she would have never allowed something like that.

"You're the only other person who'll ever see them," he said. "I want to show you how I see you."

"I'm not like those models," she protested.

"You might disagree."

"If I hate them, you'll delete them?"

"Immediately."

From several different angles and distances, Cade took

a few shots with his cell phone camera before reviewing them. "They're pretty damn good," he said.

After he was satisfied, he put down the phone and said, "I'm going to readjust you."

He redid the ankle ropes and secured them individually to the harness. Her legs were farther apart, leaving her pussy more exposed.

Then he reached for the wand vibrator.

With the way he'd used the crop on her earlier, she knew this would drive her mad, and she was right. He put it on the slowest setting, but it was enough for her to strain against her bonds.

He stopped to run additional ropes to the table, ensuring she couldn't move even an inch.

Then he subjected her to the most exquisite torture she'd ever imagined.

She screamed as he covered her pussy with the intense head, pressing it against her. Her whole body seemed to shake and she was immobilized. "Cade."

"Don't hold back."

The man was unceasing, wringing orgasm after orgasm from her.

She cried and begged for something she couldn't name.

He talked to her, encouraged her, said how pleasing she was.

Then...

The world spun crazily, as if hurtling through space. She was desperate to reach out, to hold on to something so she didn't fall off. But there was nothing...except Cade.

Vaguely she was aware of his soothing touch and voice.

Then she was in his arms, in the chair, with him looking down at her. He was bare chested, and his shirt covered her.

"Welcome back." He grinned.

"What the hell?"

"I'd say you enjoyed the orgasm torture."

"I... What?" She looked at her wrists, expecting to see

chafe marks there. But there wasn't even a single mark.

How could everything still be the same when she was so different?

After a few minutes, he left her to get a bottle of water. He opened it and stood over her, hands on his hips, until she drank.

Since her hand was shaking, he put the cap back on.

He helped her to stand and he put his shirt on her properly. Minute by minute, she got her bearings back. "That was something. Let's do it again."

As she'd hoped, he grinned.

"You're okay if I clean up the space?"

"I can help."

He shook his head, ending the conversation.

She soaked in his attentions as he handed her into the ATV. Loopy lodged herself in place and he surged forward.

Sofia was afraid she was starting to enjoy it as much as the dog was.

Back at the big house, she removed the butt plug and took a bath. Even though the bondage hadn't been all that strenuous, the bath still soothed her muscles.

As he'd done yesterday, Cade brought her a glass of wine which she sipped for the half hour that she lazed in the tub.

When she was done, she pulled on one of his T-shirts, skipped the underwear and headed up to the turret.

She heard him picking out a tune on the guitar. Until now, she hadn't been sure he actually used it.

Not wanting to disturb him, she stood at the top of the stairs, listened and watched. He was moving his bent head, as if he were someplace else, listening to lyrics only he could hear. Loopy lazed next to his chair, sprawled out on her side.

A few minutes later, as if suddenly realizing he was being watched, he glanced up and met her gaze.

"Keith Urban. *You'll Think of Me?*" she asked.

"Surprised you recognized it."

"Are you kidding? It's an oldie, and it's withstood the test of time. And you're awesome."

He shook his head. "It's fairly easy to play."

"Mind if I join you? Or am I interrupting?"

"Please," he replied, standing. He put the guitar back in its spot.

She took her customary place and Loopy moved her head. "How are you feeling now?"

"There's not much a hot bath and a glass of wine and three dozen orgasms can't fix."

A slow, smug smile filtered across his lips.

"I think I fed your ego again."

"Yeah, maybe."

"I wasn't sure whether or not you'd heard from Erin," she said.

"About?"

"Ah…"

He waited.

"She signed the contract today."

"Did she?"

From his tone, she couldn't tell whether or not he was mad. "Crap. I'm sorry if I wasn't supposed to say anything."

"I'm sure that will make Friday's family meeting rather interesting, worth going to."

"And I still need your guest list."

"You are—"

"Direct."

"Yeah. That's the word I was looking for." They smiled simultaneously. "So we'll be working together for the foreseeable future?"

"It would seem so," she replied.

"Maybe I should send my sister some flowers."

How did he manage to say things that made her so damn happy?

"I want to show you the pictures I took of you."

She wrinkled her nose. "Maybe I don't want to see them." Or maybe she did so she could make sure he deleted them.

Cade pulled his cell phone from his back pocket and

tapped through a few screens. Then he leaned forward and slid the device across the top of the trunk.

A bit hesitant, she picked it up.

But as she scrolled through the photos, she was riveted. If she hadn't been there, didn't recognize the mole on her right hip, she wouldn't have guessed it was her in the pictures.

"I told you that you're beautiful."

Through his lens, maybe she was.

The purple rope against her skin and wrapping her hair was stunning, and the arch he'd pulled her in looked more pronounced than she could have imagined.

"Model quality right there," he said.

The screen went blank and she put the phone back on the trunk.

"So. Do I have to delete them?"

"As long as you don't share them, I'm fine."

"I'm going to print one picture for my private use."

"You..." She opened her mouth in shock then slowly closed it again. "Are you serious?"

"As long as you don't mind."

Sofia couldn't believe she was considering it, yet the idea was kind of erotic. "Nothing with my face in it," she offered as a compromise.

"I'd rather have your face, but the butt bling is pretty hot, too."

"What?" She snatched the phone back. "There's no plug in there."

"No?"

She found the one he'd taken from the foot of the table and enlarged the picture. Sure enough, the little golden jewels shone from between her butt cheeks.

"That's the one," he told her. "Next time, I will coordinate the jewels with the color of your rope."

Next time...

When she was already in danger of jumping into the deep end of the emotional attachment pool with a man who wouldn't fully share himself with her. "So the picture, are you planning to put it on the shelf near the one of you and your dad?"

Silence hung. Even she couldn't believe she'd asked the question. She had a momentary twinge of regret, but she realized this conversation had been coming. He meant too much to her to let it go.

"What did you say?" His voice was chilly, unlike anything she'd heard from him before.

She could apologize and change the subject. Or she could boldly continue, hoping for the best, prepared for the worst. "When I was in your room earlier, it caught my eye." When he said nothing, she plunged ahead. "I've told you about my mom, my alcoholic father, my family. I'm curious about your dad and his death."

"Leave it." The warning in his tone was clear and steel spiked in his eyes.

"You looked happy. You both did. Like he was really proud of you."

He didn't respond.

"I know he's dead. That's no secret. What was it? A car wreck?"

"As you said, he's dead. It's no secret. And it was a car wreck."

"And?" She sought to understand him more, learn what haunted him.

"You're not going to fucking leave it, are you?"

"I can't."

"I see." Like he often did when he was being contemplative, he pressed his hands together and considered her over the top of his steepled fingers. "So you can't come to the ranch, enjoy it, enjoy this, us…"

"There is no us," she said. In frustration, she raked back her hair and bunched it into a ponytail. Even that freaking reminded her of him, so she dropped her hands.

Agitation drove her to her feet. "There can't be an us, Cade, not when you've shut yourself off from me, your family, your own damn life. You said yourself that they're worried about you. And I am, too. I can't continue to come out here and play house with you while you keep yourself holed up in this mausoleum."

"You're in dangerous territory."

Rather than anger or heat in his voice, there was more control than ever, as if he was so tight he might snap. She didn't want to be anywhere near when that finally happened.

"Am I?" She knew one thing. She wasn't the kind of woman who was capable of having anything long-term with a man who couldn't give just as fully. "You're a generous lover and I've done crazy things with you that I would have never tried with anyone else. But I've never done a one-way relationship, and I won't start now. You've given a lot, but you've demanded even more, trust that I never imagined myself capable of. Yet I get crumbs in return." From the start, he'd warned her away. She had ignored him and her own instincts time and again. "You don't know me if you don't realize how important love and family is to me, how I do nothing halfway. It's all of you or none of you."

"So what do you need to be happy here?" He came to his feet.

Loopy put her paws around her face, as if trying to block out the humans.

"I know you'd share your money, your house. But I don't want the stuff"—she waved a hand—"that money can buy."

"So what is it, exactly, that you want? Let's be clear. Is it my fucking emotions served cold on a platter for you to examine and pick through? For you to judge? For the almighty Sofia McBride to say whether or not I am allowed to be the way I am?"

"You don't know me," she snapped back, enunciating every word.

"So you want to help? Make it all better? Tell me everything's okay? That I'll get over it? That time heals all wounds? Platitudes. I've God damn well heard them all."

He continued in much quieter tones. "Like everyone else, you'll want me to focus on the good, the happiness, the laughter, the sunset, the fact I'm still here, that I have all this, that there must be some greater meaning or purpose to the whole thing."

And because maybe on some level he was right and she felt guilty about it, she wrapped her arms across her chest instead of responding.

"I'll tell you this, nothing will change history. My dad's not coming back. He was robbed of years, of the family he loved, of his potential, of the chance to grow old and maybe see his grandchildren. Do you know that kind of pain? Who have you lost? Who can you not live without that you'll never see again? Whose gravesite do you take flowers to?"

The ache, the raw devastation in his tone was real and it etched a mark deep inside her, scarring her, too. "Cade…"

"Think about that when you make your demands of me. And while you're considering that, I want you to remember that every morning I get up and I look in the mirror and I see my father's eyes looking back at me. And I know that I'm the one who killed him."

He was a fucker. A cold, hard motherfucker. In his defense, he'd never pretended to be anything else.

Cade watched her face transform, from shock, to pain, to apology, to compassion. He recognized it. He'd seen it a hundred times before from a hundred different people. The response was always predictable. And always disappointing. Except from Sofia.

"That sucks."

He blinked.

"Sucks worse than most things I've ever heard. You're right. I had no idea. I had no right to intrude. No right to demand anything from you." She drew a breath. "And you're right that there's no way I can begin to imagine that kind of pain. I'm sorry you live with it every single day. But you know what? I'm not letting you off the hook. I'm not going to give you those platitudes you expect. I'm one of those people who likes to fix things. Probably like most women, or anyone with a heart, for that matter." Tears swam in her eyes, but she dashed them away. "But I know I can't fix you. I know your family has tried. I'd be stupid to think I might succeed where they've failed."

After gulping in a breath that she seemed to force all the way to the bottom of her soul, she went on, "It would be stupid to try. And I also know that I can't keep giving and giving to a man when I have to watch everything I say. A man who will expect me to stay in bed in the middle of the night while he goes to his office, pours a whiskey and mourns. I'm simply not that strong. Nor am I strong enough to keep coming out here and pretending, hoping, wishing, dreaming that one day we can enjoy watching the sunset by the river."

She took a few steps toward him and stopped in front of him. Then she reached up and tenderly traced his cheekbone before dropping her hand to her side. "I'll tell you this from the heart. I am sorry, more sorry than you can know, that I reopened the wound."

He grabbed her wrist as she tried to walk past him. She stopped and looked at him for a moment, her beautifully sculpted eyebrows drawn together. When he gazed into her tear-filled eyes, he couldn't see the flecks in them. He opened his mouth, but he had nothing to say. Not a single fucking word, not even a nasty one.

"You warned me," she said. "You were always honest."

He let her go.

A few minutes later, he heard her boots on the stairs. He told himself to go after her, but he couldn't force himself to move. Letting her go out to her car and drive away in the dark was assholeish, even for him. But he still didn't move.

The back door slammed. Obviously confused, Loopy cocked her head and whimpered. "It's okay, girl," he soothed. Lied.

The muted sound of a car engine reached him. He went to a window and stared. Because it was dark, he could see her lights for miles. She exited the main gate, handled the bump gate like a pro then continued driving. What was he hoping? That she'd stop? Turn around? Come back? Be satisfied with the scraps of affection and the lack of emotion that he was offering?

Sofia was right. She deserved better.

Once her tail lights disappeared, he went to his study. That, too, was ironic in its predictability.

Loopy walked past, to the kitchen, maybe to the back door?

He poured himself a double of Julien's finest and sat in the chair, feet propped on the windowsill.

There was a temptation, burning and urgent, to down the

whiskey in a single gulp. But striving for a semblance of humanity, he took only a small sip. At first, anyway.

Sofia had said she was sorry she'd reopened the wound. But she needn't have apologized for that. It had never been closed in the first place. And now he had another to go on top of it.

Until he'd met Sofia, he'd never made the mistake of falling in love with a woman. He'd constructed his life carefully to avoid spending extended time with anyone, but with her determination, her sexiness, the way she'd tried to create a home in the short time she'd been at the Running Wind—from the flowers on the table to the sun tea he still hadn't dumped—she'd worked her way inside his heart.

He'd be taking bets on which one of them had been stupider.

Civility failed him, and he downed the rest of the drink.

Loopy was still sleeping near the back door when Cade went into the kitchen right before dawn.

~~~

Someone kicking the bottom of his booted foot jolted him awake.

"Rise and shine," Nathan said.

"What in the actual fuck?" Cade struggled to sit up and adjusted his hat, squinting against the glare of the late-June sun.

"If Connor were here, I'd let him take the first swing," Nathan continued, adding an annoying cheerful smile.

"That's brotherly love for you."

"I take it you forgot I was coming?"

"What?" Cade shook his head and instantly regretted it. "What day is it?"

"Saturday. You missed the family meeting, didn't respond to calls. Told your foreman, Ed, that you were taking some time off. So I thought I'd still come down and keep you company. Maybe play some horseshoes."

He scrubbed a hand down his face, feeling stubble. "Horseshoes." He had no recollection of falling asleep outside. Probably hadn't been sleep, he realized. More like a stupor, if the empty bottle of very expensive whiskey was anything to judge by.

"Shower," Nathan said. "I'll make breakfast."

"I'll pass."

"Actually, no you won't. You'll rejoin the land of the living. Coffee is the reward."

Since the scrawny Nathan probably could take him right now, Cade opted for a shower. That would at least put him on equal footing for the upcoming discussion. "How long are you staying?"

"Couple weeks."

He accepted Nathan's generous hand up. "Weeks."

"Depends." He shrugged. "Maybe longer. Audit the books. Inventory the house."

"The fuck?"

"Act like you need a babysitter, I'll fucking give you one."

He'd never seen this side of his youngest brother.

"You scared the hell out of Erin and Aunt Kathryn. Connor was making his usual lame excuses for your behavior. That's enough. Grandfather is right, you can put both of your hands up your ass and pull your head out. Or you can give up your seat on the board."

"The Colonel said that?"

"I might have improvised," Nathan said.

"Improvised?"

"A bit."

"A bit?"

"He'd have said it if he'd have thought it."

"So what did he say?"

"That you need to step into your responsibilities or get them taken away. Accused Connor of enabling you. So Erin and Aunt Kathryn were beside themselves with worry. Connor took a tongue-lashing that belonged to you, the Colonel is pissed, we were thinking of calling your mother, we talked to your foreman, and here I am. You had a hell of a Friday, big brother. Wouldn't Dad be proud?"

If Nathan had physically punched him, Cade couldn't have felt the blow more keenly.

Many times in his life, he'd been a dick. But this week, first with Sofia then with his family, he'd risen to previously uncharted heights.

"Yeah." Cade went inside and was relieved to see Loopy sleeping contentedly near her food bowl. At least she had a few chunks of dry food in there and water in her dish. Thank God he hadn't been completely derelict in his responsibilities.

Loopy yawned and stood, stretching her paws before following him.

He brushed his teeth then got in the shower and allowed the hot spray to punish him. Eventually the steam managed to lift the fog that coated his brain. He tried to piece together the events of the last couple of days.

Sofia had left late Wednesday. He'd stayed up half the night brooding, worrying about where she'd spent the night. He'd phoned her, texted her to check on her, but she'd ignored him. He'd wondered if she had gone back to her mom's house. If so, no doubt Mrs. McBride thought he was a schmuck—rightfully so. Then he'd thought that maybe she'd gotten a hotel. In Waltham? Or Corpus? He'd offered a quick prayer that she hadn't driven all the way back to Houston. It would have been two in the morning before she'd arrived.

Why the hell had he let pride stand in the way? He should have stopped her, insisted she stay.

He'd been frustrated and hung-over at work on Thursday. He'd called her again when he'd taken a lunch break, but she'd sent him straight to voicemail. By then, he had been getting worried. She'd refused all his calls. So he'd called the Houston division of Encore. He'd been told that Ms. McBride was at work but was unable to take phone calls.

Momentary relief had washed through him. But it had

been quickly followed by a flash of annoyance. It would have cost her nothing to send a text message to ease his worry. From there, regret had threatened to drag him into its familiar pit.

Cade had kept himself busy with the ranch books on Thursday evening, managing, for a while, to outrun the demons. He'd been planning to drive to Houston on Friday morning, ridiculously early, if for no other reason than he had a vehicle and could drive to see Sofia afterward. And he was curious to know why Erin had gone ahead and signed the contract, and intrigued to know what others had thought of her decision.

But he'd gone to bed too late and he'd had so much booze that he'd slept through his alarm. He'd tried calling Sofia repeatedly and heard her professional voicemail more times than he could count. At some point, he'd spiked his phone onto the ground.

After that, things became fuzzy.

As Nathan had said, their dad would have had no reason to be proud. That burned his craw as bad as anything.

He shut off the water and got out, wrapped a towel around his waist then shaved. Once he was dressed like a civilized human being, he joined Nathan in the kitchen.

A full pot of manna sat on the counter, and Nathan was wearing the Texas apron. He looked ridiculous.

"I fucked up."

"Again," Nathan said, still with that annoyingly chipper note in his voice.

Cade poured himself a cup of coffee.

"I looked at the calendar," Nathan said. "Wasn't the anniversary."

The reminder that he'd pulled a bender before was embarrassing. "No. It wasn't."

"There's usually a reason." Nathan piled an entire pan of scrambled eggs onto a plate.

"Whose henhouse did you raid? I didn't know there were enough chickens in the county to lay this many eggs."

"You need the protein."

He squeezed his eyes shut.

Nathan had already put a platter of bacon on the kitchen island. And, thoughtfully, a couple of aspirin and a glass of orange juice.

Cade hauled his ass up onto one of the bar stools and reluctantly accepted some food. When the first bite stayed down, he tried another.

Nathan refilled both their mugs before joining him.

"So you can answer the question without me repeating it, or I can ask it incessantly. Your choice."

"Too much to hope you'll go away?"

"Five hour drive before dawn on a Saturday morning after an eventful Friday night? Yeah. It's too much to ask."

They ate in silence.

After his second cup of coffee, Cade cracked. "Sofia McBride."

Nathan put down his fork. "A woman? Wait, our caterer?"

"Event planner, but yeah."

"The woman from Connor's reception? You've been seeing her? How? When? Start at the beginning."

He left out selected pieces, probably, in reality, the pieces that mattered the most. Her responsiveness, the way she gave him more than he'd ever expected or deserved.

Cade ended the story with his ending harsh words and the way he'd let her go.

"That's a bitch," Nathan said.

To his credit, he offered no advice, and Cade guessed that none was forthcoming.

"What do you want to do?"

"Turn back the clock."

"We all do."

Nathan made Cade clean the kitchen while he sat out back with the dog and more coffee.

Cade figured that was fair.

Twenty minutes later, the aspirin had started to kick in and he went outside. The sun was still a bit much, and he

293

was grateful for the hat that allowed him to block its rays.

"Your phone, I believe," Nathan said, pointing to bits of metal and glass that were on top of the table. "I'm still finding pieces."

He winced. Mostly because he'd lost the pictures of sweet Sofia in her glorious bondage. And he was probably enough of an ass that he'd never get to see her arched for him again.

"Talk to me about the expansion ideas," Nathan said, cutting into his glum thoughts.

For the next hour he discussed ideas, including some of Sofia's, such as the one for the gazebo by the river.

"Women like that shit," Nathan said. "Wedding pictures, anniversary pictures, engagement pictures, family photos, senior portraits."

"How the hell do you know about that?"

"Have a friend who's a photographer. Always looking for great places to shoot."

Then he mentioned the Koozies.

"We have some with the Donovan Worldwide logo on them."

"Even you know what it is?"

"Anyone who drinks beer knows what one is."

He frowned.

"Get all this down on a spreadsheet, let's crunch the numbers. Based on the success we've had in section one, I wouldn't say no right away. Since the Running Wind is closer to a town and access is easier, Sofia could be right that this is a good place for events as well as outdoor activities."

"What do you think about opening the house to tours?"

"Why anyone would want to visit a mausoleum is beyond me."

He'd taken exception to Sofia calling it that.

"I meant it when I said burn it down. Well, after we make sure the insurance is solid."

Cade looked at Nathan. "You seriously have no attraction to this place?"

"Hell no."

"No animosity toward me for living here?"

Nathan exhaled. "I'm going to sock you one myself."

"I'm being serious."

Nathan tipped back his own cowboy hat and seared Cade with his intense green eyes. "So am I. If had been up to me, we'd have sold the house. The land isn't in our blood like it is yours. We're grateful it matters to you."

He was dumbstruck.

"Dad loved Stormy. No one can change that. And when she refused to marry him and vanished, he married my mother. My mother, and I bet yours, loved him. Who wouldn't? From what I remember, from what I was told, he was outgoing, fun, reckless, in and out of trouble, even jail."

Cade put down the mug he'd been about ready to drink from.

"He wasn't perfect, Cade. Even if you want to think he was. He wasn't. Not ever. Story goes that he was out at the Running Wind on college break. Truth is, he was banished. He'd knocked up a woman somewhere in Europe."

Cade felt his shoulders collapse under the burden. "We have…"

"No. She miscarried. He loved women, Cade. Even when he was married to my mom, he was picked up for a DUI. The Colonel got him off. But left the hooker to fend for herself."

"The *what?*"

"You didn't hear those stories. You were insulated out here. He was a decent man, most times. And there was the Donovan image to uphold. But he had lapses. And man, he rode his motorcycle too damn fast. He was lucky he didn't die on that."

It was as if the man he'd built up, adored, had never existed.

"I've come to terms with it. He loved us. All. In his own way. We all read the coroner's report. It was an accident. A fucked-up, wished-it-had-never-happened accident.

295

If you want to carry the burden, so be it." He shrugged fatalistically. "Can't say how I'd feel in your shoes. But no one blames you. Not me, not the Colonel, not my mother."

"I got the ranch out of it."

"And? Jesus Christ, we've all got more than we can spend in a lifetime."

"I wasn't entitled to it."

"So if there'd been someone else, that kid in Europe, maybe, we should shove him aside, deny him his due?"

"God no."

"Then why you?"

∽∽∽

After they went to town for a new phone and to grab some groceries, he and Nathan played poker, fished, rode the range, reviewed financial statements. They stayed up late Saturday night talking over a beer.

For the first time he felt as if he had family. And he acknowledged that was because—until now—he'd kept them away.

He wasn't sure what the hell to do with the realization, but he slept well that night, for the first time since Sofia had been in his bed last Wednesday.

"You're a hell of a babysitter," he told Nathan late Sunday evening as his younger brother tossed his gear in the back of his pickup truck.

"I'll tell you this, the Donovans need your contribution. The Colonel isn't as healthy as he wants us all to believe. See you at the next family meeting?"

After Nathan pulled away, he called his mother and asked if he could see her. Maybe it was time to ask questions, look at facts. And maybe it was time for him to put two hands up his ass and see if he could pull out his head.

"Men blow." Zoe threw herself down on Sofia's couch.

Since it was ten o'clock and Sofia was already in her robe and planning to head to bed, the knock on the door had caught her by surprise

For a moment, her heart had stopped, and she'd thought that maybe Cade had tracked her down. Then she'd chided herself for being ridiculous.

For a couple of days after she'd left the ranch, he had tried to contact her, but she'd heard nothing since. She told herself it was better that way. But she wasn't having a lot of luck convincing herself.

After locking the door, she sat in a chair across from Zoe. "What happened?"

"I caught Todd with another woman."

"Oh, honey. I'm sorry. Wine? Coffee? Chocolate?"

"Ice cream."

"You got it." Sofia had a pint of super-premium vanilla bean in the back of the freezer, just for times like these. She'd managed to avoid opening it, but it hadn't been easy.

Figuring that no bowl would be necessary, she carried the carton and a spoon to Zoe.

Between bites, she spilled out the whole story. Todd had taken her to the nightclub for their first real date. She'd gone to the ladies' room to freshen her lipstick, and when she'd returned, he'd been practicing his vampire moves on a voluptuous blonde.

Focusing on someone else's problems was a balm to Sofia's soul, and she listened to her sister for another hour before asking the obvious question. "What happened to

Marcel?"

"He works so many hours. He's never really available"

"So what are the things that matter to you in a man, in a relationship?"

Zoe rambled, and even though she glanced at her phone when it lit up, she was strong enough to avoid Todd's first few text apologies.

"So, someone more like our father or more like a John McBride?"

"Way to go straight for the jugular, sis."

"Unless you're just having fun, these things matter. If you're having fun, recognize it, own it, enjoy it. But if you're looking for something long-term, choose a man who deserves you. One who will get up in the middle of the night with the kids or drive the catering van."

After the ice cream, Zoe was an entirely new woman. She blocked Todd's number and deleted all the messages in her phone. She even went so as far as to trashcan his pictures.

Maybe Sofia had been hasty in avoiding the ice cream.

"Have you ever been really in love?" Zoe asked, licking the front of the spoon to capture the very last bit of heavy-cream heaven.

To cover her non-answer, Sofia picked up the carton and took the spoon from her sister.

Zoe got up and followed her to the kitchen. "Come on."

"You lived with me. How much time do I spend dating?"

"OMG."

"What?"

"It's Cade Donovan! Ha! I knew it."

She shook her head and tried not to let heat chase up her cheeks to give her away. "It's not," Sofia said firmly.

"It's not?"

"No." It wasn't a lie, but damn, she wished it were.

"You spent the night there."

"He has fourteen bedrooms." Again, not a lie.

Zoe frowned with sisterly skepticism.

Sofia picked up a dishtowel and tossed it at Zoe's head.

Sofia hadn't slept for more than a few hours at a time since she'd left the ranch, and the exhaustion was beginning to wear at the edges of her energy and focus.

She prided herself on the ability to work through anything, but that had been until Cade. She imagined his scent everywhere, something probably not helped by the fact she still had his unwashed T-shirt in her closet. Every time she caught a glimpse of a rugged cowboy in a hat, her heart would momentarily be paralyzed.

Even now, she didn't question her decision to flee. Escape had been her only hope of survival.

Tonight, she'd had the right words for Zoe, mainly because she'd repeated them to herself like a mantra over the last few days.

She knew herself well enough to realize that she did want to fix him, wanted to soothe the beast inside him, hold up a bayonet to keep his demons at bay. He'd been right about everything. *Everything.* She couldn't know that kind of pain, anguish, loss. Being responsible for the death of someone she loved…? She wasn't sure she'd ever recover from that.

Sofia had realized that only Cade could save Cade, and she had no idea if he was even interested in trying. If she had stayed, he'd have destroyed her along with him.

At least she could be as strong as Zoe.

"Can I crash here?" Zoe asked.

"As long as I can, too," Sofia replied wryly.

"I know, I know."

"Go get the linens and make up the couch." With a laugh that she needed, she hugged her sister before going to her bedroom

Maybe because Sofia was thinking about Cade, she dreamed of him.

She woke up in the darkest of the night hours, aroused as she would be if Cade were in bed next to her. Though she hadn't touched herself since she'd left the Running Wind, she closed her eyes and lay on her back.

Sofia worked her hand inside her panties and ran a finger over her clit.

Images of Cade flitted through her mind. And the one that took form was the over-the-knee spanking he'd given her, teasing her, smacking her. The touch had blazed, and yet it had been so incredibly sexy.

Pretending he was directing her motions, she moved her hand faster, plunging a finger inside her pussy, then another. She jerked her hips, then smacked her pussy hard. The sting took her to even greater heights, and it was enough to push her toward an orgasm, but not enough to shove her over the edge.

She slapped herself three times, then twisted both of her nipples.

The slight pain combined with the image of him in her mind and she dug her heels into the mattress before she called out his name and careened into an orgasm.

When the aftershocks retreated, she tried to steady her breathing. But she ended up turning onto her side and hiccupping soft tears from the loneliness, for what never was, for what would never be.

❦❦❦

"Hey, boss?" Vivian knocked on Sofia's door frame and poked her head inside without waiting for an invitation. "Someone to see you."

She exhaled. Ever since Tyrone had started soliciting bids for the expanded warehouse, the site had been filled with salespeople, engineers, contractors. It reminded her of Encore's earliest days. But it turned out she'd remembered the good parts, the thrill of breaking ground, the satisfaction of watching progress happen, the shared bottle of champagne at the end of the journey.

Last week, her mother had joked that it was much like

childbirth.

"Okay," she said. "Send him in."

"Uhm..." Vivian did a little jerk with her head.

"What?" She scowled, feeling silly that she couldn't figure out what Vivian was trying to convey.

Then Cade was there, his broad shoulders filling the doorway, his presence vaporizing oxygen from the room.

She stood. "Thank you, Vivian." Sofia wasn't even sure if she'd been coherent.

"I'll, ah, be in the break room?"

"Thanks."

Vivian was the only person who knew the story about Cade, how deeply Sofia cared, how devastated she was. Still, he was their biggest client, and she had an obligation to be civil.

"Excuse me," Vivian said with a nervous smile.

Cade moved aside for Vivian. When she was gone, he stepped in and closed the door and the blinds.

"Cade," she said. Sitting would give him the advantage, but her legs wouldn't support her any longer. "Is there a problem?"

"There is."

She reached for a pen and threaded it through her fingers. Anything to keep them from betraying her nerves.

"Me."

"I'm sorry?"

Without an invitation, he sat.

"I thought if I was the best at something, maybe my dad would spend more time with me."

"Cade."

"No. Listen."

She nodded, not wanting to hear the ache in his voice.

"That picture in my bedroom? It was taken maybe an hour before his death. Donovan Worldwide sponsored race cars back then. I wanted to drive one. So he put me in one. It wasn't on the big professional circuit, but one down, with some other rookie drivers, like me. It was after qualifying, and not in my car, since mine only had one seat, but a car designed for a pro to take a passenger for a once-in-a-lifetime ride along. Someone else wrecked. I had nowhere to go. A tire got cut down, I went into the wall. The angle of impact..." He paused, took off his hat. "It was instant."

"I..."

"I woke up in the hospital hours later. And when the doctor called for my mother when I asked where my dad was, I knew. I knew."

"You don't have to tell me this."

"Yeah. I do. I was unconscious that day. And I've been that way since. It took your leaving to shake me up enough that I want to live. I owe Nathan for kicking my ass, encouraging me to look at the autopsy report. There was even a video. I've watched it six thousand times."

Her heart was suddenly careening.

"I don't deserve you. I'm probably going to be a little fucked up for the rest of my life. There will always be guilt."

"I can't imagine how there wouldn't be."

"Anniversaries of the wreck are always the worst. But if you're willing to give me another chance, I vow to do my best never to shut you out, to be the man you deserve."

"My God..."

He left the chair, got down on one knee and said, "Sofia McBride, make me the happiest man on earth. Marry me." He reached into his jacket pocket and pulled out a box. He flipped it open to reveal a stunning marquis diamond engagement ring.

"I'm not sure what to say."

"Start with yes. We can do anything from there."

"I..."

He flipped the box closed then slipped it back in his pocket before standing. This close, at his full height, he overwhelmed the space and her. He put his hands on her shoulders and drew her to her feet. "Do you need a little convincing?"

His face was set in a determined tilt that made her nervous.

"What are you thinking?" she asked.

"Like that first night at Connor and Lara's reception, you haven't kicked me out."

"True," she whispered.

"You're still here," he continued.

She licked her upper lip.

His eyes were that ferocious gunmetal color that enchanted her, wouldn't let her look away.

Before she knew what he was about, she was over his shoulder, grabbing for his waistband for stability. Even though she was laughing, she kicked. He trapped her legs with an upper arm and gave her buttocks one solid whack. "Let's go have this conversation somewhere a little more private. Give me an opportunity and I will spend the rest of my life convincing you I'm worth a chance."

"I think that's a lascivious suggestion, Sir."

"Sweet Sofia, I haven't even gotten started."

EPILOGUE

October

"Cade, really? We're going to be late to our own party."

He crossed his arms and regarded his wife, the beautiful Mrs. Sofia Donovan. "You shouldn't have bent over."

"For crying out loud, I was just putting on my boots." She scowled.

And nice ones they were, turquoise leather, handcrafted by his mother as a wedding present.

He glanced at the bed then back at Sofia.

"You're serious?" she asked.

"Do you need to be told twice?"

Even across the distance, he saw the flecks in her eyes darken. It wasn't just the words, it was the tone of voice, and she recognized it.

Sofia licked her lower lip. "Someone might hear."

Since the centennial celebration would kick off in a little less than two hours, the house was filled with family members and a few close friends. Still, the bedroom he now shared with Sofia was far enough away to give them some privacy. "I have a gag in the closet if you need it."

He crossed to the door and turned the lock before targeting her. His boots echoed off the hardwood as he demolished the distance between them, noticing the way her shoulders quickly rose and fell as she responded to him.

He shrugged out of his Western tuxedo jacket—he was wearing it far too often for his tastes—then hung it on a bedpost. "Lift your dress, Sofia."

With perfect obedience, she caught the hem and drew it up over her hips.

"Stop." He wanted to look, so he did. Her panties were a wisp of fabric, something he'd picked out for her. "I like you in thongs." That way he knew her ass was bare, waiting for his handprint. "On the bed. Face down."

With exaggerated slowness that edged toward sassiness, she turned away from him and got into position. She squirmed around as she settled herself. No doubt her movements were intentional, to snare his attention. But since the moment he'd first met her, he'd been captivated.

After moving aside the thong, he nudged her ankles farther apart, already smelling the heat of her arousal. "Tell me what you want."

She moved her head to the side so she could meet his gaze. "Fuck me. Claim me. Remind me I'm yours."

Over the months, that had become a mantra between them, words that she said to let him know she was ready for him. "I'd like nothing more." He skimmed his work-roughened fingertips up the outside of her smooth thighs then he pried apart her buttocks.

She clenched her ass cheeks before sucking in a breath, forcing herself to relax.

"You're going to be full for me today."

"I…" Sofia pursed her lips then schooled her features. "If it pleases you."

"It does." He left her long enough to grab a bottle of lube and a glass butt plug.

Her beautiful eyes widened in shock. "What the hell is that?"

"I assume your question is rhetorical."

"Cade, it's huge." She grabbed fistfuls of the bedspread.

He couldn't hide his grin. "You've had my dick up there."

"But not for a prolonged period," she protested.

"You will tonight."

Her mouth parted in shock.

He waited.

After several long moments, she sighed. "Yes, Sir."

Cade knew it wasn't possible for his dick to be harder.

He fingered her pussy, distracting her from the fear. "That's my perfect, perfect sub," he said when tension drained from her body. He left her long enough to grab a small vibrator. After turning it on to a medium-high setting, he slipped it inside her.

"Ah... Cade!"

"You can come when you want."

She jerked her hips in rhythm with the vibrations.

"Think about how much I like watching you." He lubed a couple of fingers then inserted one in her ass. After he stroked her a few times, he added the second. He took his time parting them, fucking her, opening her up for him.

"This is..."

"Tell me."

"Incredible. Almost too much."

"Good." When he had her on the verge of an orgasm, he removed both fingers. Out of her sight line, he drizzled lube down the glass.

He waited until she was on her toes, rubbing herself on the covers before saying, "You've got a horny pussy, wife."

"I need more," she whispered, voice hoarse, demanding.

How could he deny her?

He set the vibrator a notch higher. When she cried out, he began to force the glass into her tight hole.

"Damn, damn..." She squeezed her eyes shut.

This woman. Always, always, she took more than he anticipated she might. "You're almost there," he promised, soothed.

"Just get it in."

With a laugh, he continued his relentless, slow pace.

She began to thrust backward, urging him to give her more, no doubt wanting it to be over.

He managed to pry her anus apart enough to accommodate the fattest part of the plug's girth. She cried, and he gave a solid push. The glass settled itself. "Damn, that's even sexier than I imagined."

Sofia sighed. He saw her clench and unclench her buttocks

as if trying not to fight against the intrusion.

Cade brought his hands down, hard. She tossed her head as he blazed spanks across her skin.

"I love you. I love you!"

"Not half as much as I love and adore you, Mrs. Donovan." He leaned forward to kiss the side of her neck. He'd spent a lot of years avoiding emotional entanglements, but now, he wondered why. He liked being married, knowing that Sofia was there for him at the end of the day. No matter how difficult the challenges were, they faced them together. He'd never let this woman go. "I'm going to fuck you."

"Now?" Her voice wobbled, from the force of the vibrator and the girth of the plug, he guessed.

"Yeah." He unbuckled his belt then lowered his zipper. Cade didn't even have to stroke his cock to make it hard enough to penetrate her tight cunt. He removed the vibrator and plunged his cock in her.

The fit was incredible. Her pussy squeezed him, almost dragging out an orgasm before he was root-deep in her.

He grabbed her hipbones, holding her steady. He realized she hadn't yet orgasmed. "Waiting for me?"

"Trying, Sir," she replied, her voice muffled by the bedding.

"Good, good girl." He fisted his hand in her hair. "Come now." He pistoned into her and she was helpless against him.

He felt her pussy clamp down on his cock, and Sofia screamed as she orgasmed. Cade gritted his teeth, attempting to hold on for a few seconds longer. As she called his name, he lost the battle, spilling deep inside her.

Long seconds later, satiated, he pulled out then helped her to turn over and get back on the bed.

Her eyes were wide, chest rising and falling in keeping with her shallow, panted breaths.

"You amaze me," he said.

Even though he knew she wasn't cognizant of the world around her, he devoured her with a kiss, showing his love, devotion, commitment.

Tenderly, he held her, wishing he could stay in bed with her forever.

"Yours," she whispered when he ended the kiss.

"Mine," he affirmed. "Stay here." He redressed himself before going to the bathroom for a damp washcloth.

"How do you feel?" he asked once he'd bathed her pussy and cleaned up the excess lube.

"Claimed."

"Don't you forget it."

"As if I could with this thing up my ass."

He grinned.

Once she was cleansed, he pulled up her panties then offered his hand again.

She stood and went into the bathroom to tame her hair and repair the damage done to her makeup. As he often did, Cade stood there, shoulder against the doorjamb, transfixed. He watched her, marveling at the changes in his life.

Once his ring had been on her finger, he'd become impatient. She'd wanted a big wedding after the centennial celebration. With uncharacteristic impatience, he'd refused. Less than a week after he'd stormed into her Corpus Christi offices, he'd offered her two choices, set the date for no more than a month away or they were eloping.

She'd agreed to a family-and-close-friends-only event at the ranch a month after they'd announced their engagement. All the bedrooms had been filled, the way that Humphrey Donovan had once envisioned. It had been wild, crazy, fun. And he'd escorted everyone out of the front door the next morning so he could have Sofia all to himself.

Most of them had stayed away until yesterday. A blissful several months.

She loved having everyone around, the cooking, the conversation, the laughter. He tolerated it.

"I like the dress," he told her. It was short, black, fringed, sexy. With the way he was already thinking about sex, he should have encouraged her to wear jeans to cover her legs.

"Stop it," she warned, her gaze finding his in the mirror.

"What?"

"Your cock cannot be ready again," she said.

He came up behind her and bumped his hips against her buttocks. "Oh?"

"My God! Out. *Out.*" She brandished her brush.

In mock surrender, he raised his hands.

"Out," she repeated. "I mean it."

With a grin, he followed her order. He had put on his jacket and had just finished adjusting his bulldogger tie when she rejoined him, wearing a fresh coat of fuck-me red lipstick.

He swept his gaze over her, taking in the entire package, hip-hugging black dress, bare legs, turquoise leather boots, hair that teased her shoulders, a mouth he could kiss all night. "I have a gift for you."

She shifted. "The one I've got in me right now is more than enough," she promised him.

"I believe you'll like this one a little more." He went to the shelf where he had his important pictures. It had evolved since Sofia had joined him. There were photos of their wedding, her sisters, her family, including her nieces. The one of him and his father had been restored and framed. It still hurt to look at it, but he kept it there, and each day the pain, the guilt, lessened by miniscule measures.

Cade picked up a long, flat box. As she watched, he removed the lid. The stunning necklace had a diamond pendant hanging from a platinum chain. "It was Grandma Maisie's."

Her eyes widened, and she looked from it, to him. "It's gorgeous."

"Turn around, lift your hair. Let me put it on you."

"Are you sure?"

"You're my wife, a Donovan. It's yours." More and more, he was accepting his heritage, and he was learning to be proud of it.

He put the necklace on her. The pendant snuggled below the hollow of her throat, the perfect way to complete her outfit.

After she let go of her hair, he moved her in front of the mirror and stood behind her. "Now we're ready for the party."

And the future.

Boss

Excerpt

Prologue

"Is that Kelsey Lane?"

Startled, Nathan Donovan glanced up from his phone screen and looked over at his older brother, Connor. "Yeah. I just got her file."

"On a Saturday night?" Connor raised his eyebrows. "At Grandfather's centennial celebration? Better not let him see you working."

Nathan had snuck off to a corner of the big fucking tent where he'd hoped he wouldn't be disturbed. Since there were nearly a thousand guests in attendance, he should have known better than to think he could work instead of socializing and not get caught.

"Anything interesting?" Connor asked, after a glance around.

Realizing his brother wasn't going away, Nathan turned

off the screen and dropped the phone back into his pocket. "She has a master's degree. Been with Newman Inland Marine around six years, including internships. Loyal. Trusted. Exemplary record. Promotions faster than expected."

Connor nodded, as if the information wasn't a surprise.

"What do you know about her?" Nathan asked.

"Not much. Her name crossed my desk a couple of days ago. A recruiter was searching talent for BHI."

Connor's wife owned BHI, and Connor had a seat on the board of directors. As CEO, Lara counted on Connor's support and opinions. "Interesting," Nathan said. As their businesses grew, these types of conflicts were inevitable. Unwelcome, but inevitable. He knew that BHI had interests in shipping and logistics, but since they were ground-and-air based, they were at best minor competition. "What capacity are we talking about here?"

"Oil and gas."

"Interesting."

"We don't have to pursue her."

Nathan refused to stand between her and success with another company. And if her skill set would benefit BHI, they deserved the chance to woo her. "You're welcome to go after her."

Connor no longer seemed to be listening, and Nathan followed his brother's gaze. His wife Lara was talking to a tall cowboy who leaned toward her. Too close, if the sudden scowl on Connor's face was anything to judge by.

"Excuse me," Connor said, jaw set. Without waiting for a response, Connor strode toward his wife.

Thankfully, that left Nathan alone again.

He took out his phone and returned to the information on Kelsey. *Info?* If he was honest with himself, he would admit he wasn't only interested in her biography. He wanted to look at her picture.

Her smile appeared a bit forced, as if she were impatient with the photographer. Even that didn't detract from the beauty of her hazel eyes, the fullness of her lips or the sight of her long, dark hair.

Everything about her appealed to him.

If the acquisition went through, the gorgeous Kelsey Lane would be his assistant.

That was incentive to work longer and harder.

A couple whose names he couldn't remember stopped to chat. Hiding his annoyance, he put his phone away and shook the man's hand.

It took a full five minutes before their attention wandered and they excused themselves.

He wondered how many more times he would be required to smile before making an escape. Unbelievably, people were still arriving. Some were even in limos, which was supremely impractical on a ranch, not just because of the dirt roads but also the distance from a major town.

Straddling the line between irritation and impatience, he glanced at his watch. Not that it was a watch, even though it told time with the accuracy of an atomic clock. The unit was more like a mini-computer. It never needed recharging since it was powered by his body's movements. Barring that, light reenergized it. The Julien Bonds-created masterpiece wasn't just intuitive, it often anticipated Nathan's actions.

The unit vibrated. In response, he swiped his finger across the sapphire-glass surface. A tiny hologram of his sister-in-law Sofia appeared. Beneath her, in script that advanced forward as he read each word, Sofia said, *"It's not yet eight o'clock, Nathan. You're expected to stay at least two more hours. As a reminder, please ask your mother to dance. And oh, Connor just told me to lock you out of the Wi-Fi until eleven p.m., even at the guest house, so even if you run away, you won't be able to get online. He says it's for your own good."*

What the fuck? He went to swipe away the image, but she started speaking again. *"You might as well relax, have something to drink and enjoy yourself. Bye-bye!"* With a cheery little annoying wave, her image vanished.

He groaned.

Everyone apparently knew he'd rather be anywhere but here. *Fucking parties. Waste of time. Even bigger waste of money.*

He ran his finger along the inside of his shirt collar. Even though it was October, it was hotter than hell at the family's Running Wind Ranch in South Texas.

If it had been his choice, he'd have stayed in Houston to work on the Newman Inland Marine deal. It was getting close to crunch time. He was sleeping fewer and fewer hours, fueled by the challenges and opportunities. It was heady stuff. To him, it was like a drug. And he was all but shaking with the need for his fix.

As if on cue to save him, a server passed by, bearing a variety of wines all from locally grown grapes.

"Don't mind if I do." He snagged a glass of something red.

"Glad we didn't burn the ranch house down?"

At the words, he turned to see his sister, Erin. "It's not too late, is it?" he asked.

"Stop it, you cheapskate. This is fun."

"Fun?" Maybe to some people it was.

"Sofia did a hell of a job."

Even he had to admit that, despite the exorbitant cost. He'd secretly scoffed at her idea of erecting tents on the grounds. He'd even wondered aloud if the whole thing were a circus.

But the inside didn't resemble a tent. The thing was massive, had windows, tables, a dance floor, French doors and, blessedly, air conditioning. She'd even managed to get the Matthew Martin band to interrupt a nationwide tour to provide entertainment. It was world-class, from covers to their own top-ten hits, ballads to country swing, and they'd even managed a few obligatory line dances. Not bad for a band that had won country music's most prestigious award three out of the last five years.

"Granddaddy says this will be good for business."

"Not sure how that's possible when we're locked out of the Wi-Fi."

"For Christ's sake, Nathan. You won't die without your phone. Have you always been such a bore? I used to enjoy hanging out with you." She frowned. "At least I think I did. Maybe my mind is playing tricks on me."

Sometime during the evening, she'd ditched her shoes. Her hair was piled on top of her head and she'd woven some small white flowers through the strands.

She'd chosen an interesting outfit, a short leather skirt and a black corset. *Of course.* "Dressed to spite me?"

"Please." She rolled her eyes. "Get it through your thick skull. Not everything is about you."

This was an old argument. He and Erin saw financials differently. She insisted he was overly cautious, to the point of being out of step and stuffy. He didn't mind the accusation. When his father had died, Connor had inherited a company headed toward disaster. Nathan had seen how close the Donovans were to losing the hard-fought legacy that had been handed down through the generations. When he'd been appointed CFO, he'd vowed to be a good steward so that future Donovans would have something to be proud of.

Erin preferred to live for the moment, determined to do what good she could for the world. She was a dreamer. He was a planner. And when she'd approached him to invest in her friend's corset store, he'd refused.

Undaunted, she'd used money from her own trust fund to help her friend.

"So, do you like it?" she asked, interrupting his musings.

"Like what?"

"The outfit." She spun. "I'm modeling it."

"You're what?"

"Helping visibility of the shop by showing how versatile the piece is. It can be worn anywhere, even a fancy event. Corsets are not just for the bedroom."

"They should be." Or a BDSM club, which was where he preferred them. He loved lacing a submissive into one, cinching it tight so he could enjoy looking at her cleavage.

Erin smacked his arm.

"And the necklace...? Are you also modeling it?"

"Oh, this?" She touched the exquisite—and if he didn't miss his guess, fucking expensive—teardrop pendant. "No. This was retail therapy."

"Was there a reason you dropped money on an extravagant piece of jewelry?" She'd inherited a treasure trove full of stuff from their great-grandmother. Surely she could have just reset some of those stones.

"I bought it right after Connor's wedding reception," she answered vaguely.

Before he could ask anything else, she took a sip of wine. "This is good," she said approvingly before taking a second, longer drink. "So, why didn't you bring a date? That would have helped."

He regarded her. "To this command performance?"

She shrugged. "I know what you mean."

Since all of the family members had arrived Friday and planned to stay until Sunday, he'd nixed the idea of bringing a woman he barely knew to meet the family, endure endless questions and share his space.

There was little room in his life for a relationship, and he was fine with that. He adored the subs at Deviation, the city's intriguing new BDSM club. An occasional visit satisfied his primal needs. And after a few hours, he went home, even more focused on business. Scenes didn't just soothe his savageness, they energized him.

Glass in hand, he walked over to where his half-brother Cade stood talking to his mother, Stormy.

Although Nathan was a little surprised she'd accepted the invitation, he was pleased to see her. To his knowledge, it was the first Donovan event she'd ever attended.

"Stormy." He shook her hand.

"Nathan. Always a pleasure."

The woman was tall, willowy and dressed exactly the way he'd expected. Convention be damned. Her slim-cut jeans were tucked inside boots she'd likely hand-tooled herself. Her white T-shirt was form-fitting, and she wore a brown leather vest over it. She had a quick smile, a firm grip and a direct gaze. He could see why his father, Jeffrey, had fallen in love with her, even though he had been expected to marry Nathan's mother.

The Running Wind Ranch wouldn't have been what it was without Stormy's guidance. And Cade, the oldest Donovan brother, did a damn fine job of running the ranch. It had been Stormy who'd fought for her illegitimate son's inheritance and who'd instilled a love of the land in his soul. Though Nathan had little interest in that part of the business, Cade's intelligence and hard work had made it a financial success. And that, Nathan appreciated.

"Well, look who's here," Cade interrupted with a long, slow whistle.

Nathan glanced over his shoulder and saw Julien Bonds just inside the French doors. "I didn't know he was expected." A group of people moved in around him, blocking him from general view and the always-prying eye of cell phone cameras.

"Connor insisted on sending Bonds an invite," Cade replied. "No one really thought he'd show, but Sofia reserved a guest house for him, just in case. I imagine he took a helicopter from Houston." He shrugged. "I still want to see his prissy ass on a horse."

"I'll give him lessons," Stormy volunteered.

She'd spent years wrangling and was an accomplished horsewoman. If Nathan remembered correctly, she'd been the one who had taught his father to ride. That was probably the summer they'd fallen in love. "I want to ask him about a few of the watch's features," Nathan said.

"Watch? You have a Bonds watch?" Cade demanded.

Nathan flashed his wrist.

"Fuck," Cade said. "How the hell did you rate?"

"I indicated an interest in investing. He turned me down. Says he won't go public and let some board of directors interfere with his creative ideas." The man was on track to having one of the largest privately held firms on the planet. "As a consolation prize, he sent it to me for beta testing."

"And?"

"It's astounding. But..."

"But?"

"Quirky."

Cade frowned.

"Plays theme music when it's turned on. And the hologram—"

"It has a hologram?"

"Of Bonds himself. Greets you personally and suggests ways for you to improve your life." The ego was astounding. Last week, Bonds had recommended Nathan go to bed slightly earlier and sleep longer, saying his life expectancy would increase if he enjoyed more REM sleep. Bonds had added that Nathan would be twice as effective if he slept twenty percent longer, which was a good investment of his time, according to the genius.

After that, Nathan had taken the fucking thing off almost every night when he got home from the office. Problem was, it was so useful that he missed it. "Who's that with him?"

"Meredith Wolsey." Cade took a drink of beer. "Heard he brought her to Connor's reception."

"What? Bonds was there?"

Cade nodded. "They stayed on the patio. Only a handful of people saw them. I wasn't one of them, either. I heard about it from Sofia."

"Sneaky bastard."

Erin, a determined frown buried between her eyebrows, descended on their small group. "Dance with me." Erin grabbed Nathan's wrist and dragged him toward the front of the tent.

"I was just going to say hello to Julien and Meredith. Go with me? It's been a long time since you've seen him, hasn't it? Not since that night in—"

"Nathan, please," she said.

"Can't it wait?" He scowled.

Generally Erin was a great hostess, and he'd bet she'd chatted with everyone in attendance. But the way she pleaded and looked at him, eyes beseeching, he had no choice. She'd always been a pest, the little sister who could get her big brothers to do almost anything she wanted. After the death of their father, something that had devastated her and sent her to her room for weeks, she'd become even more indulged.

Cade shrugged as if to say *better you than me*.

"Now. Excuse us," she said to Stormy and Cade.

Nathan put down his wine, and she was already tugging on him. "Stop dragging me," he told her.

Her grip was desperate and her nails were digging into him. Despite the fact that he hated to dance, he went with her.

"Lead on," he said.

On the floor, to the beat of the music, he led her into a two-step. "What's the panic?"

"No panic." She gave him a huge, sunny smile.

If he hadn't noticed the way she glanced to the back of the room, at Julien and Meredith and their sudden mob of people, he might have believed she just wanted to dance. After all, she'd put her four-inch heels back on.

She lapsed into silence, and he let her, since that suited him, as well.

At the end of the number, she thanked him then excused herself before heading toward their mother, who was seated at a table with a few of her friends and his aunt, Kathryn... as far away from Stormy as possible.

When he reached Julien and Meredith, the enthusiastic greeting party had thinned, and they were standing with Cade.

Cade introduced Nathan to Meredith, an attorney he'd hired from a prestigious firm in Northern California. Julien's hand rested on the small of her back, which Nathan recognized as a move of easy intimacy. To his eye, they were much more than professional associates. And since he suspected Bonds at least dabbled in BDSM, there might be some possessiveness there too.

They made a striking couple—Bonds with his tight, slim-fitting jeans, dress shirt, leather jacket, narrow tie and trademark hideous tennis shoes, and Meredith with her open-back black gown. As dark-haired as he was, she was his blonde counterpart. A recent celebrity magazine had called them the newest power couple.

"What do you think of my masterpiece?" Julien asked as they shook hands.

"It's..." How did he tell the creator what he thought of the watch?

"You love it, don't you? I still have a few things to work out with the hologram."

"About that—"

"The tone of my voice isn't quite right when I give the daily update." He shook his head. "My engineers haven't done the synthesizing correctly."

"It's supposed to do that?" he asked incredulously. "Tell me I need more sleep?"

Julien scowled. "Of course it is. That's why people will buy it."

"I see." He actually thought some people wanted him to boss them around? Nathan wondered whether the man was certifiable or a genius.

"Overall?" Julien persisted.

"It's fucking indispensable."

Julien's mercurial frown vanished and a slow smile spread across his mouth. "Indispensable," he repeated. "Yes." Then he touched the screen of his own device. His image popped up. "Use the word indispensable in the marketing materials."

Julien's image bowed toward him. "Yes, genius."

The voice, the tone, was dead on.

Obviously the engineers had heard that term plenty.

Julien brushed the sapphire-glass surface and the

hologram vanished. "Where were we? I wanted to congratulate the Colonel."

Cade pointed out the table.

Before walking away, Julien said, "I'll upload the latest software update to you next week."

"You mean I need to download it?"

"No. It will happen automatically."

"How intrusive is this thing?"

"Check your heart rate when you see a beautiful woman and ask me then." Julien nodded politely before walking away.

"I think he wants to rule the world," Sofia said, joining them. "I caught the end bit."

"Rule it?" Nathan asked. "Dominate it is more like it."

Cade shrugged.

The band segued into an up-tempo song and announced yet another line dance.

"Show me how it's done, Mr. Donovan," Sofia said. "The only reason I accepted this job was to see you line dance. Remember?"

Proving how besotted he was, Cade tipped his hat. "Anything for my lady."

With that, as if there were no one else on the planet but the two of them, they headed toward the dance floor.

Nathan resumed his favorite position, an arm propped on one of the bar-height conversation tables.

A tall brunette wearing a sequined dress so tight it should have been impossible for her to move sashayed past him. She caught his eye and smiled. Everything about her was perfect—hair, makeup, shape.

She stopped long enough to accept a glass of wine and to look back at him, being sure he noted her interest.

Rather than engage, he checked his watch. And his heart rate.

Clearly Julien was wrong about the watch. It didn't show any reaction to the bombshell who was telegraphing her availability.

He looked back up to note that she'd moved on to someone considerably more appreciative.

Which left him free to peruse his own thoughts. There was little Nathan enjoyed more than the strategy. Except the chase.

Chapter One

Juggling two venti mochas with extra whipped cream, her electronic card key, a purse and a bag stuffed with her workout gear, Kelsey Lane exited the elevator and strode toward the set of double doors at the end of the hallway. Since it wasn't even seven o'clock, she had almost the whole building to herself, something she liked, especially on Monday mornings.

This early, if she drove, she typically didn't have to fight traffic on Houston's busy roads. If she rode the train, she could always find a seat. Regardless, she liked to get a jump on the week, organizing and preparing before the phone started to ring.

The lights were on in the office, so she tested the handle, hoping the cleaning crew was still there and that the suite was unlocked. Thankfully it was. "Good morning!" she called out so she didn't startle anyone.

With her foot, she shoved the door closed behind her.

She moved through to her desk and put down the drinks and keys before dropping her purse and bag on the carpeted floor. Then she turned to open the blinds so that she could see the upcoming sunrise reflect off the nearby skyscrapers. This had to be one of the biggest perks of her job. A spectacular view of Houston, from forty stories up.

As she turned, she noticed a potted yellow hibiscus in the corner. It hadn't been there when she'd left on Friday evening. While it was beautiful, it wasn't something that Samuel Newman would have brought in.

"Hello."

Startled by the very masculine, very sexy bass that sounded nothing like her boss's voice, Kelsey glanced up.

A man she'd never seen before filled the doorway and she sucked in a panicked gasp. His shoulders were unbelievably wide. He had on a white long-sleeved shirt with turned-back cuffs. A light gray tie was loosely knotted around his neck, and he stood with arms folded across his chest and a slight frown on his face.

Fear and uncertainty slammed her pulse into overdrive. "Can I help you?" She reached toward her phone so she could alert security about an intruder, though how anyone could have gotten past the guards in the lobby puzzled her.

"You're Kelsey Lane. And I promise you, you don't need to call for help."

Kelsey scowled. "You seem to have me at a disadvantage. Mr…"

"Donovan. Nathan Donovan."

She exhaled in a rush and moved her hand away from the phone. Of course. Though she'd never met any of the Donovan brothers, she knew their reputation. Cool. Fearless. Calculating.

Nathan, if she remembered correctly from the numerous articles she'd read in Houston's weekly business newspaper, was the youngest son. He reportedly had an uncanny eye for numbers, for investments. As the financial brain behind the family dynasty, he'd ruthlessly acquired business after business, streamlined them, sold some of them off and made others operate on thin margins, exhausting the remaining employees while terminating the rest. But one thing they all had in common after he was finished with them was profitability.

"I see you've heard of me."

"Who hasn't?" she returned. He was rumored to be outwardly friendly in a way that disguised his true Machiavellian personality. He wasn't a man to be underestimated. But the bigger question was, what the hell was he doing in Samuel Newman's office before seven o'clock in the morning?

"Was any of it good?" he asked.

"Any of…?"

"The things you've heard about me."

He looked at her through shockingly green eyes, and his gaze was so intense that she had to resist the impulse to squirm. His voice was a rich, deep baritone. Though she imagined his words were meant to keep things light and invite conversation, ribbons of unease gripped her stomach.

Rather than answer directly, she hedged, "Is Mr. Newman in there?" She leaned her head to the side, but she was unable to see past Nathan's body and into the office beyond.

Nathan scowled. "I assumed you'd be expecting me."

A moment earlier he'd seemed at ease, welcoming. But now he looked ferocious. His jaw was locked and he took a step into the room, narrowing the distance between them.

"He didn't call you? Contact you in any way?"

She shook her head.

He cursed, low and vicious, making her wince.

"Newman was supposed to tell you," he said.

"Tell me what?" Her legs no longer seemed able to support her and she sat on the edge of the polished desk.

"He no longer works here."

"But..." She grabbed for her purse and dug out her cell phone. This simply wasn't possible. "What do you mean he doesn't work here? It's his company." Newman Inland Marine had been battling some legal and financial issues, but nothing insurmountable. Or so she'd thought. She'd stayed late on Friday going over some paperwork, and she'd told her boss she had no plans over the weekend and that he should feel free to call her if he needed help with anything.

He'd looked at her over the rims of his glasses and given a tight smile before sending her on her way. When she'd said goodbye, he'd given no hint that anything unusual was happening.

She keyed in her phone's passcode then checked the display. There were no messages or missed calls.

Literally and figuratively, Nathan stood there, larger than life, giving her space to sort through things at her own speed.

"I'm afraid I'm confused." She didn't want to call Nathan a liar, but...

"Ask him." He tilted his head, indicating her phone.

After nodding, she dialed the number. She reached Mr. Newman's voice mail.

The recording was so loud she knew Nathan could hear the tinny echo. She left a brief message then followed it with a text. Not that Samuel would respond to that. He preferred to speak to people. More than once he'd said that texting and messaging were ridiculously impersonal, and he would never do business that way. He was proud of Newman Inland Marine for the way it treated its customers. Incoming calls were answered by real people, not a voice-mail system.

Which made his current behavior all the more puzzling.

"You should have been among the first people told."

She put the phone on her desk. "Until I hear otherwise, Mr. Donovan, I'm afraid my loyalties are to Mr. Newman. And I'd ask you to stay out of his office."

He gave a curt nod. "While you wait for him to call back, why not look at the sign on the door?"

After scowling at him, she pushed off the desk and walked toward the double doors. With every step, she was aware of Nathan Donovan watching her, studying her.

In the hallway, she looked at the brass plaques on the wall.

Breath rushed out of her lungs.

When she'd left on Friday evening, the wording on the top one had said *Newman Inland Marine*. It now read *Donovan Logistics*.

The second plaque—the one that had been engraved with her boss's name—had been replaced with one that bore Nathan's. The metal gleamed, new and promising.

Unable to help herself, she traced the capital *D* with a shaking finger.

Now what?

Everything Nathan had said appeared to be true. No

matter how powerful they were, Donovan Worldwide would not have been allowed to come into the office building over the weekend, replace signage and access the executive office suite. It evidently meant nothing that Mr. Newman hadn't spoken with her. And that shocked her. She was supposed to be his greatest confidante, privy to all the things that went on in the company. What else didn't she know?

She pulled back her shoulders from their dejected slump. She had no choice but to face her future. But that didn't mean she had to like it.

"Satisfied?" he asked.

He stood in the middle of the space—her space— arms folded over his massive chest. With his legs spread shoulder-width apart, he looked imposing, commanding, comfortable. As if he owned the entire freaking place. Which he appeared to.

"I'm perplexed," she admitted. Sidestepping him, she hurried toward her desk, her shoes silent on the plush carpeting. Until now, she hadn't noticed how small the area was. In her stiletto heels, not a lot of men had the ability to make her feel small. But with Nathan and his massive, more than six-foot-tall body in the center of the room, things seemed dwarfed.

Because she was a little uncomfortable, she sat in the custom, ergonomically designed chair behind her desk and reached for her coffee.

Then, because he stood in front of her and towered over her, she wished she hadn't. "Do you mind explaining things to me?" she asked.

"Why don't we go into my office?"

Her first instinct was to reply that it wasn't his. The next was to say she'd rather stay here. Then curiosity trumped both thoughts.

Coffee in hand, Kelsey grabbed her cell phone and followed him.

The sight of the office made her gasp. In just two days it

327

had been transformed.

Gone were all the framed snapshots of Samuel's friends and family. The oversize picture of him and the governor of Texas shaking hands and grinning was nowhere in sight.

And that was only the beginning of the changes.

Shelf after shelf of knickknacks and memorabilia had been removed. On Friday, every key moment in Samuel's life had been memorialized in some way, from newspaper clippings to trophies, certificates to awards.

And now... The bookcases had been ripped out. The cozy, inviting leather guest chairs facing the desk had vanished. A pair of low-slung, modernistic ones were wedged against a far wall, clearly not inviting visitors to linger.

The blinds had been replaced by a privacy screen, and a minimalistic terrarium filled with cacti sat on the window ledge. Somehow, even the scent of cigar smoke had been obliterated.

The homey green walls had been covered in a no-nonsense steel-gray paint. And the words Donovan Logistics had been stenciled on the wall in bold, black lettering.

Every trace of Samuel Newman and his caring, effervescent personality had vanished.

Nathan pulled over a chair for her. "Please. Have a seat."

She remained standing. That didn't stop him from sinking into a space-age-looking chair, crafted of steel and covered in a breathable mesh fabric. His desk and matching credenza dominated the room. And that was the only word for it. Dominated. The pieces were massive. Nathan had dual, oversize flat screen monitors, all bearing the Bonds Electronics logo. His cell phone was propped on a phone stand so he didn't even have to glance down at it when it rang.

This looked like a place from which Nathan Donovan could rule an empire.

He leaned back, silent, waiting for her decision.

Eventually, she sat. The chair wasn't as uncomfortable as it looked.

She noticed the pile of manila folders on his desk. The top one was open, and she glanced at it. Her personnel record.

Her pulse skidded to a standstill. Until now, she'd only been concerned about Samuel. But she realized Nathan probably intended to replace her, as well. Of course, her résumé wasn't up to date. She'd invested years into her current job, building the company and relationships. If she were honest, she'd probably sacrificed too much in terms of her personal life as well.

"There have already been a lot of changes," he said when she met his resolute gaze. "And Samuel impressed on Donovan Worldwide how important you will be to the success of the takeover."

He hadn't said merger. Which meant things weren't friendly. She exhaled.

"If you'd like to continue your employment, Ms. Lane, you're my new assistant."

"Your..." Kelsey wasn't often at a loss for words, so she took a drink of her mocha to buy some time. "Mr. Newman is more than a boss to me. He's a mentor. I interned here during my undergrad studies, and he hired me after I received my master's degree. I owe him a great deal."

"And you can repay it by staying on, at least temporarily."

She crossed her legs then recrossed them in the opposite direction. "I can't make any promises until after I talk to Mr. Newman."

"Of course."

Her mind raced. If she didn't know what had happened, it was likely that no one did. She had only another forty-five minutes until the rest of the employees began arriving.

"Why don't you try him again?"

It wasn't like Mr. Newman to ignore her calls. Then again, everything in the last ten minutes had been surreal. She dialed his number. This time, it rang.

Just when she was certain she would get his voice mail, he answered.

"Kelsey." His voice sounded weakened, dejected.

She knew without hearing anything else that everything Nathan had told her was true. The reality she'd been trying to deny crashed into her.

Unable to have the conversation with Nathan watching her, she returned to her desk and slumped into her chair.

"I'm a coward," he told her.

A coward?

"I meant to call you yesterday. But..." He let out a ragged breath. "Forgive me."

Betrayal and confusion rocked her. How could he do this? Not just to her, but to the entire company, hundreds of people.

"I need your help."

She squeezed her eyes shut. In no way was she prepared for this.

"Kelsey..."

Her business instincts kicked in, and she shoved aside her personal feelings. "Is there—was there—a plan to tell the company?"

"It was supposed to be different..." He paused. "I was going to come in and meet with the top management and introduce Nathan. We were going to go to the docks so he could meet the people formally. He's been out there before, a couple of weekends ago."

"Okay. And what's the new strategy?"

She heard jostling and a woman's voice. Then, "Kelsey?"

"Mrs. Newman?"

"We're at the hospital, dear."

Kelsey's jaw went slack.

"It's his heart."

Before Kelsey could utter a word, Holly went on, "The doctors say he'll be fine. But..."

Damn it.

"The company needs you."

Over the last few years, Kelsey had talked to Mr. Newman many times, stressing the need for a succession plan. She'd encouraged him to groom senior managers to take over, or

330

solicit from the outside. He'd been stubborn. He was going to live forever, and there was plenty of time.

Now, she blinked back a sudden burst of tears. There was no more time. Newman Inland Marine had a new owner, and the stress had devastated Samuel.

In the background, she could hear Samuel and Holly whispering, overlaying the hiss and beep of what had to be hospital machinery.

"Samuel wants me to tell you he's counting on you. He wants Donovan to succeed." Holly's voice was taut with emotion, maybe frustration, perhaps anger and certainly some fear.

"May I visit him?"

Holly gave the name of one of Houston's most renowned hospitals then added, "Not today, dear. Perhaps tomorrow. He needs some rest. But, Kelsey? He'll get better faster if he knows he can count on you. He's worried about the employees, as I'm sure you understand."

She gave a tight nod, even though Holly couldn't see her. "You can count on me." After a few pleasantries — platitudes, mostly — she ended the call.

Kelsey put her phone down and gave a shaky exhalation, composing herself. When she looked up, she saw Nathan standing there. "How long have you been there?" And how had he moved so silently?

"Long enough." He pulled up a chair.

More books from
Sierra Cartwright

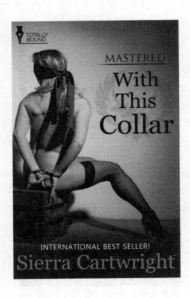

She will have nothing to do with domineering men, no matter how tall, dark, and sexy. But Dom Marcus will be satisfied with nothing less than collaring her.

bonds

crave

Is she strong enough, brave enough…

INTERNATIONAL BEST SELLER

Sierra Cartwright

She still craved him… The sight of a collar in her boyfriend's drawer had stunned Sarah. Panicking, she had fled. But no other man has ever been his equal.

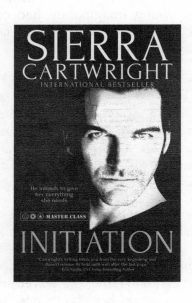

SIERRA
CARTWRIGHT
INTERNATIONAL BESTSELLER

He intends to give
her everything
she needs

⊗ ⊛ MASTER CLASS

INITIATION

"Cartwright's writing binds you from the very beginning and
doesn't release its hold until well after the last page."
-Erin Noelle, USA Today Bestselling Author

*When wannabe sub Jennifer calls him Master and begs him
to flog her, PI Logan Powell knows all his military training
won't be enough to keep his jaded heart safe.*

About the Author

NO 1 INTERNATIONAL BESTSELLER & USA TODAY
BESTSELLING AUTHOR

Sierra Cartwright was born in Manchester, England and
raised in Colorado. Moving to the United States was
nothing like her young imagination had concocted. She
expected to see cowboys everywhere, and a covered wagon
or two would have been really nice!

Now she writes novels as untamed as the Rockies, while
spending a fair amount of time in Texas…where, it turns
out, the Texas Rangers law officers don't ride horses to
roundup the bad guys, or have six-shooters strapped to
their sexy thighs as she expected. And she's yet to see a
poster that says Wanted: Dead or Alive. (Can you tell she
has a vivid imagination?)

Sierra wrote her first book at age nine, a fanfic episode of
Star Trek when she was fifteen, and she completed her first
romance novel at nineteen. She actually kissed William
Shatner (Captain Kirk) on the cheek once, and she says
that's her biggest claim to fame. Her adventure through the
turmoil of trust has taught her that love is the greatest gift.
Like her image of the Old West, her writing is untamed,
and nothing is off-limits.

She invites you to take a walk on the wild side…but only if
you dare.

Sierra Cartwright loves to hear from readers. You can find
contact information, website details and an author profile
page at https://www.totallybound.com/

TOTALLY BOUND

Home of Erotic Romance